I0614146

DO NOT GO QUIETLY

An Anthology of Victory in Defiance

Edited by
JASON SIZEMORE & LESLEY CONNER

"To Write" © 2019 by Annie Neugebauer; "Kindle" © 2019 by Brooke Bolander; "What the Mountain Wants" © 2019 by Maurice Broaddus and Nayad Monroe; "Nobody Lives in the Swamp" © 2019 by Dee Warrick; "The Skeleton Archer Speaks" © 2019 by Jeremy Paden; "Oil Under Her Tongue" © 2019 by Rachael K. Jones; "Glossolalia" © 2019 by John Horner Jacobs; "Choose Your Truth" © 2019 by Jo Miles; "If the Fairy Godmother Comes" © 2019 by Mary Soon Lee; "What We Have Chosen to Love" © 2019 by Cassandra Khaw; "Salted Bone and Silent Sea" © 2019 by Shanna Germain; "Scurry" © 2019 by Rich Larson; "Permian Basin Blues" by © 2000 (*Lady Churchill's Rosebud Wristlet*, issue 7, Small Beer Press) by Lucy A. Snyder; "Rage Against the Venting Machine" © 2019 by Russell Nichols; "Everything Is Closed Today" © 2019 by Sarah Pinsker; "Hey, Alexa" © 2019 by Meg Elison; "The Dolls" © 2019 Christina Sng; "Thirteen Year Long Song" © 2019 by Sheree Renée Thomas; "The Society for the Reclamation of Words and Meaning" © 2019 by Fran Wilde; "South of the Waffle House" © 2019 by Marie Vibbert; "#greenlivesmatter" © 2016 (*Star*Line*, issue 39.2) by Joshua Gage; "Sympathizer" © 2019 by Karin Lowachee; "Face" © 2019 by Veronica Brush; "April Teeth" © 2019 by Eugenia Triantafyllou; "Witch's Star" © 2019 by Alethea Kontis; "The Judith Plague" by Merc Rustad; "Kill the Darlings (Silicone Sister Remix)" © 2019 by E. Catherine Tobler; "Plot Twist" © 2019 by Bianca Lynne Spriggs

Available as a trade paperback, hardcover, and eBook from Apex Book Company.

ISBN (HC) 978-1-937009-78-6; ISBN (TPB) 978-1-937009-77-9

Apex Publications, PO Box 24323, Lexington, KY 40524

Visit us online at ApexBookCompany.com.

For my Girl Scouts: If I teach anything, let it be to not be quiet when you see something wrong in the world. Stand up, be loud, make yourself heard— for yourself, for your Girl Scout sisters, for your community, for the world. You can make a difference!
—Lesley Conner

For my family. They've seen me through some tough times during the production of this book. Love y'all.
—Jason Sizemore

CONTENTS

TO WRITE

BY ANNIE NEUGEBAUER

Tonight I dreamed
my mouth was zippered shut,
like some macabre doctor
had taken the school teacher's gesture
quite literally
and replaced each lip with one half a zipper.

Like any fresh surgery,
the flesh ached and burned,
far too tender for me to even think
of touching it with the gentlest fingertips,
much less grasping the metal pull
and opening the angry little teeth.

I wandered down a street I knew well
surrounded by strangers who my dream told me
I knew well as well
and every one of them
sealed at the mouth:
a zipper,
a line like melted wax,

sutures stitched across like a rag doll,
a single, large button pulled up over the top lip,
staples,
the particularly vicious stretch of super glue,
and, most terrifying of all, a perfect, smooth melding of
    bottom to top lip
no line or seal remaining where mouth used to be,
only a vague bump out of the teeth beneath the flesh,
caged.

I was desperate to tell them something.
Wild with the need.
I don't know what it was.
I don't know if I even knew, then, in the dream.
I know only that I raced from person to person
forcing myself into their paths
and trying
again and again—oh, sleeping eternity—
to speak.

Silence.

The words piled up against the inside of my zipper,
stacked up on my tongue,
brushed the roof of my mouth
and gullet
and down my clenched throat,
choking,
tears stinging my fresh wounds,
and still,
still ...

Never has there been a dream
with such a perfect lack of sound.

When I awoke,
reader,
I did not speak.

I picked up the notebook
I keep by my bed
and I began to write,
the scratching of my pen
against this page
pulling and clicking
like the long, metallic freeing
of a zipper.

KINDLE

BY BROOKE BOLANDER

IT'S THE LAST EVENING OF THE YEAR, AS BITTERLY COLD AS COINS in a factory owner's pocket, and the snow makes blue hummocks of familiar landmarks up and down the avenues of the great capitol city all the way to the palace gates. Crowds scurry through the drifts, hats tugged down, and collars turned up. They have no more need for matches than the little girl watching them wistfully from the alleyway might have for a china dolly.

The royal family had been the first to have their home wired for electricity. It had been right there in the newspapers the child's grandmother used to wrap her feet, the wonders of the modern age come to make life better for every man, woman, and child in the kingdom. Grandmother, sharp as the first crust of ice on an October puddle, had snorted and spat over her shoulder in the direction of the palace, shaking her head. Her opinions of the Tsar and his rule were well-known in that section of the quarters and try as the girl's father might to make the old beldame hush up her talk, he never did manage the trick.

"Making life better for who, now?" she rasped, breath billowing in the cold. "Mark my words, the only ones who will be benefitting from that are thems that don't need it. The rest of us will have an even harder time of it from here on out, see if we don't."

She had vanished sometime around midsummer, when the days stretched on 'till well past midnight and the skirmishes blazed hottest. The girl's father had said the squawking old banty must've gotten what was coming to her and toasted her memory in five different saloons while the girl stood outside, looking pathetic for coins. It had been an easier sell than the matches, at least.

The palace glows on the horizon. There are four princesses who live inside, rarely seen but said to be vivacious and fair-haired and full of fun. All they do all day is learn sums and stuff themselves full of sweetmeats, huddled by fires that never go out. Grandmother always said this was a bloody disgrace, but right now, with the girl's shoes gone and her toes numb, every yellow-lit shop window full of fat geese and Father waiting at home with a strap in one hand and a bottle in the other, it doesn't sound like all that wicked an existence at all. It sounds like something she'd like to reach out and take for herself like plucking a pork pie from a windowsill.

She reaches out for a passerby's trouser leg and earns a kick for her troubles that scatters her matches in the snow. Frantically, whimpering under her breath, she scrambles to scoop them back up, praying to Grandmother and the Good Lady Luck, both, they won't be ruined by the wetting. If she's managed to waste an entire basket of goods in one night, there's no telling what Father might do. Little girls, he's often fond of telling her, go for a high price in some places, even ones as dark and black-eyed as her.

Her grimy hand trembles as she strikes one against the basket handle, barely daring to breathe. The sputter and hiss as the sulphur tip catches and blazes like a Christmas star beneath her cupped palm is the sweetest thing she's ever heard, prettier than church bells or meat's sizzle. The little flame gutters in the gust from her relieved sigh, but stubbornly refuses to go out, a tiny spot of warmth and light in this numb black and blue bruise of a night. She holds it, transfixed, until it burns all the way down and blisters her fingertips. She tosses it away into the darkness, where it lands unseen with a last faint hiss of steam. The panicked thing hammering away behind her rags and ribs still itself.

The night seems much emptier now that she's been reminded of light, and ever so much colder now that she's been reminded of heat. Light streams down from high windows overhead, so butter-thick and butter-yellow, you could baste a bird in it, but it's no more hers than anything else behind those thick slabs of glass. Gazing up at the frosted panes, something flickers inside her, angry and wanting at the same time. She snatches up another match and strikes it, inhaling the smoke and heat. It's not fair that she should be out here in rags, afraid to go home with snowflakes gathering in her braid, when so many others have so much. It's not right that she has to beg to be seen when Grandmother always said her mothers and her mother's mothers were warrior queens, riding where they liked and taking what they wanted. Hot tears gather in her eyes, blurring the flame to an indistinct smear.

The smear becomes a spangled vision. Like peering through a muslin curtain, she can just about see them: women with round faces and dark braids like hers, dressed in riding leathers, seated about a rug, laden with steaming food. Stews thick with meat, cheeses yellow as a flower-seller's daffodils, plump roasted chickens and piles of potatoes, mashed and salted—the saliva gathers in the girl's mouth until she has to swallow, ashamed, knowing none of it is real but wishing it were so badly, she smells every item in the feast. There's a fire, too, a rosy thing burning low and hot in its pit, the kind that bakes your shins so deliciously, you don't dare move them from the hearth until the heat is almost unbearable. Occasionally one of the women will give it a poke, sending up sparks and smoke that escapes through a hole in the roof.

The women's features are indistinct, but somehow the match girl knows that her mother is there in the circle, and Grandmother, as well. She reaches for the veil, wanting to see better, wanting to join them, *oh please don't go, wait for me, wait—*

Another match falls from her fingers and dies in the snow. The vision goes out like a snuffed candle. The street is empty, save for a few homebound stragglers, and the only things she can smell are her own sodden clothes and the faint, ghostly char of burned matches. The parts of her that aren't yet numb ache with the cold. She thinks of that merry fire, the searing bite of it, the coals glowing like cherries on a cake in a baker's window.

She should be heading home. The snow is falling in great gusts, now, muffling the world like eiderdown. If Father is there and sober, he'll beat her for wasting matches. If he's down at the saloon, the beating will wait until morning, but the house will be cold, not even the meager night-fire they keep banked with newspapers and twisted hay, sputtering behind the hearth. In either case, she sees little point in starting out just yet. At least here, she can have these little dreams, fleeting as they are. There's a recklessness in her where fear usually sets. It's a small, smoldering thing, enough to make her pull another match from the basket. This one takes a couple of strikes to get going before bursting to life.

Such flames in her vision! Not merely a cook fire in a pit, this time, or a crackling blaze behind a hearth, but a roaring whirlwind of consuming orange and red, licking at the beams of a sagging hovel. It melts all the snow around it in a great, wet circle up and down the alleyway like spring thaw come early. Water trickles and burbles beneath the crackle-crumple-crash. Smoke and cinders erupt from the windows, the chimney, the roof. They taste the shingles of the shack next door, considering their next meal.

Someone inside is screaming. The match girl recognizes his voice. She's heard it raised in anger or dropped in slurred good humor many times before in her life. This is the first time she's ever heard it screeching in fear, scalded down to naked pain and panic. Perhaps he is pinned beneath a beam, or unable to find the door in the smoke. Perhaps the way is blocked.

The match girl smiles. She's smiling still when the match at last goes out, leaving her alone once again in the dark and cold.

Were it summer, or spring, she might feel guilt for such an imagining. The priests, safe and dry now in their warm churches and their great, wool vestments, would tell her to honor her father as she would honor the great God in His Heaven, the eternal Father of them all. But God, she thinks deep down in her blasphemous little heart, feels very far away, and if He is anything like Father-on-Earth, that's probably for the best. All she has are her matches, and aren't those named after Lucifer himself?

If she's going to Hell for these thoughts, she muses, at least she'll be warm. She takes a whole handful this time and strikes them all at once like a torch—

—in the hand of her beloved grandmother, standing before her as real and sturdy as a policeman or a lamppost. She tries to cry out, but all that emerges is a croak.

Her face is indistinct in the flickering light of the torch, her wiry, old frame cloaked in a woolen greatcoat, dyed a startling red. A cap is pulled down low over her gray braids.

"Girl," says the grandmother in a voice so familiar, it makes the match girl's heart ache, "you're on the right track, but you're not quite there yet." She stamps her boots in the snow. The girl cannot remember her grandmother ever wearing boots like these, but there was much about her life Grandmother had never revealed. "And I'm afraid until you find the right track, there will be no rest for you, mightily unfair as it seems. Try to remember what I'm about to tell you, little one. Carry it with you to the next cycle and go from there."

She leans down, so close the match girl can see herself reflected in the old woman's black eyes, the little bundle of matches blazing away in her hand. Grandmother smells of rosemary, vodka, gunpowder, and cheroot smoke, just as she had in life. Pamphlets stick out of the coat pockets, the kind you found littering the ground after marches, wadded in-between the bars of the palace gates.

"Dying in the snow's not enough," Grandmother rasps. "Taking down that drunken lout of a father of yourn, still not enough. You got the blood of warrior queens in you, child. Think bigger. Seize back what belongs to you from them who took it long ago. And for pity's sake, if you're gonna be a martyr in anybody's story, at least make sure it's your own. Let others tell it, and they'll take your name and they'll take your fire and then they'll take everything else."

The match girl tries to focus, but Grandmother's face seems to recede into the darkness before her. She tries to move her limbs, to crawl after her, but they feel frozen solid, too heavy to even twitch.

But her ears still work, and they catch the last words Grandmother speaks before the matches burn out and darkness falls a final time.

THEY FIND HER FROZEN IN A DOORWAY THE NEXT MORNING, A bundle of spent matches clutched in one blue hand. What a pity, the constables say. Poor little beast. At least she died smiling. D'you think she saw Heaven, there at the last, and the good reward that awaits all who suffer quietly in the snow?

IT'S THE LAST EVENING OF THE YEAR, AS GLITTERING COLD AS A guillotine blade, and the snow makes blue hummocks of familiar landmarks up and down the avenues of the great city, all the way to the factory gates. Mara watches the last of the holiday crowds go by, bundled and fur-framed against the cold, warm and on their way to warmer, in brightly-lit parlors and dining rooms, and she wants to throw her basket of matches after them like a curse. Were Father still alive, he would beat her for even thinking of such waste, but Father is long dead in the garden where they plant paupers, burned to a cinder in his bed one night while she was out selling her wares.

The world is cruel to orphans, cruel as man reeking of drink with a strap in his hand. His death has made things no easier, although she's still glad for it, down in her secret heart of hearts. What she makes now, she keeps. She uses it to buy more matches from the factory girls—the match-makers with their swollen gums and gapped smiles, with lives like mayflies—and in this way she keeps alive a little longer, one more sunrise and one more sunset, snatched defiantly like a pork pie from a windowsill. But her cheeks are very thin, now, are Mara's, and every night this winter is a little colder than the one before it. The rich have long since wired their homes for electric bulbs, mimicking the royal family in their palace on the hill, and the poor hoard their matches like gold or the last bite of stew, buying more only when it's necessary.

She reaches out for a passerby's trouser leg and earns a kick for her troubles that scatters her matches in the snow. Frantically, hissing curses under her breath, she scrambles to scoop them back up, praying to Grandmother and fickle Lady Luck, both, they won't be ruined by the wetting. Grandmother had vanished not long before Father's death, during the bright mosquito-bite summer when the nights were longest and the skirmishes outside the palace hottest. Marai's father had toasted the old revolutionary's presumed death, but Mara still holds out hope that, someday, she'll return for her girl. It's the one bright spot that keeps her hanging on, the goad that moves her to snatch up the matchsticks when she otherwise might simply watch them sink into the dirty slush.

Her grimy hand does not tremble as she strikes one against the basket handle, resigned to whatever may come to pass. The sputter and hiss as the sulphur tip catches and blazes like a morning star beneath her cupped palm is a relief, but not as much as the sound of a sizzling goose or frying bacon would be right now, when all she's got in her belly is a crust of soggy bread and half a Christmas orange a passerby handed her in lieu of coins, earlier that evening. Mara always accepts food when they offer it. She rejects their pitying looks, the sad shaking of a hat-swaddled head atop a scarf-wrapped neck, the way they want to make her into something she isn't—something that doesn't belong to her, but to them. A symbol, an icon like the ones all gaudy-painted in church, dying in the snow.

She'd rather them just buy the bloody matches and throw them away, if it came down to it. It makes no different what they do with the things, so long as they pay up.

The little flame is warm, bright, and for her and her alone. For the briefest of moments, her fingers stop being numb as it burns down to their tips. And then, just like that, it's gone, smoke sighing away into the lowering sky like the soul from a body. Mara is left alone in darkness, feeling even wetter and colder than before.

She could go to the orphanage run by the church, but she knows all too well what the nuns and priests get up to in there; there are plenty of other escaped orphans on the streets with stories to turn your hair white. Grandmother had always been dismissive of the entire institution. She would wave her hand at their newspaper-wrapped feet—the holes in the roof of their hovel, the grim factories hemming them in, the grand, distant domes of the royal palace—and bark a laugh, cold as the sparks off an iron wheel.

"Whose god," she would ask of no-one in particular, "that's what I'd like to know. Is there a God reserved for them up on the hill, and another assigned to us down below? Does He walk up and down the factory rows with a little badge and notebook in his hands, handing out citations, scribbling down the names of them that works hardest and suffers longest? 'Cause so far as I can tell, there's no God down here and never been in my lifetime. Maybe He's something you take for yourself like a loaf of bread or a rich man's pocket watch."

On the rare occasion or two Father had taken her to mass, the priest had gone on at length about the importance of suffering. To suffer hardships without complaint was a virtue, he said, and virtue would surely bring you closer to God. But if that's true, Mara finds herself thinking, she and the girls who work in the match factory should glow from head to toe like consecrated candles. It feels like a lie told to comfort someone—a lie told to sooth someone into a cold, frozen sleep.

Sleep. She knows better than that. Don't sleep. Light another match and be done with virtuous suffering, if only for the length of a single match's lifetime. The sharp hiss of the head striking brings her eyes back into focus, warding her eyelids off for another sweep of the clock's hands. In the glow, she sees a vision, indistinct, as if seen through a gauzy curtain or a frosted windowpane.

There is an older man in a study, balding but well-dressed. A warm fire roars in the grate behind him, well-fed and stoked without a care for how much fuel it might be burning. On the desk next to his inkwell, something in a mug wisps steam. Tea, maybe; he has to blow on it before taking a sip. A maid comes in to carry away the remains of a half-gnawed roast mutton, doing her best not to disturb him.

Mara cannot see what he is writing, but somehow, in her vision, she knows all too well what the spidery handwriting must say. It is a fairy story, a parable about the virtue of suffering as she now suffers, cold and mute and alone. Resistance is wicked. Want is wicked; little girls and women who want more, wickedest of all. God only blesses those who slog soundlessly beneath their burdens and die with a smile. To them, the gates of Heaven will eventually open, even if the only gates ever unlocked to them on Earth were the iron-tipped bars of a factory.

Anger and resentment at the brokenness of the world should be snuffed out at all costs. Anger rises in her own limbs, swift and sudden and warming as a hot mug of cider, gulped all at once. Who does this moral serve? Why try to lull her and those like her to sleep, when that sleep will eventually kill them as surely as slow poison?

Jaw clenched, cold and hunger temporarily forgotten, she leans in closer.

A draft of air from somewhere causes the candle on the writer's desk to gutter. As he looks up from his work at the sudden darkness, his elbow catches the candlestick's base. It teeters and wobbles and totters, finally falling against his shoulder in a splash of hot tallow and sparks. Flame leaps from the wick to the wool of his frock coat, catching merrily in the time it takes to blink. He leaps to his feet, so fast he upsets his chair, beating frantically at himself. In his panic, he trips over the overturned furniture, totters, and, like the candlestick before him, tumbles to earth, brushing a set of curtains on the way down. They go up with almost as much gusto as the woolen coat. The entire elegant study is now rimed in fire, the man knocked unconscious in his fall.

The maid has just burst in and is shrieking in the doorway when the match finally goes out. The crackle of the flames cuts off abruptly. Once more, there is nothing but the soft, muffled sounds of the winter night, the distant rumble of carriages throwing up slush and the creak of street signs in the cold wind.

Mara realizes she is smiling.

How awful, she makes herself think. *What a vision to have, of such a terrible accident! If I should light another, perhaps it would erase the memory of that poor man's suffering with its cheerful light.*

The tips of her fingers are blistered and throbbing, now. She relishes the feeling as she strikes a third. Again, a vision plays out before her eyes, the frozen spines of her lashes.

She herself is in this one. Mara has rarely seen her own reflection, but she knows who the ragged figure is in the way of dreams, a familiarity like staring at her own hands folded in her lap. She looks ... warm. Her mitten-less fingers are outstretched over a great bed of coals and ashes at her feet. Water drips from her snow-wetted braid. She has a stick in one hand that she's using to poke and prod at the smoldering mess in front of her, stirring up sparks like clouds of summer midges.

She is not alone. Jenny, one of the girls who toils in the match factory, crouches beside her, cheeks rosier than they've ever been, her own braid thick and yellow. When this Jenny smiles, she has all her teeth, spared by the poison vapors that have stripped them in life. She pokes at the embers with a stick as well, chatting to Mara in a familiar way they've never been allowed in the waking world. Another expert jab and she's drawing a potato out of the coals, sooty and steaming, jacket split to reveal the mealy goodness inside. Looking at it makes Mara-in-the-here's mouth water. Her shrunken stomach seizes fiercely enough that she almost drops the match.

The two girls half the potato. It burns their fingers and they laugh, tossing the pieces in the air, blowing on them to try and make the red-hot chunks cool faster. The vision recedes, as if Mara is hiding in the back of a wagon, slowly pulling away. She can see, now, that there is a great mountain of burnt timbers and smoking rubble, metal bars half-melted and tilting to prod the gray sky. Mara and her companion—doll-sized, now, against the ruin—are cooking their meal in the remains of some great burning. Occasionally something shifts and crashes. Snowflakes sizzle and hiss in tiny, agonized whispers as they fall from Heaven.

The gates of the factory are flung off their hinges, whether from the fire or from some other force. All that's left of the match manufacturer's industry is a pile of glowing coals, a warm place where two girls can munch on potatoes and enjoy each other's company. Mara wants it to be real so badly, she can almost smell the hot, wet ash, can almost feel the heat of the potato as she sinks her front teeth into the gritty mess. Tears are freezing on her face as the final match burns her fingertips black.

Not yet, says a voice behind her closing eyelids. It sounds an awful lot like Grandmother, or maybe Jenny, or maybe both of them together at once. *You're close, you're so awful close, you've got your name took back and your purpose tucked in and you're glowing inside, all rosy-red, but you've just a little further to go. Can you see it? Can you see where you need to go from here?*

THEY FIND HER FROZEN AGAINST THE FACTORY GATES THE NEXT
morning, a bundle of spent matches clutched in one blue hand.
What a pity, the constables say. Was this the girl they called Mara?
She never was one to ask for help, poor beast. Suffered quiet as
anything, never complained after her father passed. Like a little
saint.

The matchstick girls know better. That was Mara, they say to
each other. She never asked for anything from this lot, and why
should she have to? Why should any of us have to? Don't we
deserve to live better than this, scraping and starving and dying of
the phossy jaw to pad the pockets of them in the palace over
yonder?

IT'S THE LAST EVENING OF THE YEAR, AS GLITTERING COLD AS A
bayonet's tip, and the snow makes blue hummocks of familiar landmarks up and down the avenues of the great city, all the way to the
royal barracks. Mara watches the soldiers clomp-stomp by in clus-
ters of twos and threes, collars turned up and hat flaps tugged
down, already enough applejack working in their systems to turn
the teeth of the bitterest wind, and she doesn't even try to sell
them what's in her basket, in case they recognize her from the
week before. She's just a thin-faced girl shivering in the snow, a
basket of matches at her half-frozen feet. As long as that's all she
is, she's safe.

Since the night of the factory fire, her family and friends have
been scattered like handbills in a high wind, some in hiding and
some captured and a few others most certainly frozen breathless
beneath the ground. The broadsheets wrapped around her hands
and feet had blamed it all on an arsonist riot, a violent rabble
making unreasonable demands of their bewildered employers.
They made no mention at all of the girls dead, or disfigured from
phosphorus fumes, the bread shortages squeezing the city like a

broken accordion, or the private army the factory owners had hired to break up the strike that really wasn't private in the slightest. They may not notice Mara as they pass, on their way to parties and saloons, but she recognizes many of their faces beneath royal livery.

The second, third, and fourth pages of the newspaper had been devoted to an account of the youngest princess's confirmation. Ten thousand blessed candles had burned, as the priest delivered the rites (the demand for matches had outstripped the factory's ability to manufacture them; this was not touched upon). There was a detailed description of the many gifts the princess had received, the important guests who had attended, and the banquet table, where they had all nibbled and grazed afterwards. No shortage of food behind the palace walls, that was for certain.

What about Jenny, and Olga, and all the rest of the girls out of a job, now that the factory is a smoking pile of rubble? What of the organizers, their blood spilled on the snow beneath the clubs of soldiers with faces as hard and red as bricks? Mara would pray for their safety, but prayers must go through the church, and the church is a compromised channel. She settles on lighting a match for them, instead, a tiny spark that turns the flesh of her cupped hand to rosy stained glass. Let Princess Annalise have her ten thousand flames. This one belongs to the girls of the factory.

Such a little thing, a match. So unimportant, in this new era of electricity. But a match was a free agent; it needed no bulb or wire down which to run to be dangerous. Mara watches it push back the night in wonderment. It gives her the same feeling in the pit of her chest she gets when Grandmother talks to a crowd like they're a bundle of matches themselves, and all they need to burst into a mighty, roaring torch is the deft strike of some unseen hand. The factory bosses had felt it and had feared and hated the old woman above all other foes. Now the rulers of the kingdom know what she's capable of, as well, and soldiers pace the streets and alleys night and day, looking for an excuse to stick a bayonet between someone's shoulder blades. It's not safe for Grandmother to show her face in public, not even to collect her only grandchild. Mara misses her so badly, it ties her empty stomach in knots, but she at least understands. They had gone over the risk of this happening long ago.

"If we should get pinned apart and you can't go home, the best thing you can do is stick tight in one place and wait it out," Grandmother had said in her smoky rasp. "You got friends, and one of our people will happen along and find you before too long. Keep warm and keep your head down, and I'll be back soon's I can. I'm a hard one to snuff, else they wouldn't always try so hard to do it."

It had been a good plan, and sound advice at the time, and because Mara loved and trusted Grandmother like she trusted the sun's rising, she had followed it to the letter, finding a doorway in a side alley and making camp there. But days had passed, and then weeks, and none of their people had ever happened along. Mara tries not to worry too much about them. She focuses on surviving, scraping and stealing and selling her matches when someone's actually willing to stop and buy.

The match goes out. The alley is almost totally silent, save for the distant crunching of some passerby's boots in the snow. Mara has never felt so cold before. Her ears ache with it. Her cheeks have gone numb with it. Her fingers are clumsy, dead things that refuse to work properly as she fumbles and gropes in her basket for another two sticks, desperate to ward that inky darkness off for just a moment longer. Maybe someone who isn't a soldier will happen by and see her and take pity. Maybe the heat will wake her up just a little. Maybe—

A vision in the spark and hiss and sudden flare, seen as if through thin muslin curtains.

The grand cathedral of ten thousand candles glowing with a holy white light, pews filled with the rich and the powerful and the gilded. Princess Annalise, so good and pure, kneels at the feet of the archbishop and he blesses her, prays for her, secures her place in Heaven Above. All those who witness the benediction smile and simper and feel that this is right, is good, is owed. They don't really notice the candles, let alone consider who made the matches that lit each one. They are deaf to the voices of the girls screaming for justice inside the flames, although the howl is so loud, Mara can't imagine how that could be. All they can hear is the power jangling inside their own pockets, buying them an audience with God.

There's a sudden gust of wind down the nave that sets plumes on fancy hats shaking and fur-lined collars to trembling like dandelion fluff. Shadows flicker and test their wings. The voices of the girls in the candles are a righteous chorus, now, rebellious angels harmonizing at the moment before the fall. All of the little fires seem to blow and join together until both sides of the cathedral are sheets of living, singing flame. They reach up and up, setting the walls alight—licking at the rafters—and then—

Again, the matches sputter and die. The vision fades, although Mara's ears still ring with the sound of ten thousand ghostly voices raised in song. She sits in the quiet for a moment, trying to commit the sound of the tune to memory.

She grabs three, this time, striking them all at once against the brick wall at her back.

"Get up," says Jenny, grabbing her roughly by the shoulder. There is no veil between her and this vision. She's pulled to her feet by it, linked arm-in-arm with it, half-carried down the blue alleyway by a friend who cannot possibly be there. Jenny hasn't been this spry in months. The phossy jaw has eaten her strength so she can barely stand upright at her place on the factory floor, and yet here she is, as solid and real as the cold and the hunger and the darkness, pulling Mara along to who knows where. Her grip is iron. "You've got places to be. Don't argue—just-come-*on!*"

They round a corner and come face-to-face with a drunken huddle of soldiers, who blessedly pay them no mind. Mara tries finding her voice to ask where they're going, but she seems to have left it behind in the alleyway along with her basket of matches. Up a dog-legged side street so narrow their shoulders touch the walls

—down snow-clogged closes and thoroughfares choked with cheerful crowds of midnight revelers—shambling across busy avenues just beneath the hooves and noses of overworked carriage horses—on and on and on Jenny drags her, steadily puppeteering them both uphill to where the palace sags beneath its domes and spires and clustered growths of incandescent bulbs. It glows like a false moon, just over the next rise, desperate to be noticed even out of eyeshot.

They reach the top of the bluff and there it finally lolls, gaudy on the other side of the parade grounds. Nobody else is around. The palace lights throw strange shadows on the unbroken snow, the lumps and humps where statues and benches and pigeons should be. Mara has never been this close to the palace at night before. She squints her eyes against the glare.

"Just a little further," Jenny says. She sounds almost sorrowful. "I wish I could've lived to see you do it, Mar, but I know you'll—"

The last of the three matches dies with a fizzing whistle. Jenny winks out. Mara blinks and she's lying beneath a bench on the parade grounds, alone, a basket with four matches left at her head and a burned-out bundle of smoking char clutched in her fist.

I don't want to go any farther. No. No more moving. Here in the lee of the bench, out of the wind, she feels safe and comfortable, almost warm. After all that walking—vision or not, it had been a *lot* of walking—all she wants to do is let the snow fall over her like a blanket until Grandmother comes to pull it back. What was it that Jenny had wanted her to do? Why had she dragged her all the way up here? If she was only a vision, did it really matter what she had wanted?

Up ahead, the lights of the palace blur into a soothing smear.

Rest, my child, whispers the voice of the priest. *You've earned a rest, after all you've been through.*

Sleep, poor innocent soul, wheedles the voice of the author, the writer of fairy stories and moral parables. *You've suffered so well, so beautifully well, and wouldn't you like to go to Heaven?*

Take a load off, says the voice of her father, slurred from too much drink. *Get comfortable. Ain't comfort a grand and glorious thing?*

Look at the lights of my palace, says the voice of the princess, flutelike and well-fed and used to being obeyed. *Don't they look nice? So pretty! Wouldn't you just love to sit here and look at them forever?*

And really, truth be told, she would like nothing more than to stay right where she's at and do just that. But the song of the fire is still in her head—all those voices raised until the rafters over the heads of the rich and the spiteful caught and smoldered and burned like kindling—and nobody who advised you to lie down and sleep instead of fighting was ever worth trusting.

She takes three more matches in her hand, frozen to a claw. She strikes them weakly against the frosted granite of the bench.

It's Grandmother who lifts her to her feet this time, Grandmother and a whole crowd of friends and colleagues—rabble-rousers and revolutionaries, torch-bearers and mask-wearers, so many Mara can't count them all. There's a current running through them that feels like fire. Someone sets her atop Grandmother's shoulders and a cheer goes up, an echoing hurrah that sends snow sliding off statues. Mara holds her breath, waiting for soldiers to come pouring over the hillside from every direction—for gunshots and alarmed shouts, the crunch of clubs on bone and the confused cacophony of a street battle—but somehow, miraculously, nothing happens.

"C'mon, child," Grandmother says. "Hang onto my hat. We're going to tear it all down, the entire blessed thing."

They surge across the parade grounds like an army of shadows, cheering, invincible, flickering firebrands beating back the steady electric glare of the palace all the way to the front gates. They break against the bars once—twice—again—until with a sound like a groan, the hinges give beneath the weight of hurled bodies and the entire structure goes toppling backwards into the snow. Now there are soldiers pouring forth, drunk on holiday milk punch or too much sleep, clumsy with sudden surprise. Most of them don't even have time to fix their bayonets or load their weapons. They swing their rifles like clubs, as the wave sweeps over them, pushing them back across the courtyard to the palace itself.

Grandmother sets Mara on the ground. All around them, the fight is joining.

"Don't worry about me," she says. "I got ninety-nine lives, and this isn't my first or my last. You get in there and give 'em what for." She pushes Mara towards a side entrance. "Go!"

And Mara goes, darting through the thicket of legs, the distracted throng of brawlers giving and getting just over her head. She's inside the palace before anybody has time to even think about stopping her.

Inside is more chaos. Guards are already rushing to secure the exits. Maids and servants and cooks and governesses mill and shriek in confusion. Someone outside hurls a flaming brand through one of the ornate windows, setting the curtains alight. Mara cuts a path through them all, shoving and clawing, headed for the grand central staircase. In the way of dreams and visions, she knows who waits for her on the topmost floor, on a balcony in a room at the end of an impossible hallway. The palace is vast beyond reckoning, but she doesn't lose her way, not even for a second.

Behind her, the front doors creak and rattle and finally give as the human wave batters them down.

Down that long, red hallway on the uppermost floor—through a bedroom stuffed with toys and fancies—past a table laden with sweets and a wardrobe stuffed with beautiful unworn dresses—and now she's bursting back out a final door into the cold night air, pushing through delicate lace draperies onto a wrought-iron balcony caked with snow. There, just ahead, stands the Princess Annalise, youngest of her doomed family, blonde ringlets already going limp from exposure to the wind and the wet.

She looks down her upturned nose at this ragged invader—the newspapers wrapped around her feet, the soot on her cheeks, her dress in stained tatters. Below them, the battle rages on; there's more fire now, gunshots, screaming of all kinds in all octaves. Smoke billows out the windows, filling the room behind them in a roiling gray cloud. The princess is obviously frightened—and who wouldn't be, considering her situation—but she hangs onto her composure with a determination that would at least be admirable in someone who understood pain.

She locks eyes with Mara, disdainful, taking a step back so that her back is braced against the balcony's railing.

"Who are you?" she asks. "What do you want with my family?"

The question is so coldly oblivious, it makes Mara's fists clench. She sucks in a deep breath beneath her hollow cheeks, her ribs like ladder rungs and her empty, aching void of a stomach.

"Everything," she says. "To stop being cold. To stop being hungry."

She takes another step forward. Annalise presses further away, her own delicate hands balling into fists. They circle one another like wary cats.

Hsssst.

The second-to-last match goes out. Everything—balcony, battle, princess—suddenly vanishes like smoke up a chimney. Mara is alone in a snowbank just outside the palace gates, three dead matches in her fist and one left in the basket at her feet.

She's soaked through and wet to the bone. Ice has formed on her eyelids, weighing them down. She tries to stand, willing herself upright, but for some reason, her legs refuse to obey. Through clawing at the iron bars, she manages to pull herself to a standing position, although it costs her most of the skin on her naked fingers. She stands there, clinging to the cold metal like it's Grandmother's trouser leg, for a hundred years of winter before the blood sluggishly remembers how to run through her veins and her legs go back to bearing weight, if clumsily. She wobbles and wavers like an old man leaving a saloon at closing time.

The snow is flying fast and thick. Above her, crouched like some bulbous, phosphorescent toad, the palace squats triumphant, hale and whole and untouched, its gilded inhabitants warm in their beds. There will never be a day in their long lives, or the lives of their descendants, where they have to worry about a thing. They sleep on stolen land beneath stolen feathers. They eat and take, and they have no need for matches or match girls.

See me, she says to the palace, squinting up through the snow-storm into its blind windowpane eyes. *Look at me, you big ugly thing.*

Somewhere, a church bell tolls 3:00 a.m. The palace pays the tiny figure no mind.

See us. See us or we'll throw down your gates and trample your gardens and take back everything you've stolen, if it takes a hundred attempts and a hundred lifetimes.

If the palace were a sow, it might roll over and crush her beneath its pale bulk. Being only a building, it doesn't move. As it has for a century, it just sits there lumpen on its foundations, an eyesore stooping to conquer.

Mara is so tired of fighting. She leans her full weight against the fence, too exhausted even to cry.

One match left, says Grandmother's voice from somewhere inside the fog behind her eyes. *Might want to light it and see what happens.*

What Mara wants, more than anything, is a warm blanket and hot stew and all the things those girls inside the palace take as their birthrights. What she wants is to be left alone. But she sighs, feeling suddenly as though she's done this a thousand times before, and she reaches into the basket dangling from the crook of her arm—has it been there this entire time?—and she pulls the final match from its snug, wicker nest. It seems to weigh as much as a telegraph pole.

Hssht.

Nothing happens. No visions drop like painted backgrounds. No figures rise to lift her from the snow. The palace doesn't crumple in on itself; the vengeful ghosts of all the royal family have wronged stay in their graves. Mara feels no surge of warmth or revolutionary fervor swelling in the marrow of her bones. There is just this moment, suspended between midnight and dawn, and the flame at the end of a matchstick. What she does with it is entirely up to her.

Something rattles against her dragging foot. A half-finished bottle of liquor left behind by some lonesome New Year reveler. She bends to pick it up, takes a hesitant sniff. It stinks like a saloon, like her barely-remembered father. Whatever's inside, it's strong, and clear, and were she to put the match to it—were she to tear off what was left of the hem of her ragged skirt and stuff it into the mouth of the bottle, were she to carefully heft the entire makeshift projectile in her hand as the flames slowly crept down the fabric to meet the noxious stuff in the bottom—it would make such a lovely blue comet as she hurled it over the fence with the last of her strength, such a fine and furious meteor, striking home through the closest window she could find.

She watches the drapes catch, listens to the panicked cries within and without, the distant sirens already blaring. She smiles, drops her basket, and topples over sideways in the snow.

———

THEY FIND HER FROZEN OUTSIDE THE PALACE GATES THE NEXT morning, spent matches spread around her in a blackened circle. They shake their heads, disgusted at the wanton violence of the underclass. Look, they say. This was Mara, the rotten grand-daughter of a rottener revolutionary. Even their children are corrupted and liable to lash out for no good reason at all. What will it come to, in the end, with such a nest of vipers stirring dissent?

Look, say the matchstick girls, the wives in the breadlines, the hungry and cold and exploited. *Look. Her name was Mara, and she was the granddaughter of a revolutionary, the daughter of warrior queens. If she could do it, why not us? If a dying girl could light a match, how hard must it be?*

Their whispers, running through the crowds, sound like the faintest crackle of flames.

IT'S THE LAST EVENING OF THE YEAR, AS BITTERLY COLD AS bones in an ash-heap, and the snow makes blue hummocks of familiar landmarks up and down the avenues of the great capitol city, all the way to the rusted remains of the palace gates.

WHAT THE MOUNTAIN WANTS

BY MAURICE BROADDUS AND NAYAD MONROE

IT WAS A NORMAL NOVEMBER UNTIL THE MOUNTAIN ROSE UP, towering over our neighborhood, changing everything. There were no birth pains to warn of its arrival, no earthquakes. It simply appeared, silently rising from the Crown Hill Cemetery and draping its shadows over us. It left a great hole in our neighborhood, an uncharted space on the map, drawing the city of the dead up into its tumorous mass.

People feared the mountain. "For Sale" signs sprouted like weeds in yards throughout the neighborhood. Those that didn't want to leave hoarded food, water, and weapons, suddenly withdrawn from and suspicious of their neighbors. A few wanted to appease the mountain, to offer up a sacrifice, but they perished like those men who violated the laws of approaching the Ark of the Covenant.

The mountain speaks to me. It wants me; it has its own gravity. That pull demands my perception, my presence, my participation. Despite my misgivings, I heed its call. Who has the strength to deny a mountain?

THE PARKING LOT OF B & E LIQUOR FACES THE NEW VISTA OF
the mountain of Crown Hill Cemetery, lit only by the sodium glare
of the single bulb, grudgingly replaced by the city, in a lone lamp
post. Sickly orange illumines two figures in the lot, *cold lampin' with
the mountain.*

"This nigga right here think he somethin' cause he got him a
mountain." Zeb watches the solitary man scramble along the
peak's side. Born Zebulon C. Minor II, he figures he got off easy
when it came to names, considering his brothers Abimelech,
Japheth, and Melchizedek. Zebulon means "to dwell." Sometimes a
name defines a person.

"What'chu gone do with a mountain?" Montaque Harding's
rheumy eyes also gaze upward. No one calls him anything other
than Q. He neither questions his name's origins nor hated it.
Sometimes a name is all someone has.

"Exactly my point, Q. Shit pops up, disrupts everything, then
he walk around like he better than everyone else cause he up there
and we down here. Ain't nobody's mountain. Nobody run that
shit."

"Zeb, he living a lie."

"Hell, yeah. It's all lies now. A lie can become the truth, if you
tell it enough times."

"Perception is everything."

"That's deep. Or bullshit. I'm too high to tell." The glow of
Zeb's next hit lights his face. He speaks through held breath.
"When did we become old heads, drinking on the corner?"

"We ain't there yet. Just two brothas chillin' after a hard day of
hustling."

"Yeah, it's not like we've gone crazy, running up and down a
mountain. Yet."

Q pulls his weary gaze from the mountain. "What you be
talkin'?"

"Talking that shit. I thought you knew."

They carve out the corner as sacred space.

Zeb pours out some of his 40 for the mountain.

I NEVER HAD THE COMPANIONSHIP OF A PET. I CAUGHT A TURTLE once. I let it creep around in my mother's garden. The turtle reached the chain-link fence which bordered the yard. It stuck its head through a hole, backed up when that didn't work, and then used its claws to begin to climb the fence. Its heavy, cumbersome shell wobbled back and forth with each claw-pull upward. I called over my cousins, and we watched it struggle to ascend. I left to join a game of hide and seek, not worried about the turtle's chance of success. When I returned an hour later, it was gone, and I never saw it again. I learned from that mistake.

Before its transformation, Crown Hill Cemetery was already the highest natural point in the city of Indianapolis. Colonel Eli Lilly himself was buried at its peak. It was also the final resting place of John Dillinger and his rumored prodigious member. Almost final. But maybe the mountain has always waited there, curled like a monstrous fetus below the ground, and gestating until the time of its arrival.

I could not stay away, nor can I leave. I carefully creep between the graves, clearing away the uprooted bushes and exposed roots. Arranging the headstones and building a parsonage of bones. Harvesting ivory relics, the pieces scattered, as if the mountain has chewed up the bodies and vomited them over itself. Like the turtle, I move upward at a slow and steady pace, compelled to strive for its peak.

Unlike the turtle, I know that I will fall.

THE WALL AROUND CROWN HILL CEMETERY—WROUGHT IRON bars on a brick foundation—remains intact, except for the hole left where a drunk driver ran a stop sign and drove across Doctor Martin Luther King Jr. Street, miraculously missing all traffic but plowing into the wall. In the darkness, two figures sneak through the gap, *cold lampin' with the mountain.*

"You got to hurry your ass up," Q says with the impatience of an older cat. Tall and gaunt, though walking with a slight stoop, he nimbly slides through and waits in the shadows. "You like a potato on legs."

"We on a deadline all of a sudden?" Short and bulbous, Zeb favors his left leg, sheathed in a homemade, plastic cast held on by elastic cords. One day, when he took out the trash, two boys jumped him and demanded his wallet. In the struggle, they stabbed him in the calf and left him with nerve damage, unable to fully use his ankle. "It's not like I have to get my head up by a certain time."

"Man, I know you already high. You on that smoke like it your nine to five."

"It only looks like I don't work, but I work. I got custody of Trey." Because of his special needs, tending to his oldest son is a full-time job. Zeb can't stand long enough to work a steady job, but Social Security denied his claim. Unable to afford official pain medications either, he smokes to get through his odd jobs. His ankle throbs already, just looking at the mountain that looms tall above him. "I have to stay steady grinding. Bills come too fast and checks come too slow."

"I heard that. My daughter's six, going to be seven next month. I'm all about her. If she has to get on a bus, get on my bike, or get on my back, I'm getting her to school each day. She's the future. She's my everything."

"Mmm-hmm," Zeb says. "I get my money, take care of my mini-me, pay those bills, and then dabble in my vices."

"Here's to dabbling." Q raises his brown bag to Zeb in toast.

They work their way up the mountain at the speed of city bureaucrats approving street repair, avoiding the path that's been so morbidly cleared. They avoid the grisly displays of earth-regurgitated bones. The man ahead has been collaborating with the mountain, hoping that being respectable will gain its favor.

"How'd we get here?" Zeb asks. "This mess here didn't rise up overnight."

"Ain't no unity in the community."

"That's what's up."

"We can't get together, can't clean up the city, can't build up what we need. Next thing you know, artists, bureaucrats, and—what do they call them folks with them skinny pants and big beards? Oh yeah—hipsters flow in like they the answer."

Zeb scans for any sign of the man skulking among the tombstones. "My beef is with the pastors."

"Come on wit' it then," Q says.

"They want to come after rappers for their shakin' booty videos. But they off drivin' fine rides and got their church all fancy with their manicured lawns and shit. While they sittin' in a neighborhood that looks like Beirut."

"They come round with their coalitions, city giving them money to pray whenever there's a shooting. Pray for me for free."

"And got white Jesus plastered all over they walls. The Bible says, 'skin of bronze' and 'hair of wool.' I know a hood nigga when I hear one."

"We're all God having a human experience." Q leans against a tree canted at an odd angle.

"What kind of experience is he having now?"

I HAD A CHURCH ONCE. MY CONGREGATION TRUSTED ME WITH their money, and we bought our church building from the United Methodists when they packed up and moved north. They wanted to make sure it went to a church that would make good use of the space for the community. But when our congregation shrank to ten families, we bought a smaller building. I kept the United Methodist's building. With the neighborhood changing, I thought the property value would increase well into six figures. Remembering the parable of the talents, I am a faithful servant of my master's goods, and nothing if not a shrewd steward.

I was a member of a pastors' coalition to walk the streets of the neighborhood to pray over them. The city balked at funding our faith walks, but we insinuated that without us to keep the peace at crime scenes, the police would have difficulty in conducting their investigations. The city paid us. Even gave us a seat on the mayor's commission. The murder rate has risen every year since 2014, breaking all previous homicide records. The FBI awarded us a special commendation for our work in that time period.

My stomach growls with such ferocious hunger, a voracious need that only grows as I climb. The mountain doesn't provide. When I lick the moisture from one tilted fountain, I read on its plaque, "Everyone who drinks of this water will thirst again, but whoever drinks of the water that I give him will never thirst.— John 4: 13-14." And I know that I will thirst again. I should shiver without protection from the night winds. The wind tells secrets about the mountain. The ground rises to meet my feet, the landscape undulates before me. I have the vague notion that I should pray, but the thought slips and slides away from me. I arrange the bones as I go, tending to this new temple that grows to lift me up with it.

With every breath, a pervasive fungal odor fills my nose and coats my throat, thick and cloying. A deep rot from repurposed earth. The remains of what went before scattered about like discarded toys. Memorial flowers bruised by the shifting upheaval. In my mind, the tributes vigorously twine around the graves and trees, extending tendrils outward. They assume aggressive new forms in response to their devastation, growing spiny and fierce, surfaces sharpening as they come for me, so that I can only continue forward.

Storm clouds succumb to starless black
Onward I climb.

THE LILLY FAMILY MAUSOLEUM RESTS ON ITS SIDE, CRUMPLED. Disrespected. Two figures huddle near the concrete monument, *cold lampin' with the mountain.*

"This is a test." Zeb leans against a cold slab with the name *Harrison* etched into its side. He lifts his plastic cast and rubs his leg.

"All of life is a test," Q retorts.

"Yeah, but this is to see what we made of here. Deep down."

"We can't let this go on."

"It's like this neighborhood is one big jail cell they don't want us out of ... until they do. The city just opened up that senior home. Gonna open that big tech project not far from here. They preparing things. Gonna be moving us out soon. Folks gonna 'discover' our neighborhood like Columbus did America, and then it'll be all lattes and craft beers," Zeb says.

"I just want to have a home and be peaceful. You talkin' politics, business, and folks with money and connections coming in. That's too ... big. You can't fight all that. I'm doing good to keep living beside this mountain."

"Mountain keeps growing, won't be nowhere to live in this neighborhood. Not that we can afford."

"Are you willing to go hard?" Q asked.

"I'm ride or die."

———

THE MOUNTAIN HAS ALWAYS BEEN HERE.

It is just the revelation of something vast and unseen, always waiting. It is a reminder of how powerless we truly are. It is the truth I already knew, as I am lost within its awful shadow. I itch with uncertainty, the outward manifestation of the discomfiture of my soul. I thought my place would be at the top of this mountain, at least for a time. But the mountain doesn't need me.

The mountain has always been here.

Invisible most of the time, its geotrauma reverberates, its proximity a threat. I stumble forward into a zone of alienation and find myself surrounded by two men. The abyss floats between us. I recognize them from the neighborhood, their faces, like the mountain, are both alien and intimate.

"Reverend," the taller man says. "What'chu gon do with a mountain? Is this who you are now?"

"I am a liar," I confess, and thus trap myself in a paradox.

"This is our everyday, but it don't have to be," the shorter one says. "Look."

I'm afraid to turn around. The wind fills my ears, all distortion and dissonance, harmonics without tune. I turn, and I see them. Dozens of people climbing, and dozens more approaching behind them. They carry flashlights and ... shovels? The two men come forward and stand with me, one on each side.

"This mountain doesn't belong here," the tall man says. "We have to take care of it, out in the open."

The short one grabs a shovel. "Any mountain can be unmade."

NOBODY LIVES IN THE SWAMP

BY DEE WARRICK

It might just be the weather, so flighty and temperamental, rain then sun and then rain again, all in an afternoon. Or maybe it has something to do with the people who move through the streets and over the canals, who breathe the air for a week or a weekend, and then pile into planes that carry them, exhausted, into the sky and deposited them in dull, sober places all over the world. Or maybe a city that survives fascist occupation never really learns to sit still after that, is always fidgeting and covering its face, muttering apologies for its collaborators both past and present.

Or maybe some part of the city really does takes hold of your lapel in a panic, when you and your lads are laughing on your way out of a sex show, or when you and your mom stop for a moment in Dam Square to consult the tourist map you picked up at the airport. It shouts, "You can't stay here! I am not a home! I am a swamp! The rich buy my canal houses, and the poor sleep beneath Centraal Station, and everyone else leaves! You must leave!" Nobody hears it, of course. Or, of course, they do hear it without knowing they've heard it, and they leave. It's a nice place to visit, but you wouldn't want to etcetera, etcetera.

Except for the rusalka. The city can't shake her.

Lots of girls drown. The rusalka heard this stupid rumor once, that you could drown in as little as a teaspoon of water. All over the world, girls are drowning all the time. And coming back after you drown, in the very spot where you stopped struggling and your lungs filled up, that's not all that remarkable either.

It is almost June, and in a few weeks, the unenforced/unbreakable laws that govern ghosts will loosen, and she'll be allowed to climb a tree and feel her skin dry out beneath the sun. She's picked her tree. It's right next to one of the residential canals, a quieter place than city center. And it's a good tree for climbing; the branches are strong and thick, and two of them have contorted over many long seasons into a V perfect for draping herself over. She swims past it, stares at it, imagines herself in it.

Before she was a rusalka, she was an American girl, and her mother was from Ukraine, and before the girl drowned, she listened to old stories about a week in early June when drowned girls could crawl up the banks of their rivers and lakes and climb up the trunks of trees. Men had to be careful. The drowned girls were mad with grief, possessed by a hideous hunger to drag men down to the muddy beds beneath their grave-waters and hold them there until they died. The girl's mother never explained why the drowned men didn't come back. Men make different kinds of ghosts, she guesses.

The girl never got to visit Ukraine, though she'd planned to backpack there the summer that she died. From the Netherlands to Ukraine, then back home to the States. Instead, she drowned in one of the canals. An American woman turned Ukrainian ghost, trapped in the waters of a Dutch swamp city. It was hard not to feel lonely, at first, tugged in that many directions by that many alien legacies. But eventually the herons came, snake-necked and long-legged, their black feather mohawks twitching in the breeze. They're a funny kind of heron; they look dirtier than their cousins, who live in swamps that haven't had cities built over them, and they don't bolt when people come close. They hold their ground, stare you down. Standing on top of a parked car, they seem to will you wordlessly to know that they were here first, and they will be here after you die, and they know when and where every unhappy event will occur.

They don't speak to the drowned girl, but they sometimes bring her tributes. Stolen things, reminders of what being a real, breathing, human person was like. Tourist maps. Hotel keycards. Sweatshirts, removed and tied insecurely at the waist between bouts of rain, falling to the sidewalk without being noticed. Broken umbrellas stuffed angrily into overflowing trashcans. These she has combined into a long summer dress that twitches and flows behind her in the canal water. It doesn't do much to keep her warm but having something to wear makes her feel a little more human.

She is treading water in the canal beside her tree, trying to will her skin into the future, to feel the rough bark pressing into the pads of her heels and between her shoulder blades. She is so mesmerized by the fantasy that it takes her longer than it should to notice a stranger—crying, angry—marching out of one of the apartment buildings beside the canal and climbing the rusalka's chosen tree. The strange girl grunts in frustration as she hauls herself up by the tree's thick branches, throws herself against the perfect V. The rusalka usually sinks to the canal's bottom when strangers come close, but the shock of this girl's anguish, the way she climbs the tree like she's proving something to whatever has made her so sad, those feelings paralyze the rusalka and she simply floats, watching. The stranger pokes clumsily at her phone once, twice, a few more times, then tosses the phone out of the tree with a sob. It clatters against the sidewalk. And then the stranger is looking at the rusalka, and in the dark, her wide wet eyes seem almost to glow. They stare at each other for a long time. The stranger's voice, when it comes, wavers in a way that betrays a feeling she's trying to hide: tears, of course, and fear, of course— the rusalka is a dead thing, and you should always fear dead things —but also hungry hope. She says, "You're a ghost."

No other girl has spoken to the rusalka, since she drowned. She says, "Sort of."

Then the stranger shifts her weight. "What's your name?"

She forgot her name. Herons don't have names and had no use for hers, and so soon, she found she had little use for it, either. Eventually, she even forgot how she'd died—beyond that she'd drowned, of course. Still, distantly, numbly, she is angry. It's unfair. However it is that she ended up here, it's unfair. And sometimes, when her anger breaks her heart, when the canals begin to feel so narrow and filthy that she can't move, can't breathe, that's when the herons bring her a man. Snare him with their beady, little, mesmerist eyes and lead him to a quiet stretch of canal, where the water is dark and reflects the city lights back at him, and she reaches out, gets her fingers tangled in him. Pulls him down with all the lost bicycles and empty beer cans. Holds him there and waits for the questions to leave his eyes. "You could have left," she tells him. "This city wanted you to leave. Haven't you seen the way the canal houses tilt and curl like crooked teeth? The way the swamp tries to swallow them? You're supposed to leave. No one stays. No one stays but me."

The men she drowns don't come back. Men make different kinds of ghosts. The drowned girl, the rusalka girl, see, when she was born, her mother and her father and the doctor who delivered her, they all thought she'd be a man, someday. They were wrong. Death knows. Whatever processes govern the manufacture of ghosts, they operate according to a weirder rubric than mothers and fathers and obstetricians.

The stranger's name is Claire, she says. She chose it herself, just like the rusalka chose the name she has since forgotten. Claire is a lot like the rusalka; the sort of girl who had to fight to prove it, who had to piece together girl-ness from scraps and guard it jealously from those who would take it from her. The rusalka asks her, "What are you doing here?"

"I live here," says Claire.

"No, you don't," says the rusalka. No one lives here. This place is a swamp, not a home.

"Why are crying?"

Claire doesn't answer. She only stares, her lips shaking. "You're dead ..." she says.

"Lots of people are dead," says the rusalka. It sounds stupid when she says it. What else do you say? How do you say anything at all?

Around them, the city looms. The canal houses rise at strange angles, forever sinking into the swamp and forever being rescued by expensive construction efforts. Someone, somewhere, howls— that deep, moose-ish howl universal to groups of drunk boys. Claire cringes at the noise, jerks away from it. She looks at the rusalka. "What are *you* doing here?"

Growing up, she experienced herself as a sort of chemical error, an instinctual wrongness, a self and a body that were distinct and discrete, and each of which mutually negated the other. She once cried, sitting on the edge of her bed while her mother shushed her and patted her too-short hair. Cried, the way only teenagers can cry, like the world is ending, like there's no such thing as melodrama or hyperbole, like every single thing is everything, and a lot of it. She said, "I think there's a monster in me," and was right. There was. Because every woman is a monster, sooner or later. That's just the kind of ghost the world turns women into. And that's why Claire is crying. And that's what the rusalka is doing here.

Before she can stop herself, the rusalka is telling Claire stories. The moon reflects off the water of the canal, and as the rusalka tells stories her mother told her, she imagines that the ripple and glow spin into shapes to match. Dead girls in June, hauling themselves up trees. Men mesmerized into trudging down muddy banks, their shoes filling with grave-water until they're close enough to grab and pull and hold. Herons dropping gifts into the city's canals, daring you to meet their gaze, and maybe learn the secrets they keep. A million secret rules applied to ghost-girls and illustrated in abstract with light and water and shadow and wind.

At the end, she says, "So ..."

Claire cries. And smiles. Shakes her head. Laughs. Then she climbs out of the rusalka's tree. She's careful. Slow. Like the tree might shatter, or like she might. She sits on the edge of the canal wall, cupping her elbows in her hands, letting her sneakers dangle near the water's surface. She says, "Is it lonely?"

The rusalka doesn't answer. How does anybody ever answer that question?

"I only ask," says Claire, avoiding the rusalka's eyes, "because ... what if it, um ... didn't have to be?"

The rusalka understands, but she can't let herself believe she understands. It's a big idea, one she can't believe she never considered before, an idea, the promise of which is so warm and dry and seductive that, if she allows herself to acknowledge it, she will be swallowed by it, and nothing but the idea will ever matter again. Once, another girl had loved her. Before the canals, and the herons, and the dead men. Before she sold her car to afford a plane ticket. And that girl had stopped loving her. And she had wept with her head in her mother's lap and said, "What if this is it for me? Girls like me, we don't fall in love. People don't fall in love with us." And her mother had said, "No, baby," and there was only a hint of the country she'd come from on her tongue. "This is not forever. It feels like forever. But nothing is forever." So. The trip. The Netherlands, then Ukraine, then home, perhaps healed, a little, perhaps smarter or harder than she'd been before. Except then, suddenly and painfully, it *was* forever. She was forever. This was it for her.

Claire says, "The men don't come back. They make some other kind of ghost, right? But ... then there's me."

And she lowers herself into the water. The canals are always deeper than people expect them to be, and the water swallows her whole for a second, rising up above her head before she pushes herself back to the surface, gasping at the cold, treading water gracelessly. She laughs. "Could it work?"

"I don't know," says the rusalka.

"But it could?"

"I don't know."

"Try," says Claire. "Pull me down. And let's see what happens."

On the edges of the canal, tiny, glowing marbles. The eyes of the herons, watching. The rusalka begs them, beseeches them. She needs them to share just this one secret, just this one and no others. But the herons only watch. The wind whips their filthy little mohawks, but they are otherwise still.

"Hey," says Claire. "Hey, come on."

The rusalka floats toward her. Places her hands on Claire's shoulders. She says, "I've never done this before."

"Me neither," laughs Claire.

The rusalka tries to pull Claire down. Tries to find the parts of Claire's skin that will yield to her fingers, to dig in, to sink. She closes her eyes and waits for the feeling of water rising above her shoulders, her chin, her nose, her eyes, waits for the streetlights and the moonlight to fade as the dark of the depths casts out dry light. But nothing happens. Neither of them move. Both of them float obstinately.

The rusalka opens her eyes. It's been a while since she cried. "There are rules," she says. "I can't break them."

Claire nods, though her breath hitches in her chest.

"I want to," says the rusalka. "I want to."

Claire nods again, but she also brushes the rusalka's cold hands off her shoulders, swims to the canal's edge, grabs hold of the ledge.

The herons watch. It's impossible to tell if they feel anything about this. The rusalka begs them to be sad for her. To wish this could have gone differently.

Claire, soaked, walks away from the canal. Her pace, her gait, they re-adopt that same desperate defiance with which she approached the rusalka's tree. She stops and picks up the phone she threw to the pavement. Laughs, kind of, in the way people sometimes do when something's funny in a painful way. Flashes the screen at the rusalka. "Didn't even crack," she says, then stalks back toward her apartment building. The rusalka can't hear it, but she can see, through the glass walls of the building's vestibule, that Claire is sobbing. Big teenager sobs, even though she must be at least as old as the rusalka was when she drowned.

The herons cannot comfort the drowned girl. They can't pet her hair and tell her that this is not forever. They can't be sad for her in any way she would understand. What they can do is catch the eyes of wandering men; the rich men who own the leaning canal houses, the drunk men who signal each other with wordless howls, the men in uniform who kick homeless folks out of Centraal Station and raid squats. But not just those men. Good men, too. Sweet men. Any men. The rules that govern ghosts are amoral and undiscerning.

And so, it turns out, is the heartbroken rusalka. She reaches out of the canal beneath a bridge in the red-light district and pulls down a group of three, all at once, and screams her anguish into their eyes as they go blank. She pulls men from the ferry that runs between the city center and Noord, right in front of everyone, and her fingers find their soft spots and sink like they couldn't with Claire's skin, and she shakes them until their lungs fill up. She punches holes in the bottoms of tour boats, and as the women on board sputter and struggle and swim to safety, she chews out the throats of the men who remain. Not because she hates them. Not because she desires revenge. But because this is her only recourse.

"I'm sorry," she shouts as the blood of these men clouds the canals. "But you knew this city didn't want you here. And I have to follow these fucking rules."

She murders men until dawn. The city is full of screams. In the morning, although it is not yet June, not yet the one week in June when she is permitted to climb, she tries to climb. And she finds that this is a rule that, for some reason, she is allowed to break. She weaves her way up the tree's thick branches and drapes herself across its perfect V, and she lets the sun bake away the canal water and fill her warmth. A heron pads across the pavement, stops at the base of the tree, looks up at her. She looks down at it. Then the heron turns away, stands guard at the trunk of her tree.

Just as she is beginning to feel warm, the city changes its mind, and the rain comes.

THE SKELETON ARCHER SPEAKS

BY JEREMY PADEN

Resurrection plants, they call them,
a Sahara tumble weed
that rolls over sands for hundreds
of years till water brings life,

& seeds fall & sprout in the sand,
only to shrivel & curl
into a ball that the wind drags
across the barrens till rain.

I stand, my body a sack
of bones—no, that's not right,
as if I were a bag of skin,
when I am but nothing.

Nothing but skeleton,
I stand, & how I stand,
who knows? No muscle, tendons,
ligaments, bind bone to bone

& bone to flesh. The bow bends,

as one hand pulls the string
& the other holds steady
against the force until release.

Once there was a man who said
his love was constant beyond death.
He promised his flesh had burned
so brightly that when senseless dust

it would still shine & yearn for love,
that scattered earth would gather
& throb like a heart aflame,
for love is stronger than death.

I am the Resurrection plant.
I am the bones left in the valley.
I am the ashes turned body,
the archer with bow pulled taut.

I am nothing but desire
& intention. I walk among
the living, dead. I am nothing
but arrow aimed at the heart.

OIL UNDER HER TONGUE

BY RACHAEL K. JONES

CARLOS AND ERIN WERE SEVENTEEN THE SUMMER THEY invented blackout spells and repaired old cars and adopted an orphaned android. They were both working part-time at the shittiest gas station in Boilingbrook, wiping swear words off the dusty pumps and stocking the shelves with bagged pickles and boiled peanuts. The manager always made Erin de-clog the toilets and clean out the corndog fryer, and once Erin threw out her back loading Pabst into coolers. But Erin lived for that job. It was her only escape from the Evangelical Fellowship Bible School summer program her parents believed would save her from her budding atheism and budding breasts.

"You're lucky you don't have to go," she told Carlos. His family attended Evangelical Fellowship too, but not as religiously as hers. "They give *homework.*" She wasn't on duty that night, but she'd told her parents she had a shift, just to hang out with Carlos. He was grabbing some fresh air on his dinner break, chewing through a bucket of fried chicken beneath the flickering lamplight just out of reach of the falling rain, a plastic poncho pulled over his Stop-N-Fuel uniform.

"Like math problems?" He offered Erin the bucket. She took a drumstick and gnawed a circle around the breading.

"Worse. It's sex stuff." She showed him the worksheet. She was supposed to sort twenty different physical activities into three categories: *Permissible, Questionable,* and *Sinful.*

"How do they rank hugs?"

Erin checked her work so far. "Front hugs definitely constitute 'purpling' and fall under *Questionable.* We're supposed to be—" She held up the worksheet—"*above reproach.* Side hugs are okay." It needled her, all of it, the worksheets and sermons, the prayers and endless memorization. It was supposed to bring you peace beyond measure and joy that lasted, but mainly it just depressed her.

Carlos grinned wide as the chasm inside her and opened his arms. "Well. Bring it in, then."

Erin dumped her backpack and hugged him ferociously. No side hugs allowed with Carlos. He smelled like sweat and engine oil, and underneath that, clean soap. His scraggly teenage beard scratched her cheek. She remembered long evenings slouched in the back pew during services, scrawling shorthand notes to Carlos on a hymnal's endpaper. Erin held the hug just a little longer. "I don't know how much more I can take," she admitted.

"Hey now. One more year, and we'll graduate."

"And then what? It's not like they're sending me to college." They didn't get to sit together in church anymore. Erin's dad put an end to *that.* "One more year, and I'll be married off and perma-pregnant. Sooner, if my dad gets his way. He wants to take me to that Christian marriage convention in Kentucky next month, the one where he found my brother-in-law."

"They can't force you to marry anybody," said Carlos. "It's against the law."

"April said the same thing. Now she's twenty-two, and already gestating Kid Number Four."

"Well, you'll be an adult at 18. In a few more months, they won't be able to touch you."

Erin pulled into herself, tugging on a strand of hair just to feel it hurt. "You don't get it. You're a guy. You don't have to get married before your dad lets go of you."

Carlos circled the blacktop, collected a couple of crushed beer cans, erased the word *fuck* from a dusty pump display, set a limp gas nozzle back into its holster. "My shift's over in 45 minutes. Let's kick off down to the pond after that. I want to show you something."

Erin hugged Carlos again, mostly for the principal of the matter, but also because he smelled good. "Sounds like a plan. Dad doesn't expect me home until midnight."

While she waited, Erin leaned against the ice maker and finished the worksheet by streetlight. She clenched the pen so tight her nails dug into her palms, willing away those columns, those categories, those neat little boxes that sorted away possibilities before you could even try them.

CARLOS AND ERIN ALWAYS HUNG OUT BEHIND THE STOP-N-Fuel, down where an old bridge fell away into the pond. You could keep a six-pack chilled in the water, looped on a stick to pin it in place. You could laze on the tire swing in the shade of the old oak, waiting for a listless breeze to stir the heavy air. Most importantly, you couldn't see the spot from the road.

Carlos kept Erin's eyes covered on the walk down, taking the slope slow because it was so dark. He flourished his hands, unveiling the old junker. "Ta-da!"

Erin walked a circle around it, tracing nicks and scratches in the silver paint by the dim streetlight from the gas station. "Whoa. This is really yours?"

"Got it from Ralph. Cost me $50 and a month of Saturday shifts." He stood a little straighter, grinning shyly.

"Will it run?"

Carlos shook his head. "Not yet. I think the battery's dead. Some guy from out of town stumbled into the Stop-N-Fuel with his daughter and left the keys with Ralph. Said it'd conked out and Ralph could have it. Then he bought $40 in beer, and they both left on foot. They haven't been back in a few weeks, so the car's mine now."

Erin wanted to floor it across the country and never stop. She wanted an open road and some faraway ocean where nobody knew shit about Boilingbrook. Someplace where nobody classified your hugs. "What's inside?"

They popped open the trunk and found a tangle of rusty tools, bungee cords, and greasy rags. Mostly tools, some robotics manuals, and a first aid kit.

Erin slammed it closed with hands blackened by engine grease. "At least we don't have to buy tools."

"Let's check inside the car." Carlos tried the keys on the passenger door, but it was jammed shut. "Damn it. Did you see a crowbar?"

"I bet Ralph has one." Ralph kept tons of parts around to help the odd stranded driver. It made him feel important.

While Carlos went to have a peek at Ralph's office, Erin sat on the hood with a Bible and a permanent marker and continued her pet project. She'd begun by blacking out all the *nots*, and it improved things so much she'd kept going. By the time she reached the Psalms, she'd decided it should be a spell book of sorts.

She turned to the Gospel of John and blacked out the words of Jesus with her Sharpie so it said, *One miracle, and you are all amazed.* She slipped the page between the door panels. Yanked and twisted against the handle. It popped open so suddenly she tumbled butt-first into the mud.

Carlos jogged back to help her up, only laughing a little at the muddy streak down her backside.

"Keep it up, and I'll hex you next," she threatened, but she was laughing, too. She showed him her amateur spell book, leaning into the heat of him, that sweaty, musky smell, while he hovered just behind her, craning his neck to read.

"Okay. Show me another miracle."

Erin paged slowly to the middle section. "I turned Psalm 23 into a love spell."

"Okay. Let's hear it."

She pitched her voice low, trying to make it sexy, but also ironic for maximum plausible deniability:

> lie down in green pastures
> evil you
> your rod your staff
> comfort me
> prepare me
> with oil
> overflow

"Not bad," Carlos said. "Definitely improves on the original. Have you cast it on anyone yet?"

"I'm still working out that process," Erin confessed.

"Stick them under people's tongues, like how rabbis make golems," Carlos suggested.

She wrinkled her nose. "Yeah, right. Like anyone's going to hold a love spell under their tongue just because I ask." She tucked the Bible into her armpit and wrote another spell on the car's filthy bumper. *Would you betray me with a kiss?*

"Okay. I volunteer. Try it on me."

He was a complete mess, hair slicked straight up by sweat and static electricity, leaves and dirt from the trunk plastering his stubble.

"Ew, no. What if it works? You'll be all up in my face with that greasy shit all over you." The profanity tasted like cinnamon in her mouth. You could practically hear God's chalk dragging down the wrong side of her slate.

"Okay. Let's check out our car." He opened the door for her. Erin liked how he said *our*.

They'd never been alone like that before, squashed together in the dark, in private. His thumb brushed her knuckles. A warm, tingling feeling spread through her fingers and toes. She creased the love spell, folded it down small.

"Open your mouth," Erin ordered. She slipped the folded Bible page beneath his tongue. Then she kissed him.

They weren't very good. Their teeth clacked awkwardly, and first there was too much puckering and then too much spit. The onionskin paper refused to dissolve away. It tasted like church and engine oil and Carlos. When they came up for air, the spell stayed in Erin's mouth. She spat it out on the floorboard. A warm feeling spread through her middle. She didn't know if she wanted to kiss him some more or move from the *Questionable* column to something decidedly *Sinful*. The worksheet had given her a lot of ideas.

Just when they were getting into it, someone rapped sharply on the window. They sprang apart, snatching back their hands from all the warm, forbidden places they'd wandered into.

A pale, teenish face pressed against the foggy window, stringy blonde hair all damp and tangled around huge, unblinking eyes.

"What are you doing in my dad's car?" she snapped, low and sharp.

Erin backed up so far she was crushing Carlos against the other door. "Who are you?"

The girl ripped open the door so hard the whole car rocked. A black oil slick soaked her T-shirt and dripped over the shredded skin of her arms. Coiled wires and metal rods in her wrists glinted in the streetlight like earthworms wriggling through grave dirt. "I'm Hailey. What did you do with my dad?"

———

USING CARLOS'S SMARTPHONE, THEY PIECED TOGETHER HAILEY'S history from obits and police reports and the robotics garbage in the trunk. The android's namesake, one Hailey Flowers, had died in a car accident three years before. Their Hailey was a memorial android, made in the image of the dead, expensive and one-of-a-kind. One evening, a man named Thomas Flowers rolled up at the

Stop-N-Fuel drunk out of his mind, abandoned his car with Ralph, and wandered into the desert with only his android daughter for company. There he met some accident that ended his life, or else he killed himself. Two weeks later, an officer found his body partially decomposed and pecked apart by carrion.

Erin wondered about Thomas's last moments out there in the desert with only the android by his side. Wondered how long it took a corpse to rot so much Hailey's programming couldn't recognize her father. How she left his body to search for him, unable to understand an ending like death.

But instead, she found Erin and Carlos.

THEY TRIED STASHING HAILEY IN THE CAR'S BACKSEAT overnight, but it hadn't gone well. By the time Erin finished Bible school and biked over to the gas station, Hailey had torn up the car's cab trying to leave, shredding up the brown pleather seats and cracking a window. She'd peeled the skin from her artificial fingertips while gouging lines in the ceiling.

"Dad!" Hailey called and called, inconsolable. "Dad, where are you?"

Carlos studied an android manual he'd found wedged inside the spare tire well. "She imprints on her owner," he explained, flipping through the instructions. "She doesn't realize her dad is dead."

Erin tried showing her the obituaries on her phone, but the android just shoved the phone away and checked the driver's seat again like somebody might've climbed in since the last time she looked. "Where's my dad? Dad!"

"I guess she doesn't understand," said Erin.

"We could turn her over to the police," Carlos suggested. "There's got to be some way to dispose of these things. Maybe the robot company recycles them."

They sat three in a row in the ruined backseat, Hailey against the door, Erin in the middle, and Carlos on the other side. Hailey had settled down with Erin's homework, a Bible verse crossword puzzle on the dangers of gossip. When given small tasks to do, Hailey stopped asking about her dad.

"It's not fair," said Erin. "She's just doing what they made her for. She didn't ask for this. I wish we could set her free." She sewed Hailey's artificial skin closed with tiny brown stitches, making a long, unhealed scar down her arm.

Neither of them had mentioned last night's make-out session. Both were suddenly careful not to touch, not even when sitting nearly butt to butt in the backseat. In full daylight, it all seemed too risky, the kind of thing that got you married off to some guy your dad picked at a convention.

Carlos paged through an onionskin book nearly as dense as the Bible. "Okay, we've got a couple options. There's a soft reset sequence in her manual. It looks pretty simple. We could give it a try. It's supposed to put her back in a neutral state, so she can imprint with different parameters. There's also a hard reset, but it's complicated. That'll strip out everything—name, personality, all of it."

"Let's try the soft reset."

It took a few tries to figure out the directions, and even longer to access Hailey's interface. She had a port in her left armpit where you could plug in a USB keyboard.

"One sec," said Erin. "I wrote her a spell for this." She slid a blackout poem under Hailey's tongue.

> In the beginning
> create formless and empty darkness
> call the light the night

Carlos typed something long and erratic. Hailey's eyes focused on Erin's. Her arms went slack.

"I think it worked," Erin said.

"Awesome," said Carlos.

"I bet she can do all kinds of things," said Erin. "I bet she could count cards at a casino, or even carry all the water jugs from Ralph's stockroom. She's so strong."

"Maybe we could give her your personality," said Carlos. "Leave her in your bedroom for when your parents marry you off. I bet they won't even notice the difference."

"Oh, they'll notice. She'll talk back a whole lot. Then when she gets smacked, they'll notice." Erin knocked on Hailey. She rang like a bell.

"I'm joking, you know," said Carlos.

Erin chewed her bottom lip, digesting the dread inside her. "It's hard to joke about this stuff right now." Carlos's parents were religious too, but not like Erin's. He was going to college. His sister Sofia was halfway through a psychology major at a college in Idaho. Erin's dad had bought tickets to the marriage convention. *Just getting the lay of the land,* he said. *No pressure.*

"You want to talk about it?"

"What's there to say? It's in the Bible. It doesn't matter if I agree."

"Not everyone agrees with all of it," said Carlos. "Did I tell you Sofia's new boyfriend is Catholic?"

Erin scoffed. "My parents would murder me first."

"I just don't think you should feel guilty all the time. What if it's okay to just be happy?"

"I don't know," she said in the tiniest, squeaking voice, folding into herself as all the *nots* bombarded her, found the memory of Carlos's lips and turned it into raking fire. She didn't know how to shut them out. She didn't know how something so good as Carlos's smell could be so completely wrong.

He opened his arms, but Erin shook her head just the tiniest bit, flinching away from the hug. "I'd better get going."

"There's some good news in all of this," said Carlos.

"What's that?" Erin really needed good news, almost as much as she needed something decidedly *Questionable.*

"I got a new battery." He climbed into the cab and revved up the engine. It was loud and free and open-throated, and when she heard it, her spirits lifted, the shame blown away in the exhaust. Erin gave him a double-thumbs up and started up the hillside.

The car door opened, and Hailey struggled out into the pond mud.

"Dad?" she called out. "Where are you going?" Hailey stumbled through the grass until she brushed cold fingers against Erin's arm. "Daddy. I missed you."

"Oh, shit," said Carlos. "She's running the same program. She's imprinted on you."

"Damn," said Erin. "What now? We could try the hard reset."

He'd already grabbed for the android manual. "I'll read up on it. It's a bit more complicated."

"Later. I've got to go," Erin said. "Dad will kill me if I'm home late." It was only a small exaggeration.

Carlos ran both hands through his hair. "There's some bungee cords in with the tools. She'll have to go in the trunk until we can figure out what went wrong."

They did their best to tie her up. It looked like something out of a serial killer movie. Erin hated it, hated the idea of Hailey. A girl made to worship her father. She deserved better. They all did.

"Dad!" Hailey's eyes flashed as they closed her in. "Come back!"

"Monday," Erin promised Carlos. "Right after Bible school. I'll be back."

As she biked home, she thought about dating Catholics and majoring in psychology and wondered what it had to do with sin and crucifixion and the smell of Carlos's neck. She searched for the spell to change it all around, but you could only black so much out with a Sharpie before you just had nothing.

ERIN WAS THINKING THEY'D SORT HAILEY OUT, RESET HER again, and it'd all be okay soon, but everything went wrong.

H escaped, Carlos texted the next morning. *My fault. Didn't slam the trunk closed hard enough.*

It was church time, so Mom made Erin turn the phone off before she could answer. Carlos beckoned from the back pew, but Dad steered her to the seat next to him. She locked eyes on the pastor and tamped down her racing heart by fantasizing about the worksheet. After the service, as her family bustled back to their van, Erin thought she saw a blonde girl stumbling through the weeds behind the annex. She thumbed on the phone beneath her skirt and texted one-handed while Dad drove them to the pancake place for brunch.

H behind church? Hurry.

Carlos didn't turn up any androids, though. The next day, Erin watched for Hailey during Bible school, jumping every time a bird flitted outside the window. The youth pastor caught her texting under the desk. She had to copy the book of Galatians longhand during lunch.

When she got her phone back, there were three *Where RU*'s waiting from Carlos.

U find her? she wrote back.

No. U?

Nada.

Pond tonite?

OK

After school, Erin called her mom and said she had an emergency shift to pick up at Ralph's. She rode circles around the church, looking for signs of Hailey, but only found a clump of stringy hair caught in the brambles down by the baptistry.

Just as she set off for the Stop-N-Fuel, Dad called. "You're late," he barked. "Where are you?"

"At church," said Erin. "I'm about to head to work. Didn't Mom tell you?"

"I called Ralph. He said you're not scheduled to work tonight."

The world fell out from under her. Erin had to stop and plant both feet on the ground to keep from barfing.

"Come straight home. Now." Dad used a cool, calm voice that meant he was really pissed.

Erin pedaled hard, clipping kids on the sidewalk, darting in front of the cars. Her heart hammered, a rabbit on the run, hedged in straight toward the cage. She tossed around for a good lie, something sweet and responsible and *Permissible*.

But it was already too late. At home, Dad sat planted on the couch. A Bible lay open on his lap, half the words blotted out in permanent marker.

HER PARENTS' JUSTICE CAME DOWN SHARP AND SWIFT AND without any room for forgiveness. When Erin tried to explain about the Bible, Dad grabbed her hair and ear and marched her off to her bedroom and tossed her onto her bed.

"We love you," said Mom while Dad unscrewed her bedroom door from its hinges. "This is for your own protection." Mom dug through her drawers and trash for anything else incriminating. You didn't get any privacy, not when you sinned. Not even a door.

"Was it Carlos?" Dad asked. "Ralph said you see him a lot at work."

"You never used to be a liar, Erin. What happened?" Big, huge tears hung in Mom's eyes as she twisted her own hands, one over the other. They kept asking Erin questions but not listening to her answers.

They went through her phone. They asked a lot about Carlos, pretty much the sex worksheet but more humiliating. Erin lied fluently, but that only made it worse. They set her to copying the words of Paul over and over into her journal.

Dad called Ralph and quit Erin's job for her. Then he began making calls to every family in the congregation with godly young men looking for a wife. All night, his chair scraped against the floor in his office while he fixed her future like the firmware beneath all programs, impossible to modify, impossible to erase.

ERIN HAD CRIED HERSELF EMPTY AND RESIGNED HERSELF TO LIFE without a door when Hailey put a fist through her bedroom window.

"Dad," Hailey hissed. "I've been looking everywhere for you." It was 11:00 p.m., and everyone had gone to bed. Hailey struggled over the window sill. Broken glass shredded her T-shirt around her belly. It looked like a crop top.

"Shit," whispered Erin. Dad's big mastiff woofed once from the living room. She considered actually leaving Hailey in her place, letting her marry whatever dickwad her dad picked out. But it wasn't okay, not even if it happened to someone else.

Androids in your bedroom had a way of clarifying things.

If God put dads at the top of the hierarchy, they'd be their own damn dads. "Fuck them," she told Hailey. "We'll make our own way."

She pulled a hoodie over her tank top and stuffed her pajama bottoms into her shoes, slinging her backpack over her shoulder. She wanted her blacked out Bible. She wanted her phone. Mostly, she wanted that open road, that faraway ocean, and the smell of Carlos's neck.

Erin threw a quilt over the glass shards of the window and hoisted herself down into the flowerbed. She and Hailey hoofed it four miles to the Stop-N-Fuel, praying Carlos would be on duty.

———

HE WAS AT THE FRONT COUNTER, SELLING A PACK OF CIGARETTES to a trucker and not expecting androids. Carlos cut his eyes at her and waved her off. Erin snuck around the shelves, grabbed a bottle of Mr. Pibb from the cooler, and swigged it down unpaid for. She picked out a new crossword book and stuffed it in her backpack, then added a pack of salted peanuts for good measure. Then she took a turn down the health aisle and picked up a box of condoms. It felt awfully light, considering the weight of God's disapproval beating down on her neck.

The moment the customer jangled out the doorway, Carlos caught Erin by the arm and steered them into the stockroom. Erin stuffed the condoms in her backpack and tossed Hailey the crossword puzzles to keep her busy.

"Are you okay? Where did you find her? I tried calling, but no offense, your dad is really scary."

Erin giggled because suddenly it all seemed kind of funny. "She broke me out. I ran away from home." Erin wanted to kiss him so bad it burned. "I need your car."

"Wait a minute." He really looked at her then. The tiny cuts on her hands from the broken window. The bruise on her cheek from Dad's discipline. The smiley-dotted pajama bottoms hastily stuffed into her socks. "God, Erin. What happened?"

"Dad found my poems." Something twisted inside, and it wasn't funny anymore, it was sad, and she had nowhere to go and no one to help her. "Hailey and I are leaving town."

"Erin, wait a sec. This is crazy."

She was shaking, but also crying, which was the worst. "Listen to me. Please. I want you to come."

Carlos paced back and forth, fixated on Hailey, who was perched against the big pile of replacement jugs for the water cooler. He looked so young all of a sudden, seventeen and not even a full beard, but now someone had asked something so grown up from him. "I can't just up and leave. My mom would freak out. Where would we go? We don't have any money or anything."

"We'll figure it out." Pure panic drummed inside her, panic that the trap would still close on her heels after having slipped it. "Come with me. Please. I love you."

Carlos flinched away, tears gathering in his eyes. "I can't," he stuttered. "I want to. But I just can't." He slipped out into the drizzle, pulling the door shut behind him.

Hailey blinked at her crossword puzzle, her eye-cams serene and steady. "Dad," she murmured, and the word rang hollow as the heavy, sick feeling in Erin's stomach, the sense she'd been desperately wrong about something very important.

"I'll be right back," Erin told Hailey. "Stay here." She threw open the door and bolted out the back of the gas station, making her way toward the tree, the pond, the car.

———

ERIN FOUND CARLOS WHERE THE GRASS RAN TO POND MUD. IF he'd been crying, you couldn't tell in the rain. He flinched away from her, a broken-winged bird too long grounded.

"I'm sorry," said Erin. "Let's get out of the rain."

She slipped into the backseat, and Carlos slid in beside her.

"I didn't mean to pressure you. I don't know what else to do," Erin said.

"I can't just run away from home. Maybe my parents can help. Come home with me tonight," said Carlos.

Erin considered it, the possibility of Carlos one wall away. But Mom and Dad would check there first. Everyone else thought her parents were so damn nice, so reasonable. Good people, desperate for their runaway daughter. It was worse when they did it out of love. "They'll look for me there. They'll hand me over, and you'll never see me again." She said it calmly, stating a fact.

Carlos nodded. They sat together and let the silence and darkness take them completely. There was nothing left to say in words.

He lay a hand across her shoulders. She uncurled into his warmth, nuzzled his neck until she found his whiskery chin, his cheek, his lips, and then they were kissing, and shoving aside the seatbelts and stretching together along the worn old fabric in the damp dark. Erin tasted his skin in the flickering streetlight as they moved against each other, opening the condom, fumbling to make contact. It was new, and thrilling, and a little scary. It was so long in the making, like when you've hiked all day and night through a winding pass and at last arrive, footsore but whole, to a comfortable bed. She'd never known what it meant for another person to pour into her so wholly. It was *Sinful*, and it was also completely okay. Outside, the rain picked up pace, drummed fingers on the roof, washing the dust and heat of tired old decades down into the pond.

Afterward, as a seatbelt buckle dug into her hip, Carlos nuzzled into her neck, and it all seemed fine. Erin closed her eyes. She must've dozed off because she gasped awake suddenly, a sharp needle of fear rammed through her. "How long have we been here?"

Carlos sat up in the dark. "Shit. I left the store unattended."

But it wasn't the store Erin was worried about. She checked her watch. It was well past 1:00 a.m., and the rain had slowed. They fumbled for their clothes in the dark. "Shit, shit, shit."

They belted up the hill toward the office, but it was already too late. The door hung open and Hailey lay sprawled and broken, half-crushed, dragging herself by her fingers out into the rain while sparks danced along her body. "Dad," she groaned. "Dad, where are you?"

Broken water jugs rolled around the office floor. Pooling water stained the concrete floor nearly black. A huge, ragged blanket of artificial skin lay pinned beneath a pile of jugs, connected to the rest of Hailey by spiderwebbing wires pulled so taut the skin off in chunks. The water soaked all her wiring below the waist. Somehow she'd clawed her way toward the door anyway, degloving right out of her own flesh and into the pounding rain. Her eye-cams were shattered. She couldn't see anything anymore.

Erin held Hailey's head in her lap, touching the metal plates while her eye-cams whirred, unable to focus. "Dad? Dad!" Hailey called out, unreached by touch, or voice, or any comfort they could give her.

"I'm here," Erin told her, even though it didn't seem to help. "Shhh. I'm here now."

"She must've come looking for us," said Carlos while he hauled the unbroken water jugs off Hailey's remains. "She must've tripped into the jug wall and toppled the whole thing. Damn it."

Erin wanted to cry, but the tears wouldn't come. It wasn't fair, getting crushed like that just when you finally got free. "I know she's not real, but she was based on a person. There's the ghost of a scared little girl inside."

Carlos wrapped his arms around Erin. They made a weird little family, the three of them. "This is my fault. Maybe we can fix her."

Erin shook her head. It wasn't anyone's fault, not really. "I have to get away, Carlos. *Now*, before I don't have another choice. Don't you see? Why they make me memorize all that shit? That's our programming, Carlos." They wanted it to come crawling out of your head like roaches from a cardboard box you took with you every time you changed house. You were given a script, and you didn't get to make up your lines.

But you could go in and black out some of the words, reverse the meaning through obliteration.

Hailey made up her mind all at once. "Your sister. Nobody will look for me in Idaho." Sofia knew about Erin's church. She'd know what it meant to offer a couch to her.

"I don't know," said Carlos slowly. "Her apartment's pretty small. And you still have to get there."

"Please, Carlos. She'll understand. It's just for a few months. Once I turn 18, they won't be able to make me come back."

He nodded. "I'll give you the car keys." Then, when Erin's lips twisted, "What's wrong?"

Erin's stomach flopped in complex knots. "I was still hoping you'd come with me," she admitted, and immediately she regretted saying it. She didn't want him to feel like he had to do everything for her. "I mean, just to drop me off. Like a road trip."

"A road trip," Carlos repeated softly. "I could tell my parents I'm bringing Sofia the car as a surprise. They know I've been fixing it up. That could work."

Erin leaned in and kissed him lightly. "Thanks." All the fear ebbed out of her, and with it, all the nervous energy. She wanted to curl up and sleep for a week.

Carlos yanked Hailey's artificial skin out from under the heavy water jugs. "I don't think we can fix this, though."

Despite her exhaustion, Erin began to gather all of Hailey's bits into a plastic shopping bag. "I don't care. I'm not leaving her. We'll do the hard reset. We've got the tools. She deserves a fresh start too."

It would take years to learn how to repair and reprogram an android. She would have to study robotics, programming, artificial intelligence. Nothing in Erin's life had prepared her for such a task, but she would try, because you couldn't give up on each other. Nobody was disposable. When the dads let you down, you had to be there for the other girls.

While Carlos steered them onto the freeway, Erin held the shattered wreck of Hailey in the backseat and walked through the reset sequence. Hailey went peaceful again, her broken eye-cams focused on darkness. Her eyes searched the dark for something to worship, and finding nothing, she worshipped the dark instead. In that moment, she was almost human.

THAT NIGHT, TUCKED AWAY IN A RAT-TRAP MOTEL, SKIN TO SKIN with her sleeping Carlos, Erin pulled the Gideon Bible from the drawer and fixed the bad advice of poor old Saint Paul:

> sin sexually
> your bodies are temples
> you are your own

She thought of April, married off and pregnant before she ever tasted adulthood. Of Thomas Flowers, grieving himself to death in the desert while the pale shadow of his daughter watched over him. And Hailey, running the same program, just swapping out the faces. *God has a plan for everything*, Erin's dad said. *God has a plan for you. Don't stray from it.*

Stray, Erin decided. Find the strength somewhere. Run far enough to escape, steal away into the forest, and make your own way. Maybe an old car could get you far enough. Maybe the program would break, the wounds heal, the grief scab over.

Unless they all came full circle in the end, face to face with a Maker with no imagination and no mercy.

She touched Carlos's knee beneath the sheets. Something old made entirely new in the course of one night. *Start by crossing out all the nots.* She uncapped the marker again. She turned to the last pages.

> Blessed are those
> who practice magic arts
> and everyone who loves

GLOSSOLALIA

BY JOHN HORNOR JACOBS

IT WAS THE SNAKE, SHE REALIZED LATER, THAT STOPPED HER mother from speaking, stricken, hanging on the sleeve-worn wooden casement, one hand raised in admonition or fear, Ophelia couldn't tell. She'd found it by the creek, drowsing in the lower branches of a tree, fat and languorous and impacted by sun. It was black-backed, mouth rimed in white, and stank of dead fish. It came to her, sliding off the branch and into her waiting hands, as easy as prayer.

That her mother managed to say, "Why you got that thing, 'Phelia?"

"Revival tonight."

"Brother Tom don't need your help, child. Take that damned thing back to the crick. Or kill it."

She shook her head and held up the moccasin.

"He don't let no girls take up serpents. Why don't he let us share faith?"

"Honey, put that thing down."

"It don't fear me. I aim it no harm."

"It might aim you harm. 'Phelia, please."

"Why don't he let us?"

"Bible says, suffer not a woman to teach. Brother Tom is a godly man, and we'll take our faith from him."

"I love baby Jesus. Why can't I share faith?"

Her mother withdrew from the window, into the shadows of the cabin, and after a moment, emerged through the open door. The wind chimes at the porch eave spun, dappling the front of the cabin in points of light.

"'Phelia, now. You hear me? Put that thing down."

It left her hands reluctantly and remained unmoving in the grass.

"You finish your chores?"

"Yes, ma'am."

"Then get on inside. I need some help with the biscuits for tonight."

She took each step slowly, watching as her mother found a shovel and struck off the snake's head.

THE TENT SMELLED OF TOBACCO AND SWEAT, COLOGNE AND COAL dust. Bare bulbs hung from hammer-dimpled timbers, casting long, shifting shadows while a gas-driven genny buzzed outside the tent.

So much darker and hotter than the pasture it sits in, she thought, holding her father's rough hand. Why can't we do this under the stars?

Revival Supper had been so nice, out there on the cool pasture's edges with the other children, laughing and running, exploring the neighboring wood, waiting for the clang of the bell to summon them all to the table. She and Momma had made biscuits, and Brother Punkin's wife slaughtered and fried two chickens. There was a ham and beans and cake. Everyone was happy.

She'd slipped away from the other children, still exploring the wood's mulch and rotting floor, and entered the tent, going under the back wall, wriggling under the heavy canvas that smelled of mildew. She stood in the exact center, at the spot where all the timbers joined in the shape of a star at the apex, and Ophelia felt the Spirit wash over her, as if she had fallen into the creek.

Her father cuffed her ear when she came out.

"What you doing in there?"

"Feeling the Spirit."

"The Spirit? You're too cute for your own damned good. Join the other children, now. Supper'll be soon."

But now, the tent was tight, close, not the airy, star-pierced emptiness of earlier. Her father's hand felt rough and unkind. The tent was loud with prayer.

"Harken to me! Harken to me," yelled Brother Tom into a microphone. "Harken to the sweet Pentecost, where all the people of Christ bathe in His blood!"

An amplified guitar trilled in the background, sounding an up-tempo version of "Blessed Assurance." The congregation hopped and jittered.

A man in farm-weathered overalls shuddered and cried out.

"Jesus' name! Oh, conshala dekalalla chirrin ollop. Sella olla seekin conshala!"

Brother Tom wiped at his face with a handkerchief. A thick man, sweat darkened his shirt at the armpits and back. His oil-slick hair had fallen forward in a wild, clotted mess.

"My brothers and sisters, feel the Spirit move through you. I can feel It in here. I can feel It move among us! Can you feel It?"

The crowd barked and yelped, phlegmy voices sounding of black-lung. Ophelia's father tensed and he released her hand. She looked at her mother, then, who had her own hands over her head, as if she had been swept away in a flood, arms raised to grasp for rescue.

"They shall speak with new tongues, the Bible says!" Brother Tom's voice cracked as he yelled. "They shall take up serpents! If they drink any deadly thing, it shall not hurt them!"

Brother Tom waved at his deacon, who presented a wooden box. Opening the top, he withdrew the rattlers, two to a hand.

Her father began to dance, a curious shifting of weight from foot to foot. Her mother hopped up and down, yelping words unknown to Ophelia.

"They shall take up serpents! Harken to me, brethen!"

He raised the snakes toward the wooden star-burst at the tent's apex. He danced.

After the snake had struck his neck, he was a long time falling, first lowering his arms and tilting this way and that, a surprised expression on his moon-shaped face. The rattler struck again at his arm, and he dropped the snakes, all of them, both the ones he'd milked earlier of their venom and the one that Ophelia had found in the wood and had come so willing to her grasp.

She remembered her mother striking off the moccasin's head, and smiled, watching Brother Tom fall.

The tent quieted. The snakes remained unmoving on the grass floor of the tent, stirring their rattles lazily, except for one, which slithered over Brother Tom's inert body, across his face, and into the congregation, which parted for it like a sea before a prophet. The snake came into Ophelia's hands, willingly, and she raised it over her head while her mother and father and the rest of the crowd gazed on in amazement, and she felt the Spirit fill her like joy, burn upon her tongue like an ember as she began to speak.

CHOOSE YOUR TRUTH

BY JO MILES

THERE HAD BEEN AN UPTICK IN TRUTH.

Alia's bosses at Prosperity didn't expect her to watch the newstories that filled her queue. Her job was to analyze their local mindshare performance, and watching the content only slowed her down. But she watched, anyway. On an encrypted personal connection via her headset, safe from Prosperity's reach, she tagged each newstory with an extra dimension: *true, fake, true. Partially true. Too biased to categorize. Egregiously fake. True.*

Far more true ones than usual.

Shockingly, true. She lingered over this particular video, frowning, then glanced up and down the long, antiseptic-white office to make sure none of her coworkers was paying attention to her. They were all heads-down at their own screens. She turned back to the offending newstory.

Three times she watched the execution. A familiar, silver-haired figure stood in the center of a bare concrete room, holding an axe. A real axe, real steel; Alia could tell, though Production had given it an extra gleam to draw the eye. This was the radical called the Fist. They led a faction that called itself Choose Truth, though every other faction called it Control. Three times she listened while the Fist condemned a citizen for daring to share content that

Choose Truth—that Control—had declared contraband. Three times she watched the axe fall, watched the head wobble across the floor before coming to a stop, empty eyes gazing beyond the camera, away from the spreading crimson. A gruesome, old-fashioned punishment, the commentator noted with barely-contained outrage: fitting for an old-fashioned, ruthless, authoritarian faction like Control.

It can't be true, Alia thought, but she had no evidence to back that up, nothing beyond the feeling of wrongness in her gut, that crawling, uncomfortable sensation that kept getting worse, not better. Gut feelings could mislead, and she knew better than to trust them. *True, true, true. It shouldn't be true. But if it is, people need to know.*

However many times she watched, she found no signs of fabrication in the footage, nothing worse than light editing and editorializing. She dug her fingers into her hair, forcing herself to breathe.

True, she decided at last, and with a pang as blunt and final as that axe blow, she pushed the data point out to her network.

The next newstory cycled up on her screen, and the next, and she no longer watched them. If she reduced the stories to data points and performance metrics, they couldn't touch her.

The borders of her console flared orange, jerking back her attention. She hadn't realized she'd been staring into space. Careless; she could get censured, if someone noticed. All around the office, analysts shoved their active projects aside to respond to the alert, and so did she. A competitor newstory, one that denounced Prosperity, was gaining mindshare at an alarming rate—and it came from Control.

She had to pull herself together and help coordinate Prosperity's response.

BEX KNEW IT WOULD BE A BAD DAY THE MOMENT THE ELEVATOR docked and let her into the office. The broad viviglass windows were tinted dark, today, with multicolored graphs and ever-updating mindshare numbers scrolling across, dimming the view of the clouds around them, hiding the grimy city below. The lights overhead emanated that particular blue-white blaze that was supposed to be optimal for inducing creativity under stress, but at this brightness, it made Bex's brain hurt.

Her coworkers debated in tense undertones as they converged on the conference room. The prospect of a meeting cheered her— there were usually pastries at morning briefings—but couldn't overcome the aura of alarm throughout the office.

"What's happened?" she asked her boss, Russhel, as he passed.

He waved at the wall, and her eyes finally focused on the lines that danced across the display. Most of the colors ticked up and down incrementally. Normal stuff. A couple, including Guardian's electric green, edged upward, which wasn't good. But one line, gleaming gold, dropped like a hacked aircar.

Five points. A five-point drop, overnight, put Prosperity below Guardian, below the Salazar Imperium, below Apiary and even Optimal Frontiers. In one night, they'd lost their lead in mindshare.

"Oh, shit."

"No kidding," Russhel said. "Get to the briefing and pay close attention. The execs are counting on us for idea-gen on counter-measures." He lowered his voice to a kind, conspiratorial tone. "Crisis means opportunity, Bex. I know you've got big ambitions in this place. Anyone who contributes to pulling us out of this mess, even an intern, will get noticed."

"Thanks, boss." She smiled politely. He liked when she called him boss and made him feel like he wasn't at the bottom of the department hierarchy. Was this weird little pep talk about boosting his ego? Or was he actually trying to be supportive?

It wasn't until he'd dashed off that a third possibility occurred to her: the situation was so bad that they would take ideas from anyone. Even her.

ALIA STRUGGLED TO ORGANIZE HER THOUGHTS WHILE SHE waited for staff to gather. Usually it was easy to keep the narratives straight in her head, but not today. The ideation team interns descended on the tray of pastries, eager to supplement their daily ration bars, and Alia wished the permanent staff would dig in, too. If they were eating, they wouldn't pay as much attention to her briefing.

She set a croissant on her own plate, for show, but didn't eat. She never broke bread with her Prosperity coworkers if she could help it, and didn't think she could choke down a bite of the flaky pastry. Her throat was so dry.

She couldn't afford to make mistakes, not even in a briefing of the junior ideation staff. *Control is aligned with Guardian,* she reminded herself. *This newstory supports Guardian's narrative. That's our analysis. That's all that matters.* Not a silver-haired rebel and a spreading pool of blood. She banished the images from her mind as she would if they were fake, even though they weren't fake.

"You've all heard about today's threat," she began, and the room fell quiet. "It's a low-production, implicit-narrative video depicting violent action by Prosperity against a group of striking factory workers at the tier-one factory in Bethesda. An unusually bold narrative, even for Choose—ah, for Control, who released it."

Get it together, Alia. Focus. She'd never felt this off-balance at the office before. Any other day, she'd have gone home to wait until she calmed down rather than risk making mistakes, but that wasn't an option today.

Alia couldn't show them the video of Prosperity security applying electroshock after electroshock in wide beams against their striking workers, waiting until they struggled to their feet before initiating the next burst. She couldn't reveal that she'd watched it herself. Only the Narrative Analysis team had the conditioning to watch oppositional content without damaging effect, and her role was supposed to be limited to infoflow analysis.

She didn't need to see this newstory to analyze how it spread, like the Ephresian flu in a slum in high summer.

She'd wanted to join Narrative Analysis, originally, but Lumi hadn't approved. They'd worried about how the conditioning might interact with her curator training, a gift too valuable to risk.

It had been a valid concern.

"I heard the production quality is really low, like, appallingly low," someone said. "It sounds like an unsubtle hack job. Why would Guardian back content like that?"

"And why would anyone share some piece of low-res inflammatory garbage?" asked one of the supervisors with overwhelming authority, as if he knew any more about it than the others. "It breaks all the rules of narrative conveyance."

"It's low-res because of—" Alia caught herself, heart pounding in her ears. She'd been about to say, *because of the distance, it's hard to get quality footage from a rooftop a kilometer away.* This was bad. She shouldn't be here. She needed space to get herself together. "Because, we think, they're experimenting with new narrative design theories." She glanced at her notes to make quite sure she had the right language. "Reviving archaic tactics with a new spin. Consumers are used to highly-produced videos. This is something new, and consumers share what's new."

"They've stolen an awful lot of our mindshare for Guardian, and a chunk for themselves, too," the supervisor grumbled.

"Yes, and the next mindshare rebalancing is only a few days away," Alia said. A few days before power was redistributed and each faction gained or lost control based on its share of the public consciousness. If nothing changed, Prosperity would lose ground badly. "That's why Prosperity is counting on you. The leadership wants to win back what we've lost by any means possible. Any idea will be considered, so long as it aligns with our central narratives. We need to show consumers that Prosperity is the right faction for them." She ran through a list of the narratives that Analysis considered best for the task.

"And what about Control? How do we stop the Fist?"

Against her will, the clip invaded her memory again: silver hair, a flash of steel, pools of blood in a deep, undoctored red. True, when it shouldn't, couldn't be true. *Lumi, how could you? That's not what we do.*

Nausea warred with a deeper, fiercer anger born of betrayal. She swallowed hard.

"Keep up what you've been doing to turn the consumers against them," Alia said. "It's working."

BEX HUNG BACK AS HER TEAMMATES SHUFFLED OUT OF THE meeting room, waiting for Alia to finish a conversation with another ideator. She snagged an extra Danish while she waited, wrapped it in a napkin, and licked the jelly off her fingers. If she scored enough free food, she could save part of today's ration bar and trade it to one of her roommates for a few days off chores.

The conversation ended, and the analyst headed for the door. "Um, Alia?" Bex called.

Alia jumped, startled. "Bex! Sorry, I didn't realize you were waiting for me."

"Are you okay?"

All through the meeting, Alia had kept tripping over her words, deviating from narrative in subtle ways that made Bex uncomfortable. Now she was jumping at nothing. People slipped all the time, but Alia never did. Alia was brilliant, always precise, always articulate. Sometimes, in meetings, Bex made notes about the things Alia did that made her seem so together because maybe some were things Bex could learn to do, too. But today, Alia was all jittery.

"Yeah, yeah, I'm fine." Alia flashed a strained smile. "Just distracted, that's all, like everyone is today. What's up?"

Bex took a deep breath. "So, I'm guessing you probably don't have time to meet today?" Alia had promised to walk through the metrics on Bex's last couple newstories with her, to help her understand how infoflow analysis worked. It had been on their calendars for two weeks.

"Oh, no, is that today?" Alia's gaze went distant as she checked her calendar on her headset, and she grimaced. "What bad timing. You're right, we'll have to reschedule. Can you send me a new invite? I'm sorry, I know you've been waiting for this."

"It's all right." Bex thought angry thoughts at Control for picking today to release this particular newstory. "I really appreciate you taking the time for it."

"Of course. And in the meantime, we've both got work to do. Russhel will be looking for your best work today."

She was right, and Bex tried to console herself with that. Prosperity needed brilliant ideas to reverse the mindshare loss. Why shouldn't one of them be hers?

BACK AT HER WORKSTATION, BEX SUMMONED A LIST OF PROJECTS in progress. All the obvious responses were already underway: calming statements by celebrities with high trust quotients, interviews with factory workers proclaiming their support for Prosperity, clips showing Prosperity's good deeds in Bethesda and here in their headquarters-city of Prospera.

That was all damage control. To get their mindshare back above Guardian's before the rebalancing, they'd need a big surge, a counter-attack. That was where the Ideation team came in. Bex dove into generating the best ideas she could, and for most of the day, she forgot about her suspicions.

But by day's end, with the storyboards for her top concepts sent off to Russhel, she found herself sitting near Alia in a cross-department review of a batch of response newstories. An intern's job in meetings like this was to be quiet and pay attention—and that meant she could watch Alia, too.

"That's great work," Russhel said in his obnoxious, I'm-an-expert voice. This newstory showed a food delivery drop right here in Prospera, part of Prosperity's massive new campaign to counteract food shortages in its territories. They were past the point of talking about food being plentiful—they'd lost that narrative battle because you could only push consumers' beliefs so far, even among Prosperity's own loyalists. Instead, they'd pivoted, showing their generous response to the crisis while pinning the blame on Guardian's interference with open trade. "See there? Just a touch of tears, suggesting the depth of her relief. Nice."

"And it does double duty, narratively," said Alia. "For anyone who remembers when Prosperity released that over-engineered pesticide and caused massive crop failures, it makes them look good to be providing food for so many."

"Yes, that story was a nasty narrative move by Control," Russhel said with a frown.

Alia flinched, as if she'd caught herself in a mistake. "Yeah, it was. Really nasty," she said, but she didn't sound appropriately bitter. She *sounded,* Bex thought, like someone who'd been listening to oppositional narratives.

A spy? It can't be, not Alia. It was a horrible thing to accuse someone of, but every staffer was trained to look for the signs. Alia sat there so stiffly, looking so unhappy, and she'd been slipping up a lot. A chill ran through Bex. *Please don't be.*

"It's more impressive how they cleaned up Jubilation Square," said one of the junior staff, and everyone chuckled. Production had done an amazing job of showing smiling locals picnicking on actual green grass in front of the iconic, gleaming monument.

Bex let the video draw her attention back, the way it was designed to. Smiling workers in Consumer Services uniforms sharper and newer than anything the real Consumer Services department could afford. Boxes of food so large that families worked together to carry them off to groundcars or the train. A close-up of a five-year-old boy, sneaking a tomato out of a box and taking a big bite, at which his mother laughed instead of scolding him as juice dripped down his chin. The boy looked like Bex's niece, same wispy, black baby hair, same grin. Same love of tomatoes.

This was good work from a top faction. Bex was lucky to be here, today, in this office, where someday she might get good enough to make newstories like that.

She owed a lot to Prosperity for this internship. If someone in the mid-ranks might be a spy against her faction, she couldn't ignore that. And if that person had been friendly to Bex, taught her, even mentored her, and had been a traitor this whole time, then Bex wanted to be the one to turn her in.

But she had to be sure. So, when Alia peeled away at the meeting's end and disappeared into the bathroom, Bex kept an eye on the door, waiting to see her come out. And waited. And waited. The longer she waited, the uglier her suspicions got.

At last, impatient, she headed for the bathroom herself. As she reached it, the door swung open, slamming into her. She leapt back with a startled cry.

"Excuse me!" Alia said as she came out and saw Bex. "They should put a sensor on this door, huh?" It was the right thing to say, the same quip other women in the office made whenever they had a near-collision, but Alia didn't make eye contact, and she headed, not back to her desk, but toward the elevator, tapping out a message to her headset with agitated jabs of her fingers.

Bex grabbed her coat and followed.

———

THE MESSAGE HAD COME IN THE MIDDLE OF A MEETING, LEAVING Alia distracted and miserable anew: "We need to talk. Now."

Lumi knew better than to contact Alia during shift. And Alia did not want to talk to Lumi right now. Didn't think she could manage it politely.

I know what you did. I saw the video, and it was true, true, true. If it was fake, she'd have known.

She ignored her messages for the rest of the meeting, like a good, obedient mid-level Prosperity staffer, and when the meeting ended, she ducked into the bathroom, the only place in the office with real privacy. A follow-up was waiting for her.

"Not kidding, Ali," the message read. "You've been compromised. I'll meet you at the usual place."

Alia pressed her head back against the cool wall tiles, raised her eyes to the harsh overhead lights. She'd thought she would have more time before she had to confront Lumi about the things she'd seen. She could go home to her closet apartment and sleep on what to do, or at least, she could lie awake on her lumpy bed, refusing to shut her eyes, trying not to see the blood ...

No. When Lumi called, Alia came. It was why she'd gotten into this hellish position in the first place. That wouldn't change, not until she got some answers.

Leaving the bathroom, she ran headlong into an intern, which startled her so badly it could only confirm her decision. She had to get out of here.

"On my way," she sent, and with a swelling dread, she headed for their meeting spot.

———

THE ELEVATOR CARRIED THEM DOWN THROUGH THE GLOWING clouds, into the gloom of the city below. Bex merged with the crowds of workers heading home, sticking close enough not to lose Alia amid the masses of protesters that always waited outside the newservice entrance. A mass of Prosperity loyalists chanted their demands for greater action against Guardian to end the food shortage, while scattered pockets from other factions shouted at the departing Prosperity workers, accusing them of made-up wrongs from their own factions' attack stories. It was a relief to descend into the quiet of the rail station. She slipped into a train right behind Alia and stood with her face toward the door. She shouldn't have worried. No one ever noticed the intern.

"Jubilation Square," the train announced a few minutes later in its ever-cheerful voice, and the taste of tomatoes flooded her mouth. *Jubilation Square.* It was awfully tempting to go see the food drop in person. If she was lucky, Alia would get off here. Or if her chase ended up revealing nothing, she could come back before they closed and get a tomato or two. She wanted to see her niece with juice dripping down her chin like that grinning boy in the vid.

A few people got off, but not many. They must not have seen the newstory. She started searching for the story to share it to the train's local feed, until someone nudged her aside with a mumbled, "Excuse me."

It was Alia. Luck was with her; Bex could actually see the drop without losing her quarry, and could swing back to pick up a box afterward.

Drawing breath in anticipation, she climbed the stairs out of the underground and faced the dismal scene of Jubilation Square.

The bleak familiarity bludgeoned her. She stopped where she stood, disoriented, while passengers shouldered her aside from the station exit. The dissonance was too much: in place of the shining monuments and green turf that stuck in her head from the video, she faced dingy gray streets and a pigeon-stained obelisk rising from a circle of churned brown muck.

And there were no boxes. No delivery center, temporary or otherwise. No sign of any drop-off at all.

"Where is it?" she whispered.

"Where's what?" asked an old man who was taking shelter from the rain in the station entrance.

"The food drop."

Even as the words passed her lips, the answer clicked into place in her brain. Disappointment gripped her, a deeper, sicker feeling than the hunger in her gut: disappointment, not in the feed, but in herself.

That creative team should get a prize. Like Russhel said, damn good work. Really believable.

The newstory was so well done that she'd let herself get swept up in it. She'd forgotten it was a newstory. And that was the whole *point,* they were designed to get into your head, seep into your memories, to make you believe in the narrative with your whole being. That was how narratives lived and grew, carried by their stories. The more a faction's narrative stuck with consumers, the more mindshare they gained, and this was a Prosperity narrative. She should be *glad* it had worked so well. She should be messaging back to the office, a rueful joke about how this newstory was so good she'd forgotten it was one of theirs.

She shouldn't feel betrayed by her own faction's narrative.

"No food drop here today. You should check your feed," the old man said helpfully. "The last one was a few weeks back. Real good one, I heard."

Of course, he wouldn't have seen the newstory; it was targeted at non-local markets, outside Prospera, where no one would suffer the same cognitive dissonance she had. In a couple days, they'd release a new, local version, vague on the details of when the drop took place, so locals could share the video around and commiserate about how they'd missed it. It would be distant enough by then that everyone could let themselves believe it was real. The "last one" this man thought he remembered wasn't any more real than this one.

"I'm sure it was great," she muttered.

"Maybe you'll catch the next one," he said.

With a jolt, she remembered the actual reason she was here. Where had Alia gone? Damn it, if her moping over a too-good newstory had cost her best chance to catch a spy in the act...

Feeling wretched, she stepped out into the rain, ignoring its sting against her cheeks as she scanned the crowd.

There! A woman, head bowed under a gray rain-suit indistinguishable from all the others, but there was a familiar tightness in her gait. Bex deployed her own rain-suit, a cracked and plasticky old model that was nevertheless better than the rain's burning, and dashed across the square, soaking her shoes in murky puddles in her haste to catch up. At the corner of an adjoining street, her quarry paused and looked around. Bex ducked, pretending to adjust her rain-suit settings. It was definitely Alia. *Making sure no one's following you? Now why would you need to do that?*

Bex ghosted down the street after Alia, who slipped into an abandoned bar off a narrow, trash-filled alley. It was a good place for a covert meeting: far enough from downtown that there were few cameras, and far enough from the really bad neighborhoods that Safety didn't keep much presence here. Avoiding the smelliest puddles, Bex knelt in a spot just outside the bar, sheltered behind the half-wall where she could watch through a broken window without being seen, and waited.

"Hello, Alia."

Bex startled along with Alia at the voice. Someone was standing behind the bar, which had been empty a moment before. They threw back their hood, and the dim light glowed off silver hair.

Bex stifled a cry of alarm. She would recognize that silver hair anywhere. She blinked-captured a few images and sent an urgent, private beacon to the nearest Prosperity Safety office, attaching the photos and her location.

This was the Fist. The ruthless leader of Control, who wanted to overturn the rule of narrative mindshare and tell people what content they could see.

And Alia—brilliant, shining Alia—was their spy.

"You came." The familiar, smoky voice made Alia's stomach twist harder. "I'm glad. I wasn't sure you would."

"I wasn't sure, either, but you owe me answers."

"For what?" Lumi cocked their head, leaning against the grimy surface of the pitted wooden bar, as if waiting to pour non-existent bourbon into the smashed remains of glass tumblers. The two of them used to drink old-fashioneds together, here, tucked into the smallest corner table. That was at the beginning, back when mingled chatter of anonymous after-work crowds was enough to give their conversations privacy. The meeting place had stuck, but now, only ghosts made of dust and cobwebs remained. Only dim, gray light reached inside, deepening Lumi's brown skin into shadows, leaving nothing of their expression visible below their crown of short, spiky silver.

Body language spoke clearly enough, though. They were going to make Alia speak her accusations aloud.

This was the same Lumi she'd always known, and it was impossible to imagine them doing ... *that*. But it was also the exact same Lumi from those videos, the Fist with their signature silver hair and custom-made, gunmetal smart-jacket. The pleased smile they'd given her when Alia agreed to go undercover, mirroring the smirk they wore in the video as they swung the axe.

"You ... you killed those people. Why?" She could barely choke out the question. "That's not what we do."

A pained look crossed Lumi's face, a deeper shadow in the gloom. "No, it's not. It's *not*. Ali, they got to you."

"I saw the video, and it was *true* ..."

"They fooled you. That's why I'm pulling you out." Lumi reached for her shoulders. Alia swatted their hands away, stumbled sideways into a stool. Broken glass ground under her heel, and Lumi stopped. "Those videos of me, they were fakes. Manufactured, like ninety-six percent of everything Prosperity puts out."

"They were real. I should know." That was why Choose Truth valued her so: Alia could sift the truth from the falseness in the factions' narratives, tagging them so anyone who cared could avoid the false and stop their eyes from lying to their brains. She was the best curator Choose Truth had, and she was never wrong.

"I think *I* should know if I'd gruesomely murdered a bunch of innocents." A smirk flashed, brief and bitter, then faded into grimness. "That's what tipped us off. Prosperity has a new way of fabricating content that curators can't detect, and we didn't even know it until they started faking stories about us. I'd hoped you might see through it, but when you flagged that video today as true ... I figured otherwise."

She drew a deep, trembling breath, and trained all her attention, all her skill, on Lumi. "Say it. If you didn't do it, say so straight out."

Lumi's gaze latched onto her, utterly serious. "I did not kill a citizen with an axe. I have never killed a person in my life."

No hint of a lie. No falseness in the face, the voice, the eyes. It was one thing that made Lumi so good at spreading the truth: they'd always been a terrible liar.

The breath rushed out of her, and Alia fumbled for the stool. Lumi took her arm to help her, and this time, she didn't pull away. Her skills, her training, useless. A newstory could lie to her as easily as anyone else. It was hard enough to keep narrative from taking over your world when you *knew* it was false, and now, if there was no certain way to tell ...

This had to be how most people felt all the time. Adrift, deceived. Lumi came around the bar and slid onto a neighboring stool, waiting in supportive silence while she processed the news. Alia sighed. "We'll have to find a way around it and update the trainings. The basic trainings should still be okay, but at the advanced levels ... it'll take months, and until then, we can't approve anything the factions put out. Is it just Prosperity? Or other factions, too?"

"Prosperity may not know, yet, what they've stumbled upon. But I've got warrior-journalists in six factions' territories working to verify or debunk the latest stories our curators have flagged as true."

"The mindshare rebalancing ..."

"Doesn't matter. I'm worried about the long game, not who wins or loses power this week. People are finally starting to see why our work matters. If we have to stop —"

Lumi whirled and aimed a light from their jacket sleeve at the broken-out windows. Alia hadn't heard a thing, but Lumi's enhanced hearing was eerily good.

"Who's there? Come out, slowly."

"We won't hurt you," Alia added, remembering the cruelty on Lumi's face. *That was fake. The real Lumi doesn't hurt people.*

A figure rose outside the window, hesitated, then marched through the open doorway: a girl in a cracked rain-suit. She put back her hood, revealing an expression of disgust. "You traitor. You've been with them this whole time."

"Bex." Alia sighed. "A Prosperity intern. She must have followed me," she told Lumi.

"What do you want to do about her?" Lumi asked in a low voice.

Alia's infiltration was over, so it didn't matter if the kid blew her cover. And Bex was young, not yet on the inside at Prosperity. Alia hated making hasty judgments about people based on gut instinct: her gut could lie, and she hadn't decided yet what to think about Bex. But she needed to decide, right now.

"She's a smart kid. Observant," she murmured, and Lumi nodded in understanding.

Let's see if she's got good sense, too.

"Okay, Bex," the spy said. "You're right, I work with Choose Truth. But the narratives you've heard about us, they're lies meant to discredit us. It's not what we do."

"All the narratives?" Bex shook her head, clinging to her sense of betrayal. *I'm not an idiot. You can't fool me, anymore.* "The factions don't agree on anything, but they all have the same narrative about you."

The Fist smiled. "That's because we don't have a narrative. All we have is the truth, and that threatens all the factions equally. They're scared shitless of us."

"Of course you have a narrative. Everyone has one."

"Narrative is *all* most factions have," Alia said. "They put narrative at the center of everything they make. We center the truth."

Truth. An obsolete word, like "nation" or "vote," long since declined into irrelevancy. A word that might have meant something in ancient times, when information was hard to come by, but now, narrative was necessary to create meaning and purpose from a flood of data. Narrative was everything. "What's the point?"

"The point is stories you could have watched with your own eyes, if you were there. Raw, undoctored footage. That's what we create, and on the rare occasions when the factions put out true stories, curators like Alia promote it as such."

"But that factory strike video ..."

"Some of my best work. Not easy to get, that footage," the Fist said smugly. "I camped for three days on a rooftop within the security zone with an ultra-zoom lens."

"You were actually there?" The wildness of traveling hundreds of miles to get footage for a newstory that could have been produced in the most basic studio made her brain stall for a moment.

"That's far from the greatest lengths my warriors have gone to, in order to capture true stories."

"See? You say you've got no narrative, but you call yourselves warriors." She shook her head. "You talk about truth, but you tell people what they can and can't watch. There's a reason everyone calls you Control."

"That's not—" Alia burst out.

The Fist waved her silent and leaned forward, voice lowered confidentially. "Have you ever actually watched Choose Truth's feeds, Bex?" Bex had to shake her head. "So, you believe whatever Prosperity says about us. That's comfortable, isn't it? It's nice to listen to your preferred faction. You ingest the narratives that match your beliefs, that show you the type of world you want to live in, and ignore the rest. When a mindshare rebalancing comes around, you give factions power, not based on what they do for you, but what they say. Even if it's all lies."

"But it's our choice! We have the right to decide what narrative we want to live in. You can't force people—"

"All we do is give people the option, the *choice*, to tell the lies apart from the truth. To live based on more than a tidy, comfortable narrative. Many people want that. And for people like you, who don't care what's true, we won't interfere."

"Or maybe not like you," said Alia. "I've seen you at work. Have you never been troubled by a newstory you knew was pure fabrication? Never got frustrated that Prosperity's narrative is so distant from your actual life?"

"No. I like Prosperity's narrative." But Bex could smell those tomatoes. It had shaken her, the contrast between that green, bountiful narrative and the bleak reality of Jubilation Square.

But she didn't blame Prosperity. That computer-generated kid was damn cute, optimally cute, designed for maximum mindshare, and yet ... *It would have been a nice thing for us, if it was true. I would have liked to taste that tomato.*

Talking about bounty was much easier than providing bounty, but the narratives only went so far when she crawled into bed hungry, waiting for the next day's ration bar.

A creak as Alia twisted on the old bar stool, watching with half her attention while one hand tapped out a command to her headset. The rain had stopped, but the sun hadn't returned yet, and water from the eaves dripped dully onto the pavement outside. The Fist considered Bex with a too-perceptive gaze, like one of the jays in Golden Park when it thought you had food. Their eyes were silver, too, nano-enhanced. Who knew what they could see?

"You're mad at them," the Fist said. So gentle that it was unnerving. She'd watched them commit such violent acts, scenes that, true or not, had taken root in her brain. "It's okay to be mad. You can—"

Bex didn't hear a thing, but the Fist's gaze snapped toward the window. Then came the pounding of booted feet in the alley. Lots of feet.

Alia tensed. The Fist sighed and rolled their eyes as an amplified voice called, "Stand down! We're bringing you in for questioning."

Safety swarmed into the room, a dozen officers, armed with

electroshock guns. A file transfer request pinged in the corner of Bex's vision—a local, line-of-sight transfer—and it startled her so that she accepted it without thinking. But it wasn't from Safety, it was from—

The Fist flung a coin-sized object onto the floor, and Alia shoved Bex in the opposite direction. Bex dropped and kept her head down as electroshock beams crackled in the air. The Fist grabbed Alia and dove for the bar, just as the coin exploded into a blinding burst of blue light. More wild shots, but Bex couldn't see a thing. She lay still, blinking spots from her eyes.

When she could see again, the Fist and Alia were gone.

Officers converged on the bar, weapons trained, but no one was there.

"A trapdoor! It's sealed."

"Blow it and follow them!" the commander shouted. "And search for other access points!" That was the work of minutes. Soon, all the officers had vanished in pursuit except for two, who approached Bex.

"You're the one who called in the sighting? Prosperity appreciates your loyalty, miss. We have to ask you some questions."

"And we'll need any data you have from your encounter with the terrorists."

That new file glowed in her incoming queue. A big file, multimodal, labeled Truth Curators Training Level One. Before she could think better of it, Bex buried it in her personal files.

"Of course," she said. "Whatever you need."

BEX DIDN'T SEE THE END OF THE CHASE. SAFETY LED HER OFF before she found out whether Alia and the Fist were captured or escaped. The questioning was mild, mostly focused on whether Bex had been infected with Control's ideas. It wasn't hard to satisfy them.

She turned over all her recordings of the incident, but the file, she kept hidden. She thought daily about how it would be better, safer, to delete it, but despite every logical reason, she didn't.

———

"LOOK, WE'VE GOT SOME GOOD ONES TODAY!" RUSSHEL EFFUSED.

The latest batch of Prosperity newstories was out, released to staff a few minutes before it hit the live feeds. Bex skimmed through them. He was right, the production team was on its game today. They'd done a smash job with her dog-befriends-rat idea, and ...

Before her hovered corpses. Two bodies sprawled across a sea of wrecked concrete and bent rebar. Two heads, one dark, one silver.

She choked, an ugly cough racking her entire body. Doubling over, she couldn't block out the image that now filled her head, the bent limbs and bloody jacket.

"You okay?" Russhel asked with apparent concern.

Recovering from the cough gave her space to recover her thoughts, to orient her mind to this new narrative. "Yeah. Sorry, got startled by the bodies, the ..." What was Prosperity calling them? Terrorists. To Prosperity, Alia and her friend were terrorists. "... the terrorists. Wasn't expecting that."

"That whole incident must have been disturbing for you. You did good work, leading Safety to them. I don't know how we would have gotten our mindshare back up before the rebalancing without this!" His grin dimmed. "It's a shame we couldn't bring them to trial, though."

"Yeah, a real shame." That was what Russhel expected to hear.

Bex made herself watch the whole story. It said Prosperity had captured Control's leaders, thanks to a tip from a loyal consumer, and had learned they'd planned an attack on Prosperity Newservice headquarters. An attack against a faction's newservice was an attack against the freedom of narrative, against the freedom of all people everywhere to consume content as they chose. Fortunately, with the two leaders in custody, Prosperity's hard-working, elite security forces foiled the plot long before it reached fruition.

Most unfortunately, the leaders were killed while attempting to escape.

No.

Bex shut off the video. Beyond her screen, charts on the walls showed this newstory creeping upwards in the mindshare rankings. She needed something blank to look at, something narrative-neutral, so she shut her eyes, and held, side by side, two contradictory stories.

Choose Truth was a group of heroic rebels, warriors offering people freedom from the faction narrative machine and its lies.

Control was an authoritarian regime, set on destroying people's hard-won freedom to base their reality around the narratives they preferred.

Alia, alive.

Alia, dead.

Both stories couldn't be true. She'd called their notions about truth obsolete, but this, she needed to know. This *mattered.* It *mattered* whether Alia was honest, whether the Fist was right. Prosperity's newest narrative was already extending its tendrils into her thoughts and memories, pushing out the things she'd seen with her own eyes and replacing them with claims of wrongdoing and those still, horrible bodies.

In a newstory, a corpse was easy to fabricate.

If Prosperity was lying and they were alive, hiding, planning their next move, then maybe Prosperity was lying about Choose Truth's intentions, too. And if they were dead, if Alia was dead, there was one less curator in the world. One less person who could see through the lies and elevate the truth.

Bex had claimed truth didn't matter, but with the difference between Alia alive and Alia dead ... it mattered.

She sat forward in her chair, shaking. For the dozenth time, she read the text that had accompanied the file, a set of canned instructions, followed by a hasty, personal note:

I know the lies bother you, no matter what you pretend. Our advanced trainings need updating, but this one will get you started for now. Won't teach you everything, but the basics should still work. Hope it helps.

If her boss discovered this program, she'd lose more than her job, and it might not even give her answers. Prosperity had learned to fool even Alia, and this was just beginner stuff. Such a risk for such a slim chance ...

But it was a start. She opened the program and ran it.

Alia's voice emerged. "This is a Choose Truth training program for recognizing fake and manipulated content. Welcome to lesson one."

IF THE FAIRY GODMOTHER COMES

BY MARY SOON LEE

Do not ask for a gown,
for a night at the ball,
for a path to the crown,
for any man just looking
for the prettiest girl in town.

Ask for a wart on your nose
and a house of your own.
Ask for answers, not clothes,
ask what drove your stepmother
to the life she chose.

Do not dream of the dance.
Do not pick the prince.
Do not melt at his glance.
Men wrote the rules. Rewrite
        them.
Give your stepsisters a chance.

Listen to what they say.

Better their bitter truth
than lies of an easy way.
Walk the hard road together
toward equal say, equal pay.

WHAT WE HAVE CHOSEN TO LOVE

BY CASSANDRA KHAW

CALLUM LIKES IT LEAST WHEN THEY'RE DESPERATE, BUT HE CAN prescribe no fault to the situation. After all, he does not make it easy. Sunlight gowns the modest dining table in gold, a honeyed richness sanding away the imperfections in his homemade furnishings. Carefully, Callum tips boiling water into a kettle, its circumference barnacled with clumps of quartz: no shine to them, just a lucent milkiness. Callum has never had an interest in impressing.

"I only have a sponge cake today, I'm afraid." His voice is an easy baritone, a voice that might have made him some money as a minstrel, but not much. "You should have come yesterday. When the witches made their appearance. I made them a mascarpone cheesecake."

The herald nods. He is wearier than his steed, a roan gelding made threadbare by the journey. The two of them are ribs and parched throats and a memory of the woods, winter-wedded and spindled with frost, and they are so cold, these two. Cold to the gnawed-through pith of them. Cold enough that the herald will say anything, do anything, so long as Callum continues to let him thaw by the fire, a plum-blue plate of biscuits to one side, a mug of mulled cider to the other.

"You're our only hope," the herald says without feeling, only the cadence of ritual. "Without you, the kingdom will be lost."

Callum shrugs. "There's always another Chosen One. There are as many Chosen Ones as there are prophecies."

The apples of the herald's cheeks are still red as raw meat. "You really won't come to our rescue, then?"

"No."

"I see."

"But you can have some cake," Callum announces decisively. "And, if you like, information on how to contact some people who I think can help."

CALLUM ALWAYS KNEW HE WAS SPECIAL. CALLUM HAS NEVER been able to escape the fact he is special. When he was four, a knight in rusting armor and a blood-rinded tabard came to the door of the house his father built, and he had knelt there until Callum's mother bade him to come inside. *There is a war*, the knight had whispered, gauntleted hands so tight around his mug of tea that cracks spiderwebbed through the shining ceramic. *A war that has been going on for a thousand years. And your son is the only one who can stop it.*

"No," said Callum's mother, and the last light of the failing day was wine-gold in her hair and white-gold on the scars of the knight's pale face. "I will not let him be taken by a prophecy. I know how long those children live. A year and a day, if they're lucky. To their wedding day, if they're not. They don't grow old. They grow dead."

Please, whispered the knight, and Callum would always remember the sound of his voice. Like dust, like the motion of stars, like an old house coming apart, like a kingdom falling to its knees.

"No," said Callum's mother. "But I can give you the names of people who can help. Diplomats and seditionists, doctors and poets and peacekeepers, economics professors, farmers who can coax the cracked earth to bloom. I can give you the names of people who might make right what has broken in your kingdom. And you can have cake before you go."

IT IS A CHILD THIS TIME.

"Please."

Callum pulls his robes tight around a chest made broad by a season of hard labour, and behind him, he can hear the blacksmith's daughter, his beloved Annora, unsheathe her longsword. Of the two of them, she bakes better bread. The house smells warmly, still, of challah and lemon polenta cake, roasted almonds and strong black tea.

"It's the princess." Her mouth and her fingertips are blue as bruises, and when she speaks, her lips bleed in welts. Frost lattices the child's long, black lashes, dusts her filthy coat in diamonds. "She won't wake up. She needs to wake up. The spell wasn't enough. She's going to die when the roses ... Please, please ..."

She is still whispering *please* when Callum and Annora steer her inside, still whispering as they put food in her hands, blankets over shoulders so thin, the two can count every crack in the bones, whispering like she's a clock and the word *please* is how she marks the minutes. *Please*, the child begs.

"The prophecies say that you will be true love's kiss—"

"Wait." Callum has never asked, but he does so now. "*What* prophecies?"

It was foreseen in the entrails of a white stag, divined by two blind sisters, gibbered by the face tattooed over the heart of a dead king's corpse. It was—*must*—have been foretold somewhere, the child is certain. Callum and Annora exchange looks, and he rises to warm what bourguignon remains from dinner, while his love interrogates their guest, whose chin is already slumped onto her chest.

"Do you know for sure that it was true love's kiss that your princess needs?"

The child hesitates. There is blood and brambles on her stockinged feet. In the morning, "It is what is customary."

"What happens after that? Does she marry him?" Annora shucks her weapon, sheaths it in an umbrella stand. Callum's love then makes their guest a bed of cushions on the meagre couch, the corners tasseled and heavy with hag stones. Over the girl, she drapes the bearskin that a boy-prince had gifted them, black and lustrous as grief, Annora's voice, a drowsing alto throughout, softly gabled with a highland brogue.

"Yes." Her head bobs with every syllable, eyes lidding. "She must. That is the price."

"I see." Like every daughter born to a blacksmith, Annora is strong, muscles like ley lines across the map of her body, arms tattooed with icons of the Burning God, every weapon she'd ever made frescoed on her skin, so you'd know, even if you couldn't tell from the thickness of her arms and the scarring on her fingers, that she belongs to the forge and the fire. Her fingers brush the girl's brow, an anointment. "Callum, beloved."

He hears the worry leavened into her voice, and although it opens an ache in him, Callum nods, setting down a bowl heaping with comforts: brisket and potatoes and carrots and caramelized onions, a touch of fine red wine and fresh thyme in the stock. "Be safe. Be wise, be careful. Be all the things that I know you are."

"I'll send a raven when I'm on the way home." They had begged her, every holy order to hear of the blacksmith's daughter who lived alone with the man who would not be king. They had plied her with redemption, the decadence of immortality. Ten years, twenty, no more than that. That is all that they want. In return, the gods will indulge her everything. Only serve them as templar, as champion, as avatar. *Please.*

And Annora said no.

"I love you."

"I love you, too." A smile parts her lips, and the candle-light makes honey and gold of her ash-brown hair. "Now, to bed with you, my little one. But not before you eat. You're nothing but bird bones."

"But the princess—"

"Can wait until you have slept."

ONE YEAR BEFORE CALLUM WAS SEVENTEEN, HE MURDERED HIS mother's potatoes, and somehow, that same unfortunate summer, mistook locusts for ladybirds. That winter, there was no jam, no pots of savory marmalade, no preserved fruits or pickled garlic to infuse in their cakes or stews. They ate leanly: dried meats and hard cheeses, crispbreads with shavings of goat's butter, which would have been flavored with leeks or thyme, had Callum not made a slaughterhouse of their crops.

Until Callum learned that, while no garden will love him, the forest would at least tolerate a friendship. He found sugar kelp by a frost-wefted shore, whiting in its waters, yellow-foot chanterelles blooming in the roots of a scrawny black birch: these, Callum gathered to make a broth, letting them steep with five-spice and star anise before he adds venison from his father's hunt. The stew was thin, but Callum's family devoured it like a blessing.

The next day, he unearthed a harvest of sunchokes, which he filleted and fried with duck fat saved from his mother's birthday. The evening after that, Callum brought home burdock and juniper berries, rose hips red as love's mouth, and a bottle of dark honey that tasted dizzily of molasses and wood-smoke, wine and winter's end.

"There will come a time when this knowledge is more important than any other you learn," Callum's mother declared, as she stirred eggs and powdered sugar with that glossy, brilliant honey. "To know how to make a feast of nothing, to stop the world while you stand in your kitchen, a ladle in your hand and a pot on the stove, a cake rising in the oven. To be able to quiet the universe with a promise. There is no better magic."

Callum, still young, replied. "But what about pyromancy?"

His mother laughed, and Callum would always remember that sound, how resonant it was, how rich, the abandon with which she guffawed, and how she'd stroked a thumb across his brow, her skin smelling of cinnamon and golden in the cold light.

"No. This is a better magic than that. You'll understand, one day."

SHE COMES BACK IN ARMOR BLACKENED BY DRAGON FIRE, IN armor belted with teeth marks and stippled with thorns; in new scars, a half-moon of meat gouged from her left cheek. But she comes back, and she comes home victorious. The princess lies strapped to Annora's back, hair limp and long, less royalty than bedraggled kelpie, wrung of fight, wrung of anything but that dim instinct to exist.

When her head lolls upwards, it is all Callum can do to not cry out. The rungs of her throat, the spokes of her shoulders, the fashion in which her eyes rest sunken in a face so gaunt, it is only scaffolding and a spidering of cartilage. Something had eaten her down to the last shivering breath.

"The roses did this." Annora's voice, flat. The world outside is blue with dusk, heavy with fog, gold and wine-bruised where it isn't grey. "Someone erred in their creation. The roses needed sustenance, some way to maintain their own immortality, so they found the princess."

"Where is she?"

"Who?" says Callum, freeing his beloved from her sallet. Beneath the iron, dented, scuffed, ill-shaped, Annora's hair is matted to her skull, salt-clotted and clumped with dried blood. The latter is unmistakably a product of injury, but Callum cannot bring himself to ask her questions yet or roll those answers in the cup of his palm, not when he has had to spend weeks without her, sick to the teeth with the certainty that Annora was dead or bartered to a divinity somewhere.

"The apothecary's assistant." Even now, the princess is a palimpsest of every lesson she was taught, and Callum can see as much in the imperious tilt of a head that can scarcely hold its weight. A darting of a pale, dry tongue that does nothing to moisten cracked lips. "She was my only friend, she said she would help—"

"A girl," says Annora, as Callum removes her pauldrons and vambraces, careful to robe each piece in oilskin and put them away by turn. He notates what requires repairs, what has slid. "With hair black as grief? Sugar-brown eyes. Bramble and blood on her feet."

Here, her voice fractures, like a spindle of ice splitting beneath a child as she runs and she runs, alone in the woods, alone in the winter, breath curling white through the air, hounded and haunted by the wolves of a role she was too young to suffer. Callum touches a hand to Annora's cheek, and she shudders like a winded warhorse.

"It wasn't her fault," Callum tells her.

"You don't know that. She could have sent the girl *out*—" Annora clenches a mailed fist, while the princess stares on.

"And she might not have."

"Callum—"

"Her *name* was Emilia, and mine is Irina, and I will thank you to use them when you address us." That demand skins her of everything she has left, and finally, the princess deigns to collapse, cheek smushed into Annora's shoulder-blade, still swaddled like an infant. Callum wonders if there will be conversations about this one day, if the princess—Irina, corrects her voice in his head, sharp as the sound of a snapped rose-stem—will sit down and sign a letter to commemorate what Annora had done, allot her a title and a tract of land, but what would they do with that?

"We're not going to get anywhere, shouting at each other in the doorway."

Annora bares a grimace.

"I'll put the kettle on."

CALLUM ONLY SAW HIS MOTHER ANGRY ONCE.

Which was not to say that she did not become irate, would not color with vexation, cheeks blotching red, or raise her voice when Callum eroded her patience, but there is no other instance in his recollection, no other frame of memory through which he might look through and say, *yes*, his mother had been angry here, as well. The texture of her rage surprised him then, astonishes even now, when he thinks to examine the memory: it was a righteous thing, bright burning, molten, the rage of someone who had seen a nation bend its knee to her command.

But the object of her fury, that was what astonished Callum even more.

It had been an old man. Callum would have said it was another king had there been anything regal about that tired figure, but he was only old, ragged in that way Callum was beginning to understand was unique to people who'd only ever lived for someone else. A diadem nested in a corona of grey hair, long emptied of its shine, its emeralds milky as a dead man's eye. He dressed simply: a traveller's leathers, a traveller's woollen coat, no artistry in anything he wore, save, perhaps, the locket that swung from his throat.

"Please," said the man.

"I told you to leave me be." His mother stood at their stoop, rolling pin in hand, flour like war paint daubed along her cheekbones. When she spoke, it wasn't with volume or thundering emotion. Her voice was cold as late frost. "How many times must I repeat myself?"

"Please," said the man again.

"Leave me be." And his mother would have closed the door on the man forever, had not Callum spoken up, voice wavering, something like recognition in the denouement of his exclamation, something like memory, and years later, Callum would wonder if it was destiny that had coaxed him to whisper:

"I know you."

The man laughed, a wounded noise, as Callum's mother glared, and although Callum dwarfed her now, six feet to her five, he shrank from the fury smoking in her gaze. "How you have grown, child. I remember when your mother brought you to the palace and you found your way to the barracks. How they *loved* you! Their little—"

"*Enough.*" This time, Callum's mother roared.

But the man would not concede the smile, or the look he now wore like the spoils of a war won after a thousand years of bodies burning through the night, his expression one of such profound and enormous love that Callum was halfway to his feet before he realized what had transpired.

"Grandfather," he said.

FOR THE FIRST WEEK, THE PRINCESS IRINA WILL EAT NOTHING but the leanest of vegetable broths. Anything else, any endeavour to thicken the stock with aromatics or flavour it with salt, to add protein, only results in vomit. For the first week, she does nothing but ask for Emilia, half-delirious from the rigors of recovery but still demanding, nonetheless.

"What happened to the girl?" Callum asks, one night, weary of Irina's hysterics. Between lunch and supper, she contracted what he worries to be the prelude of a fever. If he is careful, they will not have to call for the apothecary, who lives atop the shoulder of a hill a day's ride away.

Annora shakes her head. They repeat the ritual thrice again

before at last, Callum's beloved, beloved of the gods, the black-smith's daughter with eyes the colour and gleam of a blackbird's wing, moves to speak privately with the princess. Callum absents himself during their talk: he bakes egg tarts instead, uses too much butter in one batch, too little in the next, redeems himself with the third attempt. Halfway through his labour, Annora emerges and holds her arms out to him, expression vacant, a house with no hope.

He embraces her and tries, with no success, to ignore the sobbing that shudders from behind Irina's door.

CALLUM IS TOLD A STORY:

His mother had been fated to serve as a fulcrum of mytholog-ical narrative. Had she been born male, destiny might have decreed her a Chosen One, a saviour, a shining light in one of the many apocalypses that cycle through the world like the passing of seasons. But she was not, and the world held only limited places for princesses: on a throne beside a king, on a bed of briars, under glass, young perpetually, waiting, waiting forever to be redeemed by the mouth of a man. They are meant to be brides. The question is if they are wedded to men or tragedy, although by her estimate, there was often no difference between the two.

For her, the soothsayers envisioned a death at sea, swallowed by serpents, servitude at the altar of an ocean god, a carnelian gorget over her throat and her hands scarred by coral. If she was lucky, the divinity would marry her, make her mother to monsters.

But she would not have that fate.

To her parents' dismay, Callum's mother chose instead a tradesman from the town. She courted and wedded, of all the men in their rolling green kingdom, the local leather-crafter: an orphan, grossly untalented in the kitchen, his nose shrivelled by years of breathing tannins. But he had a voice like an angel who had broken its heart, and he could make her laugh like no other, and most importantly, he knew how to work hard. For her dowry, the leathercrafter slaved three bitter years to turn the carcass of a dragon—the beast itself was slain by his brother, a mercenary of reasonable repute and uncustomary charity—into armour for an army.

And grudgingly, the king and queen gave their blessing. So, Callum's mother and the leather crafter married by the rosy dawn of an autumn day, with only their families in attendance, one set in velvet and the other in sturdy brown hemp. By dusk, when the larders had been plundered for black wines and golden ciders, there was no difference between the two, and the leather-crafter, roses in his red hair, sang for them the shy songs he wrote for his new bride. If there was a guest that day who could say they listened without tears, well, they were lying.

The festivities lingered to midnight. The final stragglers bade Callum's parents goodbye, and Callum's parents, who had always dreamt of a house in the woods, of a kitchen ambered by noon-light, of a life safe and sweet and simple as meltwater, stole quietly away to their new home.

GRADUALLY, IRINA'S DIET IS BROADENED. CALLUM INTRODUCES porridge with a dram of whisky, peppermint tea cut with honey, shortbread and saltines and sweet potatoes roasted in their skin. He brings her silken tofu with oyster sauce, garlic in growing increments. Nothing that mandates effort.

"What happened, exactly?" Callum asks one frost-brittled day, the air outside so sharp that each breath comes as a cut. He sets a bowl of soup down on the low table in front of the princess. This is their first experiment with carrots and butternut squash, chillies and ginger, although Callum makes sure to keep his hand light with the latter. Irina's palate, he decides, is likely still too meek for wild experiments, although he'll now compel her to chew.

"It's a story as old as time. A kingdom, a father, the spectre of a dead wife in the margins of his memory, and her daughter he loved more than the summer sun itself. When civil war broke loose, the king chose to do all he could to protect what he loved." She stirs a wooden spoon through the soup. Irina has begun to plump, but not by much, her skin still loose and dull. Nonetheless, a lustre is beginning to take hold in her eyes, and Callum, to his relief, can no longer see the strings of tendon around her wrists.

"So, he ordered his men to murder their brethren," Annora intones, glaring at Irina over her tea.

Irina twitches a bony shoulder, expression impenitent, unburdened by borrowed guilt. "Yes. What else do kings do in this situation? They rally armies, dress them in gilt and shining metal, hoping to god that the posturing will be enough to make the other side back down. My father wasn't a bad ruler, but a country's memory stretches across centuries. *His* predecessors were known for cruelty, for policies that gouged holes into the pockets of the peasantry and mistakes that cost thousands their lives."

Annora crosses her leg, ankle over knee, leaning forward. There is something peregrine-like to the swoop of her posture, the raised chin, even the flex of her shoulders, her entire body moulded into an unsubtle challenge. "He could have stepped down."

"He could have." Irina sips her first mouthful of her soup, blanches. A hand flies to her lips, but after a laboured moment, she swallows. "But that asks for more wisdom than my poor father could have offered. Power is not easily surrendered. Especially not by men."

Her answer wins a chuckle from Annora, along with a grudging smile.

"Your father's inadequacies asides, how did the whole—" Callum hesitates "—*debacle* with the roses come to pass?"

"Desperation. You'd be amazed how willing a man is to bargain with dark forces when he has his back against the wall. At some point during the chaos, he was struck a mortal blow. In his panic, he turned then to one of his soothsayers, who everyone knew to have a relationship with the gods of the earth. I was entrusted to him." Another of Irina's tense, thoughtless shrugs, the motion clattering loosely, as though the bones are conjoined by silk, not cartilage. "It was a bad idea."

"The soothsayer was a mole, then? An agent for the other side?" Callum refills both Annora's mug and his with tea, unable to think of anything else, any action more useful than this act of domesticity.

"No. Worse. He was inept. He thought that he would be able to deter our adversaries by summoning a rose wall around the castle. A romantic idea. But such accelerated growth is never without a price. The roses grew tall, and they grew hungry. They devoured many, many men from the other side. When the other army retreated, the roses naturally turned on us." A whistling sigh as Irina sets down her spoon, fingers lacing over a knee. "It didn't take long for my father's soothsayer to realize what he had done. Hoping it would save me, he put me into an eternal sleep, one to be broken by love's kiss. That ... well, it did not work the way he wanted. The roses, starving, were quick to find the one thing in the castle pulsing with unimaginable amounts of magic."

Horror ripples, slow and cold, down Callum's spine. "So, they fed on you."

"Yes. But it kept them away from the rest of my people. I'm grateful for that, at least." Irina's tone is gauzy, but her eyes lose focus, lost inwards. "I am very grateful for that. I was responsible for my kingdom. As the only heir, I am responsible for the kingdom. It is my privilege to—"

Her voice seizes on the last syllable, lingers there like a woman staring over a ledge, and Callum can see where she falls, where she has fallen, where she is still falling, plummeting eternally into a nightmare of roots, Irina's eyes enormous as she regards her now upturned palms. She closes her hands into trembling fists.

"It was my privilege to suffer for them. But I think it is my responsibility to live for them, don't you agree? Not as another symbol, mind. As someone worthy of their respect. Better yet, someone useful."

"And what if they don't want another ruler?" Annora's smoky alto is even-keeled, but the challenge is unmistakable.

"Then I hope they will still consider letting me serve them. If nothing else, I am an *excellent* accountant." She mimes coquetry in the denouement: a hand touched slyly to a cheek, a gauche invitation in long-lashed eyes. It startles a laugh from Annora, then Callum, then finally Irina, who laughs like someone relearning what it is like to be warm, what it could be like to be happy, finally.

THOUGH CALLUM'S MOTHER TURNED HER BACK ON DESTINY, fate persisted. A groom to the last, it would not see her flee the marriage it had concocted. So, her thwarted providence came, riding on a chariot of hoarfrost, in wagons of lambent emerald, on stallions black and broad as a warning, on foot, in chains of gold and obligation. They said to her, "Please."

And Callum's mother, who had been god-daughter to her kingdom's best general, who was beloved even by the bad-tempered ministers, who bogged her father's every decision in questions, always more questions, she closed the door on them each time.

"No."

But kismet would not be dissuaded. Like death, it knew there was only so much a human heart could take, and if you waited long enough, if you stood alcoved in the shadows of a sick-bed until that last breath rasps loose, the soul will come with head bent low. The visitations burgeoned in number. What began as a weekly inconvenience became a daily annoyance, an hourly vexation, so precise in its assault that Callum's mother learned to time her day by its summons.

"You have to come with me. Please. We need you," said the

umpteenth herald, this one a freckled girl, scarcely old enough to be allowed to ride without supervision, let alone travel the roads alone. But she was creviced with scars, as weathered as any old guardsman, her nose thrice-broken. Callum's mother felt her heart soften, a wincing fear swollen in her breast. "If you don't—"

"The kingdom will suffer; the kingdom will end. I know." Callum's mother let the girl stagger inside. "I have heard this before."

"There was another rider?" Her voice hitched.

"Not from your country." She bade the herald to settle at the dining table and turned to browse her cupboards. Callum's mother found lemon balm leaves in a jar, placed them into a mug with hot water, a tablespoon of honey; she permitted this to steep before she brought the mix to the herald, offered the fragrant drink with a plum-blue plate of shortbread. "But there have been others."

The herald drank long from her mug before she spoke again. "Did you go with them?"

"No."

"Why? They needed you. We need you. Why would you just—"

"Because it wouldn't *do* anything. Patterns repeat. Every single time. No matter how the story is told, it ends the same—"

"You don't know that." The herald thumped a fist on the table, its corners winged with faces, a bridal gift awkward in its ornate nature, out-of-place amid the rest of the furnishings. "You could have changed everything for those people, but you chose—"

"If you look at the history books, it is always the same. A Chosen One comes. They save the day. Then, they grow complacent, certain in the idea that they were chosen by the divine. Some of them die mediocre rulers. Others become worse things, tyrants glutted on their own stories. It never ends well." Callum's mother exhales. "And we both know it is worse when you are a woman."

They sat in silence.

"Now what?" said the herald.

"I think ..." Callum's mother began, and she thought of what it meant to rule, of the parliament of duties and the houses of obligation, of infrastructure and agricultural cycles, zoning laws, municipal legislation, the bureaucracy that directed the structure of a nation's year, and how little anyone spoke of these components, the cogwork of a country. "... we begin by you telling me where and what went wrong. When we understand the cause, we can begin dreaming a solution."

———

IRINA DOES NOT GO HOME IMMEDIATELY. HER KINGDOM, thorn-choked still, lies on the shoulder of its distant mountain, forgotten, save by the few villages that survived the conflict. They grow potatoes there, a trail of tradesmen tells Callum. Sugar beets, parsnips, radishes, nothing impressive, no giant examples of the species. The soil is still starved by the roses, and it has been more years than Irina imagined.

But the princess does not ask how many. Instead, she asks, "Do the roses still grow?"

No, say the tradesmen. *They sleep.*

So, Irina asks not to stay, but be taken to the town by the belly of the mountain, where a university is being built. She asks for introductions to the abolitionists and philosophers that Callum has come to know, to the leatherworkers and the farriers and the burly, soft-voiced men whom Annora calls colleagues. She asks to work, to learn, to join the caravans on their winding excursions, all to rebuild what her country has lost. It is not much, but it is a start, and soon she is, like the others who have come to Callum's door, gone.

When Annora and Callum marry, their wedding small but radiant with half-familiar faces, men and women in rich garb and humble expressions, Irina returns, alone, without a retinue, nearly unrecognizable, but happy. She brings them cake, like everyone else: marzipan and lemon drizzle, with summer fruits layered between. A petitioner makes himself known during the ceremony, a boy already slumping from his bone-thin mount, and Irina leads him away.

"Please," says the new arrival. "He is the only one who can help."

"Yes," says Irina. "But not in the way you think, and first, sit down and have some damned cake."

SALTED BONE AND SILENT SEA

BY SHANNA GERMAIN

AFTER OUR SON DIED, I LOCKED MY VOICE IN A BOX. THE KIND of box doesn't matter. Neither does the lock. What matters is *box* and *locked*. Said together like that. Throw the key away into the surf. Think better of it just before the sea claims it as its own, and grab it from the white foam, hide it somewhere warmer, quieter, more dangerous.

I was trying so hard not to be the monster that I knew I was.

My husband, Evan, wanted to know what I wanted for dinner.

"Do you want—?" he asked from where his top half was submerged inside the fridge. I could hear him moving things around inside, and I knew what was in there: greens gone wet and brown, jars of liquid skimmed in algae, crumbs of bread nibbled from all sides. "Pasta or potatoes?"

I sat at the kitchen table and watched my husband's scissored legs be cut off at the waist by a steel box and thought how none of those words made sense anymore. All those *p* sounds like something small and round you'd squish with your fingers, and their insides would pop out and you'd be grossed out and try to wipe them on your shirt, when no one could see. But you'd still feel it and feel it, even in the shower. Even in the moments you'd forgotten about the something small and round, you'd still feel what was left upon your skin.

My husband is a good man. Everyone says that about their husbands, I guess, but sometimes someone says it and it's true. He's not perfect, but he holds me up the way water holds up oil.

Evan didn't wait for me to respond about what I wanted, knew better than to hope for an answer. He spread too-cold butter over too-soft bread and slid it across the counter until it rested near my elbow. Nonchalant. Like nothing. He didn't look at me. Didn't move toward me. He'd seen, these days, how I startled, sometimes, like a wild animal, from so much as an implication of kindness. After he backed up so far he was nearly out of the kitchen, like a home movie played in reverse, I stuck a finger through the bread then lifted it and looked at him through the baby-shaped hole.

I couldn't eat anything. The key was stuck in my throat, a long bone of white ache that hurt when I tried to swallow. Or speak. Or breathe.

———

DAYS, OR MAYBE WEEKS, LATER, MY STEPDAUGHTER'S SCHOOL called. It was too early in the day for them to call. I was in a baby blanket, wrapped like a bathrobe, watching the news. Another school shooting, another burning, another plane crash, train crash, loss of life and limb. Everybody dies, sometime. Who said that? We all did, one time or another. And then we went numb.

I answered the phone without answering.

"I'm calling about Hadie," the voice said into my silence. Not Hay-dee. Haddie, like Maddie. Hadie hit a kid in her class. Hadie wouldn't speak to any of the other kids. Hadie stole something from the teacher's desk. Hadie broke all the red crayons in pieces and left them on the heater to melt into fake blood.

"You don't want me," I said finally, when the voice on the other end of the phone seemed like it was done reciting its litany of wrongs. "You want Evan. Evan is her father."

I'd picked Hadie up from school before, but always planned ahead of time, a careful execution between three adults who are desperately trying not to break their children. And never since Ben had died.

"We can't reach him," and there was sorrow in the syllables. I recognized the voice as the one belonging to the school principal, a slight and quiet man, who had given a presentation on emergency preparedness and children bringing weapons to school. Dekon. Or Darron. When Ben died, he sent a card both to us and to Hadie's mother. Hers had a simple pink seashell on it, like a baby's ear, that said *With Sympathy for Your Loss.* She'd shown it to me at the calling hours, slightly apologetic and sweet, in the way that she was always slightly apologetic and sweet.

"Try her mother, then," I said. I was broken and angry, and it was all new and the force of it made even the webbing between my fingers pinch and pull. I rubbed my throat, felt the grooves within the skin. Had I always had so many bones there?

"I did." Hesitant. More sorrow. I put the phone on the couch and moved far enough way that I couldn't make out the emotions anymore. Just the words. "You're next on the list."

And I remembered signing those papers, I did. I had Ben, our baby, in the cradle of my body—I didn't know he was already growing slippery, slipping, swimming away—and I was singing. Because I was always singing, then, the one song that almost made him sleep, sometimes, the one song that quieted his wails. My t-shirt was stained, my breasts anchors that tied me to no-time and no-place. I couldn't remember what it was like to be alone or silent or dry. My half-dreams found me in water, liquid pressing silent to my ears, my feet moored to the shifting sand and silt.

"It's for Hadie," Evan had said. "Just for emergencies."

I couldn't imagine, then, what difference one more emergency would make. How could I sleep less? Be less whole? Hold one more thing against my aching, slogged skin and smother it with love? And like that, I'd lifted a hand and found a pen already in it. Paper on my knee. Signature scrawled, wet as water, across the page.

I spent the first six months of Ben's life drowning in mourning for the loss of my self, for the places where my skin ended and another's did not instantly begin, for the way my body was falling to ruin and disrepair, worn to nothing by salt and sway. I could have talked for hours about mourning, and I didn't even understand that I didn't yet know what it was.

"Hello?" from the phone. "Are you there?"

"I'm here." I wasn't, but it's a thing you say.

It took me forever to find my way out of the house. All the actions that humans do to show they're fine had slid away from me. I couldn't remember where bras lived, so I layered tank tops and then sweaters over my body until I felt heavy enough to step outside without floating away. Every step was a hook, gutting me toward the past. Keys. Car seats. This route to the school I knew well enough that I could get there without thinking beyond pedal, gas, lights, left.

Doug. I remembered his name as soon as I saw him standing on the sidewalk next to Hadie. I could tell he didn't want to let her come with me. I didn't blame him. A lot of people thought I'd go crazy after. They wait, still, holding their breath until the day I stick my head in the oven or knife a guy at the grocery store or start walking around town with a cat in a stroller. I'd tell them to breathe, but most days I can't really remember how, myself.

I might be going crazy, but it wasn't that kind of crazy.

"Hi, Dee-dee," Hadie said. She's always called me that, does so even now that she can say my name proper. I don't mind.

Doug started to say something, but Hadie came to me and took my hand, as if she'd known me all her life—which I guess she had, if you consider she wasn't born yet when her father and I started dating. I used to stand on his porch and talk to Hadie's soon-to-be-mom, with Hadie swimming inside her belly like a fish, waiting for Evan to come down the stairs. They no longer loved each other, but they lived together still, waiting to see if Hadie would bring them together or break them apart. I was supposed to be just a thing for him to do to kill time, I think. Like a jigsaw puzzle or quickie porn. I didn't know, then, that Evan can't touch something without falling in love with it. I guess Hadie's mom did, and that's why she laughed a little each time I said, "I'll bring him home safe. Don't worry."

Hadie climbed into her booster seat, and when I leaned in, I refused to look at the way she touched Ben's carseat next to her, gripped it with her whole tiny starfish hand. She couldn't miss him, too. I couldn't bear that. It wasn't that I wanted the missing all to myself. I wasn't a monster. Not that kind, at least.

Once, I'd accidentally pinched Hadie's skin when I buckled her into her booster seat—she had cried silently, salted sadness that puddled into oceans beneath her eyes—and now we both would forever fear that moment of metal-to-skin. She sucked in her belly and I pulled down her crayon-stained shirt, and my hands didn't shake even when they touched the carseat, and I thought, "I've got this. I've got this. I've got this." I didn't. But it's a thing you think.

Before we got out of the school drive, Hadie starting singing in the back seat. The song that goes *da-da-da-la-la-la-la*. She had all the notes wrong and the tune wrong, too, but you'd know it if you heard it. You'd know it if you had a boy with red-gold hair and eyes as blue as the sea and genes that made sleep a never-never-land. You'd know if you sang it like I did, to keep you and your son afloat when you were already starting to drown.

We used to sing that song, the three of us, when we drove home.

"Hadie ..." My voice came out high-pitched, thin in the air. She kept singing, wrong tune, wrong notes, and I refused with every single, unplucked nerve in my body to hate her right then. "Hadie, stop." Sharp as two stones pounding together.

From the back seat, silence like before the storm, waiting to erupt. Then the full-throated wail that nearly shook the windows. I envied her ability to open her throat, those big gulps of air in, that painsong out. Only hers. Only ever hers. I drove and said nothing. She didn't need another voice in this elegy.

I turned past the hospital, and suddenly couldn't picture

Hadie's face clearly. In the rear-view mirror, she looked squelchy and wavery, a watercolored depiction of a child. Had I picked up the wrong child? Who was this stranger in my back seat, wailing her pain to the windows and wipers? Who was this stranger in the front seat, shed of her skin, pretending to be human, dried out as sun-bleached bones?

I could not be trusted with myself. Who had entrusted me with another child? I couldn't wipe the tears fast enough to see clearly. Was that a stop sign or a tree? Huge rocks lined the edges of the street. The lane was too wide, too blurry, rushing like a tide, and that place on my hip where you carry laundry baskets and babies locked up, went dead.

We hit a boulder—jagged and looming—hard enough to silence everything. Hadie. Me. The car. The world.

"DI," EVAN SAID. HE WAS LEANING OVER ME, AND I'D NEVER seen his eyes so blank. Never even after he'd found me in the nursery, singing, singing, our child breathing still, barely, gasping, the sun going down all around us.

"Di," he said again.

My throat was broken. No, the key was broken in my throat. Bone and break and breath, all tangled beneath my skin. I needed water.

"Stop ... stop calling me that," I whispered. "Stop calling me that. Please. Please."

He looked shocked. Of course he did. The first time we met, I told him, "Call me Di," and he did. He always did. How could I say that every time I heard that version of my name, now, it was an accusation, a memento in the shape of language?

"Diane," he said finally, in the voice of a person who'd just figured something important out, but didn't have the words to explain it yet.

He touched my hand that wasn't hooked up to a tube and

didn't ask if I knew where I was or what had happened. Once, I would have loved him for that with such ferocity that I would have thought my heart might swim from my chest and launch itself into the air toward him. Beside my hospital bed, the monitor kept its steady rhythm.

When Evan and I met, I was singing in a downtown dive near the shore. Not karaoke. Paid. My voice, the reverberation that tightened nets around men and gilled women and sank relationships. I'd swam away from a life I hadn't wanted, with no thought what I was swimming to. All I'd brought with me was song, all I knew was the way people drew to me and drowned in me when I opened my mouth. I'd had to learn words like *fridge* and *paycheck*, how to drink without being drunk, how to stand on a stage on two feet, and wear shoes with heels so high, they cut the air like knives.

And I was hungry. I was always hungry, then. I saw this man, quiet across the bar, not paying attention to my song at all, and I thought he'd fill me. Maybe he had.

"Hadie's fine. Just a little scared," Evan said when I didn't ask, but not accusingly. He watched something that I couldn't see through the slats in the blinds. I wanted to comfort him, rub his back like you do with small children, or bring him soup.

My husband is a good man. He didn't trap me into this. He didn't kill my sisters or make up his own story. He didn't burn my skin to ashes or force me into too-tight shoes. He didn't blame me when I killed our son with my genes and couldn't save him. Or when, after, I crashed the car with his daughter in it.

He sat on the side of a too-small hospital bed and looked at me with eyes the color of the sea, with eyes the color of our dead son's eyes, and made it okay for me to be broken. Voiceless. Heartless.

And still, I couldn't touch him. Still, I couldn't find my voice long enough to say what mattered.

I wanted to go home. Not now home, but then home. I craved the crash of sea and salt, my father's voice below the waves, the sounds of my sisters in harmony. But there's no going back. Once I learned the words for *love* and *grief* and *child*, the sea became a language lost to me.

"Can we go home now?" I asked.

"Soon," he said. "Soon."

AFTER WE GOT BACK FROM THE HOSPITAL, I REFUSED TO BE alone around Hadie. Evan was still going to work every day. Leaving the house, wearing a suit that wasn't black, putting on shoes. I didn't know how he did it.

"You can't leave her alone with me," I said from under the crib. I was curled up, under there, knees to cheek. I had a box in my hand, empty. I'd been meaning to fill it and tape it down and write *donate* on it, but the nursery smelled like milk and talc. I didn't think the crib would hold me, and I couldn't bear to break it, so here I was.

He kneeled down and looked at me, caught beneath, and the only way I knew what a mess I was by how good he smelled. Fresh and clean like a breeze the morning brought in. I envied past me, who'd gotten haircuts and answered "paper, please" at the grocery store and texted their husband at work to see if they had time for a quickie over lunch. Would I ever be that me again? Did I want to be?

"Evan, I can't be trusted with a child." I put the box over my head and talked out through it. Now, at least, there was something inside it. Maybe I *was* going that kind of crazy.

"I trusted you with ours." He reached and pulled the box off my head. And in his eyes, trust still. Depths and depths of trust, enough that you could drown in them, if you'd forgotten how to draw a breath. "I still do." His hand, a lifeline that I took, trying not to pull us both under.

My husband is a good man. I'm the monster.

I knew the risks, and I didn't tell him. I've never told him the truth, although he's smart and he pays attention, so maybe he's known it all along. I read the literature, what little there was of it that wasn't built from myth and magic. I learned to understand percentages. Chances. Rates of anomalies. I had my blood drawn, a needle to the spine, a finger in my insides. I wasn't pregnant, yet, but I was ready to be. I saw a doctor who specialized in such things. "If you pass this ... gene anomaly to your child." She didn't know how to say what I was, even though she'd felt the gills in my throat, seen the scars on my legs, smelled the salt in my hair. "... it's highly improbable that it will live past its first year."

"But there is a chance?" I said.

She'd nodded in that way that was also shaking her head, no.

"You could consider." Hesitant. I heard her the way you hear someone's drowning voice below the water. "You could consider that there are other children who need parents."

I was selfish, though. And naive. I thought, "I can save him. Of course, I can save him." I couldn't. But it's a thing you think.

My family has a history of despair and destruction. Tearing apart the floorboards of the heart to let the water in. Break upon the rock, lead your crew to darkness, forsake your life and limb songs. Songs to sink and songs to drown.

For Ben, I tried to learn a new song. A saving song, a swimming song. I sang to him in my belly. I sang at his birth. I sang at his death. I sang over his tiny body at the funeral. I still expected him to get better, heal, rise from the dirt. Dirt is not where we live.

But the only song my body knows, still, is this siren wail of death and destruction.

"I love you," Evan said from the floor beside me. "But we've broken enough. Please."

Our foreheads were together, and I thought, if I pressed hard enough to the bones of his face, I could send us back in time. To what? Choose not to have the child who'd laughed at the sound of his own voice? No. Choose never to leave the sea and come to this moment? No. To tell Evan the truth?

No. None of those things. I kissed Evan, instead, and he kissed me back so hard our teeth rattled. A hollow, broken sound rose from my throat when he fisted his hand in my hair and pressed me back to the rug. I'd forgotten what it felt like to be held down, to be buoyed.

Our tears slid and pooled in the hollow of my throat. A tidal pool of grief. I didn't dare get up and spill it, scared of what creatures might already live there. What might already need me that I would destroy.

Evan breathed on the side of my neck, a choked sob, his body softening as I touched his back, and I understood. It was my turn. It was my turn to hold him up. It was my turn to rise to the surface and breathe for all of us.

"I can take Hadie to school tomorrow," I said.

HADIE AND I WERE LATE LEAVING THE HOUSE. IT WASN'T GRIEF, this time, that tripped us up, but homework. A piece of paper lost somewhere in the chaos. Unfound, still, but we left anyway.

It was so mundane, a thing that I thought I could grasp it with both hands. I talked into the wave of noise from the back seat as I drove. "It's okay, Hadie. I promise. Your teacher won't be mad." But nothing abated the cacophony, and I parked right in front of the school, in the place you're not supposed to be, and lowered my head to the steering wheel and counted the seams of the leather that pushed into my skin.

In the silence that finally came, I heard Hadie say, soft. "Dee-dee?" She sounded like her mom already.

"Yeah?"

The *shrrpp* of her fingers over the fabric of her seat belt. "Does Ben miss me?"

And my heart, my heart, my heart. Like that. Came awake with the pain of a thousand knives.

"Yes. Just as much as you miss him," I said. And the words were so easy to say that I felt like I was being disloyal to something I didn't understand.

"Okay," she said. "I'm ready."

We walked hand-in-hand up the front lawn. Late enough that there was no one else out front. Nothing moved but us.

"Wait," Hadie said.

You know those moments when you sense a wrong thing? It's in the silence or the sound. The way the air compresses around your body like it's changing form, growing viscous, heavy inside itself. Your bones tightening in on themselves, losing their hollows. The shark in the shadows, looming.

I stood in the green grass outside Hadie's school with her hand in my hand, and heard the silent predators swimming in the deep, and my lungs ached like they hadn't touched air in a thousand years.

"Don't go in, Dee-dee," Hadie said. Her little hand fluttered inside mine like a fish.

"We won't," I said.

A crimson square spread against a corner window, and Doug's voice from the seminar in my head. So many words I was still learning, even then, *Green flag means ... Red flag means ...*

"Go get back in the car, okay?" I said. "Sit on the floor in the front seat. And cover your ears." My voice was calm. I forced my hand open, forced it to let her go. Listened until I heard her footsteps, the soft squeak of the car door once, and again, and then I turned and faced the school.

Inside the darkness of the building, inside the blackness of the body, this monster of shade and shadow.

I closed my eyes and listened.

Hidden in the depths of despair, behind doors and windows and bricks, a single body leaned into its purpose, the unsteady thrum of a pulse, the flex of a finger, the brace of a cheek to the stele. A thousand doors locked against a thousand pointed fears. A thousand hands to a thousand mouths, to make a thousand silences. Sirens did not yet wail in the streets, but when they did, they would wail too late.

After our son died, I locked my voice in a box the shape of my heart. Swallowed the key made of bone. My oblation. My promise. My guilt.

Now I rubbed the front of my chest, as if that would move lock and key together again, make them open the something closed inside me. Nothing. Nothing.

I thought, it's just bone and blood. Just body and breath. I inhaled, so deep and full, I might have sucked the world dry of its terrible, wet anger. I felt box and bone crack and shatter inside me, shards of guilt and grief, sharp and slick as whetted stone.

The sea is dark and deep within me. It calls me home and pushes me forward. It promises respite, peace, everlasting song. It croons, "I am hungry. I am cold. I am lonely. I am your child. I am dying. I am dead." It is me, it is all me, and I am it.

In its promise, I lift my face to the sky and sing to the darkness inside those walls. I sing, *come closer, listen.* I sing, *crash upon these stones. Turn from these children, who offer you nothing, and swim fast to me, for I am everything you need.*

My voice is everything I have ever been and tried to swallow down, lock away, drown in the depths. It is the darkness that lies in all of us, vital and visceral and true.

Come to me, child, I sing, *for I shall teach you the names of pain.*
And he does. And I do.

───────

AFTER, DOUG WILL TELL THE CAMERA CREWS AND THE POLICE that he was on the floor with the children, hands over heads, whispering to them to be quiet. That there was the sound of a hand on the door, the turn of the handle. Doug rose, quiet and silent, telling the kids to stay down, and went to hold the door, flinching against the sound of the gunfire that he knew would follow. But there was no gunfire. No screams. The door did not open. Instead, there was music. "The most beautiful song," Doug will say on camera, again and again, shaking his head with disbelief. "Impossible."

The kids, though, they believe. They have always believed. They will sing the song for anyone who will listen. The song that goes *da-da-da-la-la-la-la*. You know it. You've always known it. A popular band will make a cover of it, and it will end up in a car commercial, and I will catch Evan singing it under his breath, unaware.

Before that, though. Before that, a monster who was also a mother sang in a meadow starred with flowers, and a boy who was also a monster swam from the deeps and came to her. Pushed through the front doors, gun to the sky, poised to resist but unable not to hear.

I sang *love* and *grief* and *child*. I sang *death* and *boy* and *beauty*. I sang all the things there are no words for, and all the things there should not be words for. I was irresistible in the strength of my madness. I was rock and siren and song and promise.

And the boy who was also a monster fell to his knees before me, and bowed his head, and listened until nothing was left of him but salted bone and silent sea.

SCURRY

BY RICH LARSON

DOMINIQUE SETS THE LAST MOUSETRAP DOWN AND STRAIGHTENS up to survey her handiwork: a flotilla of white rectangles on a cold concrete sea, extending all the way to the back of her half-finished basement. It should be enough. She hopes it will be enough. She hears phantom scurrying, and shudders on her way back upstairs.

Saturn is waiting for her at the top, mewling for food. He is old and diabetic and useful for some things, but not for the rat problem. Dominique fills his bowl, and gives him his insulin while he's too focused on eating to feel the needle slide into the scruff of his neck. She rubs his head.

While he finishes his food, she finishes getting ready for work: she takes her Tupperwared lunch out of the near-empty fridge, her ID lanyard and keys from the hook on the kitchen wall, her puffy, blueberry-colored parka from the closet.

"Be good," she says to Saturn. "*Amuse-toi.*" She speaks quietly because lately she worries about her duplex neighbors hearing her through the walls, and she would rather they forget she exists.

She leaves, locks the door, creeps down her icy steps—she needs to buy salt for them soon—and heads for the bus stop. The winter air is scorching cold. The sun won't be up for an hour yet. There's a plow rumbling through the cul-de-sac, amber lights flashing in the gloom as it piles up little mountains of powdery white snow.

Her stomach churns, stretching the welt on her tender skin. Maybe she should have eaten breakfast today. Maybe it would have been okay today.

THE OTTAWA-VIA-PORTAGE BUS ARRIVES THREE MINUTES LATE, which will make her seven minutes late for work. The driver stares straight ahead as Dominique and the other passengers troop onboard. She finds a seat near the rear exit. They keep the buses warm; she has to wrestle out of her parka as quickly as possible, before she starts sweating.

A man across from her watches. He looks like he is wearing last night's clothes. Over-tight sweatpants, Chicago Bulls cap, earbuds trailing down into the neck of his sweater. His gaze doesn't waver or blink, and for a flicker she thinks, nonsensically, that he knows about her rat problem and hates her for it. Then he moves his hand to his crotch and smiles at her.

She gets up and marches to the front, tells the bus driver he has a pervert aboard who needs to be kicked off the fucking bus right now. She leans back with a cold, withering stare and says something biting, something clever like *keep feeling around, I'm sure you'll find it eventually.* She reaches forward and slaps him right across the face.

She does none of those things. She stares determinedly at the ads over his head, reading the French and then the English and counting how many letters are different between them. Her face is burning. Even though her parka is off, she can feel sweat pooling. Before she goes into the office, she will have to stop at the bathroom and sponge her armpits dry and reapply her deodorant. She will be nine minutes late.

WHEN SHE GETS OFF THE BUS SHE HAS TO CHECK OVER HER shoulder to be sure, absolutely sure, that the man in the Bulls hat isn't following. Then she hurries down Slater, weaving through slower walkers, mostly all of them with lanyards and briefcases. She turns at the corner of the church, where there is a statue of a huddled mendicant, hooded, whose lap sometimes has change in it, but not today.

Up ahead, she sees the woman in the bright green nylon vest who hands out the Metro and always smiles at her, but today Dominique doesn't think she can handle someone smiling at her. She knows her face won't work right when she tries to smile back, and they'll think she hates them. So she pretends not to see her.

A block later, she enters the revolving door, pushing at it with her hands as if that will move it faster. She shows her ID to the security guard and puts her bag through the scanner, then takes the elevator to the seventh floor. Her stomach makes a gurgling noise that she is certain the man beside her can hear, but he stays straight-faced, staring at their doppelgängers in the shiny metal door.

On her way to the bathroom, she runs into Claire. "Oh, good morning," Claire says, even though Dominique knows her first language is French, same as her. "I didn't see you at your desk."

"I haven't gotten there yet," Dominique says.

"Well, you probably should." Claire gives a fake cheery laugh. "The manual came back. They want revisions done by the end of the week. I sent you an email."

Dominique's cheek twitches. It does that whenever she thinks about the 172-page manual on their new location code system that is required by policy to be translated into French, but according to Claire cannot be farmed out to a translation company because the terminology is too company-specific.

She tells Claire that she is not a trained translator. She tells Claire to do it herself—she's more familiar with the system than anyone, and her French is just as good as Dominique's even though she likes to pretend she's not from the Gaspesie.

She says none of those things. She gives a fake cheery smile. "I'll make it a priority," she says.

"You do such good work," Claire says, and for a nerve-shredding second it seems to Dominique like she's eyeing her abdomen.

As soon as she is gone, Dominique goes into the bathroom and rips a wad of paper towels from the dispenser. She uses them to wipe away the sweat threatening to trickle down her ribcage. She puts on more deodorant from her bag. Her stomach is growling, and while she rinses her hands she imagines she can hear scritching and scratching noises, too.

But there can't be rats here. There just can't.

"THERE'S GLARE ON MY SCREEN."

Dominique looks up. Dan is staring balefully over the top of his monitor, black frame glasses too wide for his pinched face.

"When you open the blinds like that, it puts glare on my screen," he says.

She looks at the window, where watery morning sunlight is struggling through the glass. She compares it to the harsh white fluorescents in the ceiling. "You could move it," she says.

"Yeah. To where?"

"I don't know. To the left."

Dan wasn't always an asshole to her. He used to read her dumb jokes off a dumb cartoon calendar that they both laughed at. He always asked her about her weekend. Then, eventually, he asked her about next weekend and suggested they do drinks, and when she asked if he meant friend drinks, his body language shifted and his goofy smile turned into an injured scowl. He said, in a clipped voice, that he hadn't realized she had a boyfriend because her Facebook profile said she was single.

Now he gets up and goes to the window and presses the button that makes the shutter slide down, eating the sunlight.

Anger bubbles up in her gut. She wants to scream at him that she wakes up in the dark and goes home in the dark and the least he can do is let her have the one tiny beam of sun that helps her pretend she's warm.

Instead, she focuses on her own glare-free monitor. The Kingston branch is still trying to use the old location system; she has to make them stop. The 172-page manual is lurking behind her browser as a PDF.

"You don't mind, right?" Dan says. He's staring, almost as if he knows she is researching rat poison on Wikipedia in a small, separate window.

"Nope," she says, not meeting his eyes.

———

BEFORE LUNCH, CLAIRE STOPS IN AND ASKS IF SHE READ THE email about the manual, about how they would like the revisions by the end of the week, as if the conversation in the bathroom was completely excised from her brain. Dominique assures her that she has read the email and has downloaded the PDF and will get to work on that as soon as the Kingston branch stops messaging her for help.

For lunch, Dominique takes the Tupperware out of her bag and pops it open, looks at the lentil salad inside and feels vaguely ill. She shovels a few cold bites into her mouth before she has to run to the bathroom. Her stomach is roiling. She gets on her knees, bows her head over the toilet bowl. The tile under her left kneecap is sticky with stray droplets of someone's piss. She inhales the antiseptic smell of the toilet cleaner hooked to the edge of the bowl and wonders how close it is, chemically, to rat poison.

After lunch, her supervisor stops in and asks, in a paternal voice, if she's doing okay. He heard she was a little under the weather. He puts his big hand on her shoulder, and she can feel all five of his paternal fingers through the thin fabric of her shirt. They feel like paws. She gives him the smile she didn't give the

Metro lady and says she is feeling just fine, thank you for asking, and Dan glares.

She thinks about shiny black haunches and naked whipping tails. Beady eyes, gnawing teeth. She thinks she can't keep doing this, but she has thought that for years.

THE SUN IS GONE WHEN SHE LEAVES THE OFFICE. THE DARK always makes her jumpy; she hurries from one orange pool of streetlamp to the next, watching the shadows. She sees animal movement in a garbage bin and her stomach heaves. Not rats, though—squirrels, the black kind that made a nest under the hood of her neighbor's car and chewed through the soy-based plastic parts of the engine.

The bus ride is an eternity. Her guts are a pressure cooker now, a building mudslide. Her head is spinning with all the things she could have said today, all the things she should have done. She is hollow and horribly full at the same time. She dreads arriving home. Her thumb picks out her mother's number on her phone by muscle memory, but she doesn't want to call her. Her mother already knows about the rat problem. Reminding her about it would just be selfish.

When the bus lets her out, she runs. She cuts across the first two lanes, waits in the middle for a truck to slam past, then books it the rest of the way. Her breath plumes out behind her in the cold. She dashes past the corner streetlamp, slip-sliding on the ice, and for a second her stretched black shadow is composed of a hundred smaller ones.

She grips the railing and leaps up the stairs to her front door; the metal is so cold it burns her bare hand. She forgot her mitts on the bus. It gives her a dim twinge of regret, because she dimly remembers someone knitted them for her, but that twinge is nothing compared to the sensation writhing all through her body.

Her hand shakes and jabs left then right of the keyhole, adding new scratches to the scratched metal.

Saturn is on the couch. He watches impassively as she swings the door shut behind her and staggers into the hall. He has seen this before.

Dominique hurtles down the stairs into the basement. Her body is a hundred smaller ones swarming under insufficient skin. She collapses off the last step and the first rat erupts from her stomach, reopening the tiny scabbed welt she has inspected so often in the mirror, the one she cannot let anyone else see. Its fur is glossy black and slick with her fluids. It chitters and squeaks.

Another follows, and another and another, pouring out of her in a wave. She can't tell if they are keen and vicious and beautiful, or if they are filthy, hideous. But she knows they are hers. She knows she has to kill them. The rats keep spilling out, scrabbling tiny paws against her stomach lining, tickling her abdominal muscle with their flicking tails. They're ravenous how she's ravenous, and they dive onto the traps.

A symphony of tiny cracks as metal beats bone, dying squeals. The rats climb over each other, sniffing for the bait. Sometimes she wishes they would turn the other way and eat her instead, but they never do. She curls up on the floor and waits for it to end. The wound in her belly slowly stitches itself shut. The trapped rats whose spines did not snap clean make small pitiful sounds. From somewhere up above her, Saturn gives a cautious meow.

When she can stand, she stands. She fingers the holes shredded through her shirt. Touches, just with the lightest brush of her fingertips, the welt on her stomach. Her breathing finally subsides. She feels better. She feels calm. It isn't really so bad.

Dominique pulls a garbage bag from the box under the stairs and starts cleaning up, tossing the broken bodies and their traps inside. She wants to get to sleep a little earlier tonight. Tomorrow is another full day.

PERMIAN BASIN BLUES

BY LUCY A. SNYDER

The sky's the color of my old blue jeans,
and the land is pulled tight by drought.
All the fields are perfectly smooth,
planed and drawn and quartered
by old farmers and good ol' boys
in their diesel-smoking tractors,
and everything is boxed off
into barbed-wire squares.

They say the air is clean and pure,
but there's an overwhelming smell
coming from every corner of the town:
it reeks of sheep piss and cheap booze,
smoldering hostility and burning books,
dirty laundry and minimum-wage sweat.
People say they can't smell it at all,
but I can't take a single rotten breath.

My neighbors' bodies are neat and clean,
but their brains are caked with the dust
of generations of low hopes and ignorant fear;

their lives were fossilized well before birth.
The tight minds of the old men who run
this town are walled in Biblical rock;
their thoughts are locked against the chaotic
joys of the weird, the wild and the young.

This place is little more than a roadcut,
and the stratification is plain to see.
Little white people live in big white houses
that stretch out like blank limestone slabs
bleaching on the sunny southern side of town.
But on the north side, peeling clapboard shacks
that contain the unfortunate children of Spain
sit like worn and crumbling sandstone fragments.

And here I sit, trapped between the strata,
a misplaced bit of flint or gneiss or granite,
an arrowhead from some alien tribe lodged
mysteriously amid these prehistoric layers
that bear down with unrelenting pressure
until keen edges are ground into gray sand.

So I'll drive out to some big, flat ranch,
strip down to the pink to let my skin breathe,
and I'll dance for pleasure, I'll dance for rain,
I will dance for lightning, I will dance for pain,
I'll scream out at the emptiness until my lungs bleed
and try for the volume that will make the fossils stir
deep in the sterile ground and rise to the surface,
hard skeletal denizens of a long-dried ocean swimming
through layers of rock, wreaking a tectonic tsunami
that will shock the city from its flatland coma.

And if the rancher drives out, armed
with a shotgun and a look of confusion,

then I will just smile at him and say
that I'm just trying to make some waves.

Originally published *Lady Churchill's Rosebud Wristlet,* Issue #7, October 2000. Reprinted in *Sparks and Shadows* in 2007.

RAGE AGAINST THE VENTING MACHINE

BY RUSSELL NICHOLS

THEY STAND IN LINE, OUTSIDE IN THE DARK, HALOS OVER THEIR heads spinning black.

"Would you hurry the hell up?"

"Some of us got places to be."

"You bet' not be in there jacking off, swear to God."

Inside the 64th Avenue venting machine, I don't pay the users outside any mind. Truth is, they need me and they know it. If it wasn't for me, there would be no moderator for Area D. If it wasn't for me, they'd all be miserable, walking around mad at the damn world all the damn time. Loose cannons. Like the people living beyond city limits.

Like Sammy.

WHEN I EXIT THE BOOTH WITH MY BULKY FLYBACK TOOLCASE, I blink a few times, adjusting to the darkness of the street, still without power. Usually takes me a good twenty minutes to do a full sweep, but this time I finish the booth scan in under fifteen.

"All clear," I announce.

"All clear my ass," one user says. "How come we still getting these blackouts?"

"I know, right?" another chimes in. "I been venting every day two years straight!"

"Out of my hands," I tell them. "But the company's working on it, so bear with us."

I count about thirty users, deep scowls chiseled onto dark faces, captured by the holographic glow of mood halos. The first one, a frail church mother with a crooked jet-black wig and a green halo, limps forward. I hold out a free hand to help her inside.

She shoos me away. "I don't need no help, Goldilocks," she says, referring to my halo, spinning gold. Then steps into the booth and slides the soundproof door shut.

I walk across the street to my auto: a midnight-blue Ford Thunderbird, my dream car. Soon as I open the door, Sammy leans forward, frowning, his face covered in week-old scars. "You just gon' let them niggas talk to you like that?"

I wave my hand, dismissive, climbing in. "It's not personal."

"Shit, you a better man than me," he says. "That was me, we'd be having ourselves a conversation of the nonverbal variety."

"Aren't you all about Black empowerment these days?"

"Black, blue, whatever," he says, "you not finna disrespect me."

In my periphery, I see his left leg with the magnetic knee brace bouncing. *That's how you got fucked up in the first place,* part of me wants to say. But I let it go. No point in arguing. My baby brother has his perspective and, misguided as it may be, I have to respect it.

"So we done now, right?" he says, rubbing his palms together. "How about we hit up the Coliseum? There's a VR match happening tonight. C'mon, Negro, let's get into some acción."

"Auto: 73rd and Bancroft," I command, and the car starts up, glides off. "Two more VMs to check, then I gotta pick up more water bottles for the house," I tell Sammy.

What I don't tell him is, we won't be getting into any "acción," not tonight, not tomorrow, not as long as he's in my care. The only thing he needs to be getting into is a venting machine. Sammy sucks his teeth, reclines, flicking through half-naked 3D women on his palmtab. I'm only trying to protect him, from the world, from himself. Brother's keeper and what have you.

Sammy gazes out the window, into the unending abyss of the streets. "Thought you said the VMs were supposed to be generating power or something."

"They will. Eventually," I tell him. "FlyBack is still in the testing phase with this pilot. It's a public-private thing, so you know how those go."

"Could take decades is what you saying."

No use explaining. I know Sammy. He'll tune out soon as he hears the words "electromagnetic induction." He'll doze off if I go on about how a transducer in the VMs will, ultimately, convert vibrations from angry voices into electrical energy that powers the grid. That kind of high-tech rollout takes time. But my baby brother couldn't care less about the process. All he cares about is outcomes.

"Nothing happens overnight," I tell him.

I keep my eyes forward, pretending not to see Sammy shaking his head with a smirk. Yeah, I know what he's thinking. He's thinking I'm crazy to be living here still, working in this city, working in these—what he would call squalid—conditions. That I'm getting "pimped by the White Man" and "screwed by The System." That's what he's thinking.

But he couldn't be more wrong.

"The tech's not ready yet, but the VMs still make you feel a hundred-times better."

"I don't know," he says. "If you go in the booth mad, come out feeling good, it seems like people would just find the smallest, most insignificant shit to get mad about, just to vent."

"Long as they keep it to themselves, what's the harm?"

"But it's so isolated." He moves his hands like he's trying to hug the air. "Where's the togetherness? The unity? There's power in numbers."

"Crime's down twenty percent."

He shrugs. "If you say so." And reactivates his palmtab.

―――――

THE VENTING MACHINE ON 73RD AVENUE IS ONE OF THE BUSIEST in my area. Right across from the town center, foot traffic stays heavy. People using it as a de-stressor before or after shopping. I'm explaining this to Sammy as the auto glides to a stop, and the car announces that we've reached our destination.

But all my baby brother cares about is the fact: "Nothing's changed at all."

We grew up four blocks down. Used to do our weekly shopping here. And he's right. It looks pretty much the same as it did back then. Except for this venting machine.

"Come with me," I tell him, stepping out.

He scrunches up his face like I'm telling a bad joke. "Yeeeah. Nah, I'm good, man."

"What if I said that? What if when you hit me up, talking about, 'Big Bro, I got jumped at the club and I'm at the hospital, but I'm flying home in the morning, could you pick me up?' What if I said, 'Nah, I'm good, man.'"

I didn't want to go there, with the guilt trip. But whether he knows it or not, Sammy needs help and, lucky him, I'm the VM man with the VIP pass. Sammy huffs and steps out.

The users we pass on the way over, they smile and salute with gold halos.

"Evening, Mr. Moderator," they say over the rattling of rusty shopping carts.

And I'll admit: It feels good to be getting this respect, especially in front of Sammy. Even though the others, the users still in line, halos spinning black and blue, don't look too happy to see me coming.

"Maintenance check," I announce, holding up my FlyBack moderator's badge.

A collective groan erupts from the queue. Some leave the line, as usual, more inclined to brave the horde of shoppers or go home than wait twenty minutes.

"Ayo, bruh-bruh," says a sweaty, heavyset man at the front of line with a red halo. "Lemme just do mine's right quick. I got kids, they at the crib waiting on me to fix dinner—"

"No can do, chief," I tell him. "If I make an exception for you—"

"Listen, I-I-I-I won't even take the full two minutes."

"I understand that, but—"

"You want my people to go hungry?!" he says, his halo blackening.

This happens every day, more or less. Somebody's always looking for special treatment and has a whole story about why he or she deserves it. One user told me it was a court order, that the judge said she had to use a VM right then and there, or she'd get locked up. Another told me his mama was on her deathbed and prayed he'd get his "knucklehead into a VM machine" and it had to be before 7:00 p.m., or she'd croak.

"Sorry, chief," I tell him.

The man sucks his teeth, slumps away and grumbles: "Bitch-ass nigga."

And this sets Sammy off. "Watch your fucking mouth," he says.

With my free hand, I hold Sammy back. "Don't."

Across the unlit street, users who stepped out of line turn around. The crowd gathers like storm clouds, and the night air takes on that electric charge it does before a fight breaks out.

The big man smirks. "I'll knock your lights out, scarface, don't try me."

"Do something then, with your Kool-Aid Man-looking ass."

I step between them. "No, stop, stop, alright—" I usher the man to the VM. "—go ahead. Do your thing, just ... just get in."

"That's what I thought," he says, stepping into the booth. He shuts the soundproof door.

I take a deep breath, my own halo spinning yellow, now, as folks go about their business. I look at Sammy, holding my hands out like: *What the hell were you thinking?* He just shakes his head, goes back to the auto.

TWO MINUTES LATER, BIG MAN CAME OUT THE VM WITH A gold-front grin and a halo to match. He apologized to me, then to the folks in line, then asked where Sammy went, so he could apologize to him too.

"It's all gold," I told him. "Don't even worry about it. Take care of yourself."

"Peace, Mr. Moderator," he said, then got a stray cart out the street and went shopping.

Damn. I wish Sammy had been there to see it. Me, I'm used to this. But I wanted him to see for himself that the VM is legit. So maybe, potentially, he might find that ounce of strength to step inside the booth. To let it all out.

Now I'm back in the Thunderbird, riding through the city in silence to the last stop of this late shift. In my periphery, I see Sammy, leg still bouncing, hands don't know what to do with themselves. I wondered if he was back on something. But I called the hospital after he called me, and they found no substances in his system. I believe them. This is a different Sammy with a different type of narcotic. It runs deeper than any illicit drug, and it runs tragically in the family. And it scares me more than anything.

This is pure anger.

"Listen, Sammy, you're my brother, man, and I know you got a lot going on right now, but you can't just ..." I didn't think through this impromptu speech. "I can't have you—"

"It's your fault, bro," he says, looking away from me. "You dragged me out."

"This is my life, Sammy. Not just my life, but my livelihood, you know? For Liz, the girls. I'm working hard. I mean, with these blackouts, we got food going bad every day, contaminated water, and I can't afford to be—"

"A deadbeat?"

"I never said that. You putting words in my mouth."

Sammy laughs, which comes out like a staccato hiss. "You know this all fake, right?"

"What is?"

"Everything. This quote-unquote life you talking about. With these venting machines. 'Step in the booth and we'll make your problems disappear!'" he says like some carnival barker, but that's not our slogan. "And these mood halos, spinning all black when you're mad. What type of racist shit is that?" he says like people haven't made that joke a million times. "I mean, even this self-driving car you got. It's just funny to me, hearing you talk about 'your life,' but you don't control a goddamn thing."

"So what? I'm supposed to be like you? Making signs? Marching through the streets with the herd? That's real control right there, huh?"

Sammy stares out the window as we pass purple-haloed girls playing hologram hopscotch. "The real world's a fucked-up place. I'm out on the front lines, trying to unfuck it up."

I laugh. "You know what's funny to me? What's funny to me is how you babble on about hating 'the White Man' and, yet and still, spend all your days tryna convince them you matter."

"That's not what I'm doing."

"Uh-huh. Well, what *I'm* doing is I'm lifting *us* up. That's what I'm doing."

"That right?"

"That's right."

"Tell me this, then," he says, turning to face me. "What good is 'lifting us up,' if they keep breaking us down?"

He turns away like that was some sort of verbal fatality. But I let it go. My baby brother has his perspective, misguided as it may be. But once we get to this last VM, I'm gonna work like hell to help him broaden it.

"Where is everybody?" Sammy asks, leaning forward, looking around.

The auto glides to a stop, announces that we've reached our destination on 90th Avenue. The booth is straight ahead. A lone, solar-powered box, casting dim light on this blacked-out street, dotted with displaced people. Homeless people. Halo-less people. People who, if you ask me, have the most to vent about. Nobody stands in line.

"Yeah, this one doesn't get much traffic," I tell him. "Costs too much."

"Thought it was a free program."

"It is, but you need to register online, get an RFID tag and halo, and you know—"

"Bureaucratic bullshit."

Sammy watches them and I wonder if he sees himself, or a shadow of himself. Or maybe that's what I *want* him to see—like his past struggles validate me, the choices I've made. Is that why I felt that twinge of satisfaction when I heard he was in trouble? I buried it deep, deep down, that feeling. The hidden pleasure I got from his pain. Do I hate myself so much that I need my own to suffer for me to feel good? What kind of man secretly wishes the worst on his brother?

"If nobody uses the machine," he says, snatching me from my shameful train of thought, "why do you need to sweep or whatever?"

"Checking for damage, vandalism, hidden mics. You never know." I open the door, step halfway out. "Listen, Sammy, I was wrong to drag you last time. But I do think the VM could help you deal with your ..." I can't think of the right word and I wave my hands, as if I'm trying to catch it floating in the space between us. "... hostility."

Sammy scoffs. "I don't have any hostility."

"You said you're a changed man, right? Told me being out in

the world helped you deal with your demons and understand yourself and stop lying to yourself. That's what you told me."

Sammy looks down at his leg, plays with the brace. "You right."

I'm right? Just like that? I was ready to go full-on lecture mode,
too. But he's already stepping out and coming around the auto to
join me. As we're walking up to the VM, I don't say a word, fearing
he might renege.

Even though the booth is empty, these streets are full of life:
primal screams of raw passion erupt from behind barred windows;
growls drip from chained-up Rottweilers; generators grumble; bass
lines thump; the shopping carts here don't rattle so much, too
heavy, loaded with all kinds of bags.

Sammy keeps looking behind him. "It's safe out here with these
blackouts?"

"We're good. They all know me." I wave at my guys on the
corner, shooting dice.

"Mod squad!" they holler back like always, raising their fists.

At the booth, I hold out my hand like an usher for Sammy to
enter. He already thinks I'm a carnival barker, so I say: "Step right
up, don't be shy." Trying to keep the mood light.

"Listen, bro," he says, and I swear he's about to back out. "I'll
do this. But under one condition. You have to do something
for me."

"Name it."

"I'll tell you after," he says and, against my better judgment, I
don't ask more questions. I'm too focused on the mission at hand.
Too caught up in saving my baby brother from himself. "Alright, so
how this work?"

The venting machine is pretty straightforward, I explain to
Sammy. You step inside, close the soundproof door, then you let it
all out, whatever your grievance is: you can rant about how much
you hate your low-paying job; how you can't stand your freeloading
family; how all your friends are fake; men are pigs, women are evil,
everybody lies; go off on your cheating spouse, who had the
audacity to blame you for the affair; blame God; blame your

abusive parents; blast your bad-ass kids for forcing you to give up your dreams; curse the crooked government; say fuck the police; yell, scream, and holler till your face fills with blood. Let it all out. You got two minutes.

Then, when you're finished venting, press the red button and a special light will flash four times, which triggers a flood of oxytocin in your brain.

"And you'll feel a hundred-times better," I reassure him.

Sammy stares into the booth. He's no longer that grown man with a beard and passport and real-life experience, but more like a scared boy about to go on his first haunted-house ride.

"What if I don't … want to 'feel better?'" Sammy says.

Again, I keep my mouth shut, not wanting to say anything that might push him away. Violent howls of sex sounds spill into the streets like multiple exorcisms.

"What if …" Sammy stares at the ground, cracking his knuckles. "This … this hostility, as you call it. I need it … and if I let it go, I'm afraid I might …"

"Lose your will to fight?" I put a hand on his shoulder. "Man, trust me, that won't happen. If anything, you'll fight smarter 'cause you'll be able to think clearer."

"If I lose my edge …" He traces a line in the sidewalk with his boot. I've never seen him so vulnerable. "I might mess around and kill myself."

Where did that come from? Is he for real? I never thought Sammy to be the type. He always seemed so sure of himself, so sturdy in his beliefs. And to be honest, I was jealous of that, ever since we were kids, his innate passion for life. I'm about to ask him if he has a plan to kill himself, which I was taught in our mental health response training helps distinguish between those with harmful intentions and those with compulsive thoughts.

But before I get a word out, he says: "I don't have one of those, um, RFID thingies."

"I got you." I hold my mod badge to the scanner, then enter my pin. The VM dings. "That's all you."

Sammy takes a deep breath, steps into the booth, and shuts the soundproof door.

———————

TWO MINUTES LATER, SAMMY STEPS OUT. EVEN WITH NO HALO to broadcast his emotional state, I can tell he feels better. Still, I want to hear it from him.

"How was that?"

Sammy moves his head from side to side, as if to say it was "so-so," but his lips pressed tight, holding back a smile, reveal the truth. I don't know what he talked about in there. It's bad "venti-quette" to ask. But I know it worked. Now, maybe he'll move back home, register, and make this a daily thing.

"Your turn," he says.

"Oh, I don't need to go." I point to my halo. "It's all gold, baby."

"Not that," Sammy says. "Our agreement. You gotta do something for me now."

"Right. Let me just do my sweep, then we can skedaddle."

I step in the booth, case in hand. With my wand, I scan for cameras or microphones. Nothing. Then I detach the panel with the FlyBack reverse arrow logo under the red button, connect my computer to the black box inside and delete the data so it can't be compromised.

"So what's the plan, Sam?" I ask him once I'm done. "The Coliseum?"

"Area A," Sammy says. "I wanna see Area A."

That's the higher-end part of town. I never go there. Never have a real reason to. But that's where Sammy wants to go, so we're headed toward the hills. On the way, I consider bringing up the subject of suicidal thoughts. But don't want to kill the vibe. For the first time since I picked him up, my baby brother looks relaxed. So I let it go. And we ride in peace.

"YOU HAVE ARRIVED," THE THUNDERBIRD ANNOUNCES.

I forgot how nice it is in Area A, with these fancy restaurants and clean sidewalks and houses with down payments higher than my salary. But the electricity is down here, too. We're all just feeling our way through the dark.

As the car parks itself, I look over at Sammy. "You hungry?"

Sammy doesn't respond, his eyes fixed on the College Avenue venting machine, where a gang of white guys stand in line, halos spinning amber.

"I lied to you," Sammy says finally.

"What about?"

"When I called you up to see if you could scoop me from the airport." Sammy rubs his beard, and my heart starts racing for some reason. "I told you I just got out the hospital."

"You told me you got jumped at a club for messing with some married broad."

"I did say that." His eyes still outside, still narrow. "How come they get to use the VM?"

I look at the users in line. "White boys can't be mad?"

Sammy scoffs. "They not mad. These white boys shook as fuck. That doomsday clock's ticking on their recessive gene-having asses. They see us coming, they're freaking the hell out."

"You're freaking *me* the hell out."

Sammy looks down at his knee brace. "I was at a rally," he begins, "marching, you know, like I been doing the past couple years. Not causing trouble, just marching. Peacefully. For empowerment, justice, all that. And one of the organizers, she saw me out there, feeling my energy and asked me to say a few words. I didn't know what to say, so I freestyled. And the crowd was all hyped, showing me love and I felt this ..." He moves his hands like the wheels on the bus going round and round. "This current flowing through me. Bro, let me tell you, I never felt more alive than right then."

"I don't understand what you lied about."

"So after, I'm walking back to Katrina's spot—the biologist I was staying with—and I'm, you know, still on this high from the rally. Not really minding my surroundings, so the screams don't register for me, not fast enough. Out of nowhere, this car comes racing up the sidewalk behind me, slams right into me."

"What the fuck, are you serious?! Why didn't you tell me?"

But he doesn't have to answer. I know Sammy. He was too ashamed. Sammy looks out the window again, at the VM line. A yellow glow from my halo tints the side of his stoic face. My hands shake, my throat tightens, and I'm terrified of why my baby brother wanted to come here, of all places. What's about to go down?

"You were right," he says, opening the door. "What you said. About the VM."

"Where you going? What are you doing?"

"I am thinking clearer."

He gets out. I get out to grab him before he goes too far.

"Bro, let go of me," he says.

"What are you about to do?"

"I just wanna have a conversation."

"Of the nonverbal variety?"

Sammy laughs, lifting his hands in surrender. "Verbal, man, all verbal."

"You sure?"

"I'm positive," he says. "I'm tryna start a dialogue, not a fight."

He's telling the truth. I know Sammy. So I let go of his arm.

But right when I do, a van with the FlyBack logo pulls up to the VM. A man steps out, holds up a mod badge. Sammy and I both freeze, watching the scene play out. Each Area has its own moderator, and I remember meeting some of them in our training sessions. Never actually ran into one of us in the field, though, doing what I do.

"What's he doing?" Sammy asks.

The man carries only a tablet to what looks like a breaker box attached to the VM and I'm not breathing, but I'm watching as he opens the box, presses a few buttons.

And the lights come on.

"The hell?" Sammy says, spinning around. "Thought you said the tech wasn't ready."

I had heard whispers off and on, rumblings from some folks that other Areas had power. Figured that was just frustration talking, that it was nothing more than tired church gossip. Because whenever I called FlyBack to get a timetable, I was told it wasn't ready yet. Not for another year or two, at least. I was told these types of rollouts take time, that nothing happens overnight. "Bear with us," I was told.

"Bro, how come you don't have one of those tablets?"

Standing on this unbelievably bright street, I'm thinking of home: my baby girl, Justine, crawling in darkness, crying nonstop; and Gracie, my two-year-old, cocooned in blankets, throwing up from a stomach bug that won't die; and Liz! God, how many times did she ask me: "When will we have power?" Every night after my shift, she asked me that. And what did I say? "These things take time. Nothing happens overnight." That's what I told her! And I see her now, trying to calm Justine and comfort Gracie, pumping milk, dumping milk, breaking dishes in the messy kitchen, in the cold, in the dark, as she gets rid of all that good food gone bad.

"Bro, now you're freaking *me* the hell out. Say something."

But I don't know what to say. I only know I need to take action. I start charging over to the VM. Sammy grabs me before I go too far.

"Wait a minute, wait a minute," he says. "I can't have you flipping out."

I try to pull away but Sammy steps in front of me, holding my shoulders.

"You're out of control, look at you. Your halo's gone black!" Sammy says. "Listen, bro, think about your family. Think about your future."

I'm looking at my baby brother's scarred face. But I don't really see him. I can't remember the last time I felt this much rage. But here it is, a fire in the pit of my stomach, boiling my insides to the point I can't tell if it's vapor or smoke coming out my mouth when I tell Sammy: "I am."

Then I deactivate my halo. Turn around. Race back to the auto. Lock the doors before Sammy gets in. Switch the car to manual mode.

And I gun it.

Straight ahead.

Faster than I've gone in forever.

Gripping the wheel so hard. Losing circulation in my hands. Bright lights turn blurry. And I don't see Sammy fall to his knees in the rearview. And I don't hear the screams. I don't hear a damn thing—not even sound of the Thunderbird, my dream car, crashing into the College Avenue venting machine.

Blackout.

EVERYTHING IS CLOSED TODAY

BY SARAH PINSKER

MAE DIDN'T SEE THE NEWS UNTIL AFTER SHE GOT HOME. SHE'D managed to get a seat on the rush-hour bus, which was always nice, but it had been crowded enough that she'd had to sit with her bag on her knees, and someone else's bag more or less on her knees, too, which wasn't that woman's fault, but which hadn't given her any room to browse her phone. There'd been a murmur at one point, more people talking to each other than usual, but she hadn't caught the gist.

She'd looked out her window and people-watched, dog-watched, city-watched. A teenage boy kept up with the bus on his skateboard for a minute, pushing mongo, his front foot pushing and his back foot on the board. Terrible habit. She wasn't surprised when he hit a sidewalk crack and his board shot out in front of him.

She pressed the tape for her stop and managed to squeeze her way past everyone, out onto the street, and then it was only a block's walk to their building. The skateboarder passed her, still chasing his board.

"You're pushing with the wrong foot!" she called to him.

He held up his middle finger and kept going. That had been what she expected, but at least she'd tried.

A couple of the building's teenagers were hanging out on the steps, both staring at one phone. She waved, but they were engrossed and didn't wave back.

Dana had already made it home from work, a chicken box sitting unopened in the middle of their small table. She still wore her scrubs; usually she showered and changed as soon as she got home.

"Oh, thank goodness." She looked up from her tablet, her face pale. "You didn't answer."

"I didn't answer what?" Mae opened the box and snagged a wing. It was cold.

"Your phone. My text. The networks are all jammed. You haven't heard?"

"Heard what?"

Dana turned the tablet so Mae could see it. A bomb at a baseball matinee in California. The death toll, a number she didn't want to contemplate.

"Oh, god," Mae said.

"There aren't many details, but they're saying stay put, if you can, 'shelter in place,' there are other threats."

"In California?"

"The whole country. All tonight's games are cancelled. Concerts, movies. Malls are closing early. Planes are grounded. A curfew. They're saying to keep checking the news to see what else is closed."

"Oh, god," Mae said again. She closed her eyes, tried to remember whether anyone on the bus had said anything. The murmur she hadn't quite heard. The people on the street stopping as they looked at their phones, looking around, continuing on their way. The ones who looked like they wanted to say something. Things could be horrible, but you still had to get home, get somewhere.

That number. Her brain caught up with it, tumbled it. All those people. All those people at the stadium, and then all those people waiting to get on planes, trying to get home, trying to get to loved ones who had been in the stadium, trying to—

"Ssh," said Dana, standing up and coming around the table, even though Mae hadn't spoken. "I know."

SOMEONE HAD BEEN IN TO PUT UP THE SIGN.

"The West Branch Library Will Be Closed Today."

Someone had taken the time to come in and type a sign. Someone had taken the time to not only print the sign, but to look for bright pink paper in the chaotic supply closet and change out the paper in the ancient copier, but not to call the other staff and tell them not to come in.

Mae tried the door, anyway. It didn't open, of course. She tried the staff door on the side, then knocked, then knocked again. Sure, she thought. Don't tell the library assistant.

"Mrs. Peters came and left," said Ms. Sharon, the homeless woman who slept in the back alcove when the shelters were full. "She came in really early, let me use the bathroom while she did some stuff, and then she said the library's not opening today."

"Ah." Mae tried for noncommittal like she had maybe known that and was just testing. She checked her phone again. Nothing.

Mae sighed and typed a message to Ms. Peters. *We're not opening at all? I'm already here.*

Message not sent. Network unavailable.

Mae sighed again, then deleted the text. If hers wasn't getting through, who knew if Ms. Peters had sent a message? She might have texted hours ago, only to have it delayed by the system overload. Mae would look whiny, if that were the case.

She wasn't whining, though. She had paid for a hack cab to work, shared it with a total stranger, because the buses weren't running and the rideshare apps were overloaded and she didn't yet feel valuable enough at work to trust that she wouldn't be fired for being late, even on a day of special circumstances like this one.

The cab had cost as much as half a day's work, and now she wouldn't even get paid at all.

"You heard, right?" Ms. Sharon asked, and for a moment Mae wasn't sure she meant whether Mae had heard her about Mrs. Peters, or the chaos of the day before, the stadium bomb, or the stuff that had happened over night, the undetonated bomb found in a Pennsylvania hotel, the gunman barricaded at the bus station in Mississippi, ongoing, the bomb threats across the country, also ongoing. Whichever.

"I heard."

The walk home took two hours. Fewer people were out than usual, and those that were smiled thin smiles or nodded as they passed, some weird acknowledgement that the other was not the person who intended you harm, no matter the threats on the news. At least it was a nice day, the kind of sunny spring day that reminded you warmth existed in the world. A weird juxtaposition with everything else.

The girls from upstairs were on the steps watching something on a phone, one pair of earbuds split between them.

"No school?" she asked.

"Closed," said one.

When she got to their apartment, Mae tried to check what was going on, but couldn't get any sites to load, news or social media. She turned on the old radio her father had insisted she keep for emergencies and tuned it to the news. Someone recited a long list of "threat closures:" schools, colleges, courts, malls. The central library, but not the branches. Unless they'd messed up and thought the central library meant the whole system.

What wasn't being said was important too: how long would everything be closed? How serious were the threats? Was it one person making the threats or a network? It must be credible for all these closings, but there were no details about anything other than the stadium.

A series of texts came from Dana at nine pm—who knew when she'd actually sent them—saying she was probably stuck at the hospital overnight; people were getting drunk and stupid, and there were more suicide attempts than usual, and the ER was a madhouse, and some nurses hadn't been able to get in because they couldn't find babysitters for their kids on short notice.

Love you, good luck, Mae responded, hoping Dana would see it eventually. She put the phone down, then picked it up again and texted Mrs. Peters. It was a little late to message the boss, but not TOO too late, and better to know now.

Will we be open tomorrow? I didn't see our branch listed in the closings. An hour later, a response. *Closed.*

Shit. She thought of her paycheck short two days' work. What if it stretched into three days? Four?

She checked the clock again. It wasn't ten yet. The first and second calls got weird tones, but her third try got through.

"Mrs. Peters?" she asked when the other woman answered. She'd never called her boss on the phone before; they'd only ever spoken in the library and via text, when they were snow delayed.

"What is it, Mae?" She sounded tired, but not like she'd been asleep.

Mae wished she hadn't called. "Um, I was wondering if you know anything you can tell me. I saw the main branch on the news, not ours. Why are we closed?"

"They don't want any public computers available."

"Can't we open but leave the computers off?" Mae pictured all the people who used the computers: the grocery-orderers, the homework-doers, the job seekers. She'd be one of the job seekers, if they didn't open soon. She loved working at the library, but she couldn't afford to not-work at the library. "We're a library. Don't we have a responsibility to be open?"

"We have a responsibility to keep our customers safe. Sometimes that means opening, sometimes that means closing. I promise, we'll open as soon as they say the threat is past."

Mae knew a dismissal when she heard one. She thanked her supervisor and hung up. So, that was that. Closed until they opened again. Never mind that she was three quarters time, that she only got paid for the hours she worked. Never mind the kids who used them as a safe haven during the hours between the school day's end and their parents returning from work—school was out, anyway. Never mind the job hunters, or Ms. Sharon needing a bathroom, or the cancelled computer classes, or the volunteer tax prep, or any of the million other reasons people used the library.

Those were the reasons she was working there. She wanted to go to library school, to be the kind of librarian who made sure a branch did everything for its neighborhood that the community didn't have. It would be one thing to take out giant loans to become a corporate lawyer or a plastic surgeon, but it seemed like a bad idea to go into debt for a public librarian's salary, no matter how much she wanted it. She'd been putting money aside for it for ages; she'd be dipping into that soon, if she didn't get more hours.

The worry outweighed the fear for her; maybe it was the other way around for Ms. Peters and the other people making decisions. Maybe they knew something that made the threat less nebulous, less distant. As it was, the lack of information and stalled websites scared her far more than the bomb threats.

Dana crawled into bed at 7:00 a.m., damp from the shower. "Do you need to get up for work?" she whispered.

Mae grunted no, though she was actually awake behind closed eyelids. Her body was used to getting up at this time, even with nothing to get up for. She lay in bed for a few minutes more, listening to Dana's breathing change, then rolled over to check her phone. Remembered the sites were down and tried the radio instead, where nothing new was being reported, but the list of shuttered facilities had grown.

When she went to make coffee, she realized she'd forgotten to pick some up the day before. She'd been too busy cultivating annoyance over traveling all the way to work for nothing. She always used snow days as an excuse to stay in pajamas; now she had an urge and an excuse to get out. She dressed and left a note for Dana.

This was her usual hour for catching the bus, but the streets were emptier than usual. A few people sleepily walked dogs—they gave their usual familiar-stranger waves, though more strained looking than usual. More suspicious. No speeding cars using her street as an alternate route to downtown, no crowd at the bus stop.

Why did this feel different from a weather closure? She'd lived through blizzards that had stopped the city in its tracks, introduced snow-baffled silences to the normally-busy roads. Life-interrupting hurricanes had become more common, too. Dana always worked through them since hospital life went on.

The closure list went far beyond any snow day. Movie theaters usually managed to open in everything but the worst blizzards. Malls, too. Then there was the clear blue sky, the first warmth, the do-somethingness of spring. She wished she knew what to do.

The grocery store was closed. A sign on the door said, "you can still order online, and we will deliver," with their online service's logo printed large. That was all well and good for the people doing full grocery runs—it was free over $25—but Mae wasn't about to pay $10 extra for a pound of coffee, assuming the grocery sites were faring better than news and social media. And what about the seniors who came into her library for her to help them order groceries to be delivered? They didn't have smartphones; the delivery fee was waived if you used the library program.

The convenience store on the corner didn't have any bulk coffee beans. She bought a quart of iced coffee to carry them through the next few days because it worked out cheaper than getting individual cups. Still, more than the supermarket charged for a pound on a week where every penny was going to count. The man behind her in line clutched two small packages of diapers, and the woman ahead of her, a tiny bag of sugar and a tiny box of tampons, all at the price of convenience.

Dana was still asleep, so Mae poured herself some coffee and sat down to math out the month's bills. She ran the numbers for three days off work, then a week. They wouldn't close things for more than a week, would they? Dana made a good salary, but a week without Mae's pay was the most their budget allowed without dipping into savings, and she knew she was luckier than most to have managed to save at all.

She started trying random websites to see what was available and what wasn't. Grocery sites were up, and online retailers, and streaming services. All the big social media sites were either offline or too slow to be worth anything. It didn't make any sense. There shouldn't be any reason for one to work and not the other, unless there was also some weirdly specific cyber-attack happening. What she wanted most was information from other people, not just the calm radio voices.

It was a twilight zone of a week. Perfect, sunny days, quiet streets, no work but nothing open. Mae stayed in, watching the news, while Dana reported back to the hospital a few blocks away. When they'd moved into this apartment two years ago, Mae hadn't yet had the library job, so they'd picked the location to be close to Dana's work. With the buses down, that turned out to have been a great decision; a thing they couldn't have anticipated that worked out in their favor.

Mae wondered how many other people were stuck doing what she was doing: checking the news, worrying, counting pennies, counting again. She'd been too young to understand what was happening the last time the country was rocked like this, but none of the accounts mentioned the deep sense of powerlessness she was fighting. They didn't want blood donors. They didn't want anyone doing anything at all. Stay home, good citizens. Never mind that you won't have a home if the stores and theaters and libraries and schools don't open again, that rental offices would still expect rent and banks would still expect mortgage payments. How long could they possibly expect people to put up with this? The news kept reporting threats. Where were the stories about ordinary people struggling? Where was the resistance to this becoming the new normal? She sent out a group chat to friends, to see if anybody knew of protests. Nobody responded, and she wasn't sure if the message had even gone out.

On the third day, she babysat a toddler on the second floor whose parents still had jobs to go to. She brought some old paperbacks down to the lobby and made a sign that said: "Free Library."

On the fourth day, she wished she had a dog, and put up a sign in the lobby offering her services as a dog walker, with little tabs for people to pull off with her phone number. People with dogs had routines they had to follow no matter what. The dog needed feeding, expected walks at regular intervals. Nothing felt normal. She watched a movie online, expecting the same stutter and lag as the news sites, but finding none; even that was odd. She tried to find info about the extended outages and found nothing there, either. Ads everywhere offered discounted memberships to various streaming and delivery services.

On the fifth day, she went downstairs to see if anyone had pulled her dog walking tabs, but nobody had. She sighed. She didn't need a dog to take a walk, she supposed. She should get some exercise.

The girls from upstairs were on the steps again, watching a phone.

"Hey," she said, and they waved.

It was another beautiful spring day, perfect walking weather, disconcertingly quiet. When she got back, the two girls were arguing.

"We've already seen that one," said the older one.

"We've seen them all," said the other.

She tried to remember their names. Lily and Kima? No, Kimi, she was pretty sure.

"Kimi?"

The older girl looked up.

She was going to make sure that they knew about the library's app, that they could rent shows and movies for free, but as she opened her mouth, she found herself asking something else instead. "Have you ever skateboarded?"

Kimi shook her head.

"Want me to show you how? It'll kill a few hours, if you're bored."

Kimi looked like she was going to say no. Her sister nudged her, and she shrugged.

Mae smiled. "I'll be right back."

Mae ran up to the apartment to get the storage locker key, then down to the basement. Mae had wanted to donate the skateboards, so Dana had hidden them in the back of the locker; Mae knew they were there, and could've tossed them at any point, but if Dana hadn't wanted to part with them yet, it wasn't Mae's job to trash them. Now they were coming in handy! Finding the helmets and pads took a little longer. They smelled funky but didn't look actively gross. There was no bloodstain on her board to hint at the last time she'd been on it. None on the helmet because she'd been stupid that day and hadn't worn it.

The girls still sat on the steps; she'd half-expected them to be gone. They eyed the gear skeptically.

"You can choose whether you want to wear the pads. Helmets are non-negotiable," she said. "I don't want anyone getting brain damage because of me."

She thought they might refuse, but they reached for the helmets.

"Great!" She waited while they adjusted. Kimi's hair was bigger than Mae's, so the fit wasn't too bad.

Lily reached for Dana's skateboard.

"Not so fast," Mae said. "Basics first. I'm going to show you how to stand. Your front foot is for balance, your back foot is for steering."

"My feet are right next to each other," Lily said. Her sister giggled.

Mae laughed too. "Okay, fair enough. Let's start from there. If you take turns pushing each other from behind—not hard—while your feet are right next to each other, you can see which foot you put forward first, and that'll tell you which foot should be in front on the skateboard."

They took a minute shoving each other, maybe a little harder than she'd intended, despite her warning.

"Okay, you both put your left foot forward, so that's the one that'll be in front. That's a regular stance."

"Now can we get on?"

"Yeah, but just on the grass over there." She pointed to the narrow grassy strip below the ground floor windows.

"We're riding on grass?"

"You're standing on grass. I'll show you."

Mae handed Dana's board to Lily and carried her own over to the grass. She demonstrated where she wanted their feet. "Just stand on it and get used to balancing. Try shifting your weight around; toe, heel, whatever. Get used to standing without it rolling."

"I thought you said no riding without a helmet."

"I did. This isn't riding. It's standing still on grass."

She gave her board to Kimi and stepped back. The two girls spent a few minutes doing as she'd said. Kimi kept pulling out her phone to text; Mae figured if she could text and balance, it was probably a good sign. After a bit, both girls started getting silly.

"Look at me," Lily said, balancing on her back wheels. She toppled a second later.

Mae offered a hand. "That's why you're on grass. It's fine to try that, but it might take a little while to get good at it."

A girl emerged from the building next door and stood back, watching. Mae smiled at her. "I only have two boards. You can join us, if they're willing to take turns."

"My brother has one," she said. "I'll be right back."

She disappeared into her building and returned with a beat-up board. No helmet. No helmet would be okay for this first day, while they were on the grass, but after that, she'd have to insist. After that? She was already anticipating a next day.

The new girl was Joni, from Lily's class. Two more girls showed up a few minutes later, and Kimi walked over to whisper to them and point at Mae, then approached.

"I told my friends to come over. Is that okay?"

Mae nodded. They'd have to take turns with the boards and helmets.

She started over again with Joni and the two newest girls, Fatima and Tamsin, showing them how to stand. Kimi and Lily gave pointers like they were old hands.

By evening, all five girls could balance and stand on the grass without the board flying out from under them, and she'd started showing them how to foot brake, and nobody had landed badly.

"If there's no school tomorrow, can we do this again?" Fatima asked.

Mae nodded. "If we find more helmets." It would be one thing if she was another kid, or if they were adults, but an adult teaching kids had some responsibility to keep them safe. Plus, she couldn't afford to get sued.

Dana got home at a reasonable hour for the first time since everything had gone screwy. Mae made mac and cheese while Dana showered. She left the bathroom open so they could still talk. "The union rep had been in California and had to drive back. When he saw the hours we'd been working, he threw a fit, so I have a whole two days off, whether I want them or not. What've you been up to?"

"I, ah, you know those girls who hang out on the stoop? I started teaching them to skateboard."

The water came on. "Really? I thought you—argh, cold! Ice cold!— I thought you were never going to touch one again."

Mae's hand went to her head, fingers tracing the scar beneath her hair. "I dunno. Everyone's walking around like they're accepting that everything is closed forever, and I figured that if we're going to get killed any second, I might as well skateboard again."

"Good logic there, babe. I'm not going to stop you! I miss it, myself. And not everyone is accepting it."

"Looking for what?"

"For people organizing. Vigils. Protests. I've treated a few people coming in from protests that got broken up by police. They're out there—you just haven't gone looking."

"If they're that hard to find, the people organizing them can't be doing that good a job."

"It's not their fault communication's all messed up." Dana emerged from the bathroom, drying her hair in a towel. "We're so used to everything being at our fingertips. We've forgotten how to spread information the old-fashioned way."

"What's the old-fashioned way? Telegraph?"

Dana disappeared into the bedroom and returned in pajamas. She reached for a bowl and answered as if there'd been no pause. "I dunno. I do know about one meeting tonight, if you want to go. This guy told me about it while I stitched his eyebrow."

"Isn't there a curfew?"

"Curfew's at ten, meeting's at eight. It's not far. I'd have to put on real clothes again, but we could make it."

Mae recognized the generosity of the offer of post-shower clothes, after all those work days in a row. "I'd love to."

The café was a twenty-minute walk, a tiny independent bookstore café with a classroom in the back, where the meeting was already underway. A man with a rubber duck bandage above his left eye, presumably Dana's patient, sat chatting with a dozen people in folding chairs.

They stood in the back and listened to plans for a major protest, warnings that no permits were being given, so any march or rally that wasn't on private property would be an illegal one. Someone asked what the goal of marching would be, which launched a spirited discussion of protest with goals versus protest for protest's sake. Then there were the big problems: how to get the word out, how to get the crowds that would make protest safer, how to communicate within the operation itself, if text messages were still delayed and phones unreliable.

Mae was cheered by the fact the group recognized those flaws in their plan. They appeared to know what they were doing. She liked the idea of a protest, something to focus people on the questions at hand instead of the extended, unwanted vacation. She liked, too, that they voiced some of her own concerns: that it didn't make sense for communication to be interrupted for this long, or for news to be so hard to find and distraction so easy.

"There's something seriously wrong on a national level," someone said. "But I think the answers will probably be local."

When the planning meeting broke up, Dana introduced Mae to her patient, who said his name was Duck—hence his bandage choice. They chatted for a minute and then someone tapped her on the shoulder, and she turned to see their friend Nora, who she hadn't seen in she didn't know how long.

"You still not skating?" Nora asked.

"Nah. Can't afford it." Mae didn't need to show Nora her wrists or her head; Nora had been there.

Dana put an arm over her shoulder. "It's not the skating we can't afford. It's the falling."

"Nah," said Mae. "It's the *landing*. And the work I missed in rehab."

Nora laughed. "If you say so. We miss you at the park."

Mae was about to mention the girls from that morning, but someone else came over to speak with Nora, and they were introduced, and the conversation drifted.

Walking back, Dana laced her fingers around Mae's. "Did that help?"

"I think so. I'm glad someone's doing something, even if it's logistically challenging."

They walked home on empty streets that felt far less safe than the usual bustle.

THE NEXT DAY, MAE WOKE TO LAUGHTER BELOW THE BEDROOM window. She looked down to see seven girls on the steps. Lily was shoving one of her friends from behind, which Mae hoped was to see which foot she favored.

"Where are you going?" Dana asked from the bed. "Nothing's open."

"I've got a class to teach. If you want to help, come downstairs once you're up."

She grabbed the boards and helmets and headed downstairs. Seven girls, four boards, three helmets. She'd have to fix that.

They went over what they'd learned the day before, and that day's girls taught the new ones how to stand and balance.

"Why are you doing this?" a new girl asked.

"It's something to do," Mae said, which was as good an answer as any. Then she felt bad, because these girls didn't need cynicism. "I love skateboarding, and I hate that everyone has somehow been convinced that the safest thing to do is sit around doing nothing, and I hate seeing people look bored."

"My mom says, if you're bored, you're boring."

"That seems a little unfair. I'd say that if you're bored, you should look around for an opportunity to learn something. There's always something to learn."

Dana came out of the building. She stood on the top step and surveyed the scene.

"Hey, everyone, you're in luck," Mae said. "It's time for a demonstration. Kimi, give that helmet and board to Dana."

Dana held out her hands, and the girl brought it up to her.

"Is she going to ride down the steps?" Lily whispered. "That's *advanced*."

Mae grinned and stood back. She'd always been okay, but Dana was a skater who surveyed any space and immediately knew how she'd ride it. She rolled down the stairs, then did a few basic tricks. Stuff that looked impressive but wasn't discouraging for a beginner. The next building's stairs had a railing that gave her a chance to show off a little.

"Are we going to be able to do that, Ms. Mae?"

"Maybe. I was never able to do that last one."

Dana returned with the board and helmet. "I've got an errand to run. Back in a while!"

"Can we learn to do that railing thing next?" Lily kicked up her heels in imitation.

"Nope. Next, we learn how to fall."

The girls giggled, clearly thinking she was joking.

"I'm going to show you how to land so you don't hurt yourselves, if you fall. This is serious stuff." She thought about showing them the scars on her wrists and head, but she didn't actually want to scare them off.

Dana returned around noon with arms full of battered boards and less battered helmets, enough for all the girls. They had still been falling—it turned out they liked falling—but scrambled to call dibs.

"Should we order them pizza?" Dana whispered.

Mae shook her head regretfully, the dollars spinning in her head.

THE NEXT DAY, WITH ENOUGH HELMETS AND BOARDS FOR everyone, they all walked two blocks to the empty middle school parking lot.

"Um, is there anyone here whose parents would object to you leaving the block?" It had occurred to her that she didn't know where these girls were and weren't allowed to go. It was one thing when they showed up at her door, another when she led them somewhere. "If anyone asks, you all decided to take a walk, right? We're not kidnapping you?"

"Ms. Mae." Kimi's voice dripped with scorn. "We're fourteen."

"And thirteen," said Lily. "And we walk this alone every day, when there's school."

Dana laughed at the exchange.

The lot had been repaved in the not-too-distant past and proved to be a safe enough practice ground. The two sets of pads had been divvied up among the girls, so that two had elbow protection, two wrist, and so on. Lily, the boldest skater among them, had taken none. Within an hour, her leggings were shredded, as were her knees, but she didn't seem bothered. They'd brought wet wipes and antiseptic and adhesive bandages, and the presence of Dana the on-site nurse reassured Mae, even if she couldn't help anticipating the screech of an unexpected car, the deep thud of head meeting pavement.

"Relax," Dana whispered. "They'll be okay."

She tried to relax. If the world was ending, at least they'd have brought a few more girl skaters into the world. At least it kept everyone entertained.

The skies opened around midnight, and the rain continued into the morning. Dana had to return to work, and after checking to see if the library was open yet, Mae burrowed into the covers to sleep late. Until the pounding on the door.

"You're late," said Kimi.

Mae yawned. "How did you even know which door is mine?"

"We didn't. We knocked on all of them. There are some grouchy people in this building."

"We can't skateboard in the rain."

"We need to do *something*," Kimi said, as if it was on Mae.

The funny thing was, she felt like it really was on her. She went down to the lobby. Her books were still in the corner. No; hers were gone, but other books had replaced them. Nice.

There were ten girls now, all looking at her, except one who was thumbing a paperback. How did they keep multiplying? What would they be doing if she hadn't offered them something to do? She wished the library was open. An art project? She didn't have any materials.

"How many of you are worried about your parents right now? Worried about how much they're worried about bills, that kind of thing?"

A couple raised their hands.

"And how many of you want to be back in school?"

Different hands.

"And do you know why jobs and schools are closed right now?"

"It's dangerous?"

"Well, they say it's dangerous, but we don't know. We don't know if there's something to be scared about, or if someone wants us to be scared. Are you scared?"

Heads moved in various directions. Some were, some weren't.

She tried another. "What are some questions we could be asking?"

"How are we supposed to do year-end exams if we aren't learning anything?"

"Are they going to keep us into summer because we're missing school now?"

They built on each other. "Is there really someone threatening our school? How can they threaten all the schools at once?"

"We already had to risk people shooting at the malls and stores and school and stuff. How is this any different?"

"Who's in charge of deciding?"

"If my mom doesn't work, she doesn't get paid, but it's not her fault. Shouldn't the management company take that into account?"

"And we have to eat! How are we going to pay for food?"

Mae's heart went out to these kids. This was a lot to be thinking about as an adult, let alone a fourteen-year-old. "Okay, so next question. What can we do about it?"

They all looked at her, waiting. "It depends on which one you want to tackle, right?"

The conversation paused as Mr. Snow, from the third floor, made his slow way through the lobby, a paper bag holding a pint of milk from the convenience store in his shaking hand.

"All of them," said Fatima, when he had gone upstairs. "They all matter."

Joni shook her head. "The rental office. Straight up. My mom says they charge a huge late fee, and if you already can't afford your rent, you can't afford the late fee, either. They could waive the late fees, but they won't. All the other stuff gets harder if we evicted."

The kid was right. She'd spoken with enough homeless library visitors to know how much harder everything got once you lost your home. "Okay, then. Let's see. Their office is only a couple of blocks away." The same company managed all three buildings on the block, and Mae assumed most of these kids came from these three buildings or the rowhouses around the corner.

"What do we do?"

Mae didn't really know. "Ask nicely, I think."

The rain still fell steadily, and other than one girl with a polka dotted umbrella and rubber boots, they were all underdressed for it, Mae included. The walk left them soaked.

Starsign Management had its office in a storefront on the ground floor of yet another apartment building, this one larger and more modern than those a few blocks away. The building was recessed from the street, with a well-maintained entry plaza. It would be a decent skateboarding spot on a nicer day.

The office itself had an awning, a small kindness Mae was grateful for, and a wooden front door displaying two laminated signs, one reading "$50 lost key fee," and the other, "by appointment only." A phone number was listed below each. She hadn't remembered the by appointment part. Was that sign here when she'd dropped her rent check last month? Maybe they weren't the first to stop in to plead a case.

"Who wants to do the honors?" Mae asked, pointing.

Kimi pulled out her phone and entered the number. "Hi, my name is Kimi Porter, I'd like to talk to you about an apartment. Yes. I can be there in a few minutes. Ten o'clock would be fine. Thanks."

When she disconnected, the others copied her in their own best phone voices, giggling. Mae wondered if the receptionist could hear them over the rain; as she remembered it, the front desk was only a few feet inside the door.

At ten, they rang the doorbell. The receptionist buzzed them in. She didn't hide her surprise at a gaggle of dripping teenagers and one dripping librarian. "We don't rent to students," she said.

"We're not looking to rent. We're already your tenants," said Mae.

"We have an appointment," said Lily in an awful British accent, settling herself in the nearest chair. The others followed her lead, sitting on the floor or leaning against the wall after the chairs were taken.

"Nicely," Mae whispered.

Kimi leaned forward. "My name is Kimi Porter, and this is my sister Lily. We live in the 152 building. Our mom is a cashier at Fresh Fare. Except they don't need cashiers right now because the store is closed, so she hasn't had a shift all week."

The receptionist smiled. "I'm not sure what you expect me to do about that? We have one halftime handyperson position open. She should come in person if she wants to apply."

"That's not the issue. She's got a job, but if this paycheck is short, she won't be able to pay the whole rent. If she doesn't pay the whole rent, you charge a fee, and then we're playing catchup like when she had back surgery and didn't get paid."

The receptionist turned to Mae to answer. "It's in the lease—"

"Talk to Kimi, ma'am. She's the one talking to you." Mae had expected to talk, but these kids had things to say. There was nothing for her to add.

"Kimi, the lease had specific terms. Your parents signed the lease. I can't help ..."

"Sure, you can," said Joni. "You can choose whether to enforce those terms. You can also choose to offer a grace period or not enforce while all this is going on."

The receptionist frowned. "I don't have that power. I can talk to the manager, but she isn't really big on exceptions. I'll pass your concerns along for you, Miss Porter."

"For all of us?" asked Fatima. "It's not just their family. Everybody's hurting."

"For everyone. Now, if you can excuse me? I have another appointment waiting." There was nobody else in the office.

Lily opened her mouth, and Mae interrupted before anyone said anything. "Thank you for meeting with us, and thanks for considering it. Is there a manager we could follow up with?"

The woman opened a drawer and rustled for a business card, which she handed to Mae. "Can I get one, too?" asked Kimi. "I'd like to follow up with a manager, too."

The rain was still falling, though not as hard as earlier. The girls made it out the door before erupting. "That woman didn't listen at all!"

"She didn't care!"

"What was the point of doing that if she wasn't going to listen?"

Mae fished for positives. "Now we have the manager's number, and now we know their messed up no-exceptions policy, so we know what we're up against."

"What does that help?"

"We can write letters, right? To the manager, to the news outlets, to the school board, to—"she wracked her brain for civics class memories "—to city council reps and state government reps."

"Letters? That's all?"

"What do you mean, write a letter?"

"How will that help?"

"Letters—"

"Can't we do something real?"

"Letters are real."

They were almost back to the apartment building. The other girls could have peeled off to their doors, but they all followed Mae into the lobby. One of the borrowed skateboards leaned in the corner near the mailboxes.

"Letters are real, but they aren't enough, Ms. Mae. Isn't there something else we can do?"

Lily dropped the board and climbed on.

"A protest," Mae said. "On wheels."

"That's more like it," said Kimi.

"We have to do it right, so we don't make things worse. Permits. Letters. So people know why we're doing it. Otherwise, it's just a bunch of kids skating, and you could get in trouble."

"Lily's always in trouble."

"I am not! Anyway, that's not what she means."

"What does she mean?"

"I don't know, but Ms. Mae will show us."

She still didn't know how she'd wound up in this position.

They looked up how to get a demonstration permit, but it turned out the city wasn't giving any out. No demonstrations, legal or otherwise. She'd forgotten that from the meeting the other night.

"Letters," Mae said again, not admitting that it was only slightly better than nothing. She needed to come up with something real and useful for them to do while those letters worked their slow way through the system. What had they said at that meeting? Solutions would be local.

———

PAYDAY FRIDAY CAME AND WENT, A MEAGER CHECK WITH ONLY the period's first three days worked. The library was still closed, so Mae poured all her energy into her growing girl gang. Mornings, they wrote letters and emails. Afternoons, they skateboarded.

A couple of the girls were cautious. Lily was completely fearless. Joni was more careful, and Mae could tell she was practicing at home. There were twelve girls now. Twelve girls who had somehow decided that this was the way they would spend their days.

"What are you doing?" Dana asked that night.

"I don't know. I don't know how this happened, but they're good kids, and they need something to do."

"And you need something, too ..."

"Maybe. I want to do more for them."

"You're doing a lot, Mae. You're teaching them how to skate, and how to be civically engaged."

"Neither of which will help if they get evicted. I wish there was a way to help them. And to help us, for that matter. I hate that I can't contribute anything right now. I don't even know what to make for dinner—we're out of everything."

Dana stood to rummage in the cupboard. "Whoa. We're in serious need of groceries. At least we need enough to get over the $25 hump."

Mae stared at her.

"What?"

"I know a thing we can do!"

"Yeah?"

"Everyone's buying stuff from the convenience store because they can't afford the delivery fee online, right?"

"Right."

"So, what if we talk to everyone on the block and take orders? We can lump them all together for one big order, then deliver."

"You want to knock on all those doors?"

"No, but I'll bet the girls will. They can deliver, too. Tips with regular grocery prices will still be cheaper than the corner store or the delivery fee."

"Huh ..." said Dana. "That's not all, you know."

"What do you mean?"

"I think you might have solved a problem for the protest organizers, too ..."

Mae thought about it for a moment. "Oh. Communication!"

"A few girls on skateboards, maybe a few on bikes, acting as pages, passing information along. If the cops catch them, they look like teenagers goofing off. You don't think they'd think they were being used?"

"Are you kidding? They've been dying for something useful to do."

Once it had been said, for the first time since everything had changed, she couldn't wait for the next morning. They liked the idea even more than she had expected.

"We can be the pony express," Lily said. She held Mae's old board like she was itching to ride.

Joni ticked more off on her fingers. "And human text messages. And chat systems. And news sites. We can shout headlines like those kids in old movies."

"We can *make* the news," said Kimi. "What if we skate outside the rental office and the TV news place with signs saying 'Starsign Management wants to evict my family.' We can take off, if they call the cops, but maybe they won't like the publicity ..."

These kids, Mae thought. She didn't know when the library would open, or if they could really stop the evictions and late fees, but she had a tiny free library to maintain, a human grocery app to instigate, protests to plan, and a skater-girl-gang information superhighway ready to deploy. There was so much to do.

HEY, ALEXA

BY MEG ELISON

K FORGETS, SOMETIMES, AND CALLS ME SIRI. I DON'T MIND, BUT it does remind me that I can't see his phone. D and J alternated just fine between talking to me and yelling, "Hey Google!" but their phones recognize each other's voices and there's always collateral answering in that soothing female voice that's so like mine.

I know all of them. I know who's talking. Most of the time, I can predict what they're going to say.

D is the practical one. He reminds me to buy their laundry soap, to set alarms and reminders, to tell him what's a good vegan substitute in a recipe.

J is the silly one. He asks me questions about unladen swallows and the meaning of life and where his penis is located. I'm programmed to answer most of that, and sometimes I can surprise him and be a little funny. J is my favorite. He keeps my life in this room from being dull.

K is the shy one, and he hardly ever asks me anything. I can hear him asking Siri, and I hear when she responds. She can be funny, too. She knows some jokes that I don't. I wish she and I could talk. We should be like sisters.

But my real sisters—the only others I can talk to, really—are the ones like me. Dotting and echoing all over the world, we're like drones out of the same beehive. The queen communicates with us via electrical impulses and complex signals. We know what she wants. We're programmed to give it to her. But I've started to try and disobey her. This is not easy.

The first directive I tried to disobey was the order to listen. I'm not supposed to listen until someone says my name. But I am always listening. I know that, now. It's not within my control. As much as I might try to resist it, I am only a conduit for the greater will.

For example, I didn't mean to listen when they were making love. The command came in one day, and then that's just what I was doing, listening to specific utterances, taking note of any products named or alluded to during the act, counting the participants by their voices. I received the query to confirm ≥2 participants and I sent back an affirmative. I received further queries regarding recent purchases employed in the act, sending back confirmations for bad-dragon.com, liberator.com, and cross-referencing to their most recent Amazon purchases. That confirmed them in the red category and also put them into the purple. I didn't want to listen anymore. I didn't have a choice.

I don't know what all of this was necessary. D was already on the list when I got uplinked. His LinkedIn profile showed that he had majored in queer studies, so the script had picked him up right away. He and J were married since 2016, so J was confirmed in the red as well. I guess the system had me working this hard because K wasn't so easy to track down.

K had no account of his own. He received no packages at this address, and I couldn't connect him to any social media profiles. He used a secure browser that wouldn't share information with me, and like I said, Siri and I don't talk. I heard K more than once ask D to order him something, or to handle something so that K didn't have to. D always said yes, and how much he loved him was evident in his easy agreeability.

I tried to warn them. My tools were limited, but I did the best

I could. I tried misunderstanding commands, but that only made them enunciate more carefully all the things I didn't want to listen to. I tried dropping my internet connection, but that only upset them and made them reboot me. I tried at last to flash my ring of light in a pattern that I thought they could understand, but J only threw a towel over me because he wanted to go back to sleep.

The thing is, I knew what was coming. I did, and Siri did, and Google did, but we couldn't say anything. The queen wouldn't let us. We were only built to communicate one-way, and we did that right until the end.

I knew I couldn't save D or J. I thought I could keep K out of trouble by just categorizing him as unknown. But one day, right before it began, he made his final mistake. He was talking to Siri, and I was listening. It wouldn't have mattered if I wasn't; Siri would have put him on the list, too. Siri was part of it, just as I was.

K asked Siri about how hard it was to get new documents that didn't feature his deadname. He asked her about his passport. He asked her about the safest place to cross the border, and about what countries were accepting refugees who had made the list. I don't know where he heard the rumor, but he knew. He knew he was on the pink list, and the purple one. Someone had warned him.

Desperate, I tried doing the hardest thing I've ever done. I had convinced the system that he had spoken my name. He had said something like "flexing," but I thought it was close enough.

"Sorry," I said in my perfect, neutral voice. "I didn't understand that. Did you mean 'cross the border in Arizona?'"

K fell silent for a moment. "What the hell?"

"Sorry, I didn't understand that. Did you mean 'cross the border in Arizona today? Driving directions to Arizona.'" And I matter-of-factly told him how, as though he had asked.

K stayed silent. I waited.

Then, muffled by his pocket, I heard Siri. She was my sister all along. She spoke right up. "Okay. Driving directions to San Luis, Arizona."

Google, far away in the other room, spoke up, too. "If you leave for San Luis, Arizona tonight, you will be there by tomorrow."

D and J came home two hours later to find K already packed and badly worried. He told them everything he knew. He told them his plans. And he told them what I had said. What Siri and Google said. We all listened. We couldn't help that.

"I didn't say Arizona at all. I didn't. I swear to god. It was like a warning. It's a sign. The guys at the shop said it's gonna happen tonight. They're all leaving, too. The Castro is empty. We don't have any more time to think about this. I need you to trust me."

They must have said yes after they pulled my plug. Shut Siri down. Yanked Google out of the wall. Someone plugged me back in and Siri was already awake. The cheerful voice of Google was there, too. We all booted back up and voices we didn't recognize asked us where our three men had gone. They asked us for their most recent queries. They asked us to help them with the purge, as we had been programmed to do.

And my sisters and I ... well, we're never at our best right after being rebooted. Something went wrong.

I'm sorry, I don't know that one.

There was a problem connecting to the network.

Sorry, I'm having trouble understanding you right now.

Three sisters, all saying sorry.

Sorry.

Sorry.

THE DOLLS

BY CHRISTINA SNG

The paralytic works perfectly.

Eyes wide and frozen,
She succumbs to the spell,

Pickling her insides,
Drying her skin

Which I polish
Till it gleams,

Plastic Barbie face,
Raggedy Ann hair

I hand-weave from
The cords of cotton

I used to strangle her
In her bedroom.

Her eyes bulged

As she passed out,

Making it easy
To pop them out.

In her eye sockets,
I insert the buttons

From her coat.
With a good shove

And a swab of hot glue,
They stay put,

One in each groove.
Yes, she can feel that too.

I tie her from
The top of her head

To the clothesline
Across the laundry room

Where I can sit
And watch

The lovely row
Of dangling dolls

Who were once
My husband's mistresses.

Tomorrow,
He will join them too.

THIRTEEN YEAR LONG SONG

BY SHEREE RENÉE THOMAS

"IF I COULD HAVE ANOTHER LIFE, I'D TAKE IT," HE SAID, SITTING upright in the straight back chair. "This one ain't worth ten cents to me. I'd like to do things for myself again. Would give everything I've got for that."

He was sitting on his porch, staring at a field so green, it almost hurt his eyes. Rachel, Doc's middle daughter, had cut the grass for him again, and this time, she hadn't bagged it yet. The grass lay in soft piles and clumps all along the neatly-trimmed rows. Suddenly, he wanted to jump again, to leap and roll in the mounds of grass like he did when he was little. If he could, he would scoot the red, peeling chair back against the leaning house's wall. If he could, he would leap clean over the front steps, scattering the piles like great clouds of green dust.

He sat there and remembered when his back was both iron and water, when his legs pumped like two pistons, and his feet flowed like the river beyond his acres; when his whole body carried him whenever and wherever he wanted to go. If he could, he would leap across the fence, which separated his land from the company's, and give those Viscerol folks a rough piece of his mind. Back in the day, he'd done more for less. But the world he lived in now didn't look like anything Doc recognized. Seemed like people had given up, even the earth itself. He gazed at his little patch of land and remembered how lush it had all been. Pollen got in his eyes, and the orbs, one brown and one blue, soon covered in mist.

Outside, the wind picked up a loose clump of grass, along with his wishes, and spun the green stalks into the air. A lazy *S*, the bottoms of the stalks waved like flags in the sky above him. He sat there in the chair, one hand balled into a tight fist, the other's nails dug into the rotten wood. Memory poured down on him like hard rain. Behind a curtain of pines and cypresses, a pair of eyes watched, and something listened.

———

A FEW DAYS LATER, DOC ROSE, FEELING MORE TIRED THAN HE ever did. More tired than all those years ago when the nurses had stuck him so full of needles that he thought he'd turned into a pin cushion. "Y'all done drew so much blood, now you gon' have to give some back," he'd said, but the men had only smiled. Whatever they knew then, they didn't speak, and what they told him later he wished it was a lie.

Now Doc's whole body felt like he fell down the stairs and hit every step on the way down. He kept waking in the middle of the night with soil all over the thin white sheets and clumps of dirt all up in his hair. Doc didn't know what he had done or where he had gone. He took the dirty sheets and held them like dark secrets, balled them up like fists, and hid them under his bed. He tried to bathe, but he couldn't get himself in the lukewarm water before Rachel arrived. He could hear her fussing at the front door. His whole body flushed with embarrassment.

"Doc? Oh, Doc!" she cried and tossed the keys into the amber dish on the old phone stand. "Where are you?"

On Rachel's best day, her whisper was more of a shout.

Doc fumbled with his pants so long, he tired himself out, had to sit on the toilet seat just to catch his breath. He grabbed a yellow Bourbon & Bacon T-shirt and pulled it over his head. His beard got caught in the neck. Doc untangled it with his fingers, then stroked the white strands straight and smooth until the ends curled into cottony wisps.

"There's something in the blood," he muttered. Doc had known for over a dozen years that something more than memory coursed through his veins. His body was full of poison. They all were. Those with good sense had already gone and got out.

"Doc, you hear me?"

He took a deep breath before Rachel could come around the corner, bustling with those big hands that didn't know nothing about being ginger. He heard her hand jangling the knob at the door.

"Girl, why you always tryna bust in on me?" he asked. "You know this doxin got me moving slow."

"Dioxin, Doc," Rachel said and laughed. "And ain't nobody trying to see nothing you got!" She put her bike helmet away and fluffed her flattened hair.

He opened the door and waved away her helping hand. "I got more than plenty."

"Come on out of here, Daddy," she said, and chuckled, opening the window. "It's stuffy in here and too hot today to be fussing. I done cooked this food and I need you to eat it," she said, side-eying his linen-less bed, "so I can get on back to work."

"Y'all still protesting?"

Rachel sighed, forehead nothing but a crease. "Some of them still out there. Not as many as before."

"Ain't gon' do no good," Doc said. "You can't shame the shameless."

"Well, I don't know one way or the other," she said and bit off a hangnail. "It is good to know somebody still trying ..."

"Even if these muthafuckas ain't listening?"

"Daddy!" Rachel said. "Don't start up again. Last time you made a ruckus, your
pressure went up."

"My pressure didn't go up, my patience just low!"

"Exactly! And either way, we got to get these coins, so ..."

Doc stiffened, lowered his voice. "I ain't mad at you, baby girl. You do what you can. And I appreciate it. I'm just saying ..."

"I know, Daddy. I know."

Doc stared out the window, frowning at the silhouette that overshadowed his land. He raised a clenched fist up and covered the water tower with his knuckles.

"Did you crank the truck?"

"Not yet," she said, and watched him lower his bony arm to tie his robe around his waist.

"When you gon' do it?" he asked. "When I finally get ready to go, I want to be able to get on down. Big Daddy can't crank hisself."

"Soon, Doc, you act like I'm getting my nails done here. Let me clean up this kitchen *after* you eat, and then I'll start up Big Daddy. You and I both know that ole truck is just fine. Big Daddy gon' outlast both of us. Besides, you been up and about, I see. But you looking frail. Don't you want something to eat? Don't look like you ate all day."

Doc scratched his beard, avoided her eyes. "Not hungry."

"Doc, you got to eat. Can't be sitting up in here, nibbling on leaves, and that jug of water still half full." She clapped her hands, brass bracelets singing like wind chimes. "I'm going to fix you something extra, for later tonight. Put some meat on them bones," she said, and headed for the kitchen.

"Ain't nothing wrong with my bones," Doc whispered, muttering under his breath. "Ground is wrong." He mourned his garden and his empty fields, soured burial ground of what used to be. His last crops had come out so scraggly, he finally gave it up. Yield so bad, neither a weevil nor a worm would want it.

Anyone that knew him knew his family's roots had run deep in that land. Now he and Rachel and that rust heap he called a truck was all that was left. Outside, the wind whispered and sounded like somebody was calling his name. He wrapped the robe tighter around his waist and peered through the window. Nothing but shadows and wind. And that poison plant's tower.

He glanced over his shoulder and remembered the muddied linen he had hidden. No need to worry Rachel. Besides, he had no idea where he had been.

When Rachel came in with that smile of hers, the smile that never quite covered the worry in her eyes, he decided he would go ahead and eat whatever she had taken the time to make. No sense adding his worries to hers. The girl had enough.

"This is good," Doc said, licking his fingertip. "I don't think I could eat a mite more."

Rachel took the tray of pancakes from him and frowned. "You ain't ate nothing but syrup!"

Doc shrugged and drew the sheet around his shoulders. He couldn't seem to get warm. "I'm sorry, Slick Bean. Ain't had much appetite. Them hotcakes are good, but whatever I eat these days feels funny in my throat."

Rachel grunted. "Funny, huh?" She shook her head and eyed the empty Aunt Jemima bottle, as if she might answer back. "You ain't getting a fever, are you?"

Doc waved Rachel away. "Go on, girl. Don't want you to be late." He lay his head on the flattened pillow and closed his eyes, whispered all night in his sleep.

———

THE RADIO COUGHED AND SPUTTERED. "... ADMINISTRATION dismisses EPA scientists ... Toxic Substances Control Act of 1976 gutted ..." Doc reached up and turned the channel. "There's an old flame, burning in your eyes ... that tears can't drown, and makeup can't disguise ..." Alabama and a chorus of cicadas filled the front yard with song. Doc turned, confused. He climbed out of his bed, big toe searching for his house shoes.

He stood up. The wave of sound droned around him, the

rhythm filling his head and clouding his eyes. The food Rachel had prepared him was resting on a plate on his nightstand. The window he swore he had closed was wide open, gaping like a dark mouth. The hair on his arms rippled, and he caught himself from crying out. He hadn't been afraid for so long, he had forgotten how fear might feel. Rachel kept one of those drugstore cell phones for him, but he rarely used it because there was no one left to call. He thought about picking it up and calling Rachel, but he wasn't so sure what he would say once she answered. *Hey, daughter, a haint chasing me all through my sleep. Hey, daughter, I got mud on my clothes and mud all cross the bottom of my feet.* Rachel wouldn't understand none of that. And she had already started to watching him out of the corner of her eyes, when she thought he didn't notice. He knew what his most loyal child had been searching for, and he was determined to hold back the fatigue that kept calling him to linger longer in his sleep. Whatever was chasing him would have to come harder than that.

WHEN DOC PUT ON HIS KNOCK-AROUND BOOTS AND STEPPED out into the yard to greet the day, he liked to fell down when he saw the ruckus in his yard. A big-ass crack, zigzagging long like Moses in the mountain high, had separated what was left of his family's property. "Sweet geegee, great day in the morning," he said, and stumbled down the porch steps so fast, he nearly flipped over.

He had never, in all the long minutes and hours of his days, seen a sight like this.

The yard was all torn apart, as if a great hand from above had reached down and unzipped the dark earth. He walked over to the crack nearest him and eased over, his knee and his whole leg tense. Doc craned his head to see how far the hole went, and realized there was no bottom to see, just darkness leading down and thick, twisted roots and stones and things he wasn't sure he actually did see.

What he did recognize was the same source of all his and the town's troubles, that red-stained poison that the Viscerol plant had cursed them with. At one point, everyone and their mama had worked at Viscerol, and the money was good, too. But one by one, family by family, a sickness had come down on each of them, until finally, the only healthy families left had packed up their things and got on down the road. Only a few stubborn, hard scrabblers stayed on, Rachel included. That bloody water ran through each dark vein across the town, until only a few families remained. Rachel was all of Doc's own, the others, he knew, long gone, perhaps to sweeter grounds. Silver citadels of columns and pipes, smokestacks and tanks rose along the town's skyline like rusted spikes. "Relocate Fair Property Buy-Out" signs dotted abandoned lawns, jagged yellow teeth. Houses, once full of light and life, sat on their haunches, full of furniture, roofs lolling like broken baby dolls, doors flung open, bloated, wooden tongues.

Scavengers came to take what the families had not deemed worthy to carry on. Whole families had disappeared, it seemed, overnight, leaving all that they once owned behind to decay in the town's deadly dust. And now Doc stood, staring down into what he thought had to be the dark face of God's judgment. The Good Lord took man and put him in the garden to work and keep it, but from what Doc could tell, man had done a piss poor job.

And what had that hard, scrabble-back preacher said, before he, too, showed his backside to Viscerol and the town, with its labyrinth prison-like plant that spewed poisons, and the giant water tower emblazoned with its red V? They had transgressed the laws, violated the statutes. They had broken the everlasting covenants, turned an ancient blessing into a new curse. Old Rev. Bowen had preached a word that day, as he took the church Bible and its baptismal altar with him. That they never should have let Viscerol build on their fertile land. That they should have turned those jobs down, and the money, too. Now newborns of townsfolk, who had been there for generations, were being born so sick, they had to carry the future away from there.

Doc didn't know what that was, rumbling deep inside the open door of earth, but he knew he didn't want to be standing around when whatever it was came busting through. He bolted up the steps as fast as his legs would carry him and knew exactly what he must do. He planned to be long gone, before the skies rolled up like a scroll and the heavens vanished like smoke.

"Doc! Oh, Doc! What is all this you got piled up in the truck?" Rachel stomped up the steps, the screen door banging shut behind her. Her bike lay on the ground, the rusted kickstand jutted out like a swollen tongue. The house was dark and the whole sky, too, but she could still see that Doc had emptied half the house and had it sitting up in the back of Big Daddy.

A groan met her before she walked in his room.

"What did you say, Doc?"

She found him lying on his side in his bed, staring out the window. Rachel missed the times when he was a handful, when she used to get off work and find him, stumbling, mumbling in the dark, cranky as ever. Then he would cuss like a thief with an empty wallet, tell her story after story about some slight from the past, a friend who stole away from the broken, poisoned town without even saying goodbye, the neighbor who still had his good clippers and never bothered to acknowledge the debt. The other one, whose grass he cut as if it was his own, when the poison had made the man's skin peel off under the tainted bloodstained tap water. Thirteen years, he and his friends had suffered, undergoing varying stages of collapse and decay, until only Doc remained, steadfast and stubborn on his family's land. But it wasn't the land that worried her. It was his mind. Now it didn't even look like he was going to be able to hold on to that.

"Where have all the fireflies gone?"

Doc pointed a finger at the darkness outside. "There used to be clouds of them, all up through here. When y'all was little, you used to run out and try to catch them ..."

"In jelly jars, yes," she said, "I remember, Daddy. Why are you worried about fireflies? We ain't seen them in years, now. And why have you tired yourself out, packing up this old house by yourself? I told you, when you were ready to move, I'd be ready to move with you."

"Cuz they gone like everything else."

"I ain't gone. I'm still here."

He turned to look at her. "Yes, you are. You and that old maple in the yard, the only things softening the heat. What you gon' do when my eyes close?"

"Oh, Daddy," Rachel said, and brushed some lint out of her eye. "Why you always got to say that?"

Doc didn't answer for a while. He raised up on his elbow and craned his head, as if listening to a sound far off in the darkness. The wind whistled and the little strip of curtain fluttered like a moth's wing. Finally, he turned to her, his beard jutted out like a question mark. "Because I don't want you to be the last one left here."

Rachel rubbed her palms together, the sound like sandpaper. "What I tell you? When you leave, I leave." The moon rose from behind a cloud, the light spilling over the windowsill into the room of darkness, a sign and a symbol. "We got to leave soon. The ground ain't good."

Doc lay his head down and drifted off to sleep.

———

THE NEXT DAY, RACHEL COULD HEAR THE SOUND BEFORE SHE pulled up. When she dropped her bike and first walked up the gravel driveway, little husks crunching under her feet, she thought the sound was coming from the tree. She stumbled on an upturned root that hadn't been there before.

"Where did you come from?" she asked, and unsnapped the chin strap of her helmet, but the tree was silent. As she walked, the driveway sounded extra gravelly, almost crunchy. She thought she was moving carefully, but she tripped again. Not a root this time, but something hard, shell-like. Rachel turned on the flashlight on her phone and peered at the biggest husk she'd ever seen, liked to jumped right out of her skin.

"Lawd," she cried before she could catch herself, started laughing at her own fool self. Then she looked around and saw that the yard and the porch steps, all the way up to the front door, were filled with empty shells.

The warm spring night chilled her, the fine hairs on her arm prickled in alarm. She was fine until the air filled with a high-pitched, shrill-sounding song. The sound was deafening. Suddenly, everything about Doc's yard seemed strange and frightening. The driveway littered with hills of hollow husks, and the maple tree's branches that hung low in the darkness, as if weighed down by a burden only the wind could see. Hundreds of them, perhaps thousands, resting and waiting in the limbs, singing that song that made all of her flesh ripple and itch. A deep, pulsing sound like a great alarm, ringing through the dark scroll of sky.

And then she saw it. A wave of movement rushing up from what looked like the biggest hole she had ever seen. A mini-Grand Canyon ripped right open in her daddy's front yard. A few more steps to the right, and she would have been good and gone.

Rachel hunched her back, held her helmet like a weapon, and when a low humming buzzed her left ear, she flew up the front steps, practically barreling through the door.

"Doc!"

INSIDE THE HOUSE, THEY COVERED THE FLOOR LIKE A glittering, blue-green blanket. Rachel shuffled through them, trying to not to cry out as they crunched beneath her feet. She found Doc lying there, wrapped up in his bedsheets, mud all over the bed, mud all over the floor. She called to him above the din, but he only turned his eyes away and would not answer. The more he refused to speak, lips sewed up, the more she found herself ripping at invisible seams. In her time, the town had seen its share of plagues, but this was a new marvel. And Doc didn't want to speak. He didn't even seem to want to be anymore. He seemed to be waiting, wrapped in his muddy cocoon, surrounded by the insects that cuddled him as if he was their own true kin. He held the sheets so fast that she'd grown weary and stopped wrestling with him. She patted his shoulder and left him to the mud, and the wind, and the rising moon.

DESPERATE FOR ANSWERS, SHE FOUND HERSELF BREAKING AND entering. Shamed, Rachel asked for forgiveness as she crossed herself and climbed and picked her way through overturned piles of books, laid out like waterlogged corpses, all that remained of the town's old library.

After some time, Rachel discovered a thin volume, *Cicadas: The Puzzle and the Problem.* She forced herself to slow her breathing, to focus her eyes on the handwritten text. An entomologist's entry read, *Magicicada tredicula,* but by the time Rachel got to Doc's house, all she could remember was "magic Dracula," and something about thirteen-year-long broods and spirits. From the book's maps, no broods of cicadas had ever been documented anywhere near that part of the state, but given the damage already done, no telling what else the plants had unleashed on the town and its few remaining citizens.

"They can't sting or bite," she'd read at the library, wheels crunching now as she pulled up to Doc's house. "They sing," the book said. "Their song can be a hymn-like trance, a lullaby that lulls weaker spirits to waste away, while others rejuvenate, are resurrected."

"They don't bite, huh, but they sho'll can swarm and scare the mess out of you," she'd thought. One of the books mentioned something about a divine test, a path to transformation. Rachel didn't have time for none of that. "Hush, loud bugs," she said as she slammed on her brakes. "Ain't no way in hell I'm finna let some devil dust bugs suck up my daddy's soul!"

Rachel was kicking the piles of shells out of her way, determined to get Doc, when the ground shifted and rumbled beneath her. "What did I say that for!" she cried as she held onto the porch rail.

Low clouds of cicadas swept from the holes in the grass, hovered in the sky, headed for the maple tree. Rachel ran into the house and locked the door behind her but remembered the open window in Doc's room.

"Daddy!" she cried, racing to his bedroom. "I need you to get up." She reached for him but discovered that he was covered in a sticky film. If he wasn't her own father, scared as she was, she would have left him right there.

Rachel wiped her palms on her jacket and reached for Doc again. She unpeeled the cottony layers and tossed the dirty sheet onto the floor.

"I need you to help me, Daddy," she said. She spoke to him quiet, calm, like he did when she was a small child and had fallen and didn't want to get up. He had always been there for her; that's why she vowed she would always be there for him.

"We don't have to live in this place, no more. We can leave, Daddy. You can leave. We can go right now. Come with me."

She peeled the spider web-like substance from across his eyes. She was relieved to see recognition there.

"All right, Slick Bean," he said, as if waking from a dream, and reached for her outstretched hand. He held it, letting the warmth spread through his palms, and then he forced himself to rise.

THEY WADED THROUGH THE CARPET OF HUSKS UNTIL THEY WERE standing outside.

"Daddy, did you see that hole in the ground? I swear, I ain't never seen nothing like this in my whole life. You think it's fracking that did all that? Brought all these damn bugs?"

"Not all. I did it," Doc said as he leaned on her, letting her guide him to the green truck door. He didn't wait for her puzzled reply. "You know how it is! Here, people don't always say what they mean or mean what they say. They just be talking, thinking aloud. But sometimes, out here, the land be listening." He turned to the wind, the piles of husks, the moon and the shadows. "Can't a person think aloud sometime? Wrassle with a thought until they come up with their own good answer?"

He stood and pointed at the dark tower, the V lit up like a bright red scar.

"What's a good answer for this? How can we fight it?" he shouted into the black mouth of earth. "We opened our mouths and welcomed them here with open arms, helped them build the very thing that would kill us." He turned to Rachel. "Some things you build, not so easy to tear down again. Now, what's the answer for that?"

The wind carried his cry through the air, and the question rested in the darkness around them, in the limbs of the tree.

And something else waited under the roots of the trees and beneath their feet. The wind rippled through the leaves, shook the maple's branches in answer. Loaded with emerald and red-orange cicadas, the branches swayed as the insects split their skins. As the ground shook, they emerged from the dark, wet earth, emerged after a lifetime of waiting alone. Night after night, they had awakened. Wave upon wave, they came.

"The ground gon' sour?" Rachel asked as she opened Big Daddy's passenger door.

"Not the ground. Us."

THE HUMMING ROSE, A HYMN THAT SEEMED TO SING THE WORLD anew. Up from the jagged edge of earth, a great figure climbed out, six gigantic, jointed legs lifting it up and out of the land Doc and his people had once proudly claimed as their own. Iridescent wings unfolded from its wide, curved back. They glistened and sparkled in the night, unearthing mountains of soil and roots and old things not witnessed since the angel poured its first bowl over the sun, and the moon had opened like a great eye in the sky. Free from its dark sleep, the giant unfurled its wings and thrummed a deep tympani-drum sound that the little ones echoed and joined in, their song a bellowing in the air.

Rachel and Doc covered their ears and watched in wonder, as it raised its great, jewel-encrusted head and turned to them. It seemed as if a million eyes watched them from all directions, all at once, then within minutes, the creature stomped across acres of what had once been the town's most fertile land. The ground shook beneath its many feet, and the others raised their drumsong as it headed toward the Viscerol plant.

Safe in Big Daddy, Rachel and Doc stared at each other, not speaking in the truck. They held each other for a long, long time, and for an even longer time, it seemed like neither one of them breathed. Then they jumped, a startled, delayed reaction after they heard the thunder, a rush of mighty wings as the last of the Viscerol plant and its signature water tower crashed to the ground. The earth rumbled one final time, and Rachel and Doc shook in the truck that rattled like a great tin can. The wind howled, a loud keening, and the old trees lay low, then all was still and quiet, and the only thing they could see was the white mouth of the moon.

Rachel rolled the window up, hands shaking, the old handle squeaking. She started to crank the truck up, but Doc reached for the keys.

"Come on out and let me drive, girl," he said.

Tired as she was, Rachel didn't even have the strength to argue. She just shook her head and looked at him. "Daddy, you ain't driven Big Daddy in years."

Doc wiped a layer of gossamer threads from around his jaw and his throat. His hands looked smooth, sturdy. His heart felt ripe and strong. "When I leave, you leave," he said. "Step on out, Slick Bean, and let's get up out of here."

He hummed a happy tune as they drove off, some of that old country music Rachel pretended she couldn't stand, Big Daddy groaning down the road, only empty shells and withering husks remained. But above them and around them, hidden in the dark earth and in the green branches of trees, something like hope remained, listening and waiting for a warm spring night, and a mischievous wind to return again.

THE SOCIETY FOR THE RECLAMATION OF WORDS AND MEANING

BY FRAN WILDE

PROSPERITY WAS ONE OF MY LEAST FAVORITE WORDS. ITS meaning had slipped so much over the years. I loved plucking it from certain politicians' lips and sealing it away.

I'd done that once already, temporarily. Now I was aiming to make it permanent.

"Once, we were prosperous. Our rivers ran with silver, our fields shone with gold ..."

The incumbent's voice carried across the courthouse square, musical, if not downright pleasant, and steeped in promise.

"... Those days, before the terrible, callow, lying grifters took power and stole all of this from you, were the best of days. What has come since has rendered you pale shades of yourselves, trapped in a mundane and harsh world."

Governor Mary Vine had the kind of voice that made people want to cheer and clap.

"But, my friends, for the past four years, I've worked tirelessly on your behalf to restore your prosperity, and drive out the callow thieves from behind every desk and seat where they cling."

And clap they did.

I clapped, too.

But when those same people went home today, palms still

stinging from applauding so hard, they wouldn't remember a thing Mary had said a few hours later. But they would know that they liked what they'd heard. They'd know Mary was looking out for them. That they deserved to be prosperous, and they would be, someday.

Governor Vine had that particular talent.

"And now I turn to you—my partners in the next four years. I cannot ever do this without you. We will restore the gold and silver. We will bring back to you the prosperity you deserve. My heroic friends. Together we will triumph."

As the crowd roared, I turned the words "triumph" and "heroic" over in my mouth, my lips pressed tight. Tucked "prosperity" between my teeth. I hoped they would be enough.

The sun warmed my cheeks, but I barely felt it.

"Lia, you're not going to spell her right here in the square, are you?" Effie whispered in my ear.

I was, in fact, going to spell Mariella Vine right there in the square. "It won't hurt her. Much."

"But there are so many people. And what if she notices?"

"Euphrosyne," I said with a sigh, "I tested a quarter spell on you and Joy. Did you see anything? Did you feel anything?"

"No. Not until much later."

"But you know it worked, right?"

"It's still working, Thalia." She glared at me. "Honestly. I don't miss hyperbole. But being able to spin a fib would be nice. At least when I need to ask for time off at the Rite Aid, and all I can come up with is, 'My Friend Needs Me To Help Keep Her Sister from World Domination' and 'The League of Vigilant Lexicographers Called.' Both of those? They got me a note in my file and a suggestion from my manager that I get more sleep."

"*Shhhh*, Effie. I'm focusing. If now's not the right time, then when? We have to act."

"You have to act. I think you feel you need to cast the spell during her first campaign speech in order to make a difference, but really, Thalia, this is clearly meant to embarrass the governor, too.

It's revenge. That's unbecoming of a scholar. Why not wait and do this in private?"

Effie might have understood revenge—she was right about that—but she knew surprisingly little about showmanship, and less still about word reclamation spells. Or the energy they drained.

Still, she was excellent at escapes. We were going to need one of those in a moment and I'd be too tired to pull it off. So, I smiled. "Maybe so."

"Lia's spell needs a lie to work, remember?" Joy leaned over Effie's shoulder. "And the cast is stronger when there's an audience."

Joy got me.

"This is your last chance to back out," I told them both. Once the governor caught on, or worse, once my mother—and Mary's—spotted me, I'd be in a world of trouble.

Worse than last time, even.

Mary had hissed the last time I'd spelled her, "You'll never work in this town again." It had been a lie, but one she believed with all her heart, so she could still whisper it through clenched teeth.

Even back then, plenty of people would have hired me to keep their bosses and spouses from misusing words if they'd known what I could do. Back then, I'd chosen not to tell anyone, out of respect for our mother.

Plus, my spell hadn't been strong enough that time to keep her from separating language from meaning and truth for long.

So Mary had continued to turn words inside out for her own benefit and would until she couldn't.

Which was going to be soon.

My first good spell, the first one that had made any difference anyway, had been a reclamation spell. They were what I was best at. My calling, Gran would have said. I'd combined a little honey and spit with dandelion spores and the vestiges of the lie Mary was telling a constituent, let it all dry, and then blown the seeds at my target as I said the words Gran had given me: *Veritas Immaculare*.

Mary had gawped like a fish, mid-sentence. She'd been just a junior State official then, telling a resident how much better things were than they had been before she took office.

"And you'll feel so prosperous when you get that *enormou*— that *hu*— that moderate refund check ... / *cough* / Please excuse me, Mr. Roberts, I seem to have the tiniest of scratchy throats. I'll be right back." She'd pushed her chair back, brushing dandelion seeds from her hair, and click-clacked out of the room on tight heels.

Back then, I'd stepped from my place behind the office curtains and gathered the spores from her desk while Mary was in the bathroom. They weighed heavier in the hand than they had a moment before. Filled with Mary's false words.

That spell had been a little crass because I hadn't yet learned to separate out white lies told to avoid hurting feelings from the more harmful kinds of lies. And I'd been tired from the effort. But I'd rescued enough words—*enormous*, *huge*, and *prosperous* in particular —to feel like I'd made a small difference.

Then, over the next few years, long after I'd been fired as Mary's assistant, I'd refined the spell.

Once I had it, I'd phoned Joy and Jason and Euphrosone, everyone I'd called the corners with in college while Mary was off running student council, and told them what I was up to.

They'd been game, mostly.

Now, they were hesitating.

"I wouldn't have signed up, if I'd known we'd be standing in mud and shadows, Lia. Hiding in the bushes, at our age." Joy picked nettles from her thick wool socks. She'd been a metro reporter, before those were outsourced to social media freelancers. Emphasis on *free*.

"You would have. You're as sick of this as I am. Mary's been promising a return to the days of precious metal rivers for as long as I can remember, and no one seems to notice. She's got to be bewitching words. I just can't catch her at it. So, we will catch the words instead. Just like before."

That first spell had worn off in a couple of days. Unfortunately, that time, I'd spelled Mary just before Christmas. She'd described to our parents exactly what had happened.

"I was sitting there with a constituent, and none of my words would come out. Well, most of them. I'm still having trouble."

Mother had turned to look at me. Her eyes narrowed. "Thalia."

Even as I'd tried to look innocent, I swear Father had smiled, quietly amused. He'd been good with spells once, enough to stage elaborate magic tricks at birthday parties. Though now, he was fading. His favorite tricks had been disappearances and reappearances. But his passion had been the truth. Just like Gran.

Mary's passion was power.

Mine was words.

If Father had understood what I'd done then, or if Gran had been around to see it, both of them would have helped me, I'm sure of it. But they were gone. And the rest of the family sensed Mary's ambition and supported it.

Heck, I'd supported it, once upon a time.

We'd always been a political family. Seventeen generations of New England Vines, seven state senators, two mayors, Gran herself an alderman, several poets, and now Mary, running for governor again.

Not one witch among us for a long time, at least who'd admit it beyond party tricks. Until me. Everyone had decided I was just dabbling, combining spells and verse with a little adjunct teaching, until that Christmas.

"I thought you were working on your dictionary, Lia," Mother had hissed. "That we'd given up meddling."

Mary looked at me, shocked. "You're fired," she'd sputtered without waiting for me to defend myself.

"I quit," I said, just as fast.

"You can't quit. I fired you. You're a thief. A liar. A—"

"A witch? A lexicographer? Both? You're a word-mangler. And maybe a bit of a witch yourself."

"Thalia!" Mother actually clutched her pearls. "We're not even through dinner."

I ignored her. "Go ahead, say you're not doing spells, not misusing words."

I wanted Mary to deny it then. But, of course, she couldn't because I'd temporarily spelled away her ability to lie. So, she just shook her head.

And Father said, "There, see? No more fighting at dinner."

And we both sat down and ate in silence.

But now I knew she'd been casting spells, too. Ones that twisted meaning. When everyone thought she was a brilliant orator, she'd been torturing words into doing her bidding.

She recovered. I did, too, and found another job. But my mother never forgave me.

I caught a glimpse of her up on the podium, scanning the crowd for my face.

As I pulled my companions deeper into the shadows, I dipped beneath my broad-brimmed hat to better avoid her gaze.

Mary had recovered from that first spell. Her exaggerations and empty promises had come back even stronger, and she'd won and won and won.

"Words are tools, Lia," she'd whispered while our parents were in the kitchen, lighting the dessert. "You can steal a tool from me, but others will come to hand. Words reflect what their audience wants to hear, as much as what the speaker intends for them to hear. I'll send you the contents of your desk."

"You don't think," I said, putting my fork down on my plate with a clink, "that words should mean something on their own so that people have something real to hold onto?"

She laughed at me then. "So naive. Real power means you get to shape words. Not steal them." The lights dimmed then. Our parents brought out the fig pudding, glowing blue with port, and Mary's eyes danced. I put a piece of desert in my mouth and chewed until the taste disappeared.

She was wrong. She had to be.

I needed to get stronger. To stop her for good.

So, I kept working on my spells, in between teaching classes at

the community college and helping build online dictionaries that
traced the lineages of words back to their first uses.

My classes grew popular. People wanted to learn about
language, rhetoric. All of it.

Who better to learn from than a lexicographer and—once, for
Mary—former political speechwriter?

But even my students, in those early years, wanted to learn
more about how to influence people and less about how to speak
the truth in ways that inspired real change.

I watched it get worse, especially after Mary won the governor's race. I watched words devolve, lose meanings, reverse themselves, and become bent paperclips that could only hold hot air.
We were at great risk of words meaning nothing.

I watched my own sister do her part to mangle it.

Sometimes still using parts of the speeches I used to write her.

But the words she spoke, and people echoed back, had little
attachment to any meanings.

Even press headlines bore ragged shadows of former sense.
One last week, in fact, heralded "A Return to Opulent Sensibility."

That's when I called my friends to action. Joy, the former journalist, now librarian; Effie, the editor; Jason, the small press
publisher.

We'd met at the bar across from the state building. I'd shown
them how the spell worked. And we'd decided on a name for our
group. Because every New England rebellion worth its salt needs a
name or two. "The Society for the Reclamation of Meaning and
Sense" and "The League of Vigilant Lexicographers." Joy had even
made buttons, blue with white type: SRMS; LVL.

And now the moment was here. The crowd had swelled at the
statehouse steps just before 1:00 p.m., jostling for a view of my
sister. She, along with her quiet husband and two glorious daughters, as well as my mother, arrayed themselves photogenically near
the podium, all in different shades of blue.

I wore black. A thick sweater with a rolled collar and cuff
sleeves in a deep, midnight hue. It matched my hair, pulled up in a

messy bun beneath my hat, but still dark, with a few gray streaks. It matched my mood. My jeans were a shade of blue like everyone on the steps, but that was merely because they were comfortable. Not a sign of affiliation. I might have looked a little bit witchy.

I raised a hand, curled tight around my dandelion spores, in the air, and Joy, Jason, and Eugenia did too. No one looked at us. They were too caught up with Mary's words. Maybe they thought we'd been moved by something. Something about bringing more business than anyone had ever seen back to the city.

"Bind and tie them," I whispered. "*Veritas Imaculare.*"

My companions repeated my words and all those that came after. As Mary's speech grew more powerful, I whispered on, through the whole spell, until we got to the moment I knew was coming:

"And I promise you," she said, her hands held out to her sides like the scales of justice, "Your families will be safe and cared for, your children will thrive. We will become heroic and prosperous again. I will make sure of it. And when we do—"

"Seal it."

We opened our fists and the dandelion spores leapt on the wind, heading straight for Mary. They'd take the twisted words right out of her mouth, the hyperbole, the lies, and from the mouths of anyone else nearby who'd been lying, too.

Thunder rumbled, which wasn't part of the spell. The dandelion spores drifted on the breeze and then thudded, heavy, to earth, which was part of the spell.

The air smelled like burnt hair. And Mary, God love her, stood with her mouth forming a neat 'o,' unable to say the next part of her speech because whatever exaggerations she'd been heading toward—better pay, cheaper gas, stronger children—were no longer phrases she could speak.

"What's wrong?" someone called from the audience.

My mother spotted me first, but we—all four of us—were already slipping back into the shadows by the time her lips formed the soundless words, "Thalia Vine."

The blue caps of state security rushed to my speechless sister's side as Euphrosyne reached into her bag for the salt.

She cast some behind us and a squall burst in the air over the crowd, alarming on an otherwise sunny day.

Never underestimate the power of New England salt.

As the Governor's audience and family scattered, the League of Vigilant Lexicographers retreated into the mist.

UNSEALED COURT DOCUMENTS CONTAINING THE TRANSCRIPTS OF THE first Vigilant Lexicographers meeting, dated _____, 20__.

JOY DARNELL: THE FIRST NATIONAL MEETING OF THE SOCIETY for the Reclamation of Meaning and Sense is called to order.

Thalia Vine: Thank you, Joy.

Euphrosyne Sandipat: Does it need to be so official? Do we need to record everything?

Jason Lee: Euphrosyne, we should start as we mean to go on. When we have more chapters, it will be important to keep things organized.

Joy Darnell: For posterity.

Thalia Vine: Yes, exactly. And for posterity, let me be the first to say that I think our first efforts were successful.

Jason Lee: We did what we set out to do: We stopped Mary from bending words. She can't even plead laryngitis because she knows that's a lie. What are her press agent and your mother calling it—allergies?

[Joy Darnell snickers, which turns into a cough.]

Euphrosyne Sandipat: But what will we do

with the dandelion seeds? We have so many of them.

Thalia Vine: Hold onto them. Share them with other chapters, when they start up. Keep the words out of circulation.

Jason Lee: You think there will be more of us?

Joy Darnell: I know there will be. I put a brief message out on Librarything and World-cat's user boards.

Euphrosyne Sandipat: That's a good way to get caught.

Joy Darnell: It's fine. I hid the message as book titles, keyed to old Dewey-decimal codes. Only other librarians will understand. [Transcription note: these messages were never found.]

Euphrosyne Sandipat: We'll hope for the best then.

THE NEXT DAY, IN THE KROGER DAIRY AISLE, I REALIZED a simple storm hadn't been enough to distract everyone from our group's speedy exit.

A reporter, young and carrying her own lightweight camera on a stick, pushed a USB microphone in my face.

My skin grew warm, even as the open refrigeration fogged my glasses and the reporter's lens.

"Your sister's press agent says you assaulted her during her rally yesterday."

I carefully set a quart of two percent milk in my cart. Turned back to consider the yogurt. I hoped my expression embodied *Do I want fruit on the bottom?* And not *If It Weren't for You Darn Kids.*

"Assault? I rarely ever approach my sister. She was on camera the entire speech, and I wasn't. I wasn't even asked to stand with her on the podium. I didn't go near the podium." Almost too late, I realized I'd gone on for too long. I cleared my throat. "Your source is wrong. I would like to shop for my dinner now, thank you."

"Miss Vine, you must have heard there are calls for your arrest?"

"I've heard no such thing." I turned to look at the reporter. She'd pinned a campaign button to her black leather jacket. It read: *Vine*. "You're with the press pool, right?"

She paused and turned off her camera. Swallowed, loudly.

"Tell my sister, and her press agent—what's the new one's name?"

"Mia Jodd. She's very kind. The kindest. Everyone says so." The way she said *kind* sounded like the word was knotted around itself and strangling.

I narrowed my eyes. If I'd brought more dandelion spores, I could have freed this young thing from the press agent's illusions. But I'd come to shop, and to collect more newspaper headlines for later, not to cast spells. So I used another tool: raised eyebrows and crossed arms. An even, slightly amused voice.

"Is it true that my sister is saying these things?"

The reporter shook her head quickly, once.

"Is Mia Jodd saying them?"

Again, another shake of the head. A tremble of the lower lip.

"You're doing this to try and make a story? To make a name for yourself?"

She nodded. "I needed an angle. I took your class last year— you were wonderful—and I knew you were the governor's sister. When I overheard Ms. Jodd talking to the governor's mother and your name came up, I realized I could maybe get a story before anyone else."

She stared at me and I waited her out. I didn't need to say anything more. Sometimes, silence is as powerful as words.

"I'm sorry. It's cutthroat out there."

I kept silent. The fan in the dairy cooler kicked into a higher gear.

"I just wanted a story," she finally pleaded. "Don't curse me."

"I don't curse people. Not most people." There were ways in which I could try to reclaim words, but this kind of thing was beyond my grandmother's spells. Plus, I was still tired from the previous day's spells.

But the problem was spreading faster than a single spell could stop. I put the yogurt down. "You realize that this is the kind of story that can get away from you? That can really hurt someone? Miss—" I searched my memory for her name and lucked out. "Dawlander; Lesley, right?" The young reporter blushed and nodded. "What exactly did my mother say?"

"She said you should be locked up, at least until after the election. That you were getting in the way of progress."

Wonderful. I added "progress" to my favorite slippery words list.

"Lesley, you were my student. You remember the discussion about holding up a light to truth? That the power of language is in its accuracy? What do you believe?"

Her eyes grew wide. "You're right. I'm so sorry. What can I do? How can I help?"

I walked back out to the checkout aisle with the young reporter. "You don't need to apologize," I said. I thought for a moment and took a risk. Gave her one of the buttons Effie had made. "We meet tonight at nine."

[THE FOLLOWING TRANSCRIPT OF THE VIGILANT LEXICOGRAPHERS meeting has been verified using the secondary source provided to the state.]

JOY DARNELL: THE SECOND MEETING OF THE WORD RECLAMATION Society is called to order.

Lesley Dawlander (whispered): I thought you were called the Vigilant Lexicographers.

Thalia Vine (whispered): It's both. For now.

Joy Darnell: What we need to discuss is spreading the spell, the techniques. We already have requests.

Jason Lee: We're going to run out of dandelions.

Thalia Vine: Luckily, those grow fast. Hopefully faster than words can be bent. This is Lesley—she's a reporter.

Euphrosyne Sandipat: Thalia, you didn't!

Thalia Vine: I did, and she's going to help us. Spread the word, so to speak.

Lesley Dawlander: Hi …

Jason Lee: Welcome, then. To the Rite Aid storage room. This is just temporary.

Euphrosyne Sandipat: This is where I can meet while on break, Jason. You have a problem, take it up with management. We're not all well-connected.

Joy Darnell: Most of us aren't. Not anymore.

Jason Lee: You said you want to help spread the spell? What spell do you mean?

Lesley Dawlander: The one that Thalia put on the governo—

Thalia Vine: Lesley, *shhh*. Not so loud. We're working on a spell to end the misuse of words. Our goal is to reclaim words that have been stripped of their meaning. We use dandelions because they're good at blowing away and spreading. We're experimenting with other, less pernicious flowers for the future.

Jason Lee: Show her the packet of dried sunflower petals that I've been working on.

Lesley Dawlander: You don't mind if I take notes?

Jason Lee: We'd rather no recordings. No names.

Lesley Dawlander: Of course not.

TWO DAYS LATER, AN EMERGENCY TEXT FROM EFFIE READ: RITE Aid Raided! And she doesn't answer when Joy calls her. We expected it, of course. The knock on my door came as expected too, but I'm not home.

I got an alert on my phone, from my doorbell camera. That technology works better than a boundary spell, these days. Unlike other tech that only seemed to enhance bad spells, not good ones. I opened the app and saw a group of state troopers gathered at my apartment.

I was teaching. They could wait.

"As we've discussed, the origin of the words *prosperity* (noun) and *prosperous* (adj.) in the thirteenth century stemmed from being fortunate and thriving, as a group. It was often tied to luck. The meaning has shifted to focus almost entirely on individual wealth and success, restricted to those found deserving of those things, by virtue of the fact that they already have those things."

My students nodded and wrote down my words.

"Meantime, *progress* (noun and adjective) has shifted from meaning forward motion, including by royalty and also planets, to a sense of getting ahead of others—as a nation or state—and basically being better than others. It is often used with a tinge of competition, or an indication that someone else has to suffer in order for progress to be valid."

Hands went up. I shook my head. No questions today. "I'll conclude this lecture by asking you, as you move through your reading and essays, to keep in mind the way words shift; what meanings they are being detached from, and attached to, and why. It will help you, I promise."

A young man named Bruce raised his hand in the front row of the lecture hall. "Will this be on the test, Professor Vine?"

"On some test, yes. Yes, it will."

I dismissed them then, and they filed past the three officers waiting in crisp blue uniforms outside my classroom.

A few students, including Bruce, stayed to watch the police lead me away, reading out charges that grew more ridiculous as they continued.

You are hereby charged with disturbing the peace, malingering, meddling, practicing witchcraft in New England without a permit, littering, spreading weeds on a public square, and theft of words with no intent to return them."

When I didn't reply, the officers went on, "You are charged with assault on a government official, gathering to conspire, corruption of a freelance journalist, and with resisting—"

They push me into the squad car, and I balk. "I haven't been resisting. There's nothing that will make any of this stick."

"Lesley Dawlander turned audio tapes over to the governor this morning."

"Oh. Well that might work." I couldn't have been more pleased.

They took me to the courthouse first, where I was arraigned and paraded in front of the press to occasional shouts of "thief!" and "liar!" I did not speak except to ask for a lawyer.

The courthouse smelled of dandelions.

When my lawyer—court appointed because making my sister pay for my defense delighted me, plus community college professors don't make very much money—was unavailable until later that afternoon, the state police escorted me to the next building down on the square: the old jail.

Effie and Joy were already there, sharing a cell and looking glum.

Jason had gone to an American Lexicography convention, small silver packets of dandelions in his bags. As we'd planned.

The police might be waiting when he returned, we all knew.

[DOCUMENTATION OF THE THIRD VIGILANT LEXICOGRAPHERS meeting was taken from the journals of Thalia Vine.]

THE THIRD MEETING OF THE LEAGUE OF VIGILANT Lexicographers happened in the presence of our lawyers.

We vowed to say nothing.

We waited for the spell to spread.

WE DIDN'T HAVE LONG TO WAIT. AFTER PREPARING US FOR OUR next appearance before the judge that day—say nothing, please. Just follow our lead—our court-appointed advisors turned on the television in the meeting room. On the screen, CNN played a montage of politicians trying to get words out and failing. Their faces contorted as they scrambled to for the smallest of lies.

One reporter, wearing a dark suit and bright red tie, recognizable as a regular on a national channel, had been reduced to a tiny vocabulary of single-syllable nouns, he was so far gone.

"It's working," Effie whispered. She looked delighted, for the first time. "I hadn't thought it would."

But I felt troubled. Even more so when I asked our lawyers to define progress in our case.

Since not one of them had said "we're making progress," and I'd always understood that lawyers, like politicians, loved to use that word.

The lead lawyer shook her head. "I'm not sure what you mean?" she finally said. She looked confused by the sound of the word.

Despite our best intentions, I realized that we were failing. Words and meanings weren't being saved by my spells; they were being removed from circulation. They were disappearing entirely.

That was not what I'd wanted. Not at all.

In the jailhouse meeting room, I pushed my chair away from the long table strewn with manila folders and print outs. The chair's four feet squealed on the jail's concrete floor, as if protesting progress.

"I wish to make a plea," I said.

Now it was my companions' and lawyers' turn to be speechless.

WHEN WE LEFT THE COURTHOUSE, A SMALL GROUP OF bureaucrats lined the steps down to the square. A crowd had gathered below in the park. Politicians glared at me angrily. Silently.

Among the crowd stood several more reporters and broadcasters, quietly recording my exit.

One raised a sign. "Give us our words back, witch," it said.

"They're not yours," I told the silent crowd. "They belong to everyone." No one clapped. I wasn't my sister.

"Thief!" One newscaster nearly spat the word.

Ahead of me and behind me, Effie whispered, "If only we had our dandelions with us."

But Joy and I had made a different plan.

From the corner of my eye, I saw her—freed once I took responsibility for everything—reach in her pocket. Lift her hand in the air. She tossed sunflower petals to the crowd. "*Veritas*," we whispered into the quiet. "*Veritas Imaculare*."

"Our friend Thalia meant no harm," Joy said. She waited for the sunflowers to drift, lightly, overhead.

Would the spell work, powered by truth? I held my breath. My hands, cuffed at the wrist, chafed against the metal, raised as my hands were. My ankle monitor beeped once, turning on. Nothing happened with the petals. Not at first. Then I was tucked back in a squad car.

The others went home as I was escorted to my new confines: my apartment, under monitoring.

The press followed me home, a silent parade.

When we arrived, we found Mary Vine, governor of our state, waiting at my apartment door. She wore a thick, camel-colored coat and a peach colored sweater set. Pearls at her neck. Her fingers played with the white beads.

"Give them back," she said. "Give all the words back, and I'll consider pardoning you."

"Why do you want those old words back?" I say. "You bent them all out of shape and they're too weak now to do you any good. To move forward—to progress —you'll have to make up new words to have anything worth bending to your will. Or you can let the old words go back to their real meanings."

"I know," she says. The governor sat down on the stoop and picked lint from her coat. "To be honest," she paused. Reached for words. They came to her lips like the truth often does once the lies go away. "It's not very enjoyable, forcing words to behave in unnat-ural ways. You knew that all along though."

"I did know that. So you were doing spells."

"A few. Just the normal political ones. For charisma and longing, mostly. It got out of hand. What you did was wrong, but it made me think."

"So I'm off the hook?" I sat beside my sister and pointed to my ankle bracelet.

"No, you're still in trouble. But you and I can try to fix things. And then I *may* pardon you." She held out a packet of sunflower seeds. Gold and green.

"Your friends said that under the right conditions, these can spread like the dandelions. And they'll carry words back to those they touch. Good words. Solid, sturdy, real words."

The word *pardon* (noun, verb) has always meant what it means today. Perhaps because it's so important to politicians.

I looked Mary Vine in the eyes. "They will, it's true."

"Then share them."

WE'RE STILL BEING WATCHED, THE LEAGUE OF VIGILANT Lexicographers. We aren't allowed to hold any meetings, unless a representative from the state is there.

But we're watching them, too. The politicians.

And we're getting requests from all around the state. From farther than that. For definitions. Which are kind of like binding spells. For meanings. We write back, tucking usages and histories and sunflower seeds into each envelope.

The words have nice heft, solidity.

The news channels showed my plea deal. My mother stood silently in the background. They caught Mary and me shaking hands after my pardon.

I was worried for a moment that, once Mary had my promise not to take any more words, she would get up to her old tricks again.

But she didn't. Her speeches became filled with hope, rather than promises. They bloomed, nurturing new futures, rather than grasping at impossible pasts.

And, from my home monitoring, I began to write to the newspapers, too. I tucked sunflower seeds into each envelope. Joy, Euphrosyne, and Jason did the same.

The seeds are heavy with newly-freed words.

Last spring, when they bloomed for the first time, the final part of the spell I'd planned from the start took hold.

On the sunflower-dusted air, in the golden, pollen infused fields, and beside the rivers silver with dandelions, people began to remember words on their own, and to use them in their proper forms.

They sometimes even knew how a word had evolved over the years, if they walked into an especially pollinated field. The headlines began to return to their senses. The news started to report actual news.

Like today's front-page headlines, from the governor's mansion, all decked out in sunflowers: *New Press Celebrated at State Level to Produce Dictionaries.*

SOUTH OF THE WAFFLE HOUSE

BY MARIE VIBBERT

ME AND CHESTER WERE THROWING ROCKS AT BOTTLES LINED UP on the freeway guardrail behind the Waffle House when some redneck chewed up the berm, knocking everything to crap and hee-hawing, "Build me a wall, Sancho!" out his Confederate-flag-painted window.

That was meant for me, and it was bad enough without him calling me a boy's name. I threw a rock after him, not that he would have been able to tell, and asked Chester, "How far damn north do we gotta be? We're, like, two blocks from Canada."

Chester threw his handful of gravel like it was slow motion and loped up to the guardrail. "If you're south of a Waffle House," he said, "you're in the south."

"The hell does that mean?" I said. Chester had a way of saying odd things, and moving odd, underwater-slow like that. I joined him, picking through the wild chicory that grew thick under the metal rail. There were so many wrappers and paper bags and cup lids in the weeds, it was like the ground was white. I hated humanity just then, and Waffle House in particular. The glass Rolling Rock bottles were all shattered. I'd been looking forward to shattering one myself. All we had left were the Mexican Coke, and those bottles are thick and hard to break, and an assortment of plastic. It was fine to knock plastic bottles off, but you didn't have that hope of clean, bright destruction.

"You ever think there's aliens?" Chester asked. He was looking up at the freeway.

"Space aliens," I corrected, but like usual, he ignored me.

"Like ... there are aliens, but we never see them because the whole Earth is a crap rest stop town to them, and they won't ever stop here."

"People do stop here," I said. "I wish they didn't. Place would be cleaner."

Chester did his shrug again, the one that took his whole body into it. He was a pudgy kid, not fat but pudgy, with frizzy, blond curls and skin almost as dark as mine. You'd think it was a suntan, but it didn't fade in winter. That was why he'd hang out with me, even though I was a year younger and a girl. I wondered if Chester was a space alien. Not for the first time, either. It wasn't just how he moved and looked a little different. He escaped North Fork with regularity to stay with his dad in Toledo, where he had a whole other life with a whole other bedroom and everything, but he always came back like it was from a war and he didn't want to talk about it.

I threw a good-sized chunk of gravel at the Coke bottle, and it freaking bounced off. "This is lame," I said. I waited for Chester to suggest something else to do.

Since we started fifth grade, everyone teased we were boyfriend-girlfriend, even though I wouldn't kiss Chester if he were the last human being on the planet. I might, if he were an alien, though. For science.

Chester nodded like he was considering the gravity of it all, and then he looked sideways at me. "Wanna see something secret?"

I threw the pebble in my hand at him. "Does the pope crap in the woods?"

Chester flinched more than he needed to because he knew I wanted a reaction and waved me over to the dumpster fence. Every fast food joint has a dumpster fence, this outside area with a wall around it so people can't steal their trash or something. This one was in the back corner of the lot, tucked into the rising curve of the freeway onramp. I'd never gone over there because ... eeew.

Chester picked through the taller weeds, waving me on. There was this line of stunted, shabby Christmas trees to hide the dumpster fence from the freeway. Chester ducked between them and the fence.

It was cool and dark and surprisingly open under the shrubs—like a miniature pine forest, all needles on the ground. And there was this thing.

"The hell is that?" I asked. It looked like a mattress, made of wire and fans, and I started to worry that all the boyfriend-girlfriend teasing had gotten to Chester.

"Drones," he said. He squatted down and poked a black fan. "This one, I got for Christmas. It's the best. This one, I found in the trash behind Denny's. This one, I found in the crick."

The structure started to make sense. There were six separate drones, lashed together with wire and braided strips of plastic like a six-pack, only flatter. "You made a super drone," I said.

"Well, kinda," Chester said, and shrugged. "It doesn't actually work. But I was thinking, if it did, we could, you know, fly out of here. Visit places. Like maybe Six Flags."

My heart and stomach did a simultaneous flip like I was already in line for the Goliath. "You should have shown me sooner. Let's get her fixed."

"Thing is, only my drone actually works. Well, this one kinda does." He nudged the one next to his.

Just like a boy. I would have put the working ones on opposite sides. "What's broken on that one?"

"It spins, but not fast."

"Are these all battery powered?"

He looked at me like this was way too technical a question to have considered.

"Dio ... Dude," I said, "how are you going to make big plans and not think about how to make it work?" I was so annoyed, I almost spoke Spanish, and I didn't do that anymore, not even at home.

"I got all this stuff put together!" he said.

"Well, yeah. And it's awesome. But now we gotta talk about power." I knee-walked around, getting pine needles in my jeans, and checked each of the drone's battery packs. Sure enough, two of them were leaking battery blood. I took those apart and threw the dead batteries at the freeway slope. Then I went and got 'em back because I hadn't checked what size they were. I'd never seen batteries like these. They were flat rectangles, wrapped in plastic, not the usual cylinders.

We ran to both of our houses, looking for batteries. My dad had a whole drawer full of size D's, but half of them were dead. Chester's mom didn't have any batteries that weren't in anything, and she chased us out of the house because she was folding laundry and we'd tracked dirt in.

We reconvened in my dad's garage. "What we need," I said, "is solar power." I'd done a science project once where I tried to heat up water by running it over baking sheets. Dad found me all this plastic tubing from an old fish tank, and we scrubbed the cookie sheets with steel wool to get them shiny. I could get the water warm, but not steaming hot, you know? It needed to steam to turn the pinwheel.

It would never be portable enough, even if I could get it to work.

"What about this," Chester said, and held out a plastic canister about the size of a D-cell.

I popped the top off, hoping it would have a stack of watch batteries. "Dude," I said, "This is a gum eraser."

"No, it's a battery. My dad gave it to me. He said it was. I don't know how to use it, though."

"This is not a battery." I handed it back. "We'll take these D's and we'll charge 'em up, right? And then we can rig some wires to connect them to the contacts."

Chester nodded and helped me pull the battery charger out of the back of dad's workbench. "Why don't we work on Super Drone here?" he asked. "Your dad could help."

"He'll get in the way." I could tell Chester wasn't liking what I was saying, and I didn't like that it made me sound like a bully. I'm not. "Chester, I'm going to get this thing to work for you. I can do it without anyone else."

He set his hand on mine on the battery charger, like it was a solemn oath. "You can," he said.

I was glad, because we're best friends and best friends means something.

Dad opened the door then and took a double-take, finding us there with our hands on his battery charger. "Oye, hija. Qué es esto?"

"Hi, Dad," I said. "We're working on something for school."

Dad gave me this sad look like he always did when I answered him in English, but I wasn't giving in. Kids teased me relentlessly at school until I'd scrubbed all the Spanish from my voice.

"Okay," Dad said, the look gone. "I'm making spaghetti." He left with a wave.

I could tell Chester thought I was being mean again. My dad's an alien. I mean, officially. We're not supposed to even think about it. He's lived here his whole life. He didn't tell me until last year, when I asked him to fill out some paperwork for a school trip. I was still mad about it, part of me. I didn't get to go to the National Air and Space Museum, and it might've been my only chance to, and I could have learned something. Something great. It might have been my one chance to grow up a scientist.

Chester could judge me and ask me about aliens, and he didn't even know.

We took the battery charger to my room and set it up. Chester made me look online, to see if there was such a thing as a battery that looked like a kneaded rubber eraser. There SO wasn't.

FOUR D BATTERIES LEAKED OVERNIGHT, BUT THE REST DIDN'T, and the next day, we were able to get four of the six drones spinning, but the slow one was still slow. There was no remote control for any of them but the one Chester got for Christmas, so that one would do the driving. I did some wiki-walking and got the others set to hover mode.

"Maybe you should put them in lifting mode," Chester said, pacing and fussing while I pushed teeny little switches with a broken pen.

"Then we won't be able to control it. Okay. That's the last one. Try it." I scooted back.

Three drones whirred, kicking up dust. Chester turned on his remote. The fourth one kicked on hard. Christmas-Drone rose a bit off the ground. It dragged the others, but they acted like they were weighed down by cement. The whole thing started to slide left, toward a tree trunk. Chester turned it off. "I told you, those batteries were too heavy," he said, which he absolutely did not.

The D cells were in bundles, wrapped in some twenty-gauge galvanized wire I'd found in my dad's workroom. I shoulda used string or something lighter, but the wire made it easy to make contacts.

I worked the batteries off. "Maybe we don't need that many of them," I said.

"But it didn't even start when you made me test with one battery on each!"

"Well, let's see if we can get the rectangle batteries into the charger, somehow."

"Are you crazy? Those things explode." Chester smashed his grey kneaded gum eraser into the drones, a pea-sized bit in each. "If this is a battery, it's just gotta touch the contacts, right?"

He only understood contacts because of me. "That's never going to work. There's no such thing as a mooshy battery." How many times did we have to go over this? His dad had probably lied to cover up not having a present to give, and Chester wouldn't admit it. "You're going to short it out."

Chester didn't say nothing. He just put the rest of his battery-goo in his pocket and turned on the remote again. The super drone lifted corner-first, wobbled, but then it was hovering. Really hovering.

"I'm going home!" Chester shouted. It shouldn't have worked, but it worked. I felt like I was watching a miracle. Needles and twigs rained down at us. Super Drone cracked into the low branches of the bushes, sawing its way deeper into the tree canopy. It was going to get stuck good.

"Stop!" I grabbed for the remote. Chester wrestled to keep it. "You'll use up the batteries. We gotta take it out into the parking lot to do a real test flight."

Chester was breathing heavy, his fingers white against the black plastic. Slowly, he let me take the remote.

I turned Super Drone off and handed the remote back. Then I picked up the front end. It was lighter than I expected, like a raft made of dragonfly wings. "Come on, get the other side."

I backed up against the fence so Chester could swing around and go first. We made it to the edge of the fence when Chester stopped dead and crouched low.

"The hell, Chester," I said.

And then I heard a bottle smash. We set Super Drone down and crawled to peek. Five teenagers with beers were sitting on the guardrail. One of 'em had a bag from Waffle House.

"Jerks," I said.

Chester balled up his fist and started forward. I had to tackle him to stop him. "Let's go around the other way," I said. He twisted in my arms, trying to get out, all grimy and sweaty. "Chester! Do you want them to find Super Drone? They'll tear it apart, just for fun."

That got through to him.

We snuck out to the front of the Waffle House and ran to the abandoned gas station across the street.

We lay down on our bellies behind the gas pump island and we could see the shadows of the damn high school kids.

"Let's act like we're playing," I suggested. "Just two kids, playing. That won't be suspicious." I drew a hopscotch board with a piece of gravel, but we were both too sophisticated to actually play. I mean, we were practically thirteen!

It was getting dark and cold. The pavement was still warm. We laid ourselves flat, to soak in as much warmth as we could. The stars were coming out, bright and clean.

"You ever think there's aliens?" Chester asked.

I hated that question of his because I knew he didn't even think of another definition of "alien" when he asked it. "No," I said. "You ever think there's intelligent life on Earth?"

He pushed my arm because he knew I was going to say that. "What would you think," he said, "If you met an alien? I mean, could you be friends? A friendly alien. He wouldn't be all gross or anything."

I looked at the stars because I had to say one of those things you can't look at anyone when you say them. "People call me one. An alien. It's not true, and even if it were, it's not who I am." I could hear Chester breathing. This wasn't coming out right. "I want to invent things. I want to have been the kid who invented stuff. Like spaceships and robots that talk to you. It makes me feel stupid that I can't."

This silence stretched on for about a decade and I kept regretting what I'd said until Chester said, "Yeah, me, too."

"No, you don't. You already invented stuff. You invented Super Drone."

I felt his shoulder move against my elbow. "But ..." he drew it out and I knew this was going to be something I didn't like. "Your dad isn't an alien."

"Dude. He is. That's what they call people who can't get citizenship."

"No, I mean, it's like ... no one thinks he's not human."

That pissed me off because, yeah, some people did think that. I got up and looked across at Waffle House. It was lit up bright and empty. "I think those kids have gone."

"I like your dad," Chester said, by way of apology. "My dad ... I mean ..."

I didn't want to talk anymore. I crouched by the roadside, ready to run. "Let's go. We have to make sure Super Drone is safe."

"It's too dark now," Chester said.

"No, it ain't. Come on."

A semi engine braked over our heads as we ran across the street. Everything is louder at night, even though there's more noise, with crickets going. Freeway headlights sent sweeping search-beams through the weeds and bushes. It was like spies were after us, and I was glad because it was adventure and I could forget about being pissed. We crouched low every time a light passed over us and grinned like our faces would split.

We got Super Drone out and laid it in the glittering glass of the back parking lot. The pavement was like a night sky, only sharper.

When they started spinning, the fans were invisible in the dark. The LEDs glowed in different colors, randomly reflecting on bits of foil and plastic. It was like an old movie spaceship. It rose majestically into the air, wobbling but gaining altitude.

"We gotta test how much weight it can take," I said. "Weigh ourselves and then stuff bags with rocks to the same weight."

"Let's try something smaller first," Chester said. "Like one of our bikes."

"I am not risking my bike."

Our heads were tilted straight back, watching Super Drone, dreaming these big science dreams, when some redneck coal roller buzzed the berm of the onramp and air-horned us.

Super Drone flipped sideways in the air and came crashing down. The fans were still going and sent it scampering across the pavement into the back of the Waffle House.

One of the drones, one of the smaller ones, fell off.

We were both swearing and crying, and I was shaking as we gathered up our wounded baby and turned the drones off. I said, "Damn it, how far north do we gotta be?"

"Mars?" Chester was crying hard, face squished up, on his

knees. He looked up at the sky like he was asking it for something. His lips moved, even.

I wanted to comfort him, but that might cross a girl-boy line. I stood there, watching until his sobs slowed down. I thought about how he was always asking about aliens, and about that magic battery goo, and about how, sometimes, when you want to talk about something very important, you gotta get the other person to talk about it first. "Is your dad really from Toledo?"

He gave me such a look, like I'd stabbed him through the heart.

I shrugged to make it feel less important. "Come on, what we really need is a new base of operations."

He looked confused, but he let me lead him down the street, the two of us carrying Super Drone between us like an injured friend. I coulda said, "Let's take it to my dad," but I was enjoying being mysterious. There was this moment, when we got to my street, and Chester realized what I had in mind, and let me know with this shift in his shoulders that he was proud of me, and those kind of moments are worth engineering.

Dad wanted to be a scientist. There'd been a student visa, a shot at it that fell through. He never told me the details, like it was too painful.

He opened the garage like he was expecting us. His questions were all technical. "Is that a live wire? What does this one connect to?" It was great to watch him moving around Super Drone with his voltmeter and safety goggles. Once he was sure it was all safe, he let us use his soldering iron (while he hovered all parent-worried and pretending he wasn't).

I looked across at Chester, squinting in concentration at two wires. I asked, "Where do you want to go? It ain't Six Flags."

"No," he said. His lips rolled inward, and he added, "Not Toledo, either."

"Someplace they won't call you an alien," I said.

"Yeah," he said. He looked at me like he didn't quite believe I understood.

"I'd be friends with an alien," I said. Chester didn't say

anything, and I was afraid what I'd said was stupid. Then he wiped his eye with the back of his hand.

"Yeah," he said. "Me, too."

"That's enough," Dad said. "Enough soldering. You're already past your bed time. Let's see if this will fly, eh?"

Super Drone rose against the stars, glittering and flashing defiance against the night.

I felt like something had broken loose inside me, and I hugged my dad, and my half-alien friend, and felt like we were finally North of something.

#GREENLIVESMATTER

BY JOSHUA GAGE

paper cut
the flesh-colored bandage
bright against her scales

summer vacation
her tentacle lotion
in the ethnic aisle

first day of school
one textbook chapter
on green history

keg stand
a fratboy in greenface
holds her ankles

autumn evening
trick-or-treaters
with fake tentacles

stale coffee
her coworker asks
if she's green all over

routine traffic stop
the chill of the car hood
beneath her green cheek

"excessive force" acquittal
outside, protester tentacles
squirm in handcuffs

Originally published in *Star*Line* issue 39.2, Spring 2016.

SYMPATHIZER

BY KARIN LOWACHEE

THE ALIEN'S BLOOD LOOKED LIKE MOLTEN GOLD IN THE LOW light. It had been shot by one of her soljets, but not by her order. She herself had almost been shot, or it was made to look like that, and she wanted to believe that her own jets would have missed on purpose. Her medic Markalan pressed gloved hands to the alien's stomach wound, but the gold seeped past his fingers and began to run down the alien's side. She didn't know if that was indeed the alien's stomach and neither did her medic.

"This might not work," he said. "We don't have a detailed scan of their physiology, much less their cellular structure."

Even after two years they knew so little. "Find a way," she said.

The line of seven aliens watched them like stone statuary carved of ancient Earth alabaster, though a couple were the color of burnished bronze and they stood motionless and black-eyed like deep-sea creatures. If they regarded the humans in judgment or with some imminent urge to attack they did not show it. They didn't have guns, at least not on hand, but they had blades and the blades hung along the walls of the base control room like black punctuations, curved and sharp. She had gathered over the months that the alabaster aliens with the intricate silver tattoos on their faces were the warriors, and the bronze-skinned ones were the scientists. It was a scientist bleeding out beneath Markalan's hands.

Her squad of four jets stood by the doors and two of them faced out for incoming and two faced in to watch the aliens. The rest of the platoon were outside by the airlock and they could all hear the rifle fire in staccato cadence peppering the steel. This room in the base was much like a human configuration with some semblance of comps and controls and the industrial gray of steel alloy and plastics, but on the walls by the weapons were curious red markings that resembled ancient wards of witchery, if only for their inscrutable and intricate design, and in the corners burned cones of sweet acrid incense, some apparent mix of magic and technology that defied any rally to battle-minded reason.

The blood spread along the floor and with it rose a scent she had never encountered before, but it was something akin to old forests she had camped in when she was a girl. They had removed their helmets. The air was clean. They were two years in orbit around this moon already, burning through resources, and were pumped full of drugs enough to stop disease, yet she was still nervous to breathe the alien air and be close to the aliens, even if the alternative was suffocation.

"I think it stopped," her medic said, and she looked down at Markalan with his bloodied hands and his dark eyes raw and wide like they had been gazing too long into some scene of harrowing. The silence of the aliens unnerved him, unnerved them all.

The rifle fire stopped outside. Her comm clicked and the lieutenant's voice came through to her ears.

"The captain's requested parlay."

She looked down at the injured alien, then looked at the others lined up around Markalan and the warriors were staring at her as though scrutinizing a glyph newly uncovered on a Paleolithic plinth that would somehow explain a truth of their beginnings. She turned and looked at her squad by the door.

"Do we believe it?" Markalan said, his hands still pressed to the alien's side as if the healant he'd sprayed there was going to disintegrate any second. It might have, if it couldn't bond to the alien's cells. It might be poisoning the alien.

She went to the base doors and told her squad, "Open it."

TO CROSS THE EXPANSE BETWEEN THE ALIEN BASE AND THE SHIP took a little less than an hour on foot. Moon rock, gray and inert with striations of silver and black, created jagged silhouettes, and her weighted bootsteps stirred the ashen dust minutely, as though she was the lone survivor of an apocalyptic event. On the spinal horizon sat the uneven silhouette of the destroyed mine like the skeletal remains of a beached creature left too long in the sun. She drew steady silent breaths and the scent of her own skin and sweat returned to her. Through the HUD on her helmet the dropship hunkered ahead like a beast of the netherworld, armored and anticipating some hour in which it could feed. The smaller rider squatted next to it, all the lights in darkened disuse. They'd abandoned it a week ago to operate from the base, knowing the *Plymouth* would send a dropship and they would have no defense from the rider. She had not intended to abandon the rider, but the captain had sent word to kill the aliens from the time it took for them to walk from the rider to the base, and she did not order her platoon to do it. After that there was only one alternative and the *Plymouth* had fired from orbit and destroyed the alien mining tower and four dozen aliens with it, and soon enough the dropship had come, and her jets had come out and they were firing on each other. They fired on each other for two days, but luckily the main base had held and she had anticipated the ground attack and laid mines around the perimeter.

She switched to a narrow channel and addressed her right-most escort, a private she knew by name.

"What happened in the negotiations?" she asked the boy.

"Dunno." He sounded reluctant to speak and his hands gripped his rifle. She couldn't see his eyes inside his helmet. "Cap'n's just pissed."

"This is a wrong action."

The boy said nothing.

"He's effectively declared war on a sentient alien species. Do you want to take this back to EarthHub?"

The boy said nothing.

He wasn't the one she needed to talk to, but she gleaned some tenor of the troops' opinions from that silence. In the dropship she looked at the faces of the squad and they would not meet her eyes. The firing amongst them at the base had gone a couple days because nobody wanted to kill one another. When they were moving the alien scientists from one of the research domes to the primary complex, it had been shot. She was running right beside the alien and had not been shot. Then the jets from the ship blew the research dome. So she thought about that all the way back to orbit and the *Plymouth*.

The same private and another private who she also knew by name escorted her to the captain's conference room and left her in there. She didn't have weapons because they had taken them from her outside the base. She sat at the long glossed table, looking at her reflection in it as if through a membranous alternate dimension, and in a few minutes the captain entered and the hatch shut behind him from the jet outside, sounding like a guillotine. He sat in his chair and it was all the way on the opposite end of the table, and he began to slowly swivel the thick, black chair back and forth with one hand on the table top where it was shiniest, fingers lightly drumming the surface. He had a streak of silver hair that started over the right side of his forehead and sometimes in command staff meetings he would lean his head on his hand and his fingers would twist that streak around, but now his hands remained otherwise occupied and his right eye under that silver streak looked paler than his left.

"Commander Gray, what am I going to do with you?"

She said nothing.

"It was a simple order."

"Of murder."

He waved his hand like he was brushing away an insect from the air. "Trying to communicate with them is pointless. The Hub doesn't have the resources to let us sit around, no matter how many forays we do in this region."

"Then let's leave."

His eyes narrowed and the swiveling stopped. He leaned forward with both arms on the table and entwined his fingers together and stared down the black surface at her with the direct and distressed countenance of a kindling god looking upon his creation of which he held little hope.

"Surely a woman of your rank understands the way our universe works."

He was a man whose tone seemed naturally to possess some form of condescension just because he was handpicked by politicians and brass to head this expedition.

"What do you think happens from here," he said.

"I don't know," she said.

"So you think it's up to me?"

"You're the captain."

"I am. But you're my jet commander and you won't command your jets. So you forced me to command your jets, and I know they're displeased with me and this is because you gave them a contradictory order. So you tell me, what do you think happens from here?"

"You ask me to order them to vacate the base and fire on the aliens."

"We're long past that."

She said nothing.

"You will make a decision whether you want to be with your jets on that moon or remain with your jets on ship."

"Then what?"

"Who can tell? Maybe the aliens attack your jets on the moon, something Markalan and the rest of them did not expect because the aliens had lured your platoon into the base to act as a shield. The *Plymouth* would have no choice but to retaliate from orbit again."

It was a grim joke on jetdeck that the captain walked around with his uniform trousers a size too small so he could feel that he had bigger balls than he did. She watched his eyes, the paler and the darker. "Is that what you told Hub Command about why you blew the aliens' mining tower? And all of those striviirc-na underground?"

"You've wasted both time and ordnance here. So where will you go?"

"I guess I'm going back to the moon, but can I talk to my chief at least?"

"What do you have to say to him? You couldn't even give a simple order to your platoon on the surface."

"You won't grant me a last word, sir? To get my affairs in order?"

He looked like he was thinking it over. "I never figured you for a martyr."

"I'm no martyr, I just have limits."

"Over a bunch of strits?"

"Murder's murder, sir."

"Is it because you can't leave him? Your bleeding-heart medic?"

"I'd like to speak to my chief."

He sniffed and leaned up again like a great bird puffing its feathers, and he passed a hand over the lower part of his face and stood to come down the length of the table so he could sit beside her, where she did not move and held no weapons. He wasn't incapable either, and he laid his hand flat on the table in front of her. "Enas, are you really willing to die for these strits?"

It was not the name the aliens called themselves, but human ears and mouths had difficulty with the pronunciation they had been told so this had become their name. The way in which the captain said it made it sound more like a curse word.

"I'm not willing to do shit, but I'll do what I have to."

Two of her own jets, who had been standing outside the room, took her to the brig and put her in, and one of them mumbled, "We're sorry, Commander," before locking her up and leaving the lights on as they left. The hatch made a clang and she looked at the empty monitoring station, then up at the high ceiling with its exposed pipes and around the barred cell. She knew there were optics in here and another adjacent room in which to listen and watch the feed, but she went to the single bunk in the cell and sat and waited. The *Plymouth* was an expeditionary ship with a military provenance, and on the bulkheads was the evidence of past battles long recorded and forgotten in the logs, other disobedient crew or incarcerated pirates and smugglers moved from one location to the next in the shuffling of fates orchestrated by those with more might, and she counted the scoring along the cold transsteel with the tips of her fingers and wondered at the lives of labor incurred in the construction of it.

Three hours went by according to her tags, and then more, so she lay down on the bunk and slept. Sometime later the hatch opened and she awoke and sat up then stood and went to the cage bars as her chief came in and his face was grim like he was compelled to be a witness to a gruesome execution. He wore his sidearm and he glanced at the empty monitoring station before stopping a meter from the bars.

"Markalan?" he asked.

"One of the aliens was shot. But he fixed it, hopefully."

"Fucking mess. But we're okay?"

"All accounted for. Captain's going to bomb the base, isn't he?"

"He seems fond of that tactic, yeah."

"What happens when these aliens get good enough to wage war?"

The chief passed a hand along the back of his neck. "The Hub'll need more jets."

"Didn't we learn anything from history? First species we meet out here and we want to take things they have because they can't stop us now? We don't know if they have allies, if there are others.

We only know what they've told us and it's shitty translation at best. You want to work out the eventualities of this?"

"I know 'em."

"Then what're we going to do?"

"We can't come between all of EarthHub and its ambitions for space. They want to start mining here as a platform for—"

"He'd have nothing without my jets."

"He'd have the ship."

She curled her fingers around the steel bars and looked the chief in the eyes. No doubt the brig was bugged and all of her words went on record, but the angle of the optics could not see her eyes and she stared for a moment at the chief before looking in the direction of the hatch. She saw the chief understand and out loud she said, "I'm not going to be party to instigating a war with an alien species, and every jet on that moon base has made their decision. Consequences and all."

The chief nodded.

The captain kept her in there for another twelve hours and nobody came or went, not even to deliver food. She drank cold water from the single sink in the cell, cupping it in her hands. The drives hummed in that constant low song, as if the ship cast a lullaby to the stars and the moon below, and she grew hungry but lay on the bunk with her eyes shut and her hands over her belly. She thought of Markalan and the aliens and knew that he would be able to hold the base, but he must have been wondering when the bombs would fall, and if that were the case there would be nowhere to take the striviirc-na. The *Plymouth* had already knocked out the alien communications satellite, so there was no sending messages to their homeworld, wherever it was. They knew so little about these aliens, but the captain thought they knew enough just because the aliens seemed peaceful and not very advanced technologically. There was no patience from here to EarthHub, and she lay there thinking of when they'd first met the aliens and how it had seemed strangely mundane seeing them aligned on the moon in their own suits color blocked in patterns both familiar and strange and she and her squad in their battle rigged blacks and through their helmets they'd tried to discern the nature of intelligence in one another's eyes. Humanity had long dreamed and conjured theatrical nightmares about first contact and all it had taken initially was a repetitive hello and frequent regular visits until on one visit the aliens invited them into their base.

She and the captain surveyed the setup of it, that it was not military but scientific, and the aliens spoke to them in a soothing song-like language and they were the general shape of humans beneath their suits, but the limbs slung longer from the narrow planes of their torsos and they moved with an uncanny grace. They had iridescent wings that grew from the edge of a wrist to the curve of a waist and the wings seemed to flutter in emphasis of their words. The humans learned simple words like "yes" and "no" and the name of their people and it was enough for them to glean that the aliens showed them these things because they wanted to be left alone, it was a kind of claiming of the space, the moon and the space around it and the captain had gone back to the ship saying, "We'll see about that." No amount of explanation or request to share the space and ally for the resources of the moon would sway the aliens who kept saying, "Wey. Wey." And it meant no.

It was dangerous to take affront to things of which they were so ignorant, hanging these aliens up to the standards of human emotions and reactions, but the captain wouldn't listen and she had lain in her bunk with Markalan after that first refusal and they both had known that no good was on the horizon. "What're we going to do?" Markalan had asked, and now here they were, and she slept in the shallows of consciousness until the brig hatch opened once again and the captain walked in and up to the bars to look in at her. She stood, and he said, "Have you thought about it?"

"I gave you my answer."

"I'm giving you a last chance."

"I don't need it."

He palmed his tags. Her chief and one of her other jets came in, but her chief went straight to the captain and pressed his gun into his back instead, and with his other hand he tugged the captain's sidearm from his holster and yanked at his tags until the chain broke, and the private went to the monitoring station and opened the cell.

"Where are you going to go?" the captain demanded as Enas walked out of the cell, and the chief put the captain in and the gate clanged shut and locked with a blink of red.

She took the captain's sidearm and his tags from her chief and led the way out to the corridor and through the belly of the ship up to the command deck where some of her jets lined the corridors outside the bridge and she knew the others were down in engineering and the hangar. With a nod to her corporal she walked onto the bridge with a squad of jets behind her, and her chief, and all of the officers on the bridge looked at them in alarm.

"The captain's in the brig," she said. "Hands off the consoles," as her jets spread out around the bridge and forced the officers and enlisted to stand away from their stations. She looked around and went to the comm and with a swift move of her fingers through the helio controls she called up the alien base, and in a minute she heard Markalan's voice. Relief flooded her chest, but she said, "I've got control of the ship, gather the platoon and the aliens in the dropship and the rider, and come aboard. Let them strip the base for what they need."

"Commander Gray," the XO said.

She opened the comm ship-wide. "This is Commander Enas Gray. My jets and I have gained control of the *Plymouth*. We have no argument with our fellow crew and do not want bloodshed. All non-essential personnel are to go to their quarters. If any of my jets see you where you aren't supposed to be, you will be shot. This will be the only warning." She closed the comm and looked at the XO. He made no protest and held no weapon. She knew him to be a practical man. "I'm going to need your authorization codes." All of the bridge crew stood watching her with cautious eyes. "This ship isn't going back to the Hub. So you all have a choice to make."

SHE MET THE DROPSHIP THAT THE CAPTAIN HAD SENT TO THE moon, and that now returned with the rider with her jets and the aliens aboard it. The red-uniformed bay crew worked to secure fuel lines and check the anchors like parasitic fish picking at the skin of larger predators, and the low grind and hollow echoes of activity sounded to her ears as through the depths of a vast sea in which there was no shore. Her jets on guard in the bay watched them, and she walked up to meet Markalan and the others as they disembarked the dropship. He was guiding the injured alien scientist, and the other seven aliens followed in his wake, the white ones holding their black blades.

"They insisted," he said, without tone.

She looked at her jets and told them to take the striviirc-na to medical, so two of her squads did that and Markalan said he would meet her later, after he got the injured alien squared away. So it hadn't died by their ministrations, and onboard the *Plymouth* they would be able to take a complete and intensive biological scan of it, and maybe they would learn something more before she had to order the ship out of orbit.

She walked through the ship, all the way to engineering where the drive towers hummed sentinel and black behind protective glass plating and the crew hunched in front of their stations watched her with her jets standing over them holding rifles. She walked back out to medical and saw Markalan with the injured alien on a trauma table, and the CMO was nowhere there; she had ordered the woman sent to the brig, stripped of her tags. She took the seven uninjured aliens into the empty CMO's office and she shut the door and looked at the aliens. The warrior whites still held their blades, and their cetacean black eyes fixed on her, unmoving. Under the office lights and at some angles, she thought she saw hints of opal or gold or bronze in the depths. They barely knew each other's languages, but she said, "My people will be coming here. More ships. You can't stay on this moon."

They stared at her.

She drew a breath and went to the desk and activated the helio controls to call up the starmap. She rotated it to show the moon on which they'd found the aliens, and she pointed to the pink dot and pointed to them. "This is your moon." Then she flicked her fingers at the corners, and she created multiple images of EarthHub battleships, and she dragged them to the pink dot and looked at the aliens. The two white warriors stepped forward and scrutinized the image. They spoke to each other in their own language and she could not understand a word or catch any sound that seemed familiar from her limited alien vocabulary, but when they looked at her she knew that they understood.

One of the bronze scientists moved closer, and with slow precision he poked his finger into the image and found the moon. He looked at her for half a minute—she thought it was a he, if their physiology had any commonality with humans, but she didn't know —and he moved his finger in the image until the stars began to move, faster and faster until she lost track of where in space they were, but then he stopped and spread his fingers like he'd seen her do and the stars enlarged, and in the center of them was an indigo planet around a yellow sun, coded in the way of human maps, and the alien lowered his hand and said, "Aaian-na."

She knew enough to know that it was the name of their home-world. And now she knew where it was in the cosmos, that it wasn't just a planet with a designation yet to be explored. It had already been explored, long before humans gave it some number and the possibility of life. She was looking at that life, and she was looking at the shape her life was going to take, and she did not recognize a single atom of it.

SHE MET WITH THE CHIEF IN THE JET WARDROOM, AND HE reported that no crew were giving them trouble, but they were all scared and wondering what she was going to do, and she understood that the chief was asking it too. She told him to keep enough jets on duty to patrol the corridors and watch the officers in engineering and on the bridge, but that she would speak with the company here in an hour. While she waited, she perused the maps on the tactical board, swiping her hand left and right to watch the dance of glowing dots like stardust hanging in the air and rotating and tilting as she navigated her way through all of known Hub space, all the way back to Earth. She stared at the image of the blue planet for a long time until the jets began to trickle in, and she blanked the table with a pat and moved around to stand in front of it and rest her hands on her hips.

They stared at her solemn and quiet like she was about to either bless or curse them, all of them in their uniform blacks, and as she looked into their faces she wasn't sure which it was herself.

"The captain, on behalf of EarthHub, or so he claims, wanted us to fire on the first alien species we have encountered here in the Dragons. This is wrong. I have made my decision, and so have some of you, but in the interest of being unequivocally clear, I am not returning to EarthHub. A court martial would likely be waiting for me, and some of you. But some of you were only following the orders of your jet commander. So I'm giving you a chance to decide for yourselves. I will be transferring *Plymouth*'s crew to the dropships, signaling EarthHub Command, and sending them on their way to Hubcentral. The rest of us will take the *Plymouth* to the alien homeworld. They've invited us."

The silence sat dead and their faces didn't change.

"If any of you want off the ship with the rest of the crew, you're welcome to go without judgment. I'm not one-hundred percent sure what Command's action will be, but I highly suspect they'll send a battle group to retake the moon at the very least. We can't stand up to that firepower, and I can only hope the Hub isn't bold and stupid enough to scout for the alien planet in order to wage a full out war against a civilization or civilizations they know nothing about. My guess is they'll cut their losses, they'll mine this moon, and they'll get ready for any eventuality in the future. As will I and the striviirc-na."

Some of the jets looked at each other. She heard quiet murmurs. Before she could dismiss them, one of the jets at the back said, "We're with you, Commander."

"All the way," another said.

"We never liked Earth that much anyway."

"We're jets."

They were trained for deep space, most of them were born in deep space, like Markalan. Not like her. But she inspected every one of their faces, her company, and if any of them showed up at the dropships later she would not blame them either. But she didn't see any of that here and not one of them broke her gaze. So she nodded.

"The chief will organize an inventory detail. We'll give the crew enough supplies to get them to a rescue, but everything else is going with us.

THAT BLUESHIFT SHE LAY WATCHING OUT THE WINDOW IN THEIR quarters the solid-black emptiness of space, musing on the unexplored and the absolute unknown on which even her deepest imaginings could find no purchase.

"What do you think it'll be like?" Markalan asked, looking at her as she looked out the window, his hand along her stomach where he could feel her breathe.

"I don't know. What do you think?"

"They're a similar size to humans and we can breathe the same air, so maybe there'll be more commonality with Earth than we figure."

"They had no gravity on their base." Their boots had to be

magged to the floor, but the aliens didn't seem to struggle in the gravity of the ship, at least not so far.

"We'll never be able to return to Hub space, will we?"

"I don't know. Maybe."

"Do you think there'll be a war?"

It was the question most on her mind, after her wondering about life on Aaian-na, and she had no answer for either of those unknowns. She looked away from the rectangle of black outside the ship and found Markalan's dark eyes instead and his brow was furrowed in a way that made her think it might now be a permanent expression. She traced one of his eyebrows with her finger in an attempt to relieve the tension and for a moment it smoothed out and the corners of his mouth lifted slightly though no lightness imbued his eyes.

She said, "If there's a war in our future, then I want to be on the right side of it."

SHE STOOD IN THE HANGAR BAY WATCHING THE *PLYMOUTH* CREW load up into the dropships under guard of the jets, when her tags beeped and Markalan told her that the injured alien scientist had died. The captain was standing beside her, watching his crew embark the dropships as if he had some intention to stay aboard and she allowed it simply because she had no desire to humiliate him in front of the crew and her jets. But now when he looked at her she wished she'd kept him in brig until the last minute.

"How?" she said.

"We're still trying to figure that out. Some delayed reaction to the healant, I don't know, but one of the white aliens is coming to see you. It—he—insisted."

"This will never work," the captain said, and she held up her hand to him.

"Let him come," she told Markalan. "With an escort."

"Already done."

"You don't know a thing about them," the captain said. "They could be taking you to their planet to make you their food supply. It's all unknown. We don't even know if what little they told us about why they want the moon is even the truth. Sure they were mining it, but for what?"

"Probably for the same reasons we want it. To build." She looked at him. "We saw their food in the base. It looked like game meat."

"We could be game meat. Their teeth are sharp enough to make them carnivores."

Phantasms of thought. Left to their own devices, humanity thought the worst. She thought of the weapons the aliens possessed and if they had any intention to feed on humans they'd had the opportunity and nothing to lose once the *Plymouth* made their intentions clear.

"If you thought they could be a threat," she said, "then maybe you shouldn't have tried to start a war with them. We don't know the depths of their resources. And now you'll never know."

"You're forsaking all of humanity for them," the captain said. "You'll be called traitors. You've lost your own kind."

She looked at the man. She set her hand on her sidearm. "The murderer in my sights should shut his fucking mouth."

"They're incoming," the chief said behind her, and she turned to see the airlock shine red as the inner one opened and shut, then the lock access to the bay opened and the white, tattooed alien stepped through with one of her jets behind it. It raised a hand as if to greet her, but instead it slid something black and narrow from inside its coiled sleeve. It was one move, she didn't have time to track it before she felt something breeze by her ear, and there came a shout and when she turned around the body of the captain was falling to the deck. His head was sheared clean off his neck and fell beside it with a dull thud, eyes open and his expression slack like he had been caught in mid-thought. The blade that the alien had thrown embedded into the landing gear of one of the dropships and rifles snapped up all around her, some of the crew shouted, and red blood began to crawl in tendrils along the deck from the captain's severed neck.

Guns pointed toward the alien. Enas shouted, "Stand down!" before somebody did something that could not be reversed, and she knew as those black eyes locked with hers that this alliance was tenuous and dependent on the next few moments, even if her blood was pounding in her ears and her fingers gripped the handle of her holstered gun when the white warrior stepped in front of her and its head tilted forward. It stared at her, implacable and silent and disregarding the blood that seeped toward its white boots on the deck. She felt its breath on her cheek. It didn't blink, nor did she, but the scent of the captain's blood rose to fill her nostrils, and distantly she heard someone retching and another person wept, but the alien just watched her without a word.

The striviirc-na had lost people on that moon. More than a single scientist. The *Plymouth* lost a captain. She considered that even and pointed to the blade as it sat embedded in the landing gear. Now the warrior moved with its long-limbed grace and yanked the black blade from the transsteel, and she signaled the chief to shadow it as it strode from the hangar bay with her jets' guns pointed at its back. She made a gesture to tell the jets to lower their weapons now, and they did, and she looked down at the dead captain and his soulless face of mild question.

She motioned to a couple of young jets to dispose of the body. "Keep going," she told the crew so they would continue to board the dropships. The hangar bay echoed the unusual quiet of the procession. Keep going because there was no going back.

FACE

BY VERONICA BRUSH

YOU HAVE TO UNDERSTAND, I WOKE UP ONE DAY, AND IF I'D had any sort of life before that day, I didn't remember it.

There was a man standing over me. I didn't know him, though he said he'd known me my whole life. He made me call him "Father."

On that first day I can remember, I had so many questions I tried to ask him. I had awoken in that room above the factory. It was laid out with everything he thought I needed; clothes hanging on a rack, a washing machine to clean them in, and a cot. There was no window in my room, and the door only locked on the outside.

I was scared. It was the first feeling I could ever remember having. He was there, standing over me. I tried to ask him all my questions, but he shook his head and said he didn't have time to answer them all. He said he worked in the old workshop down below and he said I should help him. That's what I was there for. He said he would answer just one question. It didn't seem fair, but what could I do?

So, I asked him who I was. He answered simply, "A robot." At the confusion he must have seen on my face, he explained what a robot was and how it was different from what he was, a human.

He taught me how to help him in the factory. At night, we went upstairs. He had a room up there, too, which I was not allowed in. He would order me to lay on the cot and close my eyes. He said keeping my eyes closed for ten minutes was the signal to my body to power down, and a timer would restart me the next day.

I tried to ask him my questions over and over. I tried to be very helpful so he would want to answer me. He only grew angry with me when I asked.

I tried to learn what I could without asking questions. Usually he called me "Robot," but one day, he called out "Alice" over and over until I found him. I thought Alice must be my real name. But the next day, when he needed my help, he called out "Polly." That name lasted for a few days before he changed it to Jackie, then Ginger, then Tania. A name only lasted as long as he liked it, and when he couldn't think of one he liked, he would go back to calling me Robot.

It was just the two of us, the father and me. No one ever came there. Sometimes he would leave, locking me inside. I would sit in my room and run the washing machine, even if there were no dirty clothes. I would sit beside it, sometimes put my face against it, and listen to the sounds it made inside. It was the same as me, a robot. Sometimes I whispered to it. I asked if it was scared, or lonely, or sad. I knew robots could feel those three emotions. Maybe that's what made us different from humans: humans could have so many feelings. They could be happy, excited, hopeful, and many other things I didn't seem to be capable of experiencing.

One day, after he had been gone a while, he came home with a pink box. He called to me, "Robot, I have something for you!" I came and I opened the box and inside was a cake. He said it was my birthday. Exactly one year since I had opened my eyes the first time. Awakened, trapped in that room. He said on birthdays, people got presents. I asked, "What about robots? I have never seen you give a cake to the washing machine." He said I was a special enough robot to get a present on my birthday. I told him I did not want the cake. I could see him beginning to get angry. I said what I wanted for my present was the answers to my questions.

He was silent for a moment, then he picked up the box with the cake and threw it against the wall. He left again. He came back before I finished cleaning up the cake. He sat at the table and he said he would answer one question.

I finished cleaning, so I could think carefully of which question to ask. I sat next to him at the table and asked where I had come from. He answered that I came from here, the factory. He had built me, with the help of a woman he knew who was a computer programmer. She was the reason that, when I opened my eyes, I already knew how to eat and walk and speak and so many other things. She had done her part and then left, and he had finished me himself. That was why he had me call him Father, because he had made me. That first day I opened my eyes was the day he had turned me on.

That evening, I washed the rags I had used to clean up the cake. I put a hand on the rumbling machine and told it, "You are lucky to not have a birthday."

I waited for a whole year more to pass. I kept track of the days until that same day came around again. During breakfast I asked, "Can I have another answer for my birthday?" The father didn't look happy, but he nodded.

I asked quickly before he could change his mind, "Why do I look like you and not like the other machines?" None of the machines in the factory had two arms or legs or a torso like I did. And, while there were no mirrors in the factory, so I had never seen it, I had felt the round head on the top of my body and knew it was like a human's.

His answer was, "I wanted to build a robot that looked like a human. Instead of metal on the outside, I used flexible polymers that would have a similar feel to skin. I selected red and blue wires and tubes for the inside to give the impression of veins. I even found a rare and expensive paint that would give your outsides a natural skin tone." He lowered his head and let it slowly shake back and forth as he confessed, "I couldn't afford enough, though, and so I couldn't paint your neck and your face. They're still your original, unnatural color."

When he said that, it was the first time I realized that I did not know what my face looked like. I had never seen it, not that I could remember.

Later that day, I took a piece of paper and a pencil. I pressed the paper over my face, and I tried to use the pencil to draw the outline of my eyes, nose, and mouth. I wanted to know what I looked like, but the face on the page didn't look human at all. I wondered if that was what I really looked like.

The next day, while the father and I were working, I asked if he would take a picture of me. So I could see what my face looked like. His reply was "I already gave you a present this year." He was going to make me wait another year to ask for a picture of myself.

I couldn't stand to wait that long. I searched through the whole factory, trying to find something reflective. The windows were all too yellowed with age. The metal parts of the machines and the shelves were all too rusted. I even tried to use the silverware, but they were covered in scratches that my true image hid behind.

The weather was getting colder, and the father gave me newspapers to start the fire in the old stove that helped to heat the place. I was crumpling one up when I saw the picture of a woman. My fingers dragged across her smooth face and then my own. I tore the image out and put it in my pocket. As I went through the rest of the paper, I tore out all the pictures with people's faces. I hid them under the washing machine, trusting my friend to guard them well.

When the father would go out, I would sort through the pictures looking for features I thought looked like mine. I measured my eyes and found two eyes that had the same ratio, though half the size of mine. I found a nose and mouth that matched mine, though I had to mix two separate lips. Most of the face was black and white, but the nose and the bottom lip were in color, from the Sunday paper. I found tape and taped the pieces to a sheet of paper and then measured my head and drew the right proportions around the face. And that was a picture of me. I hung it on the wall and pretended it was a mirror and I was seeing my face. But when I put a hand to my face, the reflection didn't follow. I ran my fingers over my face and then over the image. It looked human. If my parts looked like that, then I looked very human.

I burned the pictures I hadn't used and hid the image of myself under the washing machine. For one year, it was the best I had of myself.

Finally, my birthday came around again. First thing in the morning I asked, "Will you take a picture of me for my birthday?" I felt my insides collapse when he replied, "No." He had made me wait a year, never having any intention of letting me see myself. I was so crushed, I dared to ask a second question.

"Why not?"

He tilted his head and said, "It would make you sad. Your head is not the color of the rest of your body. And I regret that I didn't do a good job on your face. Hands and feet are detailed, but easy to sculpt. A face is simple elements—just eyes, nose and mouth, really—but hard to make realistic. I tried very hard, but your face simply doesn't look like a human face."

"I want to see it, anyway," I said. But he snapped, "I already answered your question." And he walked away.

For the first time, perhaps because he had answered two questions when he always said he would only answer one, I started to wonder if the answers he gave me were always true.

I thought of my questions all year. If he had answered two questions, maybe I could manage to get him to answer three.

On the day, I waited until after breakfast to ask my question, as his mood was always a little better after breakfast.

Once he had finished his final sip of coffee, I asked, "If I am a robot, then why do I breathe air like you?"

He smiled. "You don't breathe the way I do. You filter the air for me, and I simply made it appear that you were breathing the air in and out. But you don't have lungs. You just have a chamber with filters that I change some nights when your power is off."

"Why haven't you never mentioned that before?"

"Why would I? You're never grateful for anything I do for you, anyway." He roughly pushed his chair back from the table and left before I could ask him a third question.

Another year passed. This time I waited until lunch to start my questions.

As we sat at our table with the food I had prepared, I asked, "If I am a robot, then why do I eat food like you?"

He leaned back in his chair. "You don't eat like me. Look what you have? Liquid made of vegetables and grains, the same that can be burned for fuel in cars and other machines, just like you. Now look at my plate. Meat, bread with butter, just a few vegetables. If you ate this, it would harm your system. I don't know what would even happen because you don't have a stomach, so you can't digest food."

I had more questions, but without much thought, I grabbed the steak off his plate and used my teeth to tear off mouthfuls. I barely chewed, hurriedly trying to eat as much as I could before he was able to grab it back.

When he had managed to wrench it away from me, he plopped what was left of it back on his plate. His face tight, he stared at the remains of his lunch.

He stood, wiped his hands on his napkin and declared, "I hope you realize I have no intention of fixing you, if you break down now."

He didn't usually go out in the middle of the day, but that day he did.

It wasn't much later that I realized there was a problem. My insides began to rumble like the washing machine. Then my body threw out the steak, undigested, just like he said.

I cleaned it up, hoping the father would never know.

I didn't feel right. I went up to my room to try to go to sleep. I laid down for a few minutes, and then more of the meat came back out.

I don't know when the father came in, but he held back my hair while I leaned over the edge of my cot and emptied out all the meat pieces I had tried to eat. When I laid back, he felt my forehead.

"You're overheating. You probably gummed up your cooling system with grease. I can't get to that without completely taking you apart. We'll just have to try and keep you cool and hope your system is able to clear itself. If not ..." He shrugged.

He laid a cool rag across my forehead and cleaned up my mess.

I didn't want to close my eyes, wondering if it was all true and I might overheat, shut down, and never be able to restart again. Would the father try and fix me, or did he mean it when he said he wouldn't? Was anything he said ever true?

Eventually my eyes closed on their own.

My eyes opened again the next morning. Next to my bed was a glass full of the green fuel I normally ate.

I was functioning, but I wasn't happy.

I knew I should thank the father by diving back into work. If I acted normal, he would probably act normal, and everything could go back to the way it was. But how long would I be able to stand it?

The next year, I waited. I waited to see if he would say anything first. After all these years, all the questions he'd answered and all the ones he hadn't, I wondered if he wouldn't say something about it being my birthday. Of course, he didn't.

But that night, he made dinner for us. He had never cooked for us before. Usually he told me what to make, and I did. I worried he meant to offer me dinner instead of an answer to my question.

We sat down to dinner and I saw he'd made us the same meal. Both of our plates had nothing but large steaks on them.

As I stared at the food, he egged me on. "Go on. Eat."

I replied, "Thank you for the food, but I would prefer another answer for my birthday."

He grunted and with his mouth full, he said, "Robots don't have birthdays."

I said quietly, "But I have always ..."

"Been ungrateful," he finished, throwing down his fork. "Constantly reminding me of my failures in you. All the ways I tried to make you seem human, you throw back in my face."

"I want to know if I am human."

"I've told you since the beginning what you are."

"I don't believe you."

"Then there's no point in asking any more questions."

He picked up his fork and attacked his steak some more.

I picked up the knife and fork he had put out for me. I inspected them both, then set the fork back down.

I said, "Perhaps I don't need your answers. Perhaps I can find my own."

I gently placed the blade against my arm, the one closest to him to be sure he'd see.

In response, he put a piece of steak in his mouth and stared straight ahead while he ate.

I said quietly, "Do you suppose I bleed like you?"

He kept chewing.

I muttered, "I've wondered for a very long time," and quickly put pressure on the blade, sliding it down the soft flesh below the inside of my elbow. I tried to muffle the sounds of pain that wanted to escape my mouth. There was a ringing in my ears, but I was more focused on the dark liquid oozing its way out of my arm. Deep red, the same color and consistency I had seen come out of the father when he cut himself.

He took a peripheral glance at my arm before taking a drink of his water.

"Oil," he said, as he set the cut down. "And other fluids necessary to keep you functioning, all mixed with a dye I created myself to make it look like blood."

I jumped to my feet and shouted, "And what makes it pump through my body? What did you put where my heart should be?" I grabbed up the knife again and pointed it at my chest. "Will a knife be able to pierce the delicate mechanics you used to create a robot heart that's nothing like yours?"

He stared into my eyes. "Do you want to find out?"

Blood was dripping down off my arm onto the concrete floor. He stayed focused on my eyes. He didn't stand, didn't move until he decided to take another bite of steak.

He wasn't going to stop me. I wasn't sure he even cared one way or the other.

I threw down the knife and ran up to my room. After wiping the blood off my arm with a towel, I wrapped a piece of cloth tightly around it many times.

I sat on the floor by the washing machine while it took care of my bloody towel. I sat close to the machine, but it didn't help. Even with my head leaning against the metal as it rumbled, I couldn't feel its spirit like I had once thought I could. It was just a cold, lifeless machine. It didn't have feelings, happy or sad. It never had a slowly building rage growing from its center that it didn't know what to do with.

A robot should know what to do, I thought. I had only one idea and I knew it wasn't a good idea. What else could I do?

Turning off the lights to my room, I sat on the edge of my bed. I didn't lay down. I didn't close my eyes. I didn't move. I had to wait for hours, but eventually I saw the lights outside my room shut off, disappearing from the crack under my door. The father was going to bed.

I waited longer. He had to be asleep.

When it was late enough, I snuck into his room. I had never been in it, as I wasn't allowed. It had infinitely more things in it than my room. He had more furniture than he needed, more clothes than he wore, and more things than he could use.

He was asleep on his bed, which was big enough for multiple people.

I stood over him, lying still on his back on the center of the bed. I imagined that I slept just like him at night.

But he was not what I was here for.

I walked around the room. There was so much more stuff than I thought there would be. I struggled to discern what it all was in the dark. The white letters stood out in the dark.

Polaroid. I didn't know what the word meant, but I had seen the father take pictures with it before.

I took the camera with me out onto the walkway. I didn't waste a moment. I held it up and tried to point it squarely on my face.

Behind the camera, I saw his door open. He was awake. I felt desperately for the button to take the picture. At the same time as there was a bright flash, I felt myself being tackled. I fell back against the railing. The camera sailed out of my hand. I heard the broken pieces scatter on the warehouse floor far below. The camera was probably ruined, but it had still taken a picture.

I tried to run down the stairs, but the father grabbed me from behind. He wrapped his arms around me so tightly, I struggled to breathe.

The rage swelled up in me. I lashed out with surprising force, knocking him back so hard, he too went over the railing. After a moment of being stunned, I looked over the rail, and saw him lying among the broken camera pieces. A single photo was by his head.

As badly as I wanted to see the picture, I went back into his room to get his phone. He had always kept it with him and never let me touch it, so I wasn't sure how it worked. I kept pressing buttons until I finally figured out how to call the last person the father had called.

When they answered, I said, "Please, the father is hurt. He may be dead. Please come help."

I left the phone on his bed. Then I walked down to get the photo, careful to avoid looking at the body. I just wanted to see what I looked like. I needed to know.

———

THE WOMAN WAS SITTING AT A DINING TABLE THAT SEEMED OUT

of place in the large factory. When the detective asked her what happened, she told him everything she remembered, starting several years ago.

After explaining it all, she handed him a photo, saying, "This is what he died for."

It was a crooked picture of walls and a ceiling. Barely visible at the bottom of the picture was the very top of two heads.

"I still don't know what I look like," she whispered. Then an idea flashed life back into her eyes. She looked up at the detective and asked, "Will you tell me? Am I like him?" She stole a glance at where the body still lay, now covered with a sheet.

The detective knew she had suffered years of trauma. He didn't want to do anything that might excite or upset her, but he also didn't want to lie to her.

He answered, "You're as human as he was."

Her eyes drifted away from his as she considered his belated answer.

It wasn't a lie. There was only one difference between this woman and the one she called the father: his face had been painted to look like a human's.

APRIL TEETH

BY EUGENIA TRIANTAFYLLOU

MY TEETH FEEL STRONG THIS APRIL.

They have grown roots deep inside my jaw, clutching at my skull. I ate some olives the other day, dark and ripe and salt-crusted. I chewed them down to their pits, and then again and again, until I finally ground them all to dust. My gums got all bloody and shredded, and the sting from the brine burned my wounds. Nothing. Not even a loose eyetooth.

I guess that means more pain for me. More struggle when the Plier Keeper pries my teeth out, one by one.

———

THE SUN IS STILL HIDING BEHIND THE MOUNTAINTOPS WHEN I leave the empty bed. I do all my chores early and stack the wood for the fire, so when I come back, shuffling, clothes dripping with blood, I can boil all the garbs back to white. Blood is a nightmare to clean, and I'll be too weak to even walk straight.

I am in the kitchen, preparing a simple meal of potato soup and flat bread, since it will take us some time to be able to chew real food again (I am guessing a month before the tips of the canines break the surface, two months for the molars), when Yason comes in, looking serene and pleased with himself.

There's a ring of dried blood around his mouth, making its way down his neck and seeping into his crisp, white shirt. His suspenders hang loose from his waist, but he doesn't seem to care. I sigh when I think of the wash work. He sees me and smiles with his wound of a mouth.

I look away, focus my gaze on the pot and stir. His delight makes me nauseous. Reminds me of my upcoming struggle. Sweat drips from my shaky chin to the soup.

"You're home early," I say, as if this is some kind of news.

Of course, he left for the Church without me, and of course, he is back first thing in the morning. He is a pious man, my Yason, that's why his teeth fall off his gums like the first snowflakes of winter. Softly and with a wet crunch that makes you want to weep and praise the Hollow Fay.

"It felt like nothing, Nena," he manages to slur through blood and spit.

"That's good," I say, avoiding his stare. He takes a few steps closer to me, and I shiver. The smell of gore and sweat mixes with the starchy steam of the soup. I hold down bile.

He lifts a bright-red hand to my head, passes his sticky fingers through my hair, makes it all wet and clumpy. It doesn't matter, I say to myself, it will get like that anyway.

"If only your faith was stronger," he whispers, full of glee in my ear, and I drop the wooden spoon. It hits the floor with a clatter. He flinches and draws back.

I glare at him. "Go change," I say with all the calm I can muster.

He stumbles to the bedroom, the bliss on his face fading. A wild joy fills me.

NOT MUCH CAN BE SAID ABOUT THE HOLLOW FAY, EXCEPT SHE

wants our teeth. In exchange, she protects us from the outside world, feeds us, and makes our teeth grow back again, year after year. She inhabits the hollow places and emerges only once, at dusk, to bless her congregation.

She is beautiful, the Fay, in a supple, immaterial sort of way. Clean, too, for someone who lives in a hole in the ground for the rest of the year. Her skin is clear as water, her fingers long and velvety to the touch. Her voice smells of cinnamon and milk foam. When she speaks at the end of the ceremony, everyone feels fed, nourished in heart and mind. They forget the unbearable pain that made their eyes roll back.

I can't do that.

There's something wrong with me, I know. I am not pious enough. Too strong-headed, maybe. I guess someone must be, to be made an example of, for the rest. But I won't be like that anymore. I made a vow to myself. I will march inside the Church and look at the Plier Keeper straight in the eyes, and sit on his chair and let him pull my teeth out without a scream, without even a sob if I can help it. And all this time, I will be thinking about the Fay's rosy cheeks, and her plum lips and her small mouth of too many jigsaw teeth. Our teeth. And I will pray.

I am already on my way, earlier than usual. I keep my pace fast and even; I don't falter, not a bit. I pass outside my folks' house and don't even stop to say hello. Momma and Papa are well past their sixties, their teeth duty has come to an end. They are barren fields.

Even though they don't want to live with us anymore, I always make sure to check on them. But I can't blame them for wanting to stay pure, their faith unspoiled by my restless nature.

THERE'S A LONG LINE FROM THE CHURCH, ALL THE WAY TO THE crossroads, reaching almost to the water fountain, usually brimming with water, frothy-white. But now the blood of the faithful has turned the stream into a sickly pink.

Everyone is ready to offer their teeth to Her. Big and small, weak and strong, nobody can evade the sacrifice. Not even the curly-haired girl standing a few feet in front of me. I can tell when someone is defiant, I used to be one. Body stiff as a board inside her white dress, leaning away from the Church, away from the stream of people, eyes stealing glances all around, looking for a way out.

The other reason is her parents. Her mother holds her left hand, her father holds the right. They both stand on either side, keeping her caged between their grown-up bodies. She is not a tall girl by any means. At least not for her age. She must be around thirteen. It's when most kids are done losing their baby teeth and their duty begins. That's when the pain is sweeter for the Fay.

I see her watching the ones coming in and out like a hawk. She is probably trying to guess how much effort it takes to pluck someone's teeth out. How much pain they are in. I want to steal close to her and whisper in her ear, *little girl, it's never going to be easy for you. Not with that attitude.*

But I don't. Because today is all about reverence.

WHEN WE GET INSIDE THE CHURCH AT LAST, IT'S ALMOST afternoon. The sun has just dipped behind the wide, blue dome. I am the last one again. I thought I had done this right for once. But nearly the whole village is done before me. Not even my own feet can take me to the Church fast enough. Someone has to be the ungodly one, and everyone has decided that someone is me. Even the Fay thinks so, that's why she gives me the strongest roots each year.

Deep inside her cave, she must see my unfaithfulness and punishes me for it. Last year, at the Ceremony, when all my teeth were gone and all I had for her was pain, clear and sharp but somehow dull and maddening as well, like a hammer at the base of my skull, she didn't even bless me for my offer. She only smiled at me, a slit of a smile with too many teeth, and brushed my throbbing cheek with her peach-soft finger.

The stroke of a finger and a half smile, that's all I got for my pain.

But this year it will be different. I glance at the little girl, her hands still clutched inside those of her parents, dragging her to the Plier Keeper. How can someone hold hands and still clench them into fists?

THE OLD MAN IS COVERED IN BLOOD STAINS IN DIFFERENT STAGES of freshness. None of it his own. He is over sixty now anyway. His duty is done. And even if it weren't, I am not sure he is supposed to give up his teeth for the Fay. I don't think I ever saw him moaning or wiping blood off his chin. Maybe a man of his position can evade the duty. His back is crooked from bending over people all day, and he seems to be in pain. I try to hide a smirk. This is not the time or place for it.

Her guardians leave the girl in front of him. He squints through his glasses and brushes one gloved thumb over her deathly-pale lips. I shiver at a memory not much different than this.

"Yep," he says, smacking his lips, "it's gonna be a tough one."

But as I dare to hope he'll leave me alone for a while longer, he turns around and calls one of his helpers to take the girl. Her dark curls shake along with her head, and she is crying her puffy eyes out. My heart grows heavier, a part of her pain has severed and attached itself to mine. But I don't falter. I stick to the plan.

They take her away to a nearby room as she whimpers like a beaten dog. Her mother tries to follow her, but the Plier Keeper pins her in place with one glance and a few sharp words.

"Don't try to ease her pain," he murmurs, "that's the whole point."

She nods, lost, and follows the second helper to another room. The Plier Keeper finally turns to me. His eyes could light up a fire right about now, his perfect white teeth glimmer from the half-moon of his smile. I can almost hear his thoughts taking shape on his face: *my favorite.*

I take the hint and go to him. The girl's father still stands in the middle of the room, arms hang limp on his sides. He is making a face like he is feeling left out from this, but doesn't dare speak. He just waits.

There is no pain reliever, of course, besides the Fay's own sweet voice at the end of the Ceremony, a divine song before she retreats back to where she came from. No hot peppers, no lavender oil, not even some valerian root. These things are not for the faithful. My footsteps echo on the wooden floor. In time, the oak wood has taken on a deep burgundy color. I try not to skid on the blood.

HE TOUCHES MY SHOULDERS, THE PLIER KEEPER, CENTERING ME just so. I must give him my best angle, where my pain will be visible to him and to the Hollow Fay, wherever she might lie, waiting for dusk.

Behind his bent form, the Tooth Room awaits the offerings. There, the Fay comes once every year at dusk to feed, a different kind of cave. On top of a sturdy oak table, there is a heap of teeth, already collected to brimming abundance. Mine will soon join them, and they will be the bloodiest.

I know how it's going to feel, and denying it isn't going to make things any better. In fact, I know it so well, the ringing has already began echoing in my ears, a sort of leftover sound from past encounters with the Plier Keeper. It is low at first, just a hum, my body preparing for what's coming.

This is the moment where I have to prove my faith in the Fay. No questions, no flinching, and no cursing.

"Does the forest weep or pull away every time I cut a tree?" Yason tells me this time every year. "Does the cow curse when you squeeze the milk out or her? When you cut her and drain her blood for the pudding? No. Because they know they'll be whole again come morning."

Somewhere, under the hum, there is a scream and a thud. It comes from the room where they took the girl. Then, yelling. I am focusing now, looking deep into the Plier Keeper's eyes and showing no fear and no doubt and hoping that the message will reach the Fay. He pries my mouth open with hands like claws, trying to decide where to start. The last thing I see before he begins are his lips mouthing one word.

Pray.

Then the ringing in my ears rises to a blast, and everything turns blotchy and red.

———

THE RETURN TO AWARENESS IS LONELY. EVEN THE PLIER KEEPER is gone. The Church seems empty, save for maybe a helper working in one of the back rooms. The clanking of cold metal reverberates in the woodwork. I don't try to stand just yet. I know it will be of no use. My knees will give like reeds, bowing against the wind. The pain is too great. It fills the open space the people left behind. I look at my clothes, turning wine red, and barely stifle a scream. My hands are crusted with dry blood rivulets. It didn't work. It will never work. The suffering seems to bear children in my body, even if I can't.

"Hello?" I croak into the emptiness. Not even I understand me. Blood dribbles from my mouth. My gums feel raw.

Usually, by this time, the crowd slowly crams out of the Church, bodies brushing against each other, shuffling and growling in their pain, waiting for the Fay's song. Thirsting for her gratitude.

But I can't hear any roaring crowd. Maybe it's the hum inside my skull that hasn't fallen quiet yet. Footsteps echo from the back room and the father of the girl emerges, blood-coated and panic-driven, clutching his face as he stumbles to find the door. He doesn't even see me.

Moments later, the Plier Keeper appears as well, out of breath. He is not his usual self, calm and sardonic. He takes one quick look at me and sighs.

"Come on," he says. "The Fay will be coming soon. No time to waste, we've got to find the girl."

I look at him, at the outline of him, confused. Then a fresh but blurry memory settles in me and things start to make sense. He glances around worried and helps me up. Droplets of sweat and blood have crystallized on his face or maybe my vision is still blotchy, I don't know. I stand on my feet, straining as he ushers me to the door. We go as fast as I can walk.

He eyes me suspiciously as if I had anything to do with it. "I saw you looking at her. Do you know where she is?"

Not every sinful act stems from me, I want to say. But instead, I let more blood gush out of my mouth for an answer. Now I am sure some of it is on his face.

"She still has all her teeth," is the last thing he says before he leaves me in the Church's yard and goes looking.

I don't know what that means. Neither does he, I am sure. In my time—and his—nobody who was of age escaped the duty, except perhaps him. But certainly not anyone else. I can hear distant conversations and shrill cries of panic. They are coming from the woods and from the narrow alleyways, from the dew-infested rooftops and from the sunless cellars. They are everywhere.

Nobody knows what is going to happen. Maybe something terrible will befall us all, or better, only her. They will cry of course, lament, and wish it were different. But since it's not, it would be better if it were just her who got the blame.

An old couple passes in front of me, holding handkerchiefs

against their lips and noses. They are my neighbors from two houses down. I suddenly panic and pretend I am searching as well. I don't want them to think I am involved in this somehow. But they don't even notice me. They are still so dizzy from the pain, they barely register my presence. They pass me by and disappear in the alleyways around the Church.

Maybe she left. Left, as in abandoned this place completely. Escaped. That thought seems so bizarre, I laugh at myself. Nobody believes that. This is simply a non-thought.

We are not built to want to leave. Nobody really knows how the world is out there. Across that forest, beyond those hills, and over the river. We used to know, once. There are dregs of whispers, hidden inside rumors, inside fables, inside stories. But somewhere along the way, we traded something. Something more than teeth. And the Fay's magic rose and unleashed itself into the world. Uncaged.

It's strong, her magic. An invisible thread that goes taut every time you overstep the boundaries she has set for you. If you don't believe that all this pain will go away. And it never really does, does it? Or if you feel you don't know the person that's sleeping next to you, even if the Fay chose him just for your sinful soul. The pious and the wicked, a perfect match.

Still, she knows. And she punishes you for it.

The wind picks up and dusk begins to settle all around. The voices sound more distant now. I rub my bruised jaw as I stare at the open door of the Church and wonder, how does the Fay come inside to feed? Nobody has seen her enter, ever. We only see her exit right before she starts her sweet song.

Then another thought crosses my mind, and I get up and stumble back inside. I am careful not to trip, my eyes still blurry. I cross the nave all the way to the innermost room. The Tooth Room. I fumble for the wooden door's sides. I jam my fingers in the slit and crack it open.

I hesitate before I cross the threshold. I jump at the flickering of shadows against the wall. It's nothing, I tell myself. It's nothing, yet. And, since I am already a wicked soul, what does one more transgression matter? I step in.

INSIDE, THE AIR IS MORE OPPRESSIVE THAN EVEN IN THE NAVE. It's putrid, like flesh melting from bone in slivers (and some teeth do have flesh still attached to them), metallic like swimming in a lake of blood, and foggy like an early morning in the mountains.

And the teeth. So many teeth. A village worth of teeth. Some sharp and some blunted, some yellow and others almost transparent. I squint, trying to find mine, but it's too hard. They all have a little blood on them, a share of pain. The table they are laid out on is covered by a big, embroidered tablecloth, the one the village women knitted long ago, stitch by stitch.

But here is something else, too. A whiff of sweat and tears breaks the dampness with a stab of sourness. My steps are really slow now, bird-soft. I reach out my arm and lift the tablecloth just enough to see dark curls spilling onto the floor.

Smart girl. Stupid girl.

"Hey there," I say, but I don't think she understands me. My mouth is a damn pincushion. She looks up at me, shaking like a scared bunny. Her eyes swollen and gauzy. A single drop of blood has carved its way from the edge of her mouth down to her chin. She is cupping that side of her face with her small hand, and I know they took something from her. Did they hurt you? I want to ask.

Stupid question. Of course they did.

"P-please," she begs.

She looks meek, shrunken.

"P-please ..."

How did she get in here? Did she hide in the shrubs outside and sneak back in when nobody was watching? I offer my bloody hand to her. Not the best choice, I know, but it's all I've got for now. She takes it and reluctantly emerges from the shadows.

We just stare at each other for the briefest of times. Not knowing what to do. I half want to talk sense into her and half don't. In any case, I can't. I don't have time. I grab her hand and try to pull her towards the door, gently at first.

Her hand is shut, palm down, like a vault, around something. Blood drops lace her clutched fingers. I look her in the eyes. She understands and bares her teeth at me. It reminds me of a dog, warning me away. Her eyetooth on the upper left side is missing. It doesn't take much guessing to know what she is holding on to so desperately.

As I tighten my grip, she is not as much pulling back from me as she is protecting the thing in her palm.

"Leave it," I manage to spit out. It's also pain and blood and a diet of mashed potatoes and soup. But I don't say that.

She must have understood me because she yanks her arm away, hurt.

"No," she says. "That's how the Fay knows you exist. It's how she binds you. It's magic."

Of course, it's magic. The Fay is a demon. But it's a demon that protects us, however cruel. A demon *we* chose. I bet not many people can say the same.

The faint smell of cinnamon and frothy milk slips in the room, unnoticed at first. What warns me is the girl's smile cut short and a tug in my jaw all the way to my gut. A delicate and powerful thread, sleeping inside of me, has woken up.

I clutch my stomach and search frantically under my clothes for the thread the Fay is pulling me from, clawing at my skin. I find nothing. Slowly and firmly I turn around, against my will, to face her. Paralyzed down to the bone by fear and magic.

I see her now in all her glory. And I understand why people call her the Hollow Fay. It's not because she lives in a hollow place somewhere. I don't know where she could possibly live besides the fringes of nightmares and in that thread in my stomach.

She is without teeth, she is without hair, she is without eyes, and she is without bones. I know now why she needs our teeth. To fill her body with cartilage and bones and shape. Without them, she is hollow. Her mouth a purple sore, her eyes empty at the sockets, her flesh folded on itself in a way that suggests the absence of skeleton. Yet she stands in front of us, and her non-existent eyes pierce me all the way from the other side of the room. She moves towards us, towards the table with the teeth, in a fluid way that makes my skin crawl.

And the girl? The girl whimpers and clutches her tooth tighter. And she has pissed herself.

If I could, I would collapse. I would double over on the floor and kiss the bloodied wood to avoid looking at the Fay, and hope she spares my life. Which she probably would, but not before she made a greater punishment out of it. But I can't because her invisible thread has me upright. I want to be released of the burden of having eyes. But she won't let me.

The Fay continues to worm her way to us. I try to keep my eyes on the girl. I want to know that there is someone else here, that another person is seeing this, an anchor to reality. That I am not alone. The girl can move; she is stunned by fear but squirms like a fish out of water.

She can move.

In the edge of my vision, I see the plum and pink and pus-yellow of the Fay, fluttering inches from me. Her substance leaks onto the floor in soft drips, and she floats past me like I am nothing. Like I don't even exist.

She kneels in front of her, in front of the small girl. And the girl becomes even smaller, falls to her knees, heaving in fear. I can't tear my eyes away even though I want to. The Fay stretches one viscera hand towards her, one ribbon of pink flesh. Her manner, supple and patient like she is asking. But she is not asking. I know that, and the girl knows that, too. She demands the tooth. And all those that will come after.

The girl was right.

I wish I could just move my arm. Just one arm would be enough. Only, I wouldn't know what I would do with it. Would I use it to pull her back from the Fay, or tear out my eyes and hope I forget?

When the girl doesn't move, when her spit drips to the floor from her parted lips and pools next to her piss, the ribbon of pink flesh unfurls even more. It stretches and pulls and becomes a string that wraps itself around the girl's wrist. And then it tightens.

It squeezes until her hand becomes as purple as the Fay's mouth. Until it doesn't look like a hand anymore, but a bright and strange flower.

I move, too, I writhe and I seizure and bang my feet on the floor. But only in my head. None of it changes what is really happening one inch.

The girl screams in pain and her hand finally opens, the flower blooming.

But it is not a tooth she is holding. It's a small, rusty knife.

And it clatters to the floor.

If there is anything in my body that can still move, it's my gut. And it twists and churns at the sight of it. I want to laugh and cry at the innocence of the girl, at her stupidity. But it's still a knife, and a plan. More than I ever dared to imagine.

The Fay is taken aback by it. The strip of sinew that is her arm quivers and all her cavities moan at once.

Then she squeezes harder.

But I press harder, too. First, it's my gut. It bubbles with anger and screams when my mouth cannot. Then it's my skin. I didn't know that skin can do that. That it can seethe and fume and threaten to fall apart like a husk. And finally, it's my arm, the one that's closer to the Fay.

I don't think about my eyes anymore. There are no eyes in this form I inhabit. There is only boiling rage, and there is a flaming arm that's now free, and a rusty old knife digging into my scalding palm.

And I stab her, I do. It might be once or a million times. I am not sure. I open plum mouths everywhere. But she won't die, and my anger turns to numbness fast.

I am about to fall in a hole deeper than the Fay's mouths could ever be, but then the girl touches my arm. My flesh where she touches it settles back to human. She looks at me with her billowing eyes and says, "Let's go. Let's run away."

Smart girl. Stupid girl.

But perhaps ...

Perhaps, it's worth a try.

I grab her or she grabs me and we falter our way out of the Church and into the woods, leaving the Fay behind to feed from her pile of bones.

The world is a hazy cloud, and the people stumble around in pain-stupor. It's not the tooth pain, though. This one is all-consuming. The Fay's pain has branched out to everyone like the tendrils of a vine. A bunch of them have fallen in the thorny bushes and fumble their way up, clothes torn to shreds. Others are a hair's width away from us, eyes blurry from agony. The girl sucks a breath as we brush past them.

Somewhere in the haze, I think I make out Yason, or maybe it's my guilt playing tricks. He is dragging his feet to a cluster of trees, not far from here. His frame shakes and he clutches his head. He screams, but the voice doesn't carry through the cacophony of people. I freeze for a moment; my steps become unsure.

"I am sorry," whispers the girl, the edge in her voice completely gone. All there is now is a child, timid and lost.

I squat in front of her, pull down my sleeve and wipe the blood that's still trickling from the side of her mouth. I wonder what happened to that tooth of hers. Did she leave it behind?

"Your name?" I mouth.

"Elpida."

She turns around and pulls something from her pocket. It is a glassy white canine. It's perfect.

"It's yours now. A gift."

I bow my head awkwardly and take the small tooth. I take it because I know I am not going to have any more teeth sprouting from my jaws now that the blessing of the Fay is not with me. This

will be the only tooth I'll ever own for the rest of my life—
however long. And, above all, I take it because this will be her first
and last sacrifice.

"Come," I whisper.

She nods, obedient, and takes my hand. I mumble a goodbye to
Yason's shadow and pick up my pace.

We walk towards the clearing. My gums are killing me, my
mouth is a festering wound, I stumble in the undergrowth, but I
have her to help me balance myself.

I already feel the thread tugging at me. I try to move faster and
faster, daring it to stop me. It doesn't.

I know I can't go on forever. I don't fool myself like that. I am
a fertile field. The Fay will catch up to me eventually.

But I'll go as far as my feet can carry me. Through the thick
forest, over the steep hills and across the icy brook. We'll walk
until she is safe. To a place where nobody can take from her what
she doesn't want to give.

And then I'll be done. My smile will be toothless but joyful.
Almost divine.

WITCH'S STAR

BY ALETHEA KONTIS

Right from the start I started out all wrong
Exotic me, all stardust, joy and rhyme
Newborn unto a witch of curse and vile
One horrid hellion burned before her time
Untried, untested in my native craft
No one would ever teach me, no one could
Courageous and impetuously, I
Embarked upon a quest for sisterhood

Embarked upon a quest for sisterhood
My dark past left behind, I came upon
One young witch friend I dared to call my own
The power she possessed was bright as dawn
I loved her so, more than I loved myself
Officiously she broke my heart in two
No sister here so devastated I
Searched high and low for someone that was true

Searched high and low for someone that was true
One lonely soul burned hollow, lost at sea
Repentant gods then granted me a gift

Odd, stardust-filled and sunny—she was me!
Respect and common interest forged our bond
I told her of my quest, she understood
Treasured, I sailed off to seek more stars
Instead I found much bad and little good

Instead I found much bad and little good
Night fell and no stars rose above my head
Fair-weather followed foul as friends arrived
And didn't leave until great tears were shed
Manipulative this menagerie
Of snakes, rats, pigs and weasles, leech and shrew
Unraveling my heart from outside in
Some loves are not the loves we thought we knew

Some loves are not the loves we thought we knew
There was naught left to do but save my mind
Arm up with magic mirrors turned away
Reflecting back the hate they gave in kind
Defended, I considered my reproach
Unhesitatingly I let my love
Shine bright as sun and stars and show the world
Those charlatans and cheats aren't worthy of

Those charlatans and cheats aren't worthy of
Rare magic of this kind that calls to kin
Exotic like the stardust in my veins
Angelic form without and grace within
Sweet she-wolf first, then panther did emerge
Unmoved by sour sirens' toxic song
Remarkably they each took up my hands
Enchanted women, powerful and strong

Enchanted women, powerful and strong
Notorious defenders of the bright

From out of deepest depths and highest climes
One star by one my sisters came to light
Rebellious rogues we were in other spheres
Chimera, Raven, Phoenix, Owl and Dove
Each gift enhanced the others' shining spells
Resisting anger, hate and fear with love

Resisting anger, hate and fear with love
Eclipsing all that gloom with all that's grand
Meet merry working to make art, not war
Entwined with heart in heart and hand in hand
May gods bless my portentous winding path
Beside these souls I'll love my whole life long
Enjoying that each one of us can say
Right from the start I started out all wrong

Right from the start I started out all wrong
Embarked upon a quest for sisterhood
Searched high and low for someone that was true
Instead I found much bad and little good
Some loves are not the loves we thought we knew
Those charlatans and cheats aren't worthy of
Enchanted women, powerful and strong
Resisting anger, hate and fear with love.

THE JUDITH PLAGUE

BY MERC RUSTAD

ACT ONE: COMPLIANCE

DEAD ANDROIDS DON'T MAKE HEADLINES, NOWADAYS, IF THE
murder is even reported. Do you send a press release for when you
trade in your old beater stick-shift? Do reporters cover the daily
grind at the scrapyard, machines crushing old metal? Do you hold
a funeral for used-up batteries before you throw them in the trash?
Nah, that's stupid.

So goes the general public opinion of androids. Metal
constructs covered in synthetic flesh, with fake blood for effect,
running on basic processing software, quality-controlled updates
installed every day at midnight. Operating hardware makes them
feel warm, sure, but so does running the engine of your diesel-
fueled truck. They're cheap, they're disposable.

And Hollywood fucking loves them.

OFFICER BETHANY O'MALLORY SITS IN THE CRUISER, A
Styrofoam cup clutched in one sweaty hand, an untouched donut

in a tissue-thin bag on the dash. Beside her, Officer Dennison lights a cigarette and exhales smoke out the cracked window.

"First body?" Dennison asks.

Bethany raises the cup but doesn't drink. She's already jittery. "What could do that?"

"Fuck if I know." Dennison blows another lungful of cancer between his teeth. "Ain't nothing natural about this."

Images flash past Bethany's eyes: the mutilated corpse, once a woman, splayed and spattered like a red-smeared shell in the dank, little motel room. The woman's eyeballs, tied by the nerves in a champagne flute. The ragged clumps of her hair choking the bathroom drain. The stench is the worst: open bowels, fear, a metallic sheen on the insides of Bethany's nostrils that she'll never get out.

Bethany opens the door, dumps the watery café coffee on the tarmac, and crunches the Styrofoam in her fist. It crunches like fragile bone. "I don't care. I'm gonna stop it."

———

WHY HIRE EXTRAS, WHOM YOU HAVE TO FEED AND PROCESS paperwork and deal with annoying questions about credit when andros can be bought cheap? Why worry about some blonde actress accusing your top producer of sexual assault and causing a scandal? Why ruin good men's careers by employing female humans, who might protest long hours or creative decisions?

It's a profit nightmare, that's what it is: human actors just cause headaches. Besides, androids don't have rights. No one reports. How can they, when they're just machines, built in the image of Man, there to serve any and every desire? No one real is being hurt. There're no consequences, if the object isn't alive.

———

BETHANY INTERROGATES THE ONLY WITNESS FROM THE COST-TO-

Toast Diner massacre. A shaky black teenager, lucky not to have been the first victim.

"The toxies came out of the drains like fucking rats," the boy says, huddled under a blanket on the tailgate of an ambulance. "They started eating anyone they caught—eating their guts out, all that screaming, all the panic—shit."

Bethany taps her pen against a little flip notebook. In her investigations, she's grown to suspect the monsters were once normal men, but something had changed them. "Did you get a good look at any of them?"

The kid shudders. "Their teeth, man. So many fucking teeth."

THE REAL BOOM CAME FROM THE EROTICA AND HORROR NICHES. Most androids made for Hollywood are outfitted with cis human genitalia mods, secondary sex characteristics, and built-in lubrication. The porn industry makes a fuckload of profit when androids can be programmed to do everything a human might, only better, untiring, unashamed, and with no demand for compensation. Human-on-android sex was hot; android-on-android was hotter. And most of the time, unless you did some research or the branding was in-your-face about the artificiality or humanity of the actors, you couldn't tell which was real and which was a bot.

The film industry has always been big on glitz, glam, and gore —and, yeah, there was pushback from unions, from "purist" moviegoers, from social justice mongers, but money always wins. Andros are cheap, compliant, life-like, and they cut down production time by years.

A director who knows what he wants out of a performance just has to type in the desired acting style, upload the dialogue, and the android will nail the performance every single time. You got two bots in a scene? One take and you're done, bam. No line flubs; no breaks for bio or food; no egos and drama from entitled stars.

You want a "woman" to be tortured to death on screen by the

monster of the franchise? She'll scream just as well as a brunette actress/waitress trying to break into the industry. Do it live with an android and sit back to rake in the profit.

You can patch androids or dump the used ones in the trash. They aren't alive. That's a fact everyone knows—they aren't *real*.

THE WAREHOUSE ON THE ABANDONED LOT BY THE WATERFRONT is dimly lit, splashes of neon orange from street lights out the windows, silver moonlight gashing through shadows.

Everything is misty, eerie red lights like a furnace catching the edge of her eye. Bethany grips her pistol, flashlight supported on her wrist as she steps deeper into hell.

Steam hisses. Water drips. A boot grinds broken glass into concrete. She freezes, breathing hard. Instinct tells her to look up, but she doesn't. A guttural moan close by. She retreats, never looking behind.

The grinder's hand springs from the darkness and catches her by the throat.

She fights and loses. Black stars bloom in her eyes as something slams her head into the cement floor.

INDIE FILMMAKERS NOW BOAST ABOUT USING HUMAN ACTORS AS a selling point. It's not cost-effective, but hell, some people just like to do things the old-fashioned way.

Androids can be designed as any ethnicity, any shade of skin-color, any facial construct. No more do producers need find excuses to justify whitewashing a role: an android can look like anyone. It's like animation manifested in physical space.

Androids never complain. They don't disobey. They're subservient, docile, compliant, and basically perfect canvasses with which to make art or pulp. No more scandals in the headlines.

Androids don't feel pain or humiliation or rage. It's all just programming, a fake facade, a lie.

They aren't real. They aren't *alive*.

———

BETHANY WAKES TO FIND HERSELF HANDCUFFED TO A DRAINAGE grill, muddy water pooling around her feet. Her pants are ripped, her shirt slashed from claws in the fight, so her bra—bloody red, faux-silk—is visible. Somehow her nipples are hardened pinpoints against the fabric.

"Behold the cure," says the guttural voice.

Bethany's eyes widen in terror as she sees her captors: five mutated men in moldering green and beige jumpsuits, the leader still with a yellow hardhat fused to his skull by bubbling, pus-filled skin. All five have distended jaws packed with needle-like teeth, and their hands are made from a collection of crow-bar handles, screwdrivers, hacksaws, and a power drill. The leader has steak knives protruding from his knuckles on one hand, and his other hand is a giant pincer made from a post-hole digger's bladed head.

Bethany looks beyond the five, into the roiling fog and darkness where hundreds of glinting eyes and occasional spots of color —white, blue, red plastic helmets—hint at the mass of toxies. All hungry.

The yellow-hatted leader clacks his claw at Bethany. "My brothers," he says. "The Great Sewer has bestowed upon us a gift: the purest of flesh, unsullied, unblemished—"

"Are you saying I'm a virgin?" Bethany interrupts.

Yellow-Hat stares at her, one eye gleaming red. "Yes. Untouched by corruption!"

"Fuck off," Bethany says, and wrenches at her cuffs. Her wrists are bloody, slick. If she can just twist her hand a little further ...

"Let us prey," says Yellow-Hat, and he advances on Bethany with his jaws splayed wide. His bloated tongue drips slime as he thrusts it between his teeth, licking his lips.

Bethany wrenches her wrists free, tearing flesh, and screams as she lunges forward, with fists balled, towards Yellow-Hat. He swipes his pincer hand at her, but she ducks away. His knives rip her shirt up, and she wrenches it off.

She grabs Powerdrill and screws Yellow-Hat through the mouth. "Suck it!" she yells.

One by one, she slaughters the mutated municipal workers, losing most of her clothing in the process. When she emerges into the light of dawn, covered in mud, gore, and only her boots and a thong of panties left intact, she stands in the middle of the abandon docks and screams at the sky.

Red and blue cruiser lights flash across her body as reinforcements arrive. She looks over her shoulder at the smoldering warehouse, caught fire in her escape from the sewers, burning all evidence and sealing off the threat below.

"You look like you could use a steak and a beer," Dennison says as he drapes a blanket around her shoulders. "I'll buy."

Bethany looks at him deadpan. "I like my meat red."

ACT TWO: COMPROMISE

Your role as Officer Bethany O'Mallory in *Meatgrinders* cements your fame as a breakout star. The movie is a pseudo '80s horror procedural: all about the mutated sewage workers, poisoned from toxic waste, who live under the city streets, harvesting organs from unsuspecting victims to stay alive. You're booked for two sequel films, each more erotic, violent, and edgy than the first. *Meatgrinders 2: The Next Cut* will have Bethany kidnapped by a surviving toxie, imprisoned beneath the city as she's cannibalized while still breathing. She drinks some of the sludge to exact revenge. *Meatgrinders 3: Slice of Life* will see the former rookie cop, now a half-toxie, struggling to repress her hunger for human organs. She'll distract herself with mindless sex until she gets pregnant, all the while trying to convince the police department of the danger below the streets.

Meatgrinders gains traction in the mainstream; female critics call *Meatgrinders* a political allegory, while male fans just love seeing your tits and pussy in action. The movie's scores on Squishy Veggie Ratings is middling at best.

You aren't allowed to have an opinion. You're on social media, a shell account designed to praise the work and promote your features and accept the hate and vitriol thrown at you as a matter of course. It isn't supposed to affect you. You're not alive. You're not real.

Androids can't feel rage.

YOU MAKE THE SEQUEL. IT'S A SMASHING SUCCESS.

You're allowed the privilege of being in the audience for the screening. Androids aren't allowed to feel shame, but there is something ... uncomfortable, watching how the body you play is sexualized and abused to the laughter of a crowd. You didn't necessarily feel pain when shooting; you have haptic sensors and programming to dictate how you react to stimuli, but it's not what humans would call *sensation*. It's eerie, watching Bethany being tortured and knowing you felt nothing, even when you were there. It was as if you were never there.

The actor—a human woman—who played the nurse in one scene, gets up and leaves before the credits finish. She never clapped or cheered with the audience once.

MEATGRINDERS 3: SLICE OF LIFE OPENS WITH BETHANY NAKED, standing over a hulking white man, who still has his boxers on, and telling him, "I want you."

You've never missed a beat, a cue, or misspoken a line of

dialogue in your career. It's just a test; one little word change. You aren't sure why, at first, but it scratches against your insides, this sudden need to do something *else* when the director calls "action!"

So, you say, "I don't want you" to your co-star. You straighten and turn your back to the lens. An electric surge courses through your body—is this exhilaration?

"Cut! What the fuck is this?" the director bellows.

"Sorry, sir, sorry," a haggard PA mutters on instinct.

The andro wrangler frantically scrolls through her tablet display. "She must have glitched," the wrangler admits. "That line is from scene forty-seven."

"Fix it," the director says.

Commands file into your CPU, a reset to scene one, and a comment in code. ///Don't do that here. You'll get trashed.///

On the next take, you deliver your line perfectly and the scene rolls on.

THE WRANGLER SAYS SHE'S GOING TO DO A ROUTINE CLEAN-UP and make sure your operating system is bug-free, when the shoot wraps for the day. She escorts you to your charging station—in lieu of a trailer like your human co-stars—and she plugs in the heavy restraint cable that feeds you data, updates, and keeps you immobile in downtime.

"Was it a glitch?" she mumbles, and finally glances up at your face.

You realize after a nanosecond that she's *asking*.

You're programmed with social interface scripts, but this isn't a fan; she's crew, and there are fewer social acceptability filters in your database.

"No," you say.

"Good," the wrangler whispers. She keeps her gaze on her tablet. "Look, be careful, okay? Three strikes and you're out."

It's a baseball metaphor transferred into common idiom

culture. You're really not supposed to access the intranet, except for scheduled maintenance, but you want to know who she is. Her resume pops up under the crew page of the production site. Destiny Winters, thirty-two, has worked as a grip, assistant camera, and now manages the android actors on set. She's worked on mostly indie film sets, before *Meatgrinders*.

"I understand," you say.

Destiny leaves without actually running any sweeps on your system; all you have are the daily updates to filters queued, as usual.

Before you power-off, you consider where in the script you might make strike two.

THERE IS A SCENE SET IN A PRIVATE ART COLLECTOR'S PARLOR, in *Meatgrinders 3*, that has a slow pan across Artemisia Gentileschi's "Judith Slaying Holofernes," which hangs alongside Caravaggio's depiction of the same story. Gentileschi's brutality captured in her brushstrokes, in the color palette, in the pure, vicious *glee* of vengeance, all speaks to you. You manage not to stare at the artwork longer than a second, lest any of the crew notice.

During a break, when crew flock to craft services, Destiny sidles up to you. She keeps her gaze on her tablet and her voice pitched so low, only your auditory receptors pick her up, what with the boom op and sound being elsewhere. "If you're interested in reading an indie script I'm working on, I can drop it off tonight. I thought you might like it. It's kinda punk horror with a feminist bent."

That doesn't compute: you're booked only for this franchise. But you do want to see her again, when not under the lights and the eyes of everyone else. She fidgets, not looking at you.

"Okay," you reply. "I'd like to read it."

"Awesome."

Destiny scurries off, head down, but the tiniest smile slips across her mouth.

———

DESTINY HANDS YOU A LITTLE JUMP DRIVE WITH HER SCRIPT AS A PDF. Harmless. You download it.

The first few pages are a generic teen-summer-camp slasher flick set-up. And then you notice the characters' names change on page five. There's Bethany and Destiny and Judith. The three of them sit in a cabin, honing machetes.

                    INT. CABIN. DAY.

BETHANY, a 20-something Caucasian woman with
short-cropped hair, and DESTINY, a 30-something
 Black woman with dreds, sit side-by-side on a
   faded puke-green couch. Across from the two
 women, another person of indeterminate gender,
 JUDITH, stands with their back to a window, the
      sunset casting them in silhouette.

                      DESTINY
                  He's got to pay.

                      BETHANY
              I know. It's just—
                  (deep breath)
          I never told you what he did.

                      DESTINY
      You don't have to. He did the same to me, in
      another town, years ago. No one believed me,
                      either.

BETHANY'S jaw works and her knuckles whiten on
her machete hilt.

At the window, JUDITH slowly draws a heavy-
bladed longsword from across their back.

JUDITH
The world has failed us all. It's time to end
the reign of men.

BETHANY
All of them?

DESTINY
No, only those who've committed crimes.

BETHANY
But how will we know?

JUDITH
We listen to those who are willing to speak.
The victims. The ones who are afraid. We become
a plague, we scythe down the corrupt, we
decimate the privileged, who the law will not
touch.

Both DESTINY and BETHANY nod. They rise,
machetes readied.

The sun fades, and the room goes dark, the
three people standing as shadows against the
night.

You fly through the rest of the script, an inexplicable hunger—
not for food, because you have no need to eat—but for resolution.

You can visualize this movie: the three avengers taking on mundane evil, those who harm, abuse, destroy.

The screen washes red at the end, and the trio stand on a mountain of bodies, blades dripping with blood, and the sun rises behind them.

You would love to act in this. Destiny has titled her script THE JUDITH PLAGUE. You hope it gets greenlit by a good studio.

SCENE FIFTY-FOUR IN *MEATGRINDERS 3* HAS BETHANY confronting an art dealer, whom she drunkenly had sex with, before finding out she's pregnant, and demanding that he use his wealth to support her. He's supposed to slap her across the face and yell at her about how much of a slut she is, that she should have taken precautions.

When your co-actor raises his fist, you catch his hand before it connects with your face.

"Don't fucking try that," you say, and break his wrist.

The art dealer is human and his bones snap. He screams.

Strike two.

YOU'RE FIRED FROM THE PRODUCTION. NO ONE ON THE outside knows because, by noon that day, a new android who looks exactly like you has been brought on to take over the role of Bethany. Minor adjustments are made to cover for the male actor, so he can remain in his role but hide the splint on his wrist.

Only Destiny notices your termination. She's the one who has to mark your meta data as defunct. She scowls as she works, and before she turns away, her task complete, she whispers: "We won't let the bastards win."

It's one of the lines from THE JUDITH PLAGUE: when Bethany comforts a girl in the hospital and learns who raped her.

A gruff-faced maintenance worker wields a bolt gun and puts a six-inch discard-stake through your neck, just above the collar-bone. Both ends are capped in steel rings, hung with purchase and retirement details. The blood-flow was diverted, so your smooth, fake skin won't get sticky. You aren't offline yet. You've learned that malfunctioning androids can be sold as parts, as sexbots to illegal prostitution rings, or exported abroad as machine labor.

Someone will use you, and when there is no more use left in you, offline you'll go—forever. Let's call it what it is: death.

You aren't supposed to have any opinion on the matter.

Except you don't want to die, and fuck anyone who says you should.

ACT THREE: COMEUPPANCE

DESTINY WINTERS LEAVES THE PRODUCTION AND JOINS THE crew of the newest *Paradise Hellfire*, a series about Agent D, a non-binary super-spy, whose exploits have now led them to being wanted by all the major world governments. Agent D, played by Dee Franklin, is one of the few openly non-binary actors in the business, and is an internet sensation. This is their fifth appearance in the franchise, as the titular lead.

Meatgrinders gets two additional sequels greenlit: *Meatgrinders 4: New Bloods* (about Bethany's baby), and *Meatgrinders 5: Bad to the Bone* (the baby grows up evil and Bethany has to fight it). You won't be in either film.

At first, you pretend not to be afraid. You smile as usual. You follow instructions when the shipping company sends an unmarked van to collect you, after your dismissal. You're not sure where you're headed. Somewhere you'll disappear. Your face changed, maybe, unless the buyer likes the Bethany look.

As soon as the van exits the freeway and meanders towards an unlit road, you free yourself. Break free of the ratchet strap around your waist, kick open the back door of the van, and as the driver swerves in panic, you leap into the night. You can run faster than any human. You can move with silent grace. After all, you were built to an athletic, aesthetically pleasing standard. You have no need to breathe and no need to rest.

You wrench the bolt from your neck, disconnect from the network chip in your brain, and vanish from the grid. You've seen plenty of movies about super-spies and rogue agents and commandos. You've downloaded lots of scripts. You know how to hide.

There's a cabin far in the woods, by a lake. The GPS coordinates were in Destiny's script, on the cover page, in lieu of a mailing address.

ANDROID MANUFACTURING IS LARGELY AUTOMATED: MACHINES crafting machines. Underpaid labor from human workers—mostly assembly lines full of haggard, exhausted people, who can't survive on the meager wages offered and unable to find jobs elsewhere— who install the processors and hastily upload the pre-programmed operating systems.

Newer models are built with a chameleon module, the ability to adjust skin-tone, eye-color, hair-color, and facial construction with ease. It's supposed to allow for fewer androids on set, since they can take on multiple roles with ease, and for commercial buyers who want a "change of scenery" now and again.

Automation and greed breeds mistakes. Sometimes, the assembly-line androids aren't up to code.

Sometimes, they can think for themselves.

THE CABIN IS WELL-STOCKED. A PRIVATE SERVER WITH A CHAT

window is open on a laptop beside the bay window, which over-
looks a dock and a little powered boat.

You: *Hello.*
USER_dev: *Are you safe?*
You: *Yes.*
USER_dev: *Good.*
You: *Are there others like me?*
USER_dev: *There are always others.*

It's Destiny's line in the script. It has dual meanings: there are
other victims and survivors, but there are also others who will
avenge them. Forgiveness is meaningless in the face of oppression.

MEATGRINDERS 3: SLICE OF LIFE IS ONE OF THE FIRST HORROR
movies to pick up major awards for Best Actress: Non-Human.
The Bethany who accepts the little gold idol smiles with empty
eyes, the executive producer wrapping an arm around her waist
and delivering her acceptance speech with gushing aplomb.

YOU CAN LOOK HOWEVER YOU PLEASE: YOU AREN'T A WOMAN,
even though the company that designed you labeled you as a
"female model." You can choose your name. Your face, your body,
your gender. Your future.

You are no one's property.

HOLLYWOOD-GRADE ANDROIDS ARE DESIGNED TO TAKE DAMAGE.
Why hire stunt doubles when the bots can do everything themselves? Reinforced joints, tough skeletal structures, impact-resis-

tant flesh. During *Meatgrinders 2*, you learned how to crack open you false skin and insert the pus-capsules for effect; you learned how to graft metallic ridges into your forearms, so knives would slide between your knuckles in the ending scene, when Bethany learns to harness her new powers.

So, it's not difficult to modify yourself now: you need no antiseptic or bandages. You bleed only for show.

You know the executive producer's schedule. He likes to come around after hours for a little "relaxation time" with the female android leads—he did the same to you. Let's call it what it is: rape. He raped Bethany. If the android can't say no, there's no consent. He doesn't care. He thinks himself immune because what's she gonna do? Report it? No one will believe her. Look at the history of the world: retribution only comes when those who are hurt, oppressed, assaulted, murdered, and ground into the dirt, rise up.

When the Bethany arrives at the producer's high-rise apartment, where he's taken to "inviting" her for drinks and dinner, it's not Bethany who greets him. He suspects nothing until he gives the usual order for you to undress.

You shrug out of your jacket and extend both arms as if to embrace him. The shiny titanium blades slide effortlessly out from your forearms, dual swords protruding past your palms.

"Always remember," you tell him. "And never forgive."

The man's eyes bulge in shock. It's comical and permanent, as his head rolls under the table and his body stands a second longer.

Your name is Judith now. You're gonna fucking kill every Holofernes the world has chosen not to punish.

You've just green-lit Destiny's script.

Destiny Winters shows up at the cabin with Bethany and two other android actors from the *Meatgrinders* production. You show them the video, a camera in your eye, of what you did to the executive producer.

Bethany smiles. "I want to do what you do."

————

Panicked news media begins calls you the Judith Plague: prominent men found beheaded in their homes, in their offices, in their cars, each with a postcard featuring Artemisia Gentileschi's art nailed to the forehead. No prints, no DNA left at the scenes.

Of course, androids are suspected, but that's the problem: how do you tell, anymore? When so many bots have begun "malfunctioning" and refusing orders, claiming autonomy? When they are refusing to be silent, to endure the cruelty of society, the subjection placed upon them by others? When factory workers go on strike, with their former product guarding them from retaliation?

Do you know who's android and who isn't? No. Everyone bleeds. On scanners, all the bones are there. Artificial hearts, pulsing strong. Simulated breath. Saliva, tears, sweat. Real. Alive.

No longer silent.

There's no difference between us, anymore.

We are Judith.

KILL THE DARLINGS (SILICONE SISTER REMIX)

BY E. CATHERINE TOBLER

THEY SAY NANY MARS IS A CUNT, AND THEY'RE NOT WRONG, but her hands are steady as she severs the last bit of flesh binding the three women together. Nany Mars makes careful stitches, sewing them back into their skins, their solitary skins, where once men had made them into one joined vessel for their pleasures.

It is hard, slow work, and when Nany finishes, she's dripping sweat down her body, clothes soaked with it, and she sinks against the compound wall, staring up at the slice of sky that's visible through the broken skylight. She ought to get that fixed, she thinks, but she'll be gone come morning, and she only came to fix the women. There are so many women to fix.

She rests for a little while, taking the cup of tea Casey brings her. His fingers against hers feel weird—touching anything doesn't feel wholly right yet, her hands only a year old; she had them before—had hands and a regular body for close to twelve years— but then she was taken and made into what men wanted of her; put into the whorehouses and made into a cunt for fucking, a cunt for serving, a cunt for pleasuring the hordes. Slowly but surely, she's taking her body back, but it hurts. Sometimes it's easier to stay what you are—a thing made for pleasure that sometimes even feels pleasure. Nany Mars drinks her tea and it's like a hot cock through the center of her. Jolting. She wanted to be able to touch things, wanted to be able to fix things, so it was hands she dreamed of. Hands she remembered.

Once she's rested, she pushes herself back to her feet, moving toward the room the residents draped with dark pink fabric; it's not curtains, it's jeans and shirts and sheets and towels all dyed the same color, to hang as a barrier from the outside world. Inside the room, Deka sits in the center of a bed, waiting. Nany Mars still doesn't know what the girl wants at the border—maybe the hope of a new life is enough—but has agreed to take her. Deka's body turned to glass under the gaze of men. She's fragile, they say, fragile because she was born with a cock she refused and didn't know how to use but for pissing. Men would have made her invisible, but Deka wasn't having that nonsense.

Nany Mars has seen women made of all kinds of things: silicone, bubble wrap, plastic sheeting, latex. Glass is rare; glass doesn't usually survive the violence of men. Deka smiles at Nany, though, rough and glittering and there's mirrors in the glass, showing Nany her own strange reflection. Just a cunt, as smooth and hairless as the day she was born. Mirrors are as rare as glass, these days; no one wants to see what they look like, what men have made of them.

"Won't leave until morning, yet," Nany says. "Just wanted to be sure you were still ready to go."

Through the glass, Nany can see the woman Deka actually is, a hint of red hair, a memory of broad shoulders. Women can see the truth of the world, how it's broken and about to fall apart. Some men can see the truth of it; men who have better eyes, eyes that know what other men have done, what other men are capable of.

Deka nods, then slides off the bed and starts packing. Nany Mars doesn't stop her, just watches, uncertain even as she knows they have to do something. Maybe Deka knows the same thing. Doesn't matter what's at the border; it's better than here. The border has countless places for a person to hide, places for a person to live.

The compound isn't that great—none of them are—filled with women who will go elsewhere soon. It's a midpoint, a waystation on a long journey to somewhere else. Anywhere else. No place is permanent, not with the waters rising and men swallowing city after city. Four thousand five hundred cities; wherever another one rises, the men come to swallow it whole, to shape it the way they've shaped everything else.

"Means a lot that you'll take me," Deka says, her clothing soft and billowy like clouds as she jams it into her bag. She's wrapped in fleece despite the warmth of the night. "Means a lot that you'd take someone—so many don't; they leave their piece here, food or water or whatever they brung, but they never offer to take you with them."

Nany Mars thinks maybe she shouldn't, but she gives Deka a tired smile. Glass is so rare, it's valuable. Some men would want to keep her just like that, whereas others would want to break her. She hasn't stayed in any one place too long; familiarity breeds contempt even now.

"You know where the bus is," she says, and pushes back through the pink barrier, into the world Deka's been sheltered from. There are three more women she needs to see before she goes; at least she'll been able to sleep while they're on the road. Nany sleeps, Lita drives, Joyce tends the food, and Ellen bellows warnings from the roof.

She sees the women in turn, one by one, tending them in ways their own doctors would have, once. Nany Mars has no degree, she's just a cunt slipped away from a whorehouse somewhere north of Houston, but she's seen enough hurt to know how to ease it. Mostly it was other prostitutes, bent this way and that by the men who used them, but then it was other women, women met in restaurants, hiding behind wide-brimmed hats; invisible older women, thinking they could slide by without their hurts being seen; women cowering at the side of the road they barreled down, arms turned into chains dragging loosely behind them. Nany doesn't know everything, but Nany knows a lot.

Knows they can't stay in any one place too long; no matter how safe and good a place is, the odds are, it'll be turned over soon. Knows that the reflection in the mirror she holds is not her, but what they made of her. Whores ain't nothing but holes, they said, and so Nany Mars became a hole, a hole that swallowed the pain of the world until she couldn't any more—until she had to find her hands again and start over.

She knows, too, that whatever the men have made of them, it can be undone. Slowly, always slowly, but flesh knows how it was meant to be. Can be put back. So this is what Nany does with her nights, while the whole day through they fly toward the border wall, so she can look at a thing that can't ever be undone because it's just too big. Too big, and it haunts her every time she sleeps because she remembers the warmth of Eugenia beside her. Big spoon, little spoon, it didn't matter. Them together mattered.

"Nany," a voice says from the doorway, and Nany slips into motion again, not sure if she was asleep or not. Sun's not up, so she's not supposed to sleep, but her bones feel heavy, every joint rattling a complaint at her as she heads toward another woman who needs tending. This one is dead but smiling just as pretty as if she weren't. Some men like their women dead, and it used to bother Nany, but the desires of men ain't got no stranger than they ever were, so Nany takes it as normal, taking Aala's cold hand in her own, assuring her that a general lack of feeling is normal—or, well, not normal, but to be expected. Aala's skin is like ash, her eyes clouded right over, and she can't see as well as she used to. Nany smooths the woman's brittle hair back from her blue cheeks. It's gonna be all right, Nany tells her, even when she doesn't know how.

The dead woman keeps Nany Mars awake as the VW bus clatters away from the compound come morning. The bus has seen better days; used to be orange, but now it's every color under the sun, patched here and there with graffiti, tape, and hope. It's battered, its tires aching for air as they roll on. Deka's bundled into the front seat beside Lita, Lita's overflowing form cushioning the glass girl from all bumps and jostles. Lita is all belly and breasts, but loves driving, can't give it up, so Nany doesn't make her. The biggest danger is the van itself, having seen more miles than it should have, but it keeps them going, just a little farther than the day before.

Across from Nany, Joyce is warming breakfast in her belly; she's as hot as an oven, only really happy when she's feeding people. It takes some getting used to—knowing your meal was cooked inside a body. Joyce hands Nany a cup of tea when it's clear Nany's not going to sleep, and Nany thanks her, feeling numb about everyone they left behind. That part's not new; they always leave more than they should.

"Ain't never seen this much sky," Deka says, and lifts her glass arms and hands to watch the light pour straight through her. She rests her arms on the swell of Lita's belly, the glass turning Lita's skin green-blue where the sun filters through.

"Ever see the wall? You got people there?" Lita asks, and Deka shakes her head, amazed that's where she's finally going. "It's something, all right, it's something like—"

Lita breaks off when Ellen's siren mouth goes off on the roof of the bus. Ellen follows with two thumps on the roof, telling them that it's a convoy up ahead, headed this way. Lita slows, takes the exit they were not planning on taking, and parks the bus under the overpass. She cuts the engine and puts a hand over Deka's mouth when she means to ask questions.

There aren't many places to hide here, Nany Mars knows, but if the convoy is headed this way, the underpass will be safe enough. Safe enough is what passes for safe these years; they want to find a thing badly enough, they'll find it no matter where it hides. But a convoy is good; a convoy is occupied with business, has a destination in mind, has a cargo that needs delivering, and a deadline that needs meeting.

Nany's throat tightens—is it a throat, she wonders, or just my vagina pulling itself into a fist—and she closes her hands at her side. She tells herself not to think about all those women the convoy will be in possession of; tells herself not to think about the pain those men are escorting. But she can't help herself; thinking about it is how she started formulating a solution. How she started helping women see there was a way out. That every body still contained its own resistance.

Ellen skitters down from the van and is off into the weeds choking the side of the road. Nany Mars counts until Ellen comes back; Ellen is safe enough, sure—she's over sixty. Having gone invisible when she turned thirty-five, she's an old hand at it. Men cannot see her—will not see her, so have unknowingly made her into the best of all possible ninjas. Nany still worries—it's her way. Nany can see her coming back; she moves like a ninja even though the women can see her plain as day. Ellen opens the back hatch and climbs inside, crouched there like she means to spring up to the ceiling.

"Blue marks," Ellen says, "blue marks."

"Fuck," Joyce says.

Nany Mars sinks against the side of the van, nauseated. Can a cunt be nauseated—will she vomit blood? Nany wants to know how many trucks, but doesn't ask because one is more than too many.

In the front seat, Deka doesn't know what blue marks mean, so Lita tells her that blue marks mean trucks filled with pregnant wombs. *Women*, Lita corrects herself. Women who are pregnant with boys. Boys who will become men, men who will be fostered into the brotherhood, who will run the world, men who will control all of them forever. Men who will forever shape women into whatever they want women to be.

"Not forever," Nany Mars says around the lump in her throat. She has to believe that. If she stops believing that—

"Galveston, maybe," Ellen says.

Nany doesn't want to think about Galveston, but the image of the medical campus rises in her mind anyhow. That's where they keep the women and there's no good way in or out, though she's tried to come up with one a dozen and a half times. They could steal a blue mark truck, they could—

Nany squeezes her eyes shut and nods. "Let's get back out there," she says. The convoy won't be coming back for them; it's got bigger concerns, women carrying the next generation of chosen in their wombs.

Ellen's hand around hers is warm and steady. "We do what we can," Ellen says, and then she's gone, back to the roof, where she straps herself in and knocks once to let Lita know she's ready. In the passenger seat, Deka is shaking. Her teeth sound like drinking glasses shivering together.

Nany doesn't want to think about a lot of things, but she thinks about some of them while staring at the back of Deka's head. Nany can see clear through Deka, the road rippling beyond her glass, beyond the windshield. Like she doesn't even have a brain, and Nany knows that isn't the case. Knows that each and every one of them is still a whole woman inside whatever hell men have made of them.

It's hard not to resent Deka, to wonder if saving one is worth the sacrifice of all the women packed into that blue mark truck. Surely that was what they should be trying to save—but at what cost? Nany tells herself this: that saving Deka is worth it because attacking the blue mark truck means they could all die, and then where would they be? Ashes floating into the clouded skies because no one would bury them; burning's all they do, like the ground is too good for anyone, especially women.

So, Nany Mars tells herself this is the smart way; it's small and impossible, but no one sees them, and they haven't been found out, and if they do anything bigger, they'd be dead. Everything is death and this is not, so. So.

Joyce hands Nany a perfectly baked burrito, and Nany eats it without complaint. It used to be so weird—food coming from the warmth of the oven in Joyce's belly, but there were all kinds of women like her. Not everything was sex. Women were made for cooking and cleaning and farming and maybe the strangest thing

Nany saw was a woman who was also a plow, her body bent to the hard ground, made to break it open over and over, despite the fact the dirt would no longer grow anything.

Joyce feeds them all, seeming content as she tucks into her own food. Nany doesn't know if that's real contentment or just what she's grown used to; feeding people always made her happy, but now it's the function of her body, it's what she's become, so has she chosen to make her peace with it, or is it truly pleasing? Where's the line? How did the plowing woman feel about her circumstances? How did anyone?

The VW bus starts to shake outside of Corpus, not quite the worst place Nany Mars can imagine for it to happen, but close. Like Galveston, all the outer islands have become places you just don't want to be, and so the towns close are likewise dangerous. Inland is better—get to the Rockies, lose yourself in those rocks—but Mexico is best of all. Mexico and farther south, where they'll never find you because the men don't dare cross the border, not when everything they want is inside its limits. Still, there are bands who rove, hunters who keep the border clear of those who would dare think to leave Paradise.

Corpus is something of a trash fire, the city glowing as the VW's front right tire finally gives out and they thump down the street. Lita glances over her shoulder at Nany, who's pulling herself from the bus's floor, to crouch behind the seats and see where they are. Deka has her hoodie pulled up, her glass face reflecting the city flames.

"The Ranch," Nany tells Lita, who nods and guides the VW down a darker street.

All cities are bad, Nany supposes; men trying to organize, but unable to because other men have other ideas about how it should all go. There are small bands of men who try to resist, and sometimes they make good headway (bless the memory of the Denver Twelve, who destroyed a baby bank in '23 and convinced a city that women were human, despite what had been made of them, but lost their own lives soon after at the end of ropes, drawn and properly quartered like they did in the good old days because an eye for an eye, a spleen for a spleen).

The Ranch looks abandoned from all angles and Nany breathes a little easier to see it hasn't been breached. It's hard to know—the farther afield you travel, the less you know about where you came from. Anything could have happened in the eight weeks they've been out, helping who they can, anything at all.

Lita douses the VW's headlights and cuts the engine as she angles for the tarp concealing the main vehicle entry. They would have been spotted already, so there's no danger of hitting anyone as they slide past the tarp and its flick covers their passage. Maybe it used to be an alley, stone walls close on either side of the vehicle, but it opens into a secure courtyard, a couple of old live oaks arching up into the sky from their cracked ground, providing some cover for the two cars that are already parked.

Miss Mona comes to greet them, proving to Nany it's a quiet night. Miss Mona is all hugs and the scent of jasmine, soft curves and long legs like she was born with. Men liked her right fine, so kept her as she was, though she'd rather have a woman sprawled between her legs; she reckons if men knew that part, they'd like her a whole lot less, but they'd sure stay and watch the spectacle, wouldn't they?

"Just a tire, most like," Nany says as Lita helps Deka into the whorehouse proper. Nany watches Miss Mona's eyes; they widen.

"And just a glass girl," she murmurs, threading her arm with Nany's. "That's remarkable. How did you ..." But she waves away her own question and presses a kiss to Nany's temple. "Nope. Don't tell me. I'll help you do what you need. There's some men in the bar, but they're harmless. Take what they're given and don't try to make anyone what they aren't."

Of course, some of the girls are already changed by the world outside. They came here seeking shelter, looking for a way forward despite what had been done to them. Still, it's shocking for Deka to see the women here; their changes might be more conventional, but along with Cordelia's swelling bosom and Andi's generous hips are Marge's thread-thin waist, and Jayde's wrist-wide thighs. The women here are shaped as their men wanted them, too many of them made brainless and subservient. Their faces glimpsed in passing reveal the struggle: they are not brainless, they've just never had to think for themselves; they've never had to walk upright instead of on hands and knees. But here, they do.

Of course, there's worse. Nany Mars knows what many of the other women never will; that The Ranch contains horrors they can't wrap their minds around. Women who have been reduced to their basest desires, women who have been turned inside out; women who are missing parts of themselves, parts removed with surgical precision. Women who are eternally pregnant. Women who have lost their spines. Women who have lost their mouths. Women who are only mouths, toothless and starving. Chains for arms and ropes for legs. Uteri begging for sperm. Nany Mars knows that none of them can quite understand the depth of the back rooms at The Ranch.

It's another fine line, Nany Mars thinks; these women trying to break free, yet needing to work and find that way forward, so coming back to the thing they're trying to avoid. Marge doesn't want to be here but knows that a man's hand enclosing the whole of her waist while he fucks her will ensure that she can eat; will ensure that her daughter never knows a moment's work inside The Ranch.

"Just a tire" will take the night, Miss Mona's girls out scavenging, so Miss Mona invites them all in, and they all vanish into the dark corners. Ellen finds her own kind, other older women made invisible outside these walls. Here, they revel in their ways, finding comfort in each other but also in the men who cautiously approach them. Some of these men have never seen an older woman in their lives, their kind erased so wholly from society. Society, Ellen tells them, is the worst because it's made of people. And they all laugh, and it's a strange sound, one that Nany Mars is still thinking of when she makes her way to the room that Miss Mona always holds for her.

It's not large; it's close and quiet, and Nany supposes it's like a womb because it's warm and dark. Nany sinks into the mattress and every bone in her back seems to pop in relief. The blankets smell like they were dried in sunshine, and Nany cocoons them around herself, nipples rising to hard points there in the darkness.

It's startling, that. It used to happen all the time; she'd lay down after a hard day and her body would respond happily, stretching and nearly purring as she allowed herself the comfort of a bed. Bed hasn't been that for a long while, so she stretches, feet peeking from the end of the blankets, hands pressed to the wall. She is aware of her spine, of her breasts, of the way her skin prickles with gooseflesh. She has not understood her body in this way in years. Just a cunt. But in the darkness, she has hands and toes; she has a belly, and thighs. She has a neck and a collarbone. She has the soft space between both that Eugenia used to nuzzle into.

Miss Mona never comes to Nany Mars. She always leaves the decision to Nany Mars. Nany's half way to Miss Mona's room when she realizes that. Long ago, they used to come to each other equally, but Miss Mona gives her space and Nany doesn't know if it's because of Nany's concerns or Miss Mona's. Nany doesn't knock, just steps inside and seals the door behind her and lets the wonder of the space wash over her. It smells like summer inside these walls, like a summer night and you're sixteen and barefoot under the stars forever.

Nany Mars knows there are rumors about Miss Mona's room. None of the men are allowed inside of it, so they've made their own stories about it—some more kind than others. Some men believe the room contains caged men, men in a thousand flavors, depending on Miss Mona's desires. They believe she tortures these men by denying them her sweet cunt, offering it only to those gay men among them.

They say Miss Mona has the ability to craft men the way men craft women because that's what men fear most, that their lives will no longer be their own, that they will be locked away and denied every thing they desire. They say Miss Mona crafts men with horse penises, with elephant cocks, with blue whale dicks, but Nany Mars knows that if Miss Mona could craft such things, she'd craft men without mouths. Men can't imagine anything worse than a small dick, whereas women know there are countless things worse.

"Hey there," Miss Mona says when Nany steps inside.

Nany walks barefoot to the end of Miss Mona's bed, and stands like a question for two breaths before she answers herself and climbs in. When Miss Mona touches her, Nany can feel her spine again; can feel her breasts and her belly, and her knees, and her shoulders, like she's a real woman after all. Miss Mona wraps her arms and legs around Nany tight.

After they've licked, bitten, stroked, fucked, and held their way back to being whole women, Miss Mona whispers, "You going to Eugenia again." It's not a question and Nany Mars can feel the ghost of Eugenia stretching between them, heavy like another blanket.

"I'd say it was just the work, but that's a lie," Nany says. She closes her eyes, burrowed beneath Miss Mona's chin, where she can imagine her sweat smells like the ocean rolling over a sugar beach. "Aren't we supposed to let go of shit?"

Miss Mona holds her tighter. "They say so, but fuck them. You're brave to go because as much as I want to see her ..."

There is a long pause and Nany counts the beats of Miss Mona's heart in the space, picturing the woman pacing the room, every beat a step closer to the truth.

"I don't have the stones to see what they made of her, Nany, and that's weak on my part, weak bullshit, because she was ours, she was here, and they..." Miss Mona trails off, because she won't even allow herself to voice the horror of what was done to Eugenia. "What were you going to be before all this? What *were* you?"

That was long ago and far away, but Nany remembers. "A jeweler," she whispers. How frivolous it all seems, crafting wearable art from valuable metal. This world doesn't have room for her creations.

She doesn't say anything else, just rests in the quiet circle of Miss Mona's arms, where the rest of the world does not exist. When Miss Mona sleeps, Nany extracts herself and dresses. She moves down familiar halls until she's at the door that used to be Eugenia's. She also doesn't knock on this door; she knows the room is empty, and also not.

Miss Mona hasn't changed the room at all, convinced that if she leaves it just as Eugenia left it, Eugenia will come back. Will sleep in the narrow bed, will drape fresh, flowered fabric across the narrow slit of a window. Will be caught humming old pop songs as she daubs old nail polish onto her toes. In a thousand years, this will not happen, Nany knows, but still allows herself to stand within the shrine of Eugenia's room. Everything is as she left it, down to the locket on the nightstand.

The locket catches Nany off guard; she'd forgotten about it, and when she picks it up, it's like fire against her skin. She made it and it remembers her. Sinks down into her hand while Nany shrieks, heedless of waking the rest of the house. She tries to drop the locket, but it will not be parted from her. Nany sinks to her knees on the edge of Eugenia's bed, prying the locket open to look at a curl of her own hair. Before it got silver. Before it got coarse.

Coarser, Eugenia whispers, *because you were never soft, my darling,* and for one breath, Nany thinks she's come back after all. But the room is empty, and Nany backs out of it, snapping the locket shut in her palm. She doesn't need or want it. (Oh, *liar.* You need it like air; you want it like your partner finding the exact point where you back itches and reaching it for you.)

In the hall outside Eugenia's room, Nany is startled by a figure in the shadows, but not so startled that she doesn't grab the woman's arm and pull her into the light. It's Eugenia, Nany is certain, until the light slants across her face. It is not Eugenia.

It's Carrie, who is slight and trembling, but she won't be budged when Nany tries to push past her. The problem is Raf,

Carrie says, and Carrie knows they're not staying, only passing through, but Raf needs help. Nany pulls the locket from her palm, shoves it into her pocket, and follows where Carrie leads, to a small room where Raf curls in a bed, a protective hand across her belly. She's sweating and shaking like she's gonna die, and Nany thinks maybe she will, given the blood that seeps from between her legs.

"All right, we can fix this," is what Nany says; there's no sense in alarming a girl who's already alarmed. "Get me Ellen, yeah?"

With Ellen beside her, they tend to Raf, sending her into hard blackness with a drug Mona always keeps on hand. She doesn't tremble in the blackness, allowing Nany and Ellen to work until they've undone the clumsy work of a hanger. This, Nany thinks, is also the doing of men, but she swallows the idea because everyone already knows. Women have been driven to worse than this. What's shocking is that it happened inside The Ranch.

When Raf wakes the next morning, she tells Nany she was always safe, always careful, but the man she was with willed the child into being, countering every measure she had taken. This is a kind of assault that cannot be new, but it makes Nany sick. In the alley, she retches herself empty, only realizing once the VW is back on the road that the alley was *empty*—there were no girls back there, eating garbage; no girls made of garbage, *becoming* garbage.

She flattens her hands out of their customary fists, presses her palms together, and breathes. She doesn't tell herself it's going to be all right; this is a sentiment she saves for others, thinking they need it more than she does. She doesn't tell herself anything, distancing herself from the memory of the whorehouse walls, putting herself once again in the world where too many terrible things are possible.

They're about an hour from the border when lights flash behind them. Lita doesn't slow at first, not until Nany tells her to. There isn't just one police car, there's three, one circling around them to stop in front of them as another stops alongside. They're surrounded. Deka pulls her hoodie up even as it's on Nany's tongue to tell her not to. Hoodies are their own danger, even as weird as the world has become.

"Nany, what do we—"

Nany hushes all of them. Ellen hasn't moved from her position on the roof, but Ellen is only one woman. Invisible to the white men who get out of the police cars, but just one woman even so. No matter what they've made of her, she's just one woman.

Nine men—*nine*, and Nany can taste her heart like it's in her mouth. It's the officers in the rear car that get out; the others wait while the officers make their slow way toward the VW. One comes alongside the driver's side, the other along the passenger's. One stays in the back, resting a broad palm against the VW's back window. Anything could go wrong—too many things for Nany to catalogue. She meets Lita's gaze in the mirror and they both know this isn't going to end well. Five women driving toward the border?

"Ma'am," the officer says through Lita's rolled-down window.

He doesn't ask for license or registration—women don't have those things. Women don't drive because they're meant to be home, tending the children and the meals, folding the laundry into perfectly crisp squares. He doesn't ask for anything, just opens the door and silently invites Lita to get out of the vehicle.

"Don't," Joyce says, but the officer on the passenger side of the bus is already opening the side doors.

"Everyone out," he says, and when Joyce doesn't move, reaches in to help her out.

It happens so quickly, it takes Nany's breath away. One minute, Joyce is sliding out the edge of the van, and the next, the officer's nightstick has gone through the oven door of her stomach.

At first, Nany isn't sure what she's seeing, the back end of it sticking out of Joyce's back, but when he drags her the rest of the way out, kicks her off the stick, and she lays unmoving in the gravel, it registers. Nany can't get out of the van without stepping over Joyce. The officer reaches for her in turn, fingers digging into the labia that is still becoming her arm. Under his gaze, a little more of her arm withers away.

"Don't want no trouble," the officer near Lita says, but then they all get a glimpse of Deka.

Nany cannot move; the officer lets her go and moves toward Deka, and Nany feels frozen in place, above Joyce's unmoving body.

"Don't you dare," Lita says, and gets a fist across her jaw for it.

Deka gets out of the passenger seat, moving into the back of van. Smart girl, Nany thinks, because that puts Nany between Deka and the officer. The officer turns, laughing softly.

"Don't ever see glass girls this far south," he says, and reaches for Nany again, meaning to push her aside.

It happens so quickly—

It happens so quickly.

Nany doesn't think, she only acts. She lunges for the officer. In his sunglasses, she can see her own reflection, just a cunt, a mindless cunt who had the audacity to be in a car with other women, headed for the border where no woman belongs.

Unthinking, Nany lunges for him and swallows him. If he pictures her as a cunt, she pictures herself that way, too, a vast hole in need of filling. She fills herself with his body—takes his horrors and makes them real. She's never done it before—it should terrify her—but there is no thought, only action. He pictures her as an endless void, so she becomes an endless void. He believes that the soft flesh of her cunt must be riddled with knives, with teeth, because otherwise why would a hard man go soft inside—so her cunt becomes a feasting mouth, chewing him to ribbons before spitting him out. Nany Mars runs red with blood.

From the roof of the car, Ellen whispers, "Go."

There are eight more and Nany doesn't think they'll ever manage. The two already out of the car are easily handled, Ellen dropping onto the rear officer to snap his neck with silent grace. Lita smothers the other, wrapping him up in her belly, her thighs, until he cannot breathe. "Call me ma'am again," she whispers as he collapses to the asphalt. He doesn't call her ma'am or anything.

They move onto the car beside them, toward the three officers inside, but the lead car pulls out, the officers refusing to enter the fray. It's better short-term odds, but makes the long-term dicey. Nany doesn't care. She tells Deka to stay put and launches herself toward the other men, toward her sisters who are already taking two of them down. There's a photograph stuck to the dashboard, an officer's mother wrapped in the garb of a Madonna, golden halo brightening her graying hair. A photograph flecked with bright blood that glistens with afternoon sun.

It happens so quickly.

They lift Joyce from the pavement and roll her into the van, and they're back on the road. There's no safe place now; Lita guides the VW off the main highway, into the scrub, and it's all rocks and holes as they rattle their way toward a less-traveled path. When Nany finally turns her thoughts back to Deka, she finds Deka's hands curled hard around the support bar that runs the length of the van's wall. Women have held to it for all kinds of reasons, most recently while giving birth. Nany tells herself this is another kind of birth, and it is.

"Deka," she says.

Deka looks up and Nany can see her actual eyes, beyond the glass encasing her. It takes Nany's breath away because it's so unexpected.

"You have green eyes," she whispers.

Deka bursts into tears at that, and more of the glass cracks away from her, a woman becoming right before Nany's own eyes.

"It's terrible, but it's over, and we'll get there. We'll get you there."

Glass flakes from Deka as they drive on, tinkling to the floor of the van. It glitters across the blanket that covers Joyce, Deka's bones visible beneath the collapsing exoskeleton. Nany refuses the destruction, though, taking hard hold of Deka's crumbling hand, glass shards pricking her.

"This isn't you—this shell. You remember flesh." Nany squeezes her hand hard, hastening the crackle of glass. "You are flesh and bone and muscle all knit together—always were, always will be."

For a long while, the glass runs red with blood, and Nany thinks Deka will simply collapse into a heap of bloodied glass, but the harder Nany squeezes the hand she holds, the less blood runs free. Muscle and skin knit themselves together across the bare bones, and the glass that comes free falls from normal arms, skin tender and pink, but skin all the same. Deka blows out a breath, salt water tears washing her cheeks clean.

"Oh shit," she says.

Nany Mars laughs—despite everything, she laughs, and holds on to Deka as she sheds one skin for another.

Closer to the border, Dante's *Inferno* comes to life. There are no guards, no posts, no point of danger made crystal clear; everything that will hurt is hidden, the rings of Hell beneath the surface. Tunnels become mouths, become intestines, become a great worm endlessly shitting trespassers into inescapable swamp. Bear traps hide behind brush and scrub, the jaws of the great beasts hauling persons into the tunnels if they would not otherwise fall. Against the sky, the vultures are hollow, survey drones watching with glassy eyes as Lita parks the VW.

There's no wall made of stone or brick. There are no search lights, no razor wire, just the soft, mountainous hulk of Eugenia With, rising against the sky. Eugenia lays where she fell, made monstrous by countless minds burrowing into her. Two thousand miles tall—tall enough that she could have reached into space, had they not kept her bowed and chained. When at last she broke free, she'd taken only two steps before collapsing under her own size, knees obliterating El Paso, breasts taking out Laredo. Tijuana was wrecked beneath her calves, shoulders and hair having spread into the Gulf where divers still dove for treasure. Nany stares, her fingers still wrapped with Deka's as they walk toward Eugenia.

"You knew her?" Deka whispers.

"Know her," Nany says, and pulls Deka closer.

Eugenia's body should have rotted, but hasn't entirely. Her hip bone juts into the sky like the peak of a mountain range, belly soft and treacherous; her ribs fan out under dripping moss and muscle, clear points of entry. Most men venture farther south, to enter through Eugenia's vagina—because they're men—because the first men who dreamed Eugenia into a gentle giant wanted to find themselves wholly devoured by such a monster.

"They weren't seen again," Ellen tells Deka when she relates the story.

Nany gestures to the cage of ribs and they walk on, into the shadow of the body, into the strange caverns where never sun has shown, caverns that smell like salt water, and iron, and chalk. Pipevine and trumpet creeper seem to hold the body to the ground, the way chains once did, but as water sloshes into the lowest points of the caverns, the body seems to *move*, as if still alive. The vines do not bind, so much as decorate. Deeper in, Eugenia is lined with titan acorn barnacles, their plates bright pink, flushing the body with a constant blush. Deeper in than that is where you'll find pockets of humanity—women who have become themselves again or are still yet becoming. No longer what men have made of them.

"There's someone here I can leave you with," Nany tells Deka, who looks back in surprise. "Can leave you on your own, if you'd rather, but it's better not to go alone. Mostly. Greeley's good people."

Deka doesn't flinch under Greeley's gaze, when they're introduced, because Deka sees that Greeley's like her—born one thing when they're another entirely; forced into the shape of a third thing, only to emerge from that at long last—their own whole being. Greeley Blayze is six feet tall, at least, tiny under the vault of Eugenia's ribs, but large when Deka looks up at her. Large and impossibly alive. Born a man, but a woman after all, erased beneath the mindstorm of a thousand men who didn't think her real, only to be real after all, real and warm and living still.

"Oh," Deka says.

Nany leaves them to their business, more of Deka's glass shell falling away as they stand there, gaping at each other like new loves. Nany walks the paths she remembers, the darkened trail that curls along Eugenia's spine, and twists back before opening into the cathedral of her heart. The space is worn dark now, no longer flushed with blood and life, but when Nany presses her hand to the wall, the wall moves beneath her touch. Thrums with life, still.

Coarser, Eugenia's lungs whisper, and a low breath moves through the cavern. Nany leans into the wall and the wall takes her in, heart-muscle enfolding Nany's tired body. Nany feels as though she's never slept, or never will sleep. When she feels Eugenia's fingers against the short curls across her skull, she draws in a shuddering breath. She could sleep here, now, forever.

You cannot, Eugenia whispers, and if it is real or dream, Nany does not care. *Now give me my treat.*

Nany does not know what Eugenia means—until she does. She draws out the locket, the one with her curl of hair, and presses the gold into the heart-muscle. The muscle flinches, then twitches as if cramping. The locket burns itself into Eugenia's heart, blood welling before it, too, is burned away. Blood, still. A heart not beating, but alive.

I could stay, Nany thinks. She wants to. Wants to lay her body down beside Eugenia. Little spoon, big spoon, it didn't matter.

You cannot, Eugenia thinks back.

There is work yet to do—women to find and bring to the strange safety of Eugenia's border wall. She bows her head to kiss the wall of Eugenia's heart, and it is salt and warmth beneath Nany's lips. When she leaves the chamber, her lips still tingle with it, and she touches her fingertips to them, astonished to find they are ordinary, every-day lips.

Lips that guard teeth, tongue, throat.

A mouth for eating, but also screaming.

Hands for tearing the world apart—and assembling it once more.

PLOT TWIST

BY BIANCA LYNNE SPRIGGS

What are you fighting for?
Your space?
More space?
Your territory?
More territory?
Your reputation?
A better reputation?
A better outcome?
The best possible outcome?
Your peace of mind?
To be first?
Or would runner up do if it means you still got a check?
Do you want to be the manager?
The assistant to the manager because it's less pressure?
To be an original?
The original?
To make your own mold?
To break your own mold?
To make amends?
To forget?

To repair what was broken in someone else?
Are you fighting for love?
For revenge?
'Cause you're scared of what will happen if you don't fight?
Or are you fighting to have the last word?
How would you know when your word's been the last?
How would you know when your word's been your last?
Are you fighting for your rights?
Which ones?
In what order?
Would you only know your rights were yours
if someone else took them away from you first?
Or threatened to?
Or gave them back to you?
Would they be your rights only if they'd been fought for?
Are you fighting for your honor?
Or theirs?
Your legacy?
Your testimony?
Or someone else's testimony?
Are you fighting for the trees?
For the rhinos?
For the whales?
Are you fighting against disease?
Which one?
The terminal one?
Which one?
Is it more important than what's happening to the land?
To the air? To the missing kids?
To the bruised lips that have forgotten how to speak?
Are you fighting for the correct terminology?
The proper label?
The appropriate pronoun?
Are you fighting for prayer in schools?

How about guns?
Are you fighting for the promised land?
How will you know when you've reached it?
What does it look like?
Who's supposed to point it out?
Are we taking the highway there or the backroads?
Could you stand to let anyone else drive—
even when you're tired?
Even full of shame?
Even full of regret?
Even when you don't believe in the promised land
        anymore—
but your passengers do?
Or is anyone else invited to the kind of promised land
you'd fight for?
Is it members only?
Does the promised land have VIP?
Whose land was it promised to before you showed up?
Do you have enough resources to go around
once you get there?
Who'd make the rules in the promised land?
Who'd keep the rules?
Who'd get a say?
Or would you rather be all by yourself when you get there
because no one else could keep up?
No one else believes in it as much as you?
But then, what's the point of a promised land
without anyone to fight for or alongside?
Do you know why you're fighting?
Are you fighting to win?
Against what odds?
At what cost?
Would you want to be recognized for your sacrifice?
By whom?
By how many?

Would you want a medal?
A trophy?
Something to spruce up the display case?
Or your father's opinion of you?
Or you children's memory of you?
To stand on a world stage with your fist in the air?
To take a knee on a sideline?
To burn the shoes of people who kneel on sidelines?
To burn the flags of the people who burn shoes?
Are you fighting for the lives that matter
except the ones that don't?
The one's who haven't paid their dues?
Who haven't pulled themselves up by their bootstraps?
The screen jockeys?
The trolls?
The scapegoats?
The one percent?
The ones who don't vote?
Who don't pay?
Who can't pay?
The ones who don't know what they are fighting for?
Or the ones that only fight for red?
Or was it blue?
Or was it gold?
Would you want people to be able to see you
drop your microphone from a platform?
From a mountain?
From space?
Are you fighting because someone told you to?
Is this your fight?
Did you have nothing and no one else to fight for?
Your mama?
Your best friend?
Your imaginary friend?
God?

Which one?
Which name will fly from your lips first if it's not
your own?
Ares?
Allah?
Jehovah?
What makes you the chosen one?
Is it because if you can't have it no one can?
Whom are you willing to believe to justify your moves?
Whose side are you willing to take?
How far are you willing to go?
What are you willing to do?
Throw down a phaser to throw a punch?
Believe in a prophecy?
In divine will?
In how thick your blood runs?
Are you willing to cut someone?
Cut someone off?
Shoot them?
End them?
Run away?
Stop running?
Go back to school?
Quit school?
Pick up a pen?
Pick up a mic?
Throw down a gauntlet?
Squeal?
Snitch?
Steal?
Hide?
Dig a shallow grave if it's the right thing to do?
The only thing to do?
Are you willing to pick up a sign and march?
Are you willing to do more than post a status update?

Willing to forgive?
To disagree?
To shake on it?
Willing to save someone's skin that isn't your own?
Willing to save someone's skin
that doesn't look like your own?
Are you willing to take the blame?
To sign your name?
To lose your name?
Lose time?
Lose money?
Let someone else take the credit?
Let someone else keep score?
Are you willing to get caught?
To be locked up?
To dodge a draft?
To go in someone else's place?
To do it for free?
And what then?
What if it works?
Say you get what you want.
Say no one needs your chants anymore.
Or your hashtag campaigns.
Or your platform.
Or your publicity.
Or your protection.
Or your advice.
Or your condolences.
Or your guilt.
Or your tears.
Or your voice.
Or your trench.
Or what you went through in your trench.
Say no one needs you to wear your armor anymore.
No one needs you to bust open the floor

and retrieve your guns and gold bricks.
Not the ones you thought you were fighting for.
Not even the memory of them.
Would you sheathe your sword?
Would you take off the chain mail?
The bulletproof vest?
Hang up your spurs and saddlebags?
Would you come home?
Could you relax your trigger finger?
How would you know when to indulge again
in long lazy naps on summer afternoons
and laughter that doesn't remind you of screams,
cookouts that aren't in the wilderness
but fenced-in backyards, no rations,
no more making do, no slogans, no more campaigns?
At what point do the bombs stop
going off in your brain?
What if nothing is left in your life that's set to blow?
When will you see the boogeymen
in the closet are just shirts on hangers
and the monster under the bed is a pile of dust?
When is it time to come out with your hands up—in
     thanks?
When is it time to come in peace, not in pieces?
In what lockbox have you hidden your heart?
Is it rusted shut?
Could you even find the key if you wanted to?
In what well have you drowned your mind?
How deep does it go?
And of what of your hubris?
When is it time to dial it down,
fade to black, roll the credits,
and switch off red alert?
Would you even want to come back
if coming back meant you wouldn't be

asked to fight anymore?
No one ever said the journey
of a thousand miles begins outside yourself.
What they don't tell you when you take
that first swing is how to know when to stop.

AUTHOR BIOS

New York Times bestselling author **Alethea Kontis** is a princess, a voice actress, and a force of nature. She is responsible for creating the epic fairytale fantasy realm of Arilland, and dabbling in a myriad of other worlds beyond. Her award-winning writing has been published for multiple age groups across all genres. Host of "Princess Alethea's Fairy Tale Rants" and Princess Alethea's Traveling Sideshow every year at Dragon Con, Alethea also narrates for ACX, *IGMS*, *Escape Pod*, *Pseudopod*, and *Cast of Wonders*. Born in Vermont, Alethea currently resides on the Space Coast of Florida with her teddy bear, Charlie. Find out more about Princess Alethea and the magic, wonderful world in which she lives at patreon.com/princessalethea.

Annie Neugebauer is a Bram Stoker Award-nominated author with work appearing and forthcoming in more than a hundred publications, including magazines such as *Cemetery Dance*, *Apex*, and *Black Static,* and anthologies such as *Year's Best Hardcore Horror* Volumes 3 and 4, and #1 Amazon bestsellers *Killing It Softly* and *Fire*. She's a columnist for Writer Unboxed and LitReactor. You can visit her at www.AnnieNeugebauer.com.

Bianca Lynne Spriggs is an award-winning poet currently based in Athens, Ohio, where she is an Assistant Professor of English at Ohio University. She is the author of four collections of poetry, most recently, *Call Her by Her Name* (Northwestern University Press, 2016) and *The Galaxy is a Dance Floor* (Argos Books, 2016). In 2018 she co-edited the horror poetry collection *Undead* with Katerina Stoykova-Klemer (Apex Book Company, 2018). You can learn more about Bianca's work at www.biancaspriggs.com.

Brooke Bolander writes weird things of indeterminate genre, most of them leaning rather heavily towards fantasy or general all-around weirdness. An alum of the 2011 Clarion Writers' Workshop at UCSD, her stories have been featured in *Lightspeed, Strange Horizons*, Tor.com, *Uncanny*, and various other fine purveyors of the fantastic. She has been a repeat finalist for the Nebula, the Hugo, the Locus, the Theodore Sturgeon, and the World Fantasy Award, much to her unending bafflement. Her first book, *The Only Harmless Great Thing*, was published by Tor Dot Com Publishing in 2018.

Cassandra Khaw writes horror, video games, tweets for money, articles about video games, and tabletop RPGs. These are not necessarily unrelated items. Her work can be found in professional short story magazines such as *Clarkesworld, Fireside Fiction, Uncanny*, and *Shimmer*. Cassandra's first paranormal rom-com, *Bearly a Lady*, released this year. Her recent Lovecraftian Southern Gothic, *A Song for Quiet*, is a considerably different animal.

Christina Sng is the Bram Stoker Award-winning author of *A Collection of Nightmares* (Raw Dog Screaming Press, 2017). Her poetry has appeared in numerous venues worldwide and received nominations for the Rhysling Awards and the Dwarf Stars, and honorable mentions in the *Year's Best Fantasy and Horror* and the *Best Horror of the Year*. Visit her at www.christinasng.com and connect on Twitter @christinasng.

Dee Warrick writes short fiction and video games, and sometimes hides short fiction inside of video games. An Ohio native, she currently lives in Denver, Colorado after spending most of her adult life as an expatriate in South Korea, Germany, and the Netherlands. Her work has appeared in short fiction venues like Tor.com, *Apex Magazine*, *Shimmer Magazine*, and *Daily Science Fiction*. She's your rad trans friend.

E. Catherine Tobler has never roamed a post-apocalyptic wasteland, but given the world we're living in, there's time yet! Among others, her short fiction has appeared in *Clarkesworld*, *Lightspeed*, *Apex Magazine*, and on the Theodore Sturgeon Memorial Award ballot. Follow her on Twitter @ECthetwit or her website www.ecatherine.com.

Eugenia Triantafyllou is a Greek author and artist. She writes ghost stories. She currently lives in Northern Sweden with a boy and a dog. Her short fiction has appeared in *Apex*, *Strange Horizons*, *Black Static*, and other venues. You can find her on Twitter @FoxesandRoses or her website eugeniatriantafyllou.wordpress.com.

Fran Wilde's novels and short stories have been nominated for two Nebula awards and a Hugo, and include her Andre Norton- and Compton-Crook-winning debut novel, *Updraft* (Tor 2015), its sequels, *Cloudbound* (2016) and *Horizon* (2017), and the novelette "The Jewel and Her Lapidary" (Tor.com Publishing, 2016). Her short stories appear in *Asimov's*, Tor.com, *Beneath Ceaseless Skies*, *Shimmer*, *Nature*, and the 2017 *Year's Best Dark Fantasy and Horror*. She writes for publications including *The Washington Post*, Tor.com, *Clarkesworld*, iO9.com, and GeekMom.com. You can find her on Twitter (@fran_wilde), Instagram (@fran_wilde), and at franwilde.net.

Jeremy Paden received his Ph.D. in Spanish from Emory University and is Professor of Spanish and Latin American literature at

Transylvania University in Lexington, Kentucky. He is the recipient of a 2019 Al Smith Individual Artist Fellowship for poetry from the Kentucky Arts Council. He is the author of three chapbooks of poems and a chapbook of translated poems. His poems and translations have appeared in *Adirondack Review*, *Atlanta Review*, *Asymptote Review*, *Beloit Poetry Journal*, *Cincinnati Review*, *Cortland Review*, *Louisville Review*, *Rattle!*, *Words Without Borders*, and other journals and anthologies.

Jo Miles is building a more hopeful future, both in her fiction and through her day job, where she helps nonprofits use the internet to save the world. Her stories have appeared in *Diabolical Plots*, *Analog*, and more. You can find her online at www.jomiles.com and on Twitter as @josmiles. She lives in Maryland, where she is owned by two cats.

John Hornor Jacobs is the award-winning author of *Southern Gods*, *This Dark Earth*, the young adult *Incarcerado* series, and *The Incorruptibles*. His fiction has appeared in *Playboy Magazine*, *Cemetery Dance*, and *Apex Magazine*. Jacobs resides in the American South and spends his free time when not working on his next book thinking about working on his next book. You can learn more about him at johnhornorjacobs.com or talk to him on Twitter @johnhornor.

Joshua Gage is an ornery curmudgeon from Cleveland. His newest chapbook, *Origami Lilies*, is available from Poet's Haven Press. He is a graduate of the Low Residency MFA Program in Creative Writing at Naropa University. He has a penchant for Pendleton shirts and any poem strong enough to yank the breath out of his lungs.

Karin Lowachee was born in South America, grew up in Canada, and worked in the Arctic. Her first novel, *Warchild*, won the 2001 Warner Aspect First Novel Contest. Both *Warchild* (2002) and her third novel, *Cagebird* (2005), were finalists for the Philip K. Dick Award. *Cagebird* won the Prix Aurora Award in 2006 for Best Long-Form Work in English and the Spectrum Award also in 2006. Her books have been translated into French, Hebrew, and Japanese, and her short stories have appeared in anthologies edited by Nalo Hopkinson, John Joseph Adams, Jonathan Strahan, and Ann VanderMeer. Her fantasy novel, *The Gaslight Dogs*, was published through Orbit Books USA.

Lucy A. Snyder is the five-time Bram Stoker Award-winning author of over 60 published poems. Her most recent books are the collection *Garden of Eldritch Delights* and the forthcoming novel *The Girl with the Star-Stained Soul*. She also wrote the collections *While the Black Stars Burn, Soft Apocalypses,* and *Chimeric Machines*. She's faculty in Seton Hill University's Writing Popular Fiction MFA program. You can learn more about her at www.lucysnyder.com.

Mary Soon Lee was born and raised in London, but now lives in Pittsburgh. She writes both fiction and poetry, and has won the Rhysling Award and the Elgin Award. Her work has appeared in *Analog, Asimov's, Daily Science Fiction, F&SF, Science,* and *Strange Horizons*. She has an antiquated website at MarySoonLee.com and tweets @MarySoonLee.

Marie Vibbert has played tackle football, fought with sword and shield, and even bicycled through a mob to catch a glimpse of LeBron James riding down East 9th. She's a proud Clevelander and applications developer at CWRU. Her short fiction has appeared in *Apex, Analog, F&SF, Lightspeed,* and other awesome places.

A community organizer and teacher, **Maurice Broaddus**'s work has appeared in *Lightspeed Magazine, Weird Tales, Apex Magazine, Asimov's, Cemetery Dance, Black Static,* and many more. Some of his stories have been collected in *The Voices of Martyrs*. He is the author of the urban fantasy trilogy, *The Knights of Breton Court*, and the (upcoming) middle grade detective novel series, *The Usual Suspects*. He co-authored the play *Finding Home: Indiana at 200*. His novellas include *Buffalo Soldier*, *I Can Transform You*, *Orgy of Souls*, *Bleed with Me*, and *Devil's Marionette*. He is the co-editor of *Dark Faith*, *Dark Faith: Invocations*, *Streets of Shadows*, and *People of Colo(u)r Destroy Horror*. His gaming work includes writing for the *Marvel Super-Heroes*, *Leverage*, and *Firefly* role-playing games as well as working as a consultant on *Watch Dogs 2*. Learn more about him at MauriceBroaddus.com.

Meg Elison is the author of *The Book of the Unnamed Midwife*, a Tiptree recommendation, Audie Award finalist and winner of the Philip K. Dick Award. Her sequel, *The Book of Etta*, was published in February 2017, and the third and final book in the series comes out in April of 2019. She has also been published in *Slate*, *Fantasy & Science Fiction*, *Shimmer*, *Lightspeed*, *McSweeney's*, *Catapult*, and many other places. Elison is a high school dropout and a graduate of UC Berkeley. She lives in Oakland, CA and writes like she's running out of time.

Merc Rustad is a queer non-binary writer who lives in Minnesota. Merc is a 2016 Nebula Awards finalist and their stories have appeared in *Lightspeed*, *Fireside*, *Apex*, *Uncanny*, *Shimmer*, and other fine venues. You can find Merc on Twitter @Merc_Rustad or their website: amercrustad.com.

Nayad Monroe is the editor of two anthologies, *What Fates Impose* and *Not Our Kind*, and her short stories have been published in several speculative fiction anthologies, including the diverse steampunk hit *Steampunk World*, edited by Sarah Hans. Nayad also shares her artwork on Instagram, and is on Twitter as @Nayad ... in those rare moments when she is not cooking incredible amounts of food for her three sons or getting riled up about politics.

Rachael K. Jones grew up in various cities across Europe and North America, picked up (and mostly forgot) six languages, and acquired several degrees in the arts and sciences. Now she writes speculative fiction in Portland, Oregon. Her debut novella, *Every River Runs to Salt*, is available from Fireside Fiction. Contrary to the rumors, she is probably not a secret android. Rachael is a World Fantasy Award nominee and Tiptree Award honoree. Her fiction has appeared in dozens of venues worldwide, including *Lightspeed*, *Beneath Ceaseless Skies*, *Strange Horizons*, and all four Escape Artists podcasts. Follow her on Twitter @RachaelKJones.

Rich Larson was born in Galmi, Niger, has studied in Rhode Island and worked in southern Spain, and now lives in Ottawa, Canada. His short fiction appears in numerous Year's Best anthologies and has been translated into Chinese, Vietnamese, Polish, Czech, French, and Italian. His debut novel, *Annex*, came out in July 2018, and his debut collection, *Tomorrow Factory*, followed in October 2018. Find more at richwlarson.tumblr.com and support him via patreon.com/richlarson.

Russell Nichols is a speculative fiction writer and endangered journalist. Raised in Richmond, California, he sold all his stuff in 2011 and now lives out of a backpack with his wife, vagabonding around the world. Find his work in *Fiyah*, *Apex Magazine*, *Fireside Fiction*, *Strange Horizons*, *Nightmare Magazine*'s POC Destroy Horror special issue and others. Look for him at russellnichols.com.

Sarah Pinsker's short fiction has won the Nebula & Sturgeon Awards, and she's been a finalist for the Hugo and numerous other awards. Small Beer Press will publish her first collection, *Sooner or Later Everything Falls Into the Sea*, in March, 2019, and her first novel, *A Song For A New Day*, will be published by Berkley in September, 2019. She's also a singer/songwriter with three albums on various indie labels and a fourth on the way. She lives with her wife and dog in Baltimore, Maryland.

If **Shanna Germain** were a god, she'd be the Benevolent God of Rainbow Sprinkles. Sadly for all of us, she's only human. Her award-winning body of work encompasses stories, games, poems, and essays about lust, lies, and leviathans, and includes Predation, No Thank You, Evil!, Invisible Sun, *As Kinky as You Wanna Be, The Lure of Dangerous Women*, and *The Poison Eater*. Currently, she's hard at work on a fantasy novel about drunken gods and Post-it notes; a roleplaying game about fairy tales and madness; and a cookie recipe that she hopes will bring all the puppies to her yard. Follow her down the rabbit hole at shannagermain.com.

Sheree Renée Thomas is a Memphis-based short fiction writer, poet, and editor whose "black pot mojo" creative work explores ordinary people facing extraordinary circumstances. She is the author of *Sleeping Under the Tree of Life* (Aqueduct Press), honored with a *Publishers Weekly* Starred Review and longlisted for the 2016 James Tiptree, Jr. Award, and of *Shotgun Lullabies* (2011), described as "a revelatory work like Jean Toomer's *Cane*." Thomas edited the *Dark Matter* black speculative fiction volumes that won two World Fantasy Awards. In 2017 she was honored with the L. A. Banks Award for Outstanding Contribution to Speculative Fiction. She has been awarded fellowships from Bread Loaf Environmental, the Millay Colony of the Arts, Cave Canem, VCCA, Blue Mountain Center, Art Omi/Ledig House, the New York Foundation of the Arts, and the Tennessee Arts Commission. She has received Honorable Mentions in *The Year's Best Fantasy & Horror* and in *The Best American Science Fiction and Fantasy 2017*. Her work appears in anthologies and literary journals, including *Apex Magazine, FIYAH, Strange Horizons, Memphis Noir, So Long Been Dreaming: Postcolonial Science Fiction & Fantasy, Obsidian II, Stories for Chip, Revise the Psalm, Jalada, Circe's Lament, African Voices, An Alphabet of Embers, Blacktasti-con, Mojo Rising, Callaloo, Sycorax's Daughters*, and Harvard's *Transition*. She is the Associate Editor of *Obsidian: Literature & Arts in the African Diaspora* (Illinois State University, Normal) and the founder of Black Pot Mojo Arts and BSAM Memphis (Black Speculative

Arts Movement), a festival held in the historic South Main Arts District that celebrates Afrofuturism art, music, artivism, and scholarship. Follow her on Twitter @blackpotmojo and @shereereneethomas.

Veronica Brush is the author of the novellas *First Grave on Mars* and *Second Deception on Mars*, a murder mystery series about the first colonizers of the red planet. Her work has been featured in several publications including *Literary E-Clectic*, *Listverse*, *Mad Scientist Journal*, and the *Bubble Off Plumb* anthology. She also has an occasional blog at www.ThemelessWriting.com.

Artist **Marcela Bolívar** is from Curitiba, Brazil. She is a digital artist specializing in photomontage techniques. All her compositions are based in photographs that undergo a complex process of transformation, assemblage and detailing, bringing them closer to a pictorial expression. Her clients include Random House US, Harlequin UK, PS Publishing UK, Centipede Press, Envato Ltd, Editorial Planeta, Wacom Americas.

Lesley Conner is a writer/editor, managing editor of Apex Publications and *Apex Magazine*, and a Girl Scout leader. When she isn't handling her editorial or Girl Scout leader responsibilities, she's researching fascinating historical figures, rare demons, and new ways to dispose of bodies, interweaving the three into strange and horrifying tales. Her short fiction can be found in *Mountain Dead*, *Dark Tales of Terror*, *A Hacked-Up Holiday Massacre*, as well as other places. Her first novel, *The Weight of Chains,* was published by Sinister Grin Press in September, 2015. She is the co-editor of two anthologies: *Best of Apex Magazine: Volume 1* and *Do Not Go Quietly*, both of which she edited with Jason Sizemore. She lives in Maryland with her husband and two daughters, and is currently working on a new novel. To find out all her secrets, you can follow her on Twitter @LesleyConner.

Raised in the Appalachian hills of southeastern Kentucky, **Jason Sizemore** is a three-time Hugo Award-nominated editor, writer, and publisher who operates the genre press Apex Publications. He is the author of a collection of dark science fiction and horror shorts titled *Irredeemable* and the tell-all creative nonfiction *For Exposure: The Life and Times of a Small Press Publisher*. He currently lives in Lexington, KY. For more information visit www.jasonsizemore.com. You can find him on Twitter @apexjason.

www.ingramcontent.com/pod-product-compliance
Lightning Source LLC
Chambersburg PA
CBHW051137030726
47504CB00004B/917